# WELCOME TO SANCTUARY CITY

*SCREENPLAY*

**DIRECTOR'S COPY**

*Written By*

*Paul D. Escudero*

Based on the novel Sanctuary City by Paul D. Escudero
DEC 2023

WORKBOOK PRESS LLC
187 E Warm Springs Rd,
Suite B285 Las Vegas NV 89119 USA

Website: https://workbookpress.com/
Hotline: 1-888-818-4856
Email: admin@workbookpress.com

Ordering Information:

Quantity sales. Special discounts are available on quantity purchases by corporations, associations, and others. For details, contact the publisher at the address above.

Library of Congress Control Number:

ISBN-13:        978-1-963718-51-5   Paperback Version
                978-1-963718-52-2   Digital Version

REV. DATE: 04/23/2024

Verbose copy. This screenplay is written in two forms:

Verbose: Director's copy – published and printed.
Summary: For Producers, Actors, and Production Staff (electronic copy only) contact me direct for the Summary Copies after contract signed for movie.

NOTE TO DIRECTOR AND PRODUCER:

The original Novel SANCTUARY CITY was almost 600 pages font size 10. That makes it a very large Novel. As such Sanctuary City was split in half and will be two movies, the first is WELCOME TO SANCTUARY CITY. At a later date the second half of the Novel will become a screenplay. Most likely unless a studio requests change of the name before its published, will be known RETURN TO SANCTUARY CITY.

Eventually when the sequel to Sanctuary City is produced simultaneously with the Novel a third and likely fourth movie in the series will be produced. When you read the original Novel, you will discover its set up nicely for a sequel.

Since Evo Kaplan turned into Dranzonians Public Enemy Number One during Sanctuary City, there will be lots of opportunities for the sequel.

FADE IN:
EXT.  OUTER SPACE  - INTERGALACTIC SPACE TIME – DAY

Note to Director: Paul Escudero's MUSIC "Welcome to Sanctuary City" starts at the beginning of the movie. This is the theme song for the movie. It is performed again at the end of the movie starting 90 seconds before the credits start flowing at the end and replays until the end of the credits.

"Welcome to Sanctuary City" piano track audio will be provided to the studio that films this screenplay. By the time the shooting starts a recording star may have recorded the song with exclusive use allowed by Paul D. Escudero to insert in this movie. Permissions for the recordings do not relinquish Mr. Escudero's intellectual property rights to the song.

Part of the "Welcome to Sanctuary City" is in this Cinematic book trailer for review to understand the essence of the DRAMA:

Sanctuary City Book Trailer v2.mp4 (dropbox.com)


EXT. CGI. SPACE–PRAXISVLASIA EXPANSIVE VIEW OF HUGE REVOLUTIONARY SPACE FLEET APPROACHING EARTH LIKE

PLANET PRAXISVLASIA (pronounced Praxis-vlasia)


VOICE OVER (MALE VOICE)
The Dranzonian Empire recoiled rather quickly from the initial setbacks created by fratricidal warfare. With great care and efforts, the Dranzonian Empire managed to barely hold on to the industrial center and the Dranzonian Capital, Praxisvlasia. The loss of Praxisvlasia would have been a psychological defeat and most likely cause the Empire to collapse, much like the way the Vandals did to the Roman Empire on planet Earth.

The failure of the Revolutionary Guards to grab the industrial heart of the Dranzonian Empire, resulted in Dranzonians being able to construct replacement ships for the fleet in a timely manner. Even though fleet personnel were thinned out by the desertion of the revolution sympathizers, through conscription and coercion, replacements slowly trickled in to beef up the manning of the Dranzonian ships that were extremely automated but still relied on humanoids to manage and operate the complicated weapons systems.

Richard Wagner - Ride of The Valkyries - YouTube

VOICE OVER (MALE VOICE)

It came down to the wire, though. In the **Battle of Praxisvlasia**, one of the fiercest and deadliest in galactic history. Revolutionaries, who were over-confident, and hell bent on conquest planning outcome of a new Empire with a different political system waged space battles as if nothing else mattered. Tactics were thrown out the window as their over-confidence spilled over into enthusiastic and later desperate waves of attack.

EXT. CGI. SPACE – THE PLANET PRAXISVLASIA IS SHOWN GROWING IN SIZE AS IF A SPACECRAFT WAS APPROACHING. USE THIS MAN OF BIRDS VIDEO AS AN EXAMPLE TO BUILD THE PLANET IMAGE:

Man of Birds: Traveling to the Stars by Paul D. Escudero | Book Video Trailer - YouTube

VOICE OVER (MALE VOICE)

*Performed while the planet expands in size as the fleet approaches.*

Setting up for the battle, mainly due to the political correctness of the Revolutionary Guards' General Staff, one might say that were overwhelmingly made up of traitor officers who were unable to make it to the top of the Dranzonian Empire Galactic Space Command, dithered and over-planned to minimize casualties within the Revolutionary Guards.

EXT. CGI. SPACE - EXPANSIVE VIEW OF DRANZONIAN EMPIRE FLEET LAUNCHING FROM THE EARTH LIKE PLANET PRAXISVLASIA

VOICE OVER (MALE)

The Revolutionary Forces dithering on the attack extended the elapsed time of the battle, which allowed the Dranzonians enough time to deploy more ships and back-fill empty slots in formations to give them a slight numerical advantage.

EXT. CGI. SPACE - PRAXISVLASIA EXPANSIVE VIEW: DRANZONIAN EMPIRE SPACE CRUISERS SHOOTING BLUE LASERS AND SPACE ROCKETS AT REVOLUTIONARY GUARDS SPACE BATTLESHIPS

VOICE OVER (MALE)

The Revolutionary Guards' INTEL greatly underestimated the Dranzonian home world Praxisvlasia order of battle. That was a grave mistake, because the Revolutionary Guard deployed the spear of their attack in what they thought was overwhelming strength ended up as nothing more than a force that could barely obtain a stalemate.

EXT. CGI. SPACE - PRAXISVLASIA EXPANSIVE VIEW: MULTIPLE SCENES FROM EACH WARING SIDE SHOWING SHIPS DESTOYED INTO SPARKLING DEBRIS, SHOWING FIREWORKS, SHOCKWAVES.

VOICE OVER (MALE)

Unfortunately for the Revolutionary Guard, they were far away from supplies and their supply chain was hampered by the unavailability of transports, which they failed to obtain during the uprising because they placed too much emphasis on capturing combat capable ships.

EXT. CGI. SPACE - PRAXISVLASIA EXPANSIVE - REVOLUTIONARY GUARDS SPACE BATTLESHIPS LAUNCHING SALVOS OF SPACE ROCKETS. ROCKETS LEAVE BEHIND GLOWING CONTRAILS.

VOICE OVER (MALE)

Most of the space docks and shipyards were located at Dranzonian Empire Planet, Praxisvlasia sector. Only a paltry flow of Revolutionary Guard transports could be constructed in time for the battle.

EXT. CGI. SPLIT SCREEN SHOT. SPACE - PRAXISVLASIA

Note: Revolutionary Guards spaceships on one side and Dranzonian spaceships on the other side facing each other.

VOICE OVER (MALE)

The Revolutionary Guard never calculated the possibility they would need vast resupply because of their over eager misjudgments and lack of valid INTEL, set the stage for an eventuality they never anticipated.

EXT. CGI. SCENES OF REVOLUTIONARY GUARDS, ROCKETS HITTING, DRANZONIAN EMPIRE SPACE CRUISERS CREATING LARGE EXPLOSIONS.

15 SECONDS LATER.

<u>CGI.  SCENES OF DRANZONIAN EMPIRE SPACE CRUISERS HITTING
TARGETS ON REVOLUTIONARY GUARDS SPACE BATTLESHIPS WITH
LASER AND BEAM WEAPONS SETTING OFF EXPLOSIONS.</u>

In this scene, six missiles strike the side of a REVOLUTIONARY
GUARDS space battleship followed momentarily by a massive explosion
that turns into plasma and a temporary sun that lasts for several seconds
then fades.

<u>EXT. SPLIT SCREEN SHOT: TOP/BOTTOM SPLIT. DRANZONIAN
SPACEWARSHIPS ON TOP, REVOLUTIONARY GUARD SPACE-WAR-
SHIPS IN THE BOTTOM HALF (GIVING A WIDE PERSPECTIVE).</u>

<u>EXT. CGI.  SCENES OF REVOLUTIONARY GUARDS ROCKETS HITTING
TARGETS ON DRANZONIAN EMPIRE SPACE CRUISERS.</u>

<u>EXT. CGI. SPACE BATTLE LASTS UP TO THREE MINUTES.</u>

VOICE OVER (MALE)

After numerous attacks and satisfactory defense of Praxisvlasia,
the Revolutionary Guard Force Commander, General Guodu
Jiaolu, realized he had to abandon the attack and move his force
away from the battle zone if he were to have a force left, which
would be needed to defend the Revolutionary Empire from the
Dranzonians, who would likely try to regain their lost worlds.
Also, General Guodu Jiaolu soon realized that Dranzonians
would chase the remnants of his fleet to the far corners of the
Empire to catch and punish them. It was a bitter speech he had
to make to his staff.

<u>INT. REVOLUTIONARY GUARDS COMMAND SHIP</u>

GENERAL GUODU JIAOLU

Comrades and patriots, I did look   forward to sleeping on
soft beds in Praxisvlasia and enjoying the plunder that would
immediately be ours, but unfortunately, the battle has not turned
out the way we planned.

Revolutionary Guards General Guodu Jiaolu paused and looked around the
control room of his command ship and everyone had it on their faces. They knew
the battle was lost and prayed General Guodu Jiaolu would retreat before they
were all killed.

GENERAL GUODU JIAOLU

We cannot continue the fight without possibly suffering material
damage to the fleet we need to have available to defend our
Empire and our home worlds and planets.

There was a dreadful silence in the large command ship command center where all offwatch officers and even those currently at battle stations were observing, some of which was done remotely on video screens scattered throughout the ships.

GENERAL GUODU JIAOLU
We are now going to disengage the Dranzonian Fleet and return to our worlds and regroup and rethink our  next moves. The extraction plan is now being sent to all ships and a rear guard is being established so that Our fleet may maneuver and avoid further battle.

Everyone in the control room looked astonished. Despite the screening of personnel to provide General Guodu Jiaolu with the toughest and strongest people in the force to be on his staff, there were a couple people teared up.

GENERAL GUODU JIAOLU
I order this course reversal with a heavy heart. Many of you have fought rather superbly, and your heroism has been second to none. However, due to our intel failure, we did not arrive with an overwhelming force like we planned.

General Guodu Jiaolu understood the significance of this failure that now appeared to be a blunder.

GENERAL GUODU JIAOLU
Due to our long supply lines, we cannot remain here fighting a war of attrition knowing the Dranzonians can build more ships and add personnel to replace any ships we might damage.

EXT. CGI. 15 SECONDS SPACEPRAXISVLASIA  ADDITIONAL SCENES OF SPACE BATTLES.

GENERAL GUODU JIAOLU
We do not have enough firepower to punch through the Dranzonian defenses to take out the planet. Therefore, to remain here is a recipe for disaster. We are better suited to leave now, regroup, re-plan, and come back later with a bolder plan.

The Revolutionaries didn't know they had the Dranzonians on the ropes and just a few more attacks were all that would have been needed to shake the foundation of the Dranzonians and complete the objectives of this phase of the battle. Had they done so, they would have been sleeping in soft beds that night.

INT. DRANZONIAN COMMAND SHIP - SPACE

The Dranzonians were almost in a state of shock when word quickly spread from ships communications:

DRANZONIAN COMMANDER
(Fleetwide announcement)
The Revolutionaries Space Fleet maneuvered and appears to be leaving Praxisvlasia.

VOICE OVER (MALE)
With a heavy heart and a sigh of relief, the Dranzonians were elated; the outcome was in their favor.
Unfortunately, the leadership on Praxisvlasia refused to allow their fleet to chase after the Revolutionaries to inflict irreparable damage that might have led to restoration of the Empire at that time. By being far too timid, the Dranzonians lost their opportunity to inflict a death blow to the Revolutionary Guard Force, which could have manifested the end of the Revolutionary Empire.

The Revolutionary Guard ultimate failure during the Battle of Praxisvlasia resulted from flawed intelligence. An immediate effort was put forward to bolster the Revolutionary Empire's ability to conduct espionage or sabotage. They went looking for Talent.

## EXT. PRAXISVLASIA – DAY EVO KAPLAN LEAVING HIS APARTMENT BUILDING AND WALKING DOWN A SIDEWALK.

Evo Kaplan, a former Dranzonian spy down on his luck was soon identified as some of the talent the Revolutionary Empire's Secret Service sought.

Evo started out doing well with the Dranzonian Secret Service including participating in well over 500 missions before he was terminated.

Almost one quarter of the original Secret Service personnel were terminated because there was evidence, they either condoned the revolution or gave material support to it.

Immediately after the Dranzonians were able to establish some semblance of security, most of and all known revolutionaries had fled Praxisvlasia. Many revolutionaries feared arrest and subsequent firing squad during the ongoing martial law.

The upper management for the Dranzonian Ministry for State Security immediately started a sophisticated purge of those undesirables whose loyalty could not be established.

Evo Kaplan at first wasn't a whole-hearted supporter of the revolution; in fact, he was merely aloof because of his introverted personality and didn't like to be pushed around. He was known to be a maverick and had a growing record of insubordination with his supervisor Reginald Heiqishi, who took advantage of the purge to get rid of Evo Kaplan. In many other instances similar skullduggery occurred, and old scores settled.

Evo Kaplan was soon out of a job and out of a career, with little hope of securing a new position in the vacuum of revolution and severe damage to the economy that it caused. Evo Kaplan found himself in a situation he didn't care to be in. Having been used to living well, he was suddenly cast into poverty and resentment.

The purge wasn't successful in identifying all the potential moles. Members of the Dranzonian Secret Service who resented the heavy handedness in the purge and were sympathetic to people such as Evo Kaplan were sometimes recruited by Revolutionary operatives. They in turn provided incredible intel in the form of identification of almost the entire roster of Secret Service operatives and those purged, as well as their home residence, where they could be surreptitiously contacted and recruited in a veiled manner.

From then onward, the Revolution began a systematic and comprehensive operation to establish contact with individuals such as Evo Kaplan to recruit him.

The Dranzonian Ministry for State Security needed to have sophisticated operatives inside the Secret Service, and they also needed numerous well-trained spies to penetrate all other areas of government and business. In a matter of time, the Dranzonian Ministry for State Security Secret Service knew all of Evo Kaplan's story thanks to a terrible data breach where the Revolutionary Spies got copies of all their personnel files.

<u>EXT. PRAXISVLASIA EVO KAPLAN WALKING BY A PARK ON HIS WAY TO A FOOD COURT.</u>

Evo Kaplan remembered how his career started out, on a high note and he was on his way to destiny.

Evo Kaplan was a history major in college with a math and physics aptitude. The Dranzonian Empire Secret Service liked recruiting people with a history or law background. They would also recruit military members for clandestine paramilitary operations. By the time the Dranzonian Empire Secret Service recruited Evo Kaplan, he was already a black belt in martial arts, which they knew in his background check prior to contacting him.

One didn't apply to the Dranzonian Empire Secret Service. Every single employee, whether it be for scientific study, legal, or space related Dranzonian Empire Secret Service missions, was identified and screened and selected by the Dranzonian Secret Service Resources Division that spied on virtually everyone.

Sophisticated algorithms filtered through the compendium of people and at the same time analyzed the current makeup of the force to derive all the manning structures needed, whether it be temporary or permanent. The temps were always recruited from within. The permanent employees had to be recruited from outside the agency.

It was not uncommon for the Dranzonian Empire Secret Service to steal, or "recruit" as they would call it, from the military or other agencies. When they took a military member, who would most likely participate in multiple clandestine paramilitary operations, they were loaned to the Dranzonian Empire Secret Service. By design their orders were "indefinite."

Every time the joint chiefs made an inquiry into the status of their service member, the Dranzonian Empire Secret Service simply responded, "That person is currently on a classified mission." Even if that same person was still on the planet, it didn't matter.

<u>EXT. PRAXISVLASIA FOOD COURT – DAY – EVO KALAN ORDERING A MODEST MEAL.</u>

Quite a few of these recruits also went through biological three-dimensional biological printing cosmetic surgery, and many liked their new looks better and never changed back, allowing better concealment, and avoiding former spouses since they got a free identity change in the process!

One could say it smelled a lot like the French Foreign Legion, where people joined to change their identity to escape legal proceedings. Unfortunately, that person could never leave except to a war zone for fear of capture.

Evo Kaplan was identified while in graduate school studying galactic history. When he registered his martial arts black belt, which was a legal binding act that all martial arts schools were required to do since they were giving that person lethal combat capability, their names into a database.

When Evo Kaplan received his first degree in history, his name was placed into a database that tracked historians. The government then monitored his college transcripts following his progress through his more advanced degree, which further elucidated the essence of his academic achievements including foreign languages. The sophisticated computer algorithms created compound databases, whereby they took multiple points of interest that intersected.

As an example, a historian with martial arts black belt and a minor in mathematics and foreign languages. The computer algorithms then took job descriptions and matched the compound points of interest with job descriptions deriving a potential candidate to fulfill that billet.

<u>EXT. PRAXISVLASIA FOOD COURT – DAY – EVO KALAN CARRIES HIS MEAL TO FOOD COURT TABLE.</u>

EVO KAPLAN started daydreaming about what brought him to this circumstance as he reflected on his past.

VOICE OVER (MALE)

Evo Kaplan surveillance files were suddenly in a compound database and went into another database under description: *objective personnel recruitment.* A background check immediately started without the recruit knowing he was under any kind of scrutiny.

Since the Dranzonian Empire Secret Service could access any data storage on the planet, or monitor any communications, and perform surveillance on anyone at any time; it didn't take long to discover who the person's family was, his inner circle of friends, his college professors, especially those he had the most acute relations with, like in the history department at the university.

Thus, before any recruiter ever confronted Evo Kaplan, they already had his dossier, and the recruiter had carefully read it along with recommendations and had with him allowable indoctrination materials used in the recruitment process.

In Evo Kaplan's personal situation, with only one remaining family member who was terminally ill, there wouldn't be a family to investigate. His background check was substantially simpler. His lack of political involvement was also a plus because he was unlikely to fall into the Revolution mindset that was then sweeping the Empire, including the first salvo of the civil war starting on Zuanshicheng, Revolutionary Empire home world and capital.

During the winter break, which allowed students to visit their home worlds and get out of the horrible weather that marked that period of weather patterns for Praxisvlasia, Evo Kaplan would have a lot of free time, and his recruiter knew it. Evo Kaplan saw no need to travel the long distance to Vergentia, a Dranzonian Empire World where he grew up because his relative, an uncle, was terminally ill and very well might be dead and cremated by the time he got there.

Avoiding that winter break travel, he could concentrate on his studies and work on the thesis he was writing as a requirement for graduation, which would occur, if all things went right, in six months. Evo Kaplan's dormitory roommate had already left on the holiday, and he was alone in his room when the doorbell rang. Looking through the security optics at the door, he saw a well-dressed man carrying a pouch or streamlined briefcase. Evo Kaplan opened the door.

EVO KAPLAN
Is there something you need?

STRANGER
Are you Evo Kaplan?

EVO KAPLAN
Yes.

STRANGER

May I have a few minutes with you? I have something I wish to discuss with you.

It was not uncommon for corporate recruiters to start canvasing graduate students at this time, since they would be available to start work in a short period of time and in some cases could start working part time as an intern.

                              EVO KAPLAN
                            Sure, come on in.


The well-dressed recruiter and Evo Kaplan went into Evo's dormitory room and Evo gestured to the man.


                              EVO KAPLAN
                        Would you like to sit down?"


There was a large table in the middle of the room that had several books and papers on it where it appeared someone was researching and working on a project.


                              STRANGER
                            Yes, thank you.


The man pulled out a brief out of his case.


                              STRANGER
                I know you realize at this point in your education, you would
                start to have recruiters show up on your doorstep attempting to
                hook you before their competitors do.

                I wasn't expecting many corporate recruiters because I'm a
                history major and most likely schools and universities would
                most likely seek me.


                              STRANGER
                I represent an organization that is like a university, with all the
                vigor and challenges associated with it.


                              EVO KAPLAN
                        And exactly who is that?"


                              STRANGER
                Have you ever entertained the notion of working for a
                government agency?


                              EVO KAPLAN
                            No, not really.

STRANGER
Here's a little pamphlet I've brought along to kind of give you
the gist of what we do.

The man handed Evo Kaplan the briefing, which was nicely bound in professional
looking covers, almost as if it were a hard-bound book.

Evo's heart almost dropped when he saw the title:

*"Considering a Career with the Secret Service."*

As he opened the brief and casually looked at some of the zingers in the high gloss
pages, he felt an emotion like never before in his life. There was intense curiosity,
as well as fear.

The man sitting across from him was now more than intimidating. If was no
different than a Spanish Matador looking into the eyes of a bull for the first time.

KAPLAN
You represent the Secret Service?

SECRET SERVICE REP
That's correct. I'm a recruiter for the Dranzonian Empire Secret
Service.

EVO KAPLAN
I couldn't accept a job offer from anyone until I finished my
master's degree.

SECRET SERVICE REP
We wouldn't expect you to leave the campus until you have
finished and received your degree. But we wanted to contact
you now, get you to make a commitment, then prepare you for
your training as soon as you finish here.

EVO KAPLAN
If I agreed to join the Secret Service, what would I have to do?

SECRET SERVICE REP
It would be impossible for me to explain it all to you here in a
short period of time. If you are sincerely interested, we know
that you have ample time now with your winter break, and I
would arrange to fly you to our headquarters where you would
get an indoctrination and begin the process.

EVO KAPLAN
What happens after the indoctrination?

 We would then fly you back here so you could continue working on your academics and finish up. As soon as you graduate, we would then send you to our training center and you would begin your life as a Secret Service agent."

EVO KAPLAN
I suppose I could go for indoctrination.

SECRET SERVICE REP
When could you be ready?

EVO KAPLAN
Anytime, really. I have quite a bit of free time now since the campus library will be closing tomorrow for a week so that librarians can take off for the holiday."

SECRET SERVICE REP
Would it be okay for me to arrange transportation for you, say, tomorrow morning?

EVO KAPLAN
Sure, why not?

SECRET SERVICE REP
One other thing.

EVKAPLAN
Yes?

SECRET SERVICE REP
It would be in your best interest not to inform anyone what you are about to embark upon. For your own personal safety in the future, where our enemy's data mine everything, you should not discuss with anyone your intentions of becoming a Secret Service agent.

EVKAPLAN
Yes?

SECRET SERVICE REP
Also, it's our policy to never divulge to anyone outside the agency the identity of any Secret Service agent, and that includes you notifying any friends or relatives."

EVO KAPLAN
What do I tell them?

SECRET SERVICE REP
We will provide you with a cover story. For now, in case someone asks you where and why you are traveling tomorrow, simply tell them a corporate recruiter is taking you on a trip to present an opportunity for you. And by agreement of non-disclosure, you can't name the company.

EVO KAPLAN
I do not have anyone I'll be meeting before tomorrow.

SECRET SERVICE REP
All right, Evo Kaplan, tomorrow morning someone will ring your doorbell and you will be taken to the space port for transport to headquarters.

EVO KAPLAN
Am I going to another planet?"

SECRET SERVICE REP
No, it's just a long distance so you will be flying on an orbiter to get there quickly.

EVO KAPLAN
All right.

SECRET SERVICE REP
One other thing. I would like that brief back. It would not be good for you to have that laying around here in case your roommate spotted it.

Evo Kaplan handed the brief to the Secret Service recruiter, who put it in his briefcase. The man stood up and walked toward the door, which Evo Kaplan opened and watched him smartly walk away.

Evo's life as a Dranzonian Secret Service Agent began then, and he never would have predicted the terrible outcome that would be his destiny.

Even though Evo Kaplan was moderately upset with the treatment he received, along with the perceived defamation and vilification in an all-out character assassination so that his supervisor Reginald Heiqishi could arrange for him to be purged with all the other undesirables, he still maintained a shred of patriotism and loyalty.

Evo Kaplan's loyalty was waning by the day as his personal poverty grew to the point it seriously affected his ability to maintain even modest living standards.

Well-trained spies do not always detect when they are being recruited. The process is very complex and complicated because there is great risk in the event the target of the recruitment decides to notify officials and agree to become a temporary operative or double spy to bag a potential intelligence asset.

The Revolutionary Spy Recruiter had to go slow. There must be multiple contacts and socializing to disarm the psyche of the person and gradually prepare them for the next level in the recruitment process.

Sometimes recruiting a spy turns out to be quick, but sometimes it's painfully slow. People in the field in the spy business have their protocols and rule of thumb to adhere to. Otherwise, they run the risk of compromise.

In the business of cloak and dagger, anonymous people, or others referred to as spooks, because nobody really knows their identity. If a recruiter is compromised, they are also often killed, especially since there is no identification and record to who the individual really is.

Where there are stringent laws such as in the case of the Dranzonian due process, which was considered one of the most advanced and compassionate in the galaxy, the Secret Service knows it's considerably easier and simpler to merely dispose of a body than to attempt the complicated route of due process in the legal system. They also know nobody will ever miss a spook since they have a phony ID and the perpetrating enemy will never attempt to recover a spook because that in itself would be an admission to participation in a nefarious process.

Evo Kaplan had a lot of Revolutionary surveillance on him. They always knew where and when to find him. In his case, Evo Kaplan's recruitment started with hunger pain.

<u>EXT.   PRAXISVLASIA FOOD-COURT - DAY</u>

-

VOICEOVER

Without a lot of credits saved up, Evo Kaplan, watching his savings slowly dwindle down, was desperate to find a source of income. Evo carefully planned out his meals and sometimes had extremely insignificant meals just to hold him over for a day, Evo Kaplan was at an outdoor public food court table typically shared with a dozen or more strangers, starting to eat his modest and minimal meal, when a well-dressed gentleman sat down  on the same table directly across from him.

GENTLEMAN

That looks like enough food for a couple of pigeons.


EVO KAPLAN

Well, it's all I can afford. I must space out meals. I do not have
an income.


GENTLEMAN

Yeah, it's been tough on a lot of people since the Revolution.
Say, let me buy you a wholesome meal. Maybe that will help
put you back on your feet again.


In the past, Evo Kaplan would have told the stranger to get out
of his face and might have entertained the notion to simply
kicking his ass, but hunger has a funny way of working on one's
personal psyche.


EVO KAPLAN

Normally I wouldn't accept gifts from strangers, but I've
not eaten well lately. If you want to buy me one of those box
lunches, I'll take one.


GENTLEMAN

Sure, I'll be right back.


Evo Kaplan watched the man get up and make his way over to a food counter that
sold box lunches that had everything in them one needed, including an RFI sticker
for a drink dispensary. Moments later the man walked back to the table with two
box lunches.


GENTLEMAN

Here you go, the drink dispensary sticker is on the box lunch so
you can go select which drink you want.


The man followed Evo Kaplan to the drink dispensary, where they both received
the drinks of their choice, and they made their way back to the park-like bench in
the food court area.


Evo didn't pay too much attention to the man as he opened his box lunch and
started removing items to eat. It wasn't fancy, but it hit the mark. This would be
the most substantial meal Evo Kaplan had in over a week.


As the hunger pains started to rescind, Evo Kaplan then started to morph into a
suspicious personality of the traits of a good spy. It was the eternal spy in his soul
that drove him to analyze the stranger and size him up.

Evo Kaplan might not be employed, but that didn't mean he wasn't still a good spy. Even though Evo Kaplan was just now becoming penniless, he at least kept his dignity and kept up his personal hygiene, though in coming days it would start to get rougher if he didn't find employment.

EVO KAPLAN

So, who are you and what do you want?

Evo Kaplan knew this man had targeted him for some specific reason, as there were plenty of bums around, the stranger could have fed.

GENTLEMAN
I know a way of spotting talent. I'm always on the lookout for talent where I can place that individual. in interesting scenarios that provide mutual benefit.

EVO KAPLAN

I see. What specific areas of interest?

GENTLEMAN

A lot of different opportunities come along in technology, finance, security, you name it.

EVO KAPLAN

Are there some of those opportunities available now?

GENTLEMAN

I always find opportunities. That's the business I'm in.

EVO KAPLAN

What made you decide to approach me?

GENTLEMAN

I first saw you from a distance, thought you were a normal person out enjoying your day, then I watched. you order your food, and the contents immediately gave me the notion you might be in a stressed situation, like a lot of people these days since the Revolution.

EVO KAPLAN

Okay, but why me? Surely there are a lot of ordinary people that have done what I did today because a lot of people are walking around hungry these days.

GENTLEMAN

Yes, they are, but they clearly don't take the time to keep
themselves clean and pay attention to their personal hygiene
like you.


EVO KAPLAN

Why is that so important to you for this possible job?


GENTLEMAN

That tells me you probably have high standards and even though
you are currently in a distressed situation, you could probably
be recruited and placed where you would be beneficial to a third
party in their endeavors.


EVO KAPLAN

So, what specific would you have for me?


GENTLEMAN

I have not determined that yet. I need to find out a little about
yourself, your education, former employment history, and a few
other required pieces of information.


EVO KAPLAN

You probably wouldn't believe me if I told you.


GENTLEMAN

No, I would believe you. In the situation now here at Praxisvlasia,
we have a lot of displaced people. Some very interesting with
incredible backgrounds. To no fault of their own, the revolution
has placed them into stress.


GENTLEMAN

What kind of work did you do in the past?


EVO KAPLAN

I'd rather not say it here in public. If we can go someplace
where we can have a private discussion, say a public park, I'd
feel more comfortable disclosing my personal history.


Kaplan wasn't afraid to go somewhere with this well-dressed man because as
a trained martial artist, he knew he could probably kill him within a minute.
But it would be good to find out if this was legitimate and could possibly lead
to something that would help him recover from his personal financial disaster
bestowed upon him by his former supervisor Reginald Heiqishi, who he was just
now figuring out used the purge to get even.

                              GENTLEMAN
There's a park a couple blocks up the street. After you finish
eating, let's go there to talk.

                              EVO KAPLAN
                               Alright.

The two men stood up about five minutes later and began their walk toward the
park. On the way they engaged in some small talk.

<u>EXT. WALKING TO CITY PARK FROM THE FOOD COURT – DAY AROUND
LUNCHTIME</u>

                              GENTLEMAN
Did you grow up here on Praxisvlasia?

                              EVO KAPLAN
No, I came from an off world, Vergentia. Do you know where
it is?

                              GENTLEMAN
Yes, I stopped there once on a trip to the Pleiades. Cluster
where I was sent on a scientific discovery investigation on an
unnamed planet.

Evo Kaplan had not put on his spy thinking cap in a while since he was effectively
out of the business, and he wasn't looking around like he would have two years
before to notice if he was being followed. The men arrived in the park a short
while later several hundred yards ahead of the security detail sent along to protect
the recruiter and, if necessary, assist in his extraction and deposit him to a safe
house.

<u>EXT. AT PRAXISVLASIA CITY PARK - DAY</u>

                              GENTLEMAN
What did you study in Vergentia?

                              EVO KAPLAN
Communications and languages.

                              GENTLEMAN
How many languages do you know?

                              EVO KAPLAN
I'm certified in fifteen languages.

GENTLEMAN
Who certified you?

EVO KAPLAN
Ministry for State Security.

GENTLEMAN
You were a government employee?

EVO KAPLAN
Correct.

GENTLEMAN
What happened? Why are you not with the Government any longer?

EVO KAPLAN
I was purged like a lot of others because I could not prove my loyalty and my supervisor Reginald Heiqishi hated my guts because I often made him look stupid before he got a promotion and became my boss.

GENTLEMAN
Yea, that crap happens now and then. When did you get removed?

EVO KAPLAN
About six months ago.

GENTLEMAN
And with fifteen languages nobody would hire you?

EVO KAPLAN
Who would I tell them to call for a reference? My old supervisor, Reginald Heiqishi?

GENTLEMAN
Yeah, I can see where that could be dicey. What did you do for the Ministry for State Security?

EVO KAPLAN
This is the part you probably will have a hard time believing.

GENTLEMAN
I think I will believe you. Go ahead and tell me.

EVO KAPLAN
I worked for the Secret Service.

GENTLEMAN
Did you have some type of desk job?

EVO KAPLAN
No, I was a field operative.

GENTLEMAN
How many clandestine missions did the Ministry for  State
Security send you on?

EVO KAPLAN
I wasn't there for a very long time, I'm still relatively young.
But I would estimate five hundred plus missions, ranging from
days to weeks.

GENTLEMAN
Did you have any major activity during the Revolution?

EVO KAPLAN
Sure, I was the person who managed to keep the MSS operations
center online even though it was under perpetual attack through
espionage and sabotage.

GENTLEMAN
I bet those were tough times.

EVO KAPLAN
I got to see a couple of my best friends killed.

GENTLEMAN
They were Secret Service?

EVO KAPLAN
Yes.

GENTLEMAN
How did they get killed?

EVO KAPLAN

They killed each other. One was a Loyalist; the other friend was a Revolutionary.


GENTLEMAN

What did they do? Shoot at precisely the same time?


EVO KAPLAN

They both had their laser pistols on full power and burned holes in each other's chests faster than they could feel it, then fell over dead.


GENTLEMAN

How do you feel about the Revolution?


EVO KAPLAN

I wasn't for it prior to being terminated. I would imagine there are a lot of people that were purged that are not happy with our government.


GENTLEMAN

Here's my business token, and a few credits to help you stay alive for a few days. I think I might have work for you, a man of your credentials. Contact me in a couple of days and we'll meet and I'll probably have something for you where you don't have to worry about personal finances any longer.


EVO KAPLAN
I appreciate that.


VOICE OVER
(As Evo exits the park and Evo walks home.)


The recruiter turned around and walked back toward the two men who were now on the other side of the park sitting on a bench, as if they were simply two strangers out enjoying the lovely weather.

These elderly men appeared to pay no attention to the recruiter as he walked past. Evo Kaplan watched the recruiter leave and after he was several blocks away, Evo too continued as he headed toward the dump he lived in, which was all he could afford.

Though the credits the man gave him would, of course, make Evo Kaplan's life much better for the next few days. If Evo Kaplan was careful, he could stretch those credits for at least a week.

As Evo Kaplan turned a couple blocks further away, heading for his temporary residence, which was the worst slum he had ever lived in his lifetime, the two elderly men sitting at the park bench got up and walked in the direction of the recruiter. They eventually got to a public conveyance center near the food court and took the transportation to a location where he got off and made his way to a safe house. The gentleman also got public conveyance but went to a different safe house.

The first step in the recruitment process was completed. The Revolutionary recruiters were somewhat elated that Dranzonian Empire's Secret Service would toss out one of their best spies. It's these types of individuals who become the best recruits and ultimately do the most damage to their former agencies.

Evo Kaplan arrived home, still living as a former spy who had left behind his spy craft and was now on the cusp of misery as his life had unfolded in ways he never imagined.

Part of Evo Kaplan's problem was his bitterness as well, as it's almost impossible for a former Secret Service operative that was purged to ever have an employment history, making it almost impossible to find a job.

Furthermore, since there was massive unemployment caused by the financial collapse caused by the revolution, there might not be any jobs to be found. The same sort of conditions that led to the revolution were now being magnified, and incompetence at the top of the government was preventing the steps needed to be taken to restore the public's faith and get the economy working again.

Experts had been warning their leaders that if they didn't start taking massive actions soon, they very well could see a second revolution, which would finally put the nail in their coffin and result in the total collapse of the Empire. The Revolutionaries would then have no problem waltzing in and taking over the Empire.

The squalor conditions that Evo Kaplan lived in felt depressing. The unfurnished apartment was nothing more than a roof over his head, but even that was tenuous if he didn't soon find a source of income. He was, though, suddenly hopeful, and happy that the chance encounter today achieved something at least and the box lunch filled him up nicely to the point he now felt about leaving the world behind and laying down and taking a nap.

The next day Evo Kaplan considered contacting the recruiter, but he remembered the man had said to call him in a couple days. One problem Evo had was he had to pawn his personal communicator to get funds to eat just the prior week. He made up his mind he would wait for the second day then use a public communicator, which was hard to find these days, and contact the recruiter.

Evo Kaplan recalled there was a public communicator by the food court he had been at. Evo decided he would take the time to exercise, especially since he was no longer starving, and he could accomplish a workout.

VOICE OVER

Evo Kaplan went back to Praxisvlasia City Park. There he jogged around the park a bit, then he went to an open area far away from most of the people and practiced his martial arts forms. The muscle memory created by practicing these forms created a lethal weapon. Evo Kaplan knew he had over a dozen special moves he could use to disable almost any opponent, even another martial artist.

In the spy business the person with the first punch usually lived and the other died. Speed was critical. The muscle memory helped Evo deliver those devastating blows, usually in a couple milliseconds. His hands and feet moved so fast that opponents could not see the hand or leg movement as it was applying its terrible blows.

Offset one hundred yards away was two elderly seemingly innocuous-looking men, probably retirees. Evo didn't know but he was now under constant surveillance. His future employers were most interested in how Evo Kaplan was handling himself in the circumstances he found himself in.

People undergoing severe mental stress because of financial situations like Evo Kaplan could simply stay home and brood all day long.

But a genuine professional and someone who wants to maintain their proficiency in martial arts ignores all the negatives and goes out and participates in a regiment of daily activity that will preserve their basic status and proficiency in something as vital as tools in the trade.

As Evo performed his workout, he was unaware he was being filmed and that the video would be carefully gone over by professionals, who would write a report on the efficacy of the routine that Evo performed.

Providence was on Evo Kaplan's side because he put his expertise and determination into his workout, and professionals who knew the forms and the muscle memory understood this was the real deal, the man was maintaining proficiency of a deadly killer.

EXT. PRAXISVLASIA. FOOD COURT - DAY

VOICE OVER
Two days after the initial meeting, Evo Kaplan went to the food court. He was surprised the credits the man gave him was far more than he would ever imagine coming from a stranger.

Evo purchased a box lunch, and the printout showing how many credits were left on the token was surprising. Evo could probably eat the rest of the month if he ate modestly and didn't overdo it.

That fateful moment came at the completion of the box lunch. Evo Kaplan spotted the public communicator and approached it. He placed his credit token in front of the communicator, which remotely accessed it and asked for the number to call.

As soon as Evo stated the number, the voice analysis of the phone system encoded his words and placed the call to the number requested. Shortly the phone rang and there was an answer. A nice female voice answered on the other end.

UNKNOWN FEMALE
Hello. Evo Kaplan?

EVO KAPLAN
Yes.

UNKNOWN FEMALE
Mr. Catamountz will be right with you. One moment, please.

VOICE OVER
Evo wondered why a female would be answering and how she knew who he was.

Less than a minute later, the voice on the other end of the phone was unmistakably the man he had met a couple days earlier.

                    MR. CATAMOUNTZ
Evo Kaplan, I'm glad you called. I think we may have an assignment for you.

                    EVO KAPLAN
                That's great! What kind of work?

                    MR. CATAMOUNTZ
Say, where are you now? Perhaps we can meet. I'd like to talk to you about this opportunity in private.

                    EVO KAPLAN
Sure, no problem. I'm currently at the Praxisvlasia food court where we met a couple days ago.

                    MR. CATAMOUNTZ
All right. I can be over there in about ten minutes. Say, remember the park where we talked?

                    EVO KAPLAN
        Yes, just a couple blocks away from the food court.

                    MR. CATAMOUNTZ
            Right. How about meeting me at that park.

                    EVO KAPLAN
            Sure thing. See you in about ten minutes.

The communicator suddenly shut off, as it was apparent that the man on the other end, had ended the call. Evo Kaplan proceeded to walk to the park.

<u>EXT. AT PRAXISVLASIA CITY PARK.</u>

                    VOICE OVER
(During Evo and Mr. Catamountz arrival at the park)
By the time Evo Kaplan arrived at the Praxisvlasia City Park, a couple old men were once again sitting at the park bench, all smiles, minding their own business, hardly talking.

Evo walked about fifty yards further and found an empty park bench and sat down and waited. True to his word, Mr. Catamountz pulled up on a semi-empty street in a rather fancy land conveyor that stopped twenty yards directly in front of him and got out of the back seat after his driver opened the door.

Mr. Catamountz evidently has some wealth, Evo Kaplan thought. Evo Kaplan now knew the man went by the name Catamountz. Evo had never heard of him before.

Mr. Catamountz approached Evo Kaplan sitting on the park bench.

MR. CATAMOUNTZ
Thanks for calling me. I believe I've found an assignment for you that will be worth your while.

EVO KAPLAN
Oh yeah? What kind of work?

MR. CATAMOUNTZ
I figure a position in security would suit you well.

EVO KAPLAN
What levels of income do security people make these days?

MR. CATAMOUNTZ
You'll make more than you did working for the Secret Service.

EVO KAPLAN
Where would I be assigned?

MR. CATAMOUNTZ
Eventually right here in Praxisvlasia.

EVO KAPLAN
I see. When would I start work?

MR. CATAMOUNTZ
You can be on the payroll right now if you want.

EVO KAPLAN
I don't have anything better to do. I suppose I can.

MR. CATAMOUNTZ
Good, why don't you get in the vehicle with me, and I'll take you to where I can get you set up and working.

EVO KAPLAN
Alright.


Mr. Catamountz led Evo Kaplan to the vehicle where the driver dutifully waited, and opened the rear door and gestured to Evo to get in. Evo climbed in and the driver shut the door, then walked to the other side and opened the door for Mr. Catamountz.

The car was soon on its way to a semi-empty expressway. A year ago, this would have been almost bumper-to-bumper traffic. But since then, due to the revolution, there was massive unemployment and people could no longer afford the fuel since the saboteurs had destroyed ninety percent of the fuel production on Praxisvlasia.

Fuel production making synthetic hydrogen fuel out of the vast ocean salt water was slowly coming back online. Currently  percent of the capacity has been restored and the government was claiming that within another ninety days fifty percent would be restored and expected fuel prices to start coming down.

The government only allowed the companies to raise prices exponentially to help force conservation. They were not out of the woods yet and the latest skirmishes with the Revolutionaries conveyed the notion: *Don't let your guard down.*

Thanks to the massive unemployment and excessive fuel prices, the freeways were almost abandoned, and they were able to shoot across the city in a few minutes. Soon the driver was exiting onto a local road that led up into the hillside. Momentarily they were pulling into the large circular driveway of a mansion.

The car came to a halt in front of the main entrance. People with uniforms stood like guards in front of the entrances. The driver opened Mr. Catamountz's door first, then walked behind the vehicle and opened the door for Evo Kapla

EXT. AT UNKNOWN MANSION PRAXISVLASIA - DAY


MAN IN A UNIFORM
Follow me, Evo Kaplan


The Man in a Uniform  and led Evo Kaplan into the mansion and into the corner room that appeared to be some kind of personal library and study. A good-sized table was in there and some nice-looking people, including a very attractive woman, stood there waiting for them. As soon as the woman spoke, Evo knew this was the lady he talked with earlier on the public communicator.


INT.  OFFICE IN THE MANSION PRAXISVLASIA - DAY

XING GANMAO
Hello, Evo Kaplan. I'm Xing Ganmao, project coordinator.


EVO KAPLAN
You must be the person I talked with on the communicator a short time ago.


XING GANMAO
Yes, that was me.


EVO KAPLAN
I understand I'm being offered a position in security. Is it for this facility?


XING GANMAO
No, it's quite a different location, but before you actually start work assignments, we want to transport you off planet, where we want to send you for training.


EVO KAPLAN
What kind of training do I need? I do martial arts and am an expert in the use of over forty different types of weapons, including lasers and projectile shooters, from when I worked for the Secret Service.


XING GANMAO
As you know, Evo Kaplan, from your days in the Secret Service, it is a changing galactic empire.


EVO KAPLAN
Yes, I'm quite aware of the change that's occurring.


XING GANMAO
You must be made aware of geopolitical issues and other factors. All the expertise you require needs to be developed in total secrecy.


EVO KAPLAN
Alright.


XING GANMAO
A lot of lives could be at stake, including your own. Therefore, we want you to be fully prepared to deal with all the factors you will soon face.

EVO KAPLAN
I think I can handle it when do I start?


XING GANMAO
As soon as you sign the contract, we'd like to schedule you on
an off-planet transport leaving in a few hours. Do you have any
pressing personal matters you need to attend to before we ship
you off.


EVO KAPLAN
I live in a dump, and I don't have many furnishings. I would not
be leaving much behind for the landlord to confiscate.


XING GANMAO
If you wish, we will collect all your personal items. and put
them in storage for you.


EVO KAPLAN
I need to make arrangements to pay my landlord.


XING GANMAO
Don't worry about that. We'll take care of that for you.


EVO KAPLAN
I have a couple months of back rent I need to pay.


XING GANMAO
Consider that taken care of, we'll handle it. Do you want access
to that apartment when you get back from training? Or would
you like us to find you a better place to live since your salary
will be more than sufficient to get a fully furnished apartment
in the Grazdang area?


Evo Kaplan was taken back with those remarks. To be able to afford living in
Grazdang, is considerably more than he was making working for the Secret
Service. This new job was suddenly getting interesting!


EVO KAPLAN
I suppose if I'm going to be gone for a while, just place my few
meager articles in storage and I'll look for a place to live after I
get back from training.


XING GANMAO
Certainly, we'll do that. Now come over and review your work
contract, then sign it and we'll proceed to make reservations for
your travel. I'll now introduce you to Brenda Broyals.

With the contracts signed, Evo Kaplan was led back outside to the front entrance and introduced to Brenda Broyals.

                              XING GANMAO
                         Brenda, this is Evo Kaplan.


                             BRENDA BROYALS.
                  Good to meet you Evo, please get in the vehicle, it's going to
                  take us to the space port.


Evo Kaplan entered the Vehicle and Brenda Broyals joined him. They were immediately on their way to the space port.

EXT.  EVO KAPLAN GETS INTO CAR WITH ESCORT BRENDA BROYALS
- DAY

Shortly after introductions the female escort Brenda Broyals was now sitting in the back seat of the vehicle, next to Evo Kaplan. Evo Kaplan felt it was rather odd he was being escorted to his training with the formidable Brenda Broyals who he knew nothing of.


                             BRENDA BROYALS
                  We have a connecting flight on the way and will arrive in about
                  a week at a neutral planet Zanziltar.


                               EVO KAPLAN
                  Will we be hassled at the space port for leaving the planet?


Evo Kaplan asked, remembered from his secret service work *planetary exits* had been a problem for a lot of people as the government was trying to snag traitors on their outbound passages.


                             BRENDA BROYALS
                  The government of Zanziltar remained strictly independent and
                  refused to side in with the Dranzonian Empire or the Revolution.


                               EVO KAPLAN
                                Why is that?


                             BRENDA BROYALS
                  Their motive, of course, is they offer intergalactic banking.


Evo Kaplan knew about intergalactic *banksters* from the days when he was still working for the Secret Service.

EVO KAPLAN
I know a lot of criminals store their wealth in Zanziltar banks
because the privacy laws on planet Zanziltar are stricter than
anywhere else.

The roads were still almost empty of traffic, so travel to the space port was rather
prompt. Evo Kaplan was traveling basically with the shirt on his back. He didn't
have much to take anyway, having pawned off most of his personal effects to get
credits just to survive.

EVO KAPLAN
I'm traveling kind of light. I've been through a tough time. I
hope I can get some personal items in Zanziltar.

BRENDA BROYALS
Everything you need there will be provided. In my travel case I
have a few items for you to use on the way there.

EVO KAPLAN
That's good. I would sure hate to go a week without brushing
my teeth.

BRENDA BROYALS
Not a problem. One of my jobs is to make sure you have what
you need to survive and fit in. I do have a change of clothes for
you. for your arrival in Zanziltar so that you do not stand out.

EVO KAPLAN
That's nice of you.

Brenda Broyals and Evo Kaplan soon arrived at the space port where Evo quickly
noticed a transport sat there, which he was probably scheduled to go on. The space
port departure area was almost empty, but there were a few individuals checking in.

On all intergalactic flights, due to the lengthy nature, each person had to carry
their luggage onto the spacecraft. You were limited to how much you could carry
in one trip. There were no round trips or carrying racks allowed. That kept the size
and weight of the non-human cargo brought onboard down to a minimum.

 As Evo Kaplan looked around and observed the few travelers proceeding through
the security check point, he noticed they were all dressed well in expensive
clothes. No doubt bankers are carrying the loot off planet to avoid government
seizure.

It was well-known that since the peak of the revolution, people were scared and
there was quite a business of bankers taking depositors money to Zanziltar for safe

keeping, because nobody knew for sure who was going to win. It was a foregone conclusion that if the Revolutionaries had defeated the Dranzonian Empire, all their wealth would be confiscated.

<u>INT. PRAXISVLASIA INTERGALACTIC SPACEPORT</u>

BRENDA BROYALS
I have all our travel documents. Just follow me through security.

EVO KAPLAN
All right.

VOICE OVRER
(While going through security check point)

Evo Kaplan now started to analyze the situation he was in. Whoever Mr. Catamountz was and what he really was involved in now, starting to seem larger than life. The fact they had generated travel documents meant they must have planned this for a while.

Evo had been caught up in the extraordinary evolution of this experience and had not taken the time to gauge Brenda Broyals, who now led him to the security checkpoint official checking all exit vouchers.

Everyone leaving the planet had to be cleared with a state seal on the document. Either Catamountz and his group had some great connections, or they were the best counterfeiters in the world.

Along with the counterfeit document, they also had to have a programmed RFI chip imbedded in the paper for the scanner.

The facial recognition technology would also identify the travelers, and because Evo Kaplan was a former Secret Service employee, his travel was always tagged by immediate reports to the Secret Service.

What Evo Kaplan didn't know was the security checkpoint was manned by a Revolutionary operative, and this date and this flight had to be selected to match their travel with the insider mole being at the gate to allow them to board the spacecraft.

What Evo Kaplan also didn't know was the security checkpoint employee was doing at that moment was ignoring the FLASHING PROMPT on his computer terminal stating in bold letters: DETAIN EVO KAPLAN AND TAKE HIM TO SECONDARY SCREENING.

Someone from the Secret Service would detain and question him on why he was leaving the planet and in particular: Why was Evo Kaplan going to Zanziltar?

SECURITY CHECKPOINT
REVOLUTIONARY OPERATIVE
Everything looks in order. You are allowed to proceed.

The security man handed Brenda Broyals back the papers she had for the two of them, apparently traveling as a *couple*. Evo Kaplan didn't quite know or understand what was going on at that time and showed no outward stress, as he assumed everything was in order.

VOICE OVER

Evo Kaplan also didn't know that Secret Service would send agents to Zanziltar a couple days later to track him down and discover exactly why Evo Kaplan was there.

It would not be the first nor would it be the last time one of the innocently purged Secret Service agents who were upset over their mistreatment decided to become in the employ of the Revolutionaries.

VOICE OVER

Unfortunately for the Dranzonian Secret Service, Mr. Catamountz, and his group *the FIRM* knew the Secret Service would be hot on Evo Kaplan's trail, so when Evo and Brenda arrived at Zanziltar Intergalactic Spaceport, they would be whisked away to an undisclosed location and simply disappear during their entire stay.

After cooling their heels in Zanziltar, the Secret Service agents would travel back to Praxisvlasia, mildly angry at being sent on a wild goose chase. Any record of Evo Kaplan arriving no longer existed. There was no trace of him.

*The conclusion was: there was a misread of credentials at the space port and someone else traveled to Zanziltar.*

The trip to Zanziltar was typical of a long flight with one stopover.

<u>INT. INSIDE INTERGALACTIC PASSENGER TRANSPORT.</u>

BRENDA BROYALS AND EVO KAPLAN BOARD THE INTERGALACTIC PASSENGER TRANSPORT.

VOICE OVER (FEMALE)
The Intergalactic Passenger Transport Evo Kaplan boarded with Brenda Broyals was over five hundred long and eighty feet wide capable of above light speed, though it would not go that fast on this trip. Half of the cabin seated passengers were required to sit during takeoff and landings allowing the transportation company to minimize *Stowaways*.

The trip to a space station stopover on the way was uneventful. Evo napped and slept most of the way.

VOICE OVER (FEMALE)
Upon arrival to the distant Space Station, Travelers were allowed off the ship and could buy gifts at a duty-free shop. Food on the space craft was not all that great and designed to protect digestive systems to help minimize issues with the sanitary system. Brenda Broyals and Evo Kaplan knew they would have a chance to eat galactic class cuisine when they arrived at the space port and didn't eat much of the food the transportation company offered.

<u>INT.  SPACE STATION - EVO KAPLAN AND BRENDA BROYALS DEPART THE  INTERGALACTIC  PASSENGER  TRANSPORT   AND  ENTER  THE SPACE STATION</u>

BRENDA BROYALS
Let's go to a restaurant and get some good food.

<u>INT. EVO KAPLAN AND BRENDA BROYALS WALK INTO A RESTAURU-ANT – DAYLIGHT WITH ARTIFICIAL LIGHTING ON SPACE STATION.</u>

After Brenda Broyals and Evo Kaplan were seated and orders taken, Evo Kaplan looked over Brenda, who was facing him. In the short time they had been together, this was the first close-up where he could observe her carefully.

<u>CLOSE ON BRENDA BROYALS</u>

Brenda Broyals had a beautiful face, and she had no makeup on since, being on a ship for seven days, she really had no reason to decorate herself. It was typical of women to travel long distance in plainness. But even without all the extra ingredients, Brenda had some distinct looks that didn't require augmentation to expose the essence of her beauty.

The Intergalactic Passenger Transport Spacecraft had water recyclers, so people could attend to their personal hygiene and take showers in the artificial gravity created for everyone's comfort and safety. The intergalactic passenger transport was often called a *pigs and people* craft, had a seat and a bunk for everyone. The bunk rooms were bathed in infrared light so that security personnel could monitor and make sure some perpetrator didn't attempt to climb into a berth not designated for them.

Prior to liftoff, a self-locking plastic hand band was placed on everyone that had an RFI device on it to track each person, and their travels through the Passenger Transport and were monitored and recorded for security purposes. Those plastic bands were cut off from the passengers as they were disembarking the ship at their destination.

Looking around the restaurant, Evo Kaplan could see there were many people, besides him and Brenda, still wearing their plastic wrist bands. They would be getting back on a ship to travel to their destination.

EVO KAPLAN
Tell me, how long have you known Mr. Catamountz?

BRENDA BROYALS
Several years.

EVO KAPLAN
He seems like a very nice person.

BRENDA BROYALS
He certainly is.

EVO KAPLAN
Do you know anything about the training where Mr. Catamountz
is sending me?

BRENDA BROYALS
If I did, it would not be appropriate for me to discuss it with you
in a public forum, especially until you go through it.

EVO KAPLAN
I see. Is there an element of physical training since this relates
to security?

BRENDA BROYALS

Like I said before, it would not be appropriate for me to discuss it with you in public. Your trainers will explain everything to you.


EVO KAPLAN

Did you attend the training?


BRENDA BROYALS

If I did, I would not be permitted to reveal it to you.


CLOSE ON  BRENDA BROYALS


VOICE OVER (MALE)

Brenda smiled, hoping Evo Kaplan would stop asking questions. She knew there was a possibility they were tailed to their destination and even the slightest hint would betray them, and the next thing she would know is she would be in a filthy Dranzonian Empire prison where they didn't particularly treat Revolutionaries well. The fact she was a pretty female meant there would be other abuses as well.

Evo sized up Brenda as he reflected that he once read men think about sex consciously or unconsciously once every fifteen seconds. Evo Kaplan thought, a*nyone who tangles with Brenda will probably be in for the ride of their life.*

Some of Evo Kaplan's past experiences working for the Secret Service started to affect the way he was now starting to notice. His mind had entered surveillance mode and was looking around carefully in a not-too obvious manner.

Evo Kaplan looked for signs of clandestine activity, perhaps someone following them or some intelligence apparatus at work. If there had been any Secret Service personnel here, Evo Kaplan would no doubt recognized the Secret Service personnel since it's a small club, unless they had received significant cosmetic surgery, which happens from time to time as they reinvent spies to do new operations.

Nothing stood out; there was no hint of any indication an intel apparatus was in their vicinity. Evo knew too there were now two large competing INTEL organizations: The Dranzonian Empire Ministry for State Security and the Revolution Empire, Secret Service.

Between the two warring factions combined, there were now just about the same number of spies as there had been before. The question is: who was the good guy and who is the bad guy now?

If Evo Kaplan did come across former Ministry for State Security Secret Service agents, how would he know they had not defected to the Revolution Empire Secret Service? That caused Evo Kaplan to create an emotional thought about his past. *My former supervisor Reginald Heiqishi screwed me over and I didn't deserve it.*

*Why should it matter who I work for in the future?*

Evo Kaplan didn't quite know for sure what he would be doing in his new job, but one thing he did know for sure: whatever Mr. Catamountz was involved in, entailed a significant amount of money, and he was going for security training. *Perhaps I'll be a bodyguard?*

The two finished their meal. Brenda paid for it with a company credit token. Must be nice to be walking around with an unlimited company expense credit token, Evo Kaplan thought.

BRENDA BROYALS
I think we should get back to our ship. The Passenger Transport is probably reboarding passengers.

EVO KAPLAN
After you.

<u>CLOSE- ON EVO KAPLAN.</u>

Evo Kaplan delayed getting up until Brenda was up and starting to move toward the exit. Evo Kaplan then took a precious moment to look over Brenda's contours and make a mental estimation of her size, shape, and invocativeness.

VOICE OVER (MALE)
She looks really healthy, and probably works out every day.

VOICE OVER (FEMALE)
Having men check out Brenda Broyals body was nothing new to her. Brenda had been thoroughly trained as an operative to exploit men's weaknesses.

Brenda Broyals had no doubt Evo Kaplan was stealing glances at her posterior.

*If it helps keeping that puppy in line, that's okay with me,* Brenda thought, and had the forethought to proceed earnestly to the space craft to avoid delaying its launch, which usually upsets the other passengers when a passenger showed up late and they had to delay launch. The rest of the journey would be hell-to-pay if you were that passenger.

As they approached their gate, over the intercom made the announcement.

SHIP'S INTERCOM
Ladies and gentlemen, we are now re-boarding the flight to Zanziltar. Everyone, please proceed to the boarding gate and take your launch seat.

VOICE OVER (FEMALE)
Everyone had a private secure bunk to lay down in during the flight. There was a requirement everyone had to be in their seats during the spacecraft launch. The bunks were made up by flight attendants with new linen and open for view so that they could catch anyone trying to sneak aboard the flight.

The Intergalactic Passenger Transport company and government took stowaways very seriously. On Intergalactic Passenger Transports, there were not the typical cargo holds of most Intergalactic spaceships. Passengers had to hand carry onboard their belongings and were given up to four cubic feet to stow all their personal effects, which was part of their berth arrangement laid out in segments next to their seats.

<u>INT. INTERGALACTIC PASSENGER TRANSPORT - SPACE</u>

VOICE OVER (FEMALE)
Shortly after everyone was seated, the spacecraft was given authorization to depart the Dranzonian Empire space port to the obscure planet Zanziltar. The stopover would not have been done except for the fact it was right on the way and other connecting flights passengers boarded flights to Zanziltar at this location.

There were now a few more passengers and the flight were almost full. The combination of anti-gravity machine and the unique Dranzonian propulsion systems allowed the craft to take off down a runway and land just like an aircraft or from a space station like they were now leaving.

The space station strategically located from planets had different types of craft coming and going, providing planetary to galactic transfers. When launching from a planet, the windows would be useful for five minutes, then the radiation shields would slide down, covering them to protect passengers as the craft traveled through space and sometimes through radiation gradients caused by cosmic events.

VOICE OVER

As soon as the craft was away from the space station and accelerating, the fasten seat belt sign went out and people were free to move about the cabin, some of which elected to get in their berth and take a nap. With the lunch Evo Kaplan just finished, it seemed to him the most appropriate thing to do now was to get horizontal and take a nap and get his mind off things.

The flight was uneventful. A few hours prior to landing at Zanziltar, the pilot over the intercom suggested passengers get up and take care of their business now so they would all be buckled in for planetary re-entry.

BRENDA BROYALS

Let me get you your change of clothes. Come with me.

VOICE OVER

Brenda Broyals, then stood up and walked to next to her berth opened the storage locker and pulled out a box and handed it to Evo Kaplan, who took it to the bathroom he shared with a dozen other passengers in their cubical area. He would take a quick shower then change into his newly provided clothes, wondering if they would fit.

Little did Evo Kaplan know the Revolution knew everything about him. They had broken into his apartment back on Praxisvlasia and carefully went through all his belongings, finding out everything about him possible, including his clothing sizes.

Evo Kaplan didn't know he had no secrets left.

After taking care of business and the shower, Evo Kaplan felt rather pleasant as the water on his body released multitudes of endorphins, he tried on his change of clothes. Surprisingly they fit perfectly! But the style was something quite foreign. Evo Kaplan had never seen men wearing shirts and slacks of this type, including fabric and colors and patterns.

<u>INT.  SPACE PORT LOBBY ZANZILTAR – DAY</u>

Evo Kaplan exited the Intergalactic Passenger Transport and walked into the lobby. He quickly understood why he was given a change of clothes. He looked like everyone else. His Zanziltar-style clothing was to help conceal the fact he was from Praxisvlasia and blend in well with the locals.

Brenda Broyals also had on new clothes that resembled the local customs. Anyone curious would naturally think they were a Zanziltar couple arriving back from a holiday. Evo Kaplan was now starting to realize there was more to the game being played than he had previously imagined.

Had it not been for his utter moment of vulnerability and desperation, he would never have gotten himself into something of this nature, and he was now starting to analyze what it could possibly really mean.

VOICE OVER (MALE)

Evo Kaplan was shooting in the dark, totally unknown to what his future held. What Evo knew was people got recruited for clandestine operations usually became Victims when they were the most vulnerable.

Victims usually had something going on to be coerced into participation. Trafficking people, prostitution, slaves, and child soldiering was a good example of coercion, and they usually all had one thing in common: *desperation.*

Evo Kaplan's desperation was fearing starvation and running out of options. When Evo thought about how the Secret Service treated him and the fact coming from that community made it real hard to get a job, especially with fifty percent unemployment. The resentment almost made Evo's blood boil. Evo was the perfect candidate for recruitment, and his handlers would play on that resentment in the days to come.

Evo Kaplan's transformation would be quite fascinating. His last supervisor Reginald Heiqishi just helped create an adversary the Dranzonians could ill afford to cope with. In firing Evo Kaplan, an incompetent supervisor Reginald Heiqishi had done more damage to the Secret Service than most moles.

In due time when the Ministry for State Security Secret Service fully analyzed the defection, they would have to investigate all the causes and effects. That supervisor would not do well in the aftermath of such an investigation and a critique of him that followed.

BRENDA BROYALS
Just follow me.


<u>EXT.  PUBLIC CONVEYANCE AREA  ZANZILTAR - DAY.</u>


Brenda led Evo Kaplan out of the Space Port arrival lobby out onto the public conveyance area.


<u>INT.   PRIVATE VEHICLE  - ZANZILTAR ROAD NETWORK – DAY.</u>


A very nice rich-looking private vehicle pulled up making no noise, obviously electric powered, and stopped. The driver got out, walked over, and opened the passenger door of the extended vehicle that contained smoked glass windows that worked one way— only passengers could look out. Brenda obviously knew this person and walked directly over and got in the vehicle.

Evo Kaplan followed Brenda Broyals and about one second after he was inside, the driver shut the door and immediately walked over to the driver's side and got in and drove off. Zanziltar was bustling with activity. Little did a lot of the people in plain view realize, one-third of them were Revolutionaries; the other third were Dranzonians and the rest locals.

A lot of money was changing hands during the Revolution. A lot of weapons were being purchased along with information. The spy business was as good as it could be. Unfortunately for the short-sighted Dranzonian Secret Service, most of that money and activity was being spent and done by other entities. Had they not purged a single Secret Service agent, they would now be far better off. The unintended consequences were enormous.

Thanks to the foresight of dressing like Zanziltarians, Evo and Brenda did not stand out. If someone were looking for Praxisvlasians, they would have clearly missed the couple who blended in well because their natural attire conformed almost to Zanziltar standards.

The vehicle traversed through a major metropolitan area. Congestion was heavy, but the toll road they were on kept it down to tolerable levels. They briskly went through the city and out to the outskirts towards a mountainous region. In a short while they were climbing up a road on the foothills heading to a sparsely populated area fenced off for multiple estates with large properties.

In a while the automobile pulled into a Zanziltar Chateau. It was clear this was used as a base for activity, as there were numerous fancy-looking vehicles parked outside by the entrance. It could easily be a banker's convention taking place by the looks of the types of vehicles scattered around the premises.

BRENDA BROYALS
We get out here.

EXT. *THE FIRM'S* (SPY AGENCY) ZANZILTAR CHATEAU - DAY

Brenda led Evo Kaplan to the front entrance and into the FIRM's Chateau (training campus) that was teaming with opulence.

INT. SPY AGENCY'S ZANZILTAR CHATEAU - DAY

As expected, there were maybe twenty people inside, Evo Kaplan quickly observed. They were obviously busy, and everyone got quiet as they walked through the very large entrance way on their way to a hallway that seemed to be one hundred feet long. From the outside the building looked impressive. From inside it was even more impressive! Evo caught the view of two individuals he immediately recognized. They were former Dranzonian Secret Service agents.

VOICE OVER (MALE)
This was obviously a set up. They must have known all along who he was. Now the day of reckoning is happening. He was probably in over his head in some nefarious activity, which would not end well. *Perhaps Mr. Catamountz wasn't such a nice guy after all?*

It appeared obvious now to Evo Kaplan this organization  the "FIRM" recruited him because he was a spy and even though he had been though all kinds of training on how to spot recruitment and how to avoid it, he just blew basic spy 101, and here he was now trapped, probably going to do something he doesn't want to do and will severely regret.

*Like all good recruiters, they have something to coerce him,* Evo Kaplan thought. Evo's first thoughts were he only signed one page of the contract. They could easily change the other pages and if he threatened to quit, they would simply hand his contract over to the authorities back in Praxisvlasia.

*Did I just make the most stupid blunder of my life?* Another lesson learned is double spies often have no idea who they really are working for. Double spy's handlers use them in  very sophisticated manners and make them believe their allegiances are with someone not involved.

Fear struck Evo Kaplan as he suddenly realized this FIRM in a Zanziltar Chateau in an Intergalactic Sanctuary City, could be a Revolutionary Guards operation.

They may or may not reveal who they really are, but since they are just like me, they most likely could be a Revolution Empire Secret Service Section. The most painful betrayal possible!

Brenda led Evo into a room that could pass for a private study of a mogul. The bookshelves were full of all types of books. Even at a reasonable distance the names of classics stood out. The desk was clean with no loose papers on it.

Whoever used this room had great organizational skills. Nothing was left to chance or compromise. Whoever worked in this room left it sterile every time they departed.

BRENDA BROYALS
Have a seat, Conrad Fanzui be right in.

Brenda sat in the furthest seat, giving the interviewer a direct view of Evo Kaplan when he soon sat down. Moments later the person of interest arrived and sat down at the desk with a file and started flipping through a few pages. At the distance Evo Kaplan could not help but see his own picture was pasted inside the dossier in several instances. Overall, it was probably one and a half inches thick.

*They really have been studying me*, Evo thought, now realizing the enormity of all that was transpiring. After a moment the man looked up, and if Evo Kaplan ever thought he could read evil in someone's eyes, now was the time. No doubt this person now had life or death options for Evo.

CONRAD FANZUI
You came highly recommended.

EVO KAPLAN
By whom, may I ask?

CONRAD FANZUI
Those are privileged sources we can't divulge, as we promise anonymous sources their information is safe with us. We must adhere to that policy to stay in business.

EVO KAPLAN
What kind of business is that?

CONRAD FANZUI
The FIRM is in the same business you are in.

EVO KAPLAN
Until I was hired for this job, I was unemployed.

CONRAD FANZUI

Evo Kaplan, you were a proud member of the Dranzonian Empire Ministry for State Security, Secret Service Branch, according to your statements to Mr. Catamountz.

EVO KAPLAN
That's true.

CONRAD FANZUI

We hired a couple of your former coworkers who were purged the same time you were.

EVO KAPLAN
I noticed a couple guys I recognized coming in here.

CONRAD FANZUI

Yes, they were questioned about you. I believe you went on quite a few missions with one of them.

EVO KAPLAN

I suppose that since I was purged, I'm no longer obligated to adhere to my confidentiality clause with the Secret Service. Did he indicate what kind of missions we did?

CONRAD FANZUI

The FIRM's business requires information that is essential. We pressed him for all the details and since he, like you, were purged and no longer feels obligated to the confidentiality clause in his former contract, admitted to much of everything the two of you did together.

EVO KAPLAN

I see. Since you already know everything, I did, there should be no purpose in me admitting to anything I did in the past.

CONRAD FANZUI

If you are worried, we would use that information against you to coerce you to work for us or do something we wished you to carry out, you are sadly mistaken. We do not need to coerce you. You signed the contract and if necessary, I'll now tell you how we'll enforce that contract.

Evo looked in the eyes of the man who hadn't even introduced himself and could see the evil flowing out of it. If there was a living hell and a living devil, he was sitting next to him.

EVO KAPLAN
I can imagine how you enforce contracts.

CONRAD FANZUI
You being a former Secret Service operative, you should be well versed in such matters, because leading up to the Revolution the Secret Service conducted countless missions, some of which you were part of that one could state showed no mercy on its victims.

EVO KAPLAN
In my business it was kill or be killed. I only did it in self-defense.

CONRAD FANZUI
It doesn't matter why you did it, we just established you are a hired killer.

<u>C.U. EVO CAPLAN'S FACE WHILE HE IS THINKING.</u>

VOICE OVER (MALE/EVO CAPLAN'S)
*Perhaps living hungry and in poverty suddenly felt more compelling than now. I wonder now that they figure I'm stuck with them, will they tell me who they really work for?*

Evo Kaplan was wondering such questions, the PERSON OF INTEREST (aka Conrad Fanzui) suddenly let down his mask a bit.

CONRAD FANZUI
By the way, my name is Conrad Fanzui. I run the FIRM's organization here at Zanziltar.

EVO KAPLAN
Conrad Fanzui, are you my new boss?

CONRAD FANZUI
No, Evo your boss traveled with you to Zanziltar.

EVO KAPLAN
Brenda Broyals is my boss?

CONRAD FANZUI
Yes. Brenda Broyals has had seven days to observe you. She'll be taking you to your quarters now and will make all the arrangements for you.

EVO KAPLAN
That's nice to know.


CONRAD FANZUI
One thing we know is that since you were purged out of the
Secret Service and have not had physical conditioning at the
levels you maintained while working. So, the first order of
business is to get you back into tip top shape.


EVO KAPLAN
And after that?


CONRAD FANZUI
The next thing is technology changes rapidly during wars and
revolutions. You are now obsolete. For the next few weeks, you
will be spending time getting. back up to speed on many aspects
of the spy business.


EVO KAPLAN
That makes sense.


CONRAD FANZUI
 You have not deployed on any dangerous missions in well over
a year. We just can't throw you out to the wolves and hope you
survive.


EVO KAPLAN
I appreciate that.


CONRAD FANZUI
For a while you will be sent out on teams to help you get back
into the swing of things before, we send you out alone on
assignments.


EVO KAPLAN
After I receive all this training and get up to speed, where will I
live and what will I be doing most of my time?


CONRAD FANZUI
It's our intentions to ultimately send you back to Praxisvlasia as
your home base. You will be a deep undercover operative. and
activated from time to time when we need a man of your talents
for projects.

                          EVO KAPLAN
In the spy business there is always someone we are helping and
someone we are hurting. Who are those people?


                        CONRAD FANZUI
Good question. Whoever is the highest bidder obtaining the
FIRM'S contract, and we do what they want or provide the
information they seek.


                          EVO KAPLAN
So, we could be going up against the Dranzonian Empire or the
Revolution?


                        CONRAD FANZUI
We have no allegiances except to money. Whoever pays us gets
our services. The FIRM is an independent Intergalactic Spy
Network. Our purpose and focus are to make money and lots
of it as fast as we can. Brenda Broyals will go over banking
details on how you will be compensated and where your wealth
will be stored.


                          EVO KAPLAN
So, if we get a task from the Revolutionaries, it's not that we
have a moral link to them and would not be doing them a favor,
it's just for the money?


C.U. CONRAD FANZUI


                        CONRAD FANZUI
That's correct. The revolutionaries are no better than the
Dranzonians. They both have issues. We do not have to have
philosophical connections with people who pay us. We just do
it for the money.


                          EVO KAPLAN
Is that why the Firm is here in the Sanctuary City, Zanziltar
where the evil bastards store their wealth in case they end up on
the losing side of the war?


                        CONRAD FANZUI
Evo Kaplan, you are closer to the truth than you realize.


C.U. EVO KAPLAN

VOICE OVER<br>(EVO KAPLAN'S VOICE)

Somehow Evo Kaplan knew Conrad Fanzui was lying. He was probably a Revolutionary Empire surrogate and time would tell when he tipped his hand. *Maybe if I stuck it out here a while and learned this organization well, I could use that to get back into the Dranzonian Empire Secret Service. If I came home with the goods, I might be able to force them to reverse their decision on my purge.*

CONRAD FANZUI

Brenda, why don't you show Evo to his living quarters and help him get set up.

BRENDA BROYALS<br>On my way, Mr. Fanzui.

CONRAD FANZUI<br>Thank you, Brenda.

Conrad Fanzui stood up and walked out of the room through a side door to another part of the building.

<u>EXT. THE FIRM'S OPEN WORKOUT AREA BEHIND THE MANSION - DAY</u>

Brenda led Evo through the back entrance of the large estate, down a walkway past a good stand of trees, and behind a hill, and there stood a variety of buildings out of public view. What stood out was down the hillside a short distance was a park-like lawn large enough to be a soccer field with what appeared to be a jogging/running track around it. On the far side of the field was what appeared to be numerous physical fitness workout equipment. Brenda handed Evo a small hand-held communicator.

<u>EXT.  AT THE DOOR TO EVO KAPLAN'S NEW LIVING QUARTERS - DAY</u>

BRENDA BROYALS

Here's a communicator. It has a lot of functions not normally available to the public, and we'll go over it with your training.

Evo Kaplan looks over the communicator briefly.

BRENDA BROYALS

This is your living quarters, Number Six. Place your hand over the palm reader and I will program it for you.

Evo placed his hand on the palm reader.

BRENDA BROYALS

Activate palm print, certification code 894856, Brenda Broyals.

HIDDEN SPEAKER

Remove hand from palm reader.

Evo Kaplan removed his hand from the palm reader.

HIDDEN SPEAKER

Place your hand on the palm reader again.

Evo Kaplan placed his hand back on the palm reader and approximately two seconds later he heard instructions from the speaker.

HIDDEN SPEAKER

You are the authorized resident. You may now enter.

A solenoid activation sound was then heard augmented by the speaker and Evo grabbed the door handle and opened the door.

BRENDA BROYALS

Go on in and let me show you a few items about your residence.

INT.  EVO KAPLAN'S NEW LIVING QUARTERS IN THE SPY TRAINING FACILITY - DAY

Evo Kaplan and Brenda Broyals walked in the living quarters, which was well furnished. All the furniture was in spectacular shape and looked very expensive.

BRENDA BROYALS

Here's your bedroom through this door.

Brenda opened the door and gestured for Evo to walk in and look. The Bedroom looked like an expensive hotel room on some of the best planets.

BRENDA BROYALS

Your bathroom is through that door. It is restocked when you<br>are away during the day. You have maid service, and they<br>will replace any items that become empty, such as toothpaste,<br>bodywash, shaving cream, et cetera.

Evo walked over, opened the door, and looked inside, and saw there were plenty of towels and a lot of necessities prepositioned.

BRENDA BROYALS

There is a cafeteria down the walkway in the direction we were walking to your quarters. You can order just about any type of food there, as we have a full-time chef. We expect you will be too busy to do matters such as cooking and cleaning. We do all that for you so that you can dedicate your time to professional undertaking.


EVO KAPLAN

I'm ready to experience my ability without being held back by my former incompetent boss.


BRENDA BROYALS

You will find all the clothes you need here. We provide that too. We want to make sure you fit in where you will be going to do your assignments. We program your wardrobe to what you will be doing as well.


EVO KAPLAN
That's understandable.


BRENDA BROYALS

In the closet is workout clothes for physical training and martial arts training. Tomorrow morning, we start with physical training, and afternoons you will be receiving martial arts training to get your proficiency back up. In case you are injured, we have staff doctors.


EVO KAPLAN
Okay.


BRENDA BROYALS

One final thing, you can contact me on your personal communicator any time you need. Just say 'call Brenda' and I will be connected.


EVO KAPLAN
All right.


BRENDA BROYALS

You will be receiving security briefings every day, usually after martial arts training. One thing you need to understand is people here have a lot of tasks unrelated to others, as we have over fifty contracts going in parallel all over the galaxy, and in some cases far out of the way places.

EVO KAPLAN
I would assume so.


BRENDA BROYALS Nobody needs to know what you are doing.


EVO KAPLAN
That's correct. My survival depends on nobody. knowing what I do.


BRENDA BROYALS
They all have been trained in their security briefings to not ask you questions about your work assignments, just like you will be trained not to discuss with them what their assignments are. We are all spies here doing dangerous work. Compartmentalization is very important, otherwise leaks could wreck an ongoing operation resulting in deaths.


EVO KAPLAN
Sure, no problem.


BRENDA BROYALS
What you have done in the past is also off limits.


EVO KAPLAN
That's understandable.


BRENDA BROYALS
Even though you recognize a few former Dranzonian Secret Service guys here, you are not to approach them and discuss your past.


EVO KAPLAN
I'm not interested in meeting them.


BRENDA BROYALS
Nobody needs to know your past, and we do not want anyone to know you were once a Secret Service operative.


EVO KAPLAN
Right, and that is important to me to bury my past.


BRENDA BROYALS
Your past is effectively buried. Your identity will be changed, just like the Foreign Legion. Evo Kaplan no longer exists.

EVO KAPLAN
That's fine by me. In a way the Secret Service allowed me to
die from starvation.

BRENDA BROYALS
You will be given a new identity. Since that hasn't happened
yet, until we give you a new temporary identity, your alias now
is John Youling.

EVO KAPLAN
Will I eventually be allowed to leave here?

BRENDA BROYALS
When your contract is up or when we send you on an assignment,
you will leave here.

Evo Kaplan suddenly had severe regrets. His six-year contract with this spy
agency was a long time. Out of hunger pains he created a personal disaster!

BRENDA BROYALS
Relax for the rest of the day. I'll come by tomorrow morning at
6:00 A.M. and escort you down to the workout area so we can
begin. your physical training.

EVO KAPLAN
Alright.

BRENDA BROYALS
Your workout clothes are in the closet with pairs of running
shoes, you will need in the morning.

EVO KAPLAN
Okay, I'll be ready, but not sure my time clock will be.

BRENDA BROYALS
Understand you will be suffering from space lag for a while, but
exercise will help you adjust quicker.

EVO KAPLAN
Sure.

BRENDA BROYALS
Okay, see you tomorrow.

Brenda turned and walked out of the entrance and turned right, apparently heading back to the mansion where she most likely had an office.

<u>EXT. WALKING OUT IN THE SPY TRAINING CAMPUS AREA - LATE AFTERNOON</u>

A while later Evo left his quarters and walked in the direction Brenda had said was a cafeteria. In due time he found it and went inside.

<u>INT. SPY TRAINING CAMPUS CARETERIA - LATE AFTERNOON</u>

The cafeteria was essentially empty, as it wasn't during normal meal hours, but the staff was there to assist him.

CAFETERIA EMPLOYEE

Hello sir, what can I do for you?

EVO KAPLAN

I'm new here, just checking things out. Got off a transport a while ago and have not had a meal in a while and was getting hungry.

CAFETERIA EMPLOYEE

Have a seat and we'll bring you a menu.

EVO KAPLAN

Thank you.

VOICE OVER (FEMALE)

The cafeteria employee walked around and grabbed a menu and took it to the table. Everyone within the compound was tracked by facial recognition software. When the cafeteria employee walked back over to the terminal and initiated a transaction, which recorded the meal service so that logistics people could apply supply chain management and re-order all the appropriate substances, he also saw the identity.

The person's name was John Youling, which people who had been working here a long time understood was a temporary name and an operational name would soon be provided and encoded in all their site apparatus.

More importantly, the identification specified the cafeteria was available all hours per day for John Youling. There were no restrictions, which meant this guy was a spook.

The menu was prepared and printed in two languages: standard and Zanziltar language.

Unlike any other menu Evo had ever seen, there were no prices. Evo Kaplan, (a.k.a. John Youling), ordered a meal and was soon pleasantly surprised the chef knew his business.

After his meal, Evo walked back to his room and checked out all the amenities, including an entertainment center where he soon was watching some video, and was happy that shows that were played on Praxisvlasia just six months ago when he still had video service before he had to pawn all his personal electronics was playing here locally. Any shows he missed after selling his video equipment could now be seen.

The space lag was getting to Evo Kaplan, so he decided to take a shower then get some rest. Between the early dinner and the shower, Evo was feeling better than he had in a long time. He slid between the sheets and was soon sound asleep. Evo Kaplan should have known the level of surveillance on him. He was being monitored, every move he made. His surveillance team logged the time when Evo Kaplan went to bed.

Evo Kaplan would get a good equalizer sleep and be ready to start his physical training, which he didn't mind. Eating well and having physical training was far preferable to the almost emaciated state he was slowly sliding into just a week ago.

Evo Kaplan's living quarters where he now stayed was very comfortable, with the temperature set for 72 degrees. No sooner than climbing between the sheets, Evo conked out and was sound asleep. His bed was very comfortable, and a deep sleep ensued. Evo woke up around 5:30 A.M.

Knowing that Brenda would be there at 6:00 A.M., Evo Kaplan wasted no time making himself ready, with shorts and a T-shirt, and workout shoes. *They know everything about me, including shoe sizes, Evo Kaplan reflected.*

<u>EXT.   SPY TRAINING CAMPUS WORKOUT AREA - MORNING</u>

VOICE OVER (FEMALE)
Right at 6:00 sharp, Brenda showed up with her workout clothes on, and the two left Evo Kaplan's living quarters and walked down to the workout area and started stretches followed with some running. They then did a variety of exercises.

The workout lasted until it was time to break for lunch. Evo was sore as hell already! Lunch was good and soon they were back down to an area where martial arts training was going on.

Tips on throwing, grappling, kicking, and punching were explored. In martial arts it's all about muscle memory. Evo Kaplan worked on techniques with his instructors, and they soon took note he was actually pretty good.

Just because Evo Kaplan was purged out of the Secret Service had no bearing on his martial arts skills.

Evo Kaplan quickly demonstrated he was fast, alert, and did a great job of predicting opponent's moves. By the end of the training session, Evo Kaplan was exhausted. Evo Kaplan's trainers knew they didn't have to worry about motivating him, as he conducted himself in a very exemplary fashion.

Next it was a couple hours of security refresher. A lot of information on espionage and sabotage was discussed. It became clear to Evo that he could one day be tasked to sabotage something. The consequences could be enormous, especially if he was caught. These routines went on for several weeks, each day stepping up the intensity a notch or two. Then they added an hour of weapons training to fill out the day.

After a couple days with a laser pistol and a projectile firing device, Evo felt at home with weapons. He might have been rusty, but he never forgot his training.

Brenda had observed a lot of training over the past five years and instinctively drew the conclusion Evo Kaplan was one of her best trainees. He was another example that Dranzonian Secret Service did, in fact, train their personnel at a high level. Too bad they were so stupid they purged this patriot. Little did the Dranzonian Secret Service know they threw one of their better operatives into the hands of the enemy.

Now it was time to start developing Evo Kaplan for missions. The way the recruitment process worked, he would get deep into espionage and get so used to it, Evo would never suspect the motivation, or the partisanship involved. And as Evo Kaplan sunk deeper and deeper into the morass of anti-Dranzonian Empire espionage, he would one day figure out Evo Kaplan's working for the enemy. By then it would be too late, as the Dranzonians would be seeking him to exterminate him and anyone else in the Revolutionary Empire Zanziltar Intelligence Operations Directorate.

**REVOLUTION INTELLIGENCE SERVICE ZANZILTAR OPERATIONS**

VOICE OVER
The Dranzonian Empire Ministry for State Security Secret Service Branch recognized there was some type of Revolution Empire Section, Secret Service Zanziltar operation going on.

However, the Dranzonians were unsuccessful in locating it and Zanziltar officials went out of their way to never side with or assist any foreign power as they strictly maintained their neutrality.

The capital city of Zanziltar was referred to as SANCTUARY CITY.

Such a SANCTUARY CITY posture was necessary to ensure their banking sector remained the bank of last resort for the galaxy. Such circumstances were the catalyst to not only ensure their survival, but also their viability as the major holder of wealth of the richest in the Galaxy.

The rank-and-file Revolutionaries were strictly naïve. The centers of power in the Revolutionary Empire, five-member Committee for State Security and the newly anointed chairman, Cornelius Xie de Hundan, lived rather lavishly and they shared the spoils with those closest to the chairman.

The Revolution turned into a pyramid scheme, with people near the top receiving most of the wealth obtained by a variety of methods. The average revolutionary would be considered Proletariat on Earth, and almost all the Dranzonians would be viewed as the Bourgeoisie class.

Cornelius Xie de Hundan was no different than Karl Marx. He understood the value of the low morals of useful idiots.

The failures in life these Revolutionaries realized by the time they were forty years old made them feel they missed out on the finer aspects of life because of their vast exposure to negative influences. The seething resentment of the Bourgeoisie Dranzonians festered year after year until finally societal safeguards broke down and large-scale insurrection manifested.

VOICE OVER
The Five Members of the Committee for State Security were the organizers and leaders of the insurrection that morphed into a major Revolution.

Long before they achieved their power and influence over the Revolutionaries, they had been friends and co-conspirators together. The Five Members of the Committee for State Security only trusted each other, and when the time came to impose their will over one-half of the remnants of the Dranzonian Empire, it seemed natural for them to share power like they always had.

Unfortunately, there was a second uprising, and the Revolutionaries were being opposed, fearing a new Revolution that would fragment their gains earned through the blood, sweat, and tears of many brave men and women who gave it all for their freedom and redesigning the Empire in the political structure they felt was more useful to the broader population.

As a reaction to the Second Revolution that was beginning, the Five Members of the Committee for State Security knew they had to appoint one person with dictatorial powers to squelch the ring leaders of the Second Revolution. It did not take long for the five-member Revolutionary Empire Committee for State Security to appoint their leading general, Cornelius Xie de Hundan, and give him such broad powers.

Cornelius Xie de Hundan, being a student of history, knew his next step was consolidation of power. Hence, he sent the other members of the Committee for State Security on a multi-year fact-finding journey to the distant corners of the Empire, and in their absence absolute power was corrupted completely.

VOICE OVER
Thanks to the five-member Committee for State Security visits, one planet in particular, Stonue, was viewed as a major problem for the Revolutionary Empire. Cornelius Xie de Hundan, being a clever man, realized he couldn't just go in and wreck Stonue. Such savagery would not be accepted by other worlds.

Therefore, Cornelius Xie de Hundan knew his only other option was to deal with its leaders. Assassination, coercion, and other traditional methods were all on the table. The Revolutionary Empire had communications links to Zanziltar via captured relay stations outside of Dranzonian Empire areas they could operate. Conrad Fanzui was contacted via secure communications and given his marching orders.

SPLIT SCREEN SHOT: SPY TRAINING MANSION & CORNELIUS XIE DE HUNDAN'S HEADQUARTERS – DAY.

CORNELIUS XIE DE HUNDAN
(XIE DE HUNDAN pronounced
SHAY DA HUN DONE)
Conrad Fanzui, this is Cornelius Xie de Hundan.

CONRAD FANZUI
Your excellency, what can I do for you?

CORNELIUS XIE DE HUNDAN
The situation on Stonue is becoming intolerable. The Stonues refuse to accept orders from the Revolution, and I do not want other planets to copy their temperament.

CONRAD FANZUI
Understand.

CORNELIUS XIE DE HUNDAN
How soon can you put a task force together?

CONRAD FANZUI
We are always ready to serve the Revolution. It's all up to you in how you prioritize it. We have many other operations on-going, but if you tell me to place this operation in the TOP TEN, we can execute the operation immediately.

CORNELIUS XIE DE HUNDAN
Yes, consider it now part of the top-ten.

CONRAD FANZUI
We will begin operations immediately. What specifically is your goal?

CORNELIUS XIE DE HUNDAN
I want the Stonue world leader Chuo Wanpi removed; any way possible.

CONRAD FANZUI
And after that?

CORNELIUS XIE DE HUNDAN
We'll figure out our next move when we find out what we can expect Chuo Wanpi's successor to agree to.

Cornelius Xie de Hundan then shut off his communicator and sat back and smiled. Being a dictator was far more pleasurable than a yes-man to the Committee for State Security. He then started thinking about his next moves. He knew Conrad Fanzui was loyal and proven it to him time after time as they slowly took down the Dranzonian Empire. If it were not for just one failure at the battle of Praxisvlasia, the Dranzonians would be no more.

Conrad Fanzui wasted no time in swinging into action. He called Brenda Broyals into his office.

<u>INT. SPLIT SCREEN BRENDA BROYALS AND CONRAD FANZUI</u>

BRENDA BROYALS
Yes Conrad, what can I do for you?

CONRAD FANZUI
We have a new task.

BRENDA BROYALS
What's it this time?

CONRAD FANZUI
You are going to put a hit team together and send them to Stonue.
They are to take out Stonue's recalcitrant leader, Chuo Wanpi.

BRENDA BROYALS
If I recall correctly, he's a very popular leader. It would almost
be a suicide mission. Getting off the planet after they kill Chuo
Wanpi will be virtually impossible.

CONRAD FANZUI
I agree. This might be  a good set up to the Revolutionary
Empire Fleet visit the planet to put down the insurrection and
arrest a group of people claiming they assassinated Chuo Wanpi
in a coup.

BRENDA BROYALS
What do we do with them?

CONRAD FANZUI
Keep the killers in safe houses until the fleet arrives and starts
doing a house-to-house search for the killers, and they can arrest
our people and take them back to Zuanshicheng (pronounced
Zoo Awn She Chang) to stand trial, convict them, then execute
them, and scatter their ashes in the desert.

BRENDA BROYALS
Would we kill our spies?

CONRAD FANZUI
No, of course not. The public will not know they were not
killed, and of course you will fabricate an identity for them like
you usually do.

BRENDA BROYALS
I'm a little short on personnel, our TOP-TEN missions have drained most of our experienced agents.

CONRAD FANZUI
I read your reports on Evo Kaplan. Evo Kaplan was a legitimate Secret Service operative and most likely did missions at least this difficult and probably much harder.

BRENDA BROYALS
Yes, our subsidiary sustainment team went through all the Evo Kaplan records we obtained from one of our operatives inside the Secret Service branch where Evo Kaplan's files are kept. I provided a report on all his missions found in his personal classified actions file.

CONRAD FANZUI
Yes, I read that report thinking about staffing this mission. Evo Kaplan certainly did some rather fascinating missions, which begs the question why the hell they would purge him.

BRENDA BROYALS
That's easy. I did my own checking. His former supervisor, Reginald Heiqishi, used the opportunity to settle an old score. In the process he gave us one of his best men. Hopefully he will do that a few more times.

CONRAD FANZUI
You feel that he's developed far enough along to assign him to this mission?"

BRENDA BROYALS
He's much more experienced than half the people now working for you. We might as well check out how well our investment turned out.

CONRAD FANZUI
Yes, his recruitment was rather expensive.

BRENDA BROYALS
And dangerous. We got lucky and were not spotted. How soon must we deploy?

CONRAD FANZUI
I think Cornelius Xie de Hundan expects the assassination to be done this week.

BRENDA BROYALS
That's kind of short notice.


CONRAD FANZUI
It's not the first time you have been up against the clock.


BRENDA BROYALS
Nor will it be the last time.


<u>EXT. IN THE REVOLUTIONARY EMPIRE SPY CAMPUS OUTDOOR TRAINING AREA - AFTERNOON</u>


VOICE OVER (FEMALE)
Just as Evo Kaplan was starting to feel melancholy about his situation, thinking his training would linger for months, Brenda surprised him that day right after martial arts training.


BRENDA BROYALS
Today will be the last day of training for a while.


EVO KAPLAN
Why is that?


BRENDA BROYALS
This evening after you eat and rest a while, you will be summoned to the Zanziltar Operations Planning Center for special briefings.


EVO KAPLAN
What's that all about?


BRENDA BROYALS
For security reasons, we cannot discuss it now. When  you are in the secure rooms of the Zanziltar Operations Planning Center, you will be briefed on your personal disposition and what is in store for you.


Before Evo Kaplan could think of another question to ask, Brenda turned around and walked away from him as she appeared to be heading back to the mansion.

Evo went back to his quarters, showered, put on street clothes, and then made his way to the cafeteria to get a healthy meal.

Evo Kaplan had a strenuous workout and didn't have a big appetite but didn't want to screw up his time clock he had established for his daily routine. He saw some familiar faces, but the atmosphere and the culture here was synthetic as well as reeking of privacy. Simply put, there were no conversations.

However, in another hour, Evo would be sitting across a table from a few of these same individuals as they discovered they were all part of a new team and they were now planning the operation, with help from the intel staff and the technologists who would outfit them with the equipment they needed.

After a small meal and a little rest, Evo Kaplan was summoned by Brenda Broyals who informed him of his new identity for the mission: Proctor Pugong.

Evo made his way to Zanziltar Operations Planning Center. It was a short walk and not far past the cafeteria, well camouflaged and built into the side of a hill. From above it could not be seen by satellites. The walkway was covered to protect members from the rain but also to prevent observation from satellite, which would give away the number of people who were walking around the complex.

Unless you were inside, you would not know what all was there. All the plunder from the numerous Dranzonian Empire worlds easily paid for the clandestine building of this center. Even clandestine construction workers were flown in.

As good as Zanziltar intel was, they even failed to detect the construction of the site and the crowning achievement of the Revolutionaries was to bring in power plants to that outsiders would never know the extent of the development. The Zanziltar Operations Planning Center detected everyone with facial recognition but required a palm print for entry. It all happened automatically.

ZANZILTAR OPERATIONS PLANNING CENTER<br>
SECURITY SYSTEM SPEAKER

Proctor Pugong (a.k.a. Evo Kaplan), place your right hand on
the palm reader.

When Proctor Pugong's (a.k.a. Evo Kaplan) identity was confirmed, the solenoid operated door opened, and Evo was prompted.

ZANZILTAR OPERATIONS PLANNING CENTER<br>
SECURITY SYSTEM SPEAKER

Proctor Pugong, you may enter. Directions will be provided
inside at the security watch station.

<u>INT. ZANZILTAR OPERATIONS PLANNING CENTER – EVENING</u>
And soon a Zanziltar Operations Planning Center Security Officer at a booth just inside spotted Proctor Pugong (a.k.a. Evo Kaplan), he gave him directions to the room where he would start indoctrination.

SECURITY OFFICER
ZANZILTAR OPERATIONS PLANNING CENTER
Proctor Pugong, take the hallway to your right and proceed to room 108, there is someone there waiting for you.

Evo walked to the room where he would start intensive indoctrination.

SPECIAL AGENT "C"
Evo Kaplan?

EVO KAPLAN
My identity has been changed, I'm now Proctor Pugong.

SPECIAL AGENT "C"
Hello, Evo Kaplan. I'm "C." I gave you the name Proctor Pugong for this mission.

EVO KAPLAN
Pleased to meet you, C.

SPECIAL AGENT "C"
Evo Kaplan, your new identity will remain as Proctor Pugong until we need to change it again. You will now use the name Proctor Pugong. None of the other team members except Brenda Broyals is to ever know your real identity of Evo Kaplan.

EVO KAPLAN
Not that I mind, why is Brenda Broyals going on this mission?

SPECIAL AGENT "C"
We are only risking taking her along with the knowledge  of your true identity so that she can evaluate your performance during the operation.

EVO KAPLAN
Alright.

SPECIAL AGENT "C"
Here is a personal documents holder that has all your new identity artifacts and records. No other articles are authorized to be on you when you deploy from here.

EVO KAPLAN
Okay.

SPECIAL AGENT "C"
As a precaution in case, you forget to remove something out of your pockets, a change of clothes will be provided to you in the deployment room, where a doctor will give you a final check for your health status.


EVO KAPLAN
Okay.


SPECIAL AGENT "C"
All your possessions required for the trip will be prepacked for you, and here's a list of articles you will have in your travel luggage. Please review it this evening, and if there are any items not listed you feel you should have with you, please inform the control center watch officer in the front entrance.


Evo nodded and glanced down at the list that appeared to have been prepared very methodically.


SPECIAL AGENT "C"
This might seem a little strict but  suffice to say we have had operatives caught carrying unauthorized materials with them that helped the enemy detect they were agents.


EVO KAPLAN
It's like the Dranzonian Empire Secret Service does to deploying agents. I wouldn't expect anything less.


"C" then led Evo Kaplan, (a.k.a. Proctor Pugong), into a conference room. Brenda Broyals and other team members were in the room sitting at the long table where soon a holographic video was then played that one would feel was a documentary.


The target of the assassination Chuo Wanpi images and a brief history were shown. A detailed list facts about Chuo Wanpi's were shown, including images of his mistress Noreen Taiyanghua.


TEAM MEMBER
Why are you showing us his mistress? What does Noreen Taiyanghua have to do with the hit?


SPECIAL AGENT "C"
Chuo Wanpi visits his mistress about once a week in a secluded residence on the outskirts of Wuxing, the capital city of Stonue. Our plan is to hit him while he's nestled with his lover and make it appear like a murder-suicide perpetrated by his spouse.

TEAM MEMBER
How could his spouse get near the place with Chuo Wanpi's security men in place?


SPECIAL AGENT "C"
Chuo Wanpi is playing a dangerous game. He's a politician and normally would have about fourteen in his security detachment. But since the sleaze is sneaking out to visit Noreen Taiyanghua and is worried about his political enemies discovering what he's doing, he's going incognito with only two security officers.


Pictures and diagrams were now displayed.


SPECIAL AGENT "C"
The home is secluded on an empty road with the nearest home over one mile away. We'll make it look like the spouse shot the two security men who usually hang out at the front entrance of the home and walked in and shot the two lovers in bed with a laser pistol.


TEAM MEMBER
How would this woman kill two agents swiftly?


SPECIAL AGENT "C"
We'll use a very strong laser pistol model that a woman of her means can obtain especially from the black market so that a burn through on the bodies will be complete, insuring death.


TEAM MEMBER
What about Chuo Wanpi's spouse?


SPECIAL AGENT "C"
We'll make it look like she shot herself in the bedroom with her husband and the mistress.


TEAM MEMBER
When is this scheduled?


SPECIAL AGENT "C"
In about a week to account for the time it takes to get there and positioned to a safe house then deployed to the home to do the hit, with time to spare if required.


TEAM MEMBER
How are we going to get from the safe house to the hit and back?

SPECIAL AGENT "C"
There actually will be several safe houses, and you will only
know which one you are going to in the event you are captured.
You will be sent to your safehouse upon arrival on the planet.


<u>INT. ZANZILTAR OPERATIONS PLANNING CENTER CGI. EVENING</u>


A SIMULATION OF THE HIT SHOWN ON HOLGRAPHIC VIDEO TO THE
HIT TEAM.


Everyone closely observed the ongoing presentation showing how the operation
would unfold.


SPECIAL AGENT "C"
The team will be broken up into three sections and converge
onto the residence in a Terrain Sportster and park out of view
of the home in two different directions. Looking at the map of
the residence shown now, you will see the road going past the
home that runs north and south. Every team member will carry
a laser pistol, but we want Proctor Pugong to do the shooting.


TEAM MEMBER
Why isn't Brenda Broyals a shooter, she's the best shot we have.


SPECIAL AGENT "C"
Brenda Broyals will shoot only as a backup and an absolute
necessity.


SPECIAL AGENT "C" was hoping there would not be any more dumb questions
so he could get this briefing done.


SPECIAL AGENT "C"
Team Alpha will ride past the home on their Terrain Sportsters,
which is not unexpected.


There are rider enthusiasts who go over this road from time to
time as part of their hobby and would not be unexpected.


The guards have seen Terrain Sportsters off and on because we
have used them to do drive by in surveillance on the home as
our special Terrain Sportsters are equipped with sensors and
surveillance equipment to confirm the presence of Chuo Wanpi
in the home.


SECOND TEAM MEMBER
How will the sensors pick him up?

SPECIAL AGENT "C"
That's compartmentalized information. I'm sorry, we can't tell
you how the system works, but it does work well.

The team members were mildly astonished, they had never deployed with such
an extravagant equipment before. It implied nobody was safe anywhere, it would
be impossible to hide.

SPECIAL AGENT "C"
Team Charlie will park their Terrain Sportsters in a driveway
approximately two miles from the home on the road shown as
Point Xray on the map.

THIRD TEAM MEMBER
Why is Team Charlie stationed so far away?

SPECIAL AGENT "C"
Team Charlie's purpose is early warning and rear guard to warn
us of approaching vehicles or law enforcement.

SPECIAL AGENT "C" could now see he was starting to get everyone's
concentration. "C" could tell by their body language they were now deeply
involved mentally in the briefing. Assassinations often cause people to be
animated.

SPECIAL AGENT "C"
Team Bravo will stop one half mile short of the home, which
happens to coincide with a curve in the road, which is out of
sight for the security men.

SPECIAL AGENT "C" pointed with his laser pointer onto the holographic map
areas he was addressing.

SPECIAL AGENT "C"
Each member of all teams will have a special communicator we
can send remote self-destruct commands. After this meeting
one of our technologists will give you all training on the
devices used in the operation.

PROCTOR PUGONG, (a.k.a. EVO KAPLAN)
What are these Terrain Sportsters? I've never driven one before.

SPECIAL AGENT "C"
These Terrain Sportsters are all computer controlled. All you

need to do is get on the Terrain Sportster and it will do all the driving. for you. The Terrain Sportsters can operate like a drone with an agent assigned to remotely drive it via a satellite link.

FIRST TEAM MEMBER

Doesn't using satellite links pose vulnerability. to being captured?

SPECIAL AGENT "C"

To single us out and detect us would be like finding a needle in a haystack, but not knowing which haystack to look for it.

FIRST TEAM MEMBER

The Terrain Sportsters have considerable computational ability and the artificial intelligence built in and surpasses most humanoid robots.

PROCTOR PUGONG, (a.k.a. EVO KAPLAN)

Who in the team will be driving the Terrain Sportsters?

SPECIAL AGENT "C"

As a standard procedure, none of our operatives drive the Terrain Sportsters; they are all remotely controlled for all operations.

PROCTOR PUGONG, (a.k.a. EVO KAPLAN)

Why do you do that?

SPECIAL AGENT "C"

Simply put, we control where you are going, you have no choice. I think you can figure out the rest.

VOICE OVER

Chills suddenly went down Evo Kaplan's spine as he realized they could drive the Terrain Sportster directly into incoming vehicles if they wanted to silence their operation.

The Revolutionary Empire had a brutal reputation with their spies. Evo hoped this was not a Revolutionary Empire operation because he knew he was in over his head.

Evo Kalan no longer had control of his own destiny. Being hungry back on Praxisvlasia no longer seemed so bad after all.

After many more details of the planned assassination were discussed, the meeting ended with an admonition that nobody was allowed to discuss the mission under any circumstances. After most of the team was out of the room and Evo following along, Special Agent "C" addressed Brenda and Proctor.

SPECIAL AGENT "C"
Brenda and Proctor, please wait for a minute. I wish to talk with you privately.

BRENDA BROYALS
Yes, sir.

A moment later the rest of the team was gone and just C, Brenda, and Proctor Pugong (a.k.a. Evo) was present in the room with SPECIAL AGENT "C"

SPECIAL AGENT "C"
Brenda, I want you to call transportation services and have them bring up two Terrain Sportsters to the front entrance, and I want you to escort Proctor on a ride through Zanziltar City so he can get the feel of riding one of these Terrain Sportster devices.

BRENDA BROYALS
Right away, sir.

Brenda Broyals turned and looked at Evo Kaplan with a devilish smile.

BRENDA BROYALS
Follow me, Proctor.

EXT. OUTSIDE THE MANSION AT THE CIRCULAR DRIVEWAY - EVENING.

Soon the two were out at the front entrance and two security men pulled up with Terrain Sportsters and got off. These machines would make an Earth person's off-road rider dream come true. It was impossible to see how the things worked; there were no apparent wheels or noise, and when the security men got off, it was quite apparent these things were also very stable.

BRENDA BROYALS
Get on that Terrain Sportster and put on your safety harness. You will be needing it.

The Terrain Sportster had a nice conformal wind screen so bugs in the face and eyeballs were unlikely. *I wonder how fast one of these babies goes.* Evo thought.

The safety harness was self-explanatory, plus the Terrain Sportster operating system had voice and coached Evo through the process of hooking it up properly. Sensors would then indicate they were safe to proceed. Just like an entertainment park ride, great care was given to figure out the best safety for riders.

BRENDA BROYALS

You will be driven by autopilot. I will control my Terrain Sportster. I have your Terrain Sportster set up for *convoy mode*. Artificial intelligence in it will drive you safely following my Terrain Sportster.

EVO KAPLAN<br>I think I'm ready,

Brenda smiled and started her Terrain Sportster in forward motion. Evo Kaplan would soon learn he didn't like his Terrain Sportsters set for *convoy mode*, where the Sportsters would simply follow Brenda at a safe distance and controls would be activated accordingly utilizing artificial intelligence for collision avoidance.

Riding down the curving driveway seemed uneventful. The ride had a pleasantness to it. At the end of the private driveway, Brenda turned right, and Evo's Sportster followed her. He was holding on to the controls in a sense like a motorcyclist would on Earth or Praxisvlasia many years ago. Zanziltar is where the rich boys and girls with fancy transportation played. Other people on Zanziltar had similar Terrain Sportsters and strange looking vehicles that appeared streamlined.

Most of the traffic appeared to be rational, but a few rich young adults growing up terribly rich and spoiled zipped past at alarming speed. Evo thought, *those riders on Terrain Sportsters must be going two hundred miles per hour!*

Brenda was letting Evo get used to riding this strange Terrain Sportsters device and drove along in the opposite direction of the city, ostensibly heading out to the countryside.

VOICE OVER

In a sense, roads on Zanziltar were like Germany's autobahn on planet Earth. There were no speed limits, so if you were smart you stuck to the slower lanes unless you wanted to go fast. In a short while some hot shot sped past Evo and Brenda like a hot sirocco coming out of the desert. That must have triggered a sensation in Brenda because she immediately accelerated at a wicked pace.

Evo was pushed hard back in his seat as his convoy mode Terrain Sportster lock stepped with Brenda's Terrain Sportster and applied the five-thousand-horsepower available.

Sixty to two hundred and fifty miles per hour in three seconds was quite a sensation.

Evo would never lie and say he wasn't scared at that moment. It almost seemed insane. Revolutionary Empire Zanziltar operations took street models and supped them up exponentially. They spent ten times the cost of the Terrain Sportster for the modifications. Performance was necessary because failure was not an option.

The Revolutionary spy ring had to make almost every operation with overwhelming superiority, whether in numbers, stealth, or performance. Because of the terrible consequence of failure, no expense was denied if it was necessary to complete the mission in the way C wanted it done.

With triple the horsepower the punk had that earlier zipped past, Brenda had no issues quickly catching and passing. When the punk decided he wanted to race and sped up to three hundred miles per hour, Brenda left him in slip stream as she temporarily sped up to five hundred miles per hour using computer assist, which used radar and infrared to navigate the Terrain Sportster safely around other transportation devices that seemed to be crawling along compared to them.

The punk quickly gave up. Brenda thought the punk probably scared himself trying to keep up. Brenda then pulled back on the throttles and soon they were coasting along at one hundred and sixty miles per hour, which covered a lot of territory quickly.

Soon the two came up to an exit, which Brenda took. They were now on a narrow winding road going up a mountain hillside.

A person could imagine it looked like a one-lane road going up rural mountains where if two cars met, one of them had to back down to a passing section. Brenda went softly for a while, allowing Evo to regain his composure and hopefully not poop his pants. After five minutes or so, Brenda figured she had given Evo Kaplan more than enough time to recalibrate his stamina, then she performed what such a device was meant to be able to do on this narrow windy road. It was safe to say that within five minutes, if there was ever a time in his adult life where Evo considered crapping his pants, it was now.

One thing this demonstration did was convey to Evo that authorities at Wuxing would have a hell of a time apprehending them if they got a head start. Unless there were air assets already deployed to track them, they would disappear quickly.

Evo Kaplan imagined that after the Terrain Sportsters got ahead a couple miles, they could simply turn into a safe house parking garage and step out of their coveralls and disguises and walk out the back door to their handlers, who had an escape route all worked out.

Brenda then slowed and steered her Terrain Sportsters up to an area that had a beautiful view and pulled over and stopped the Terrain Sportster. She got off the device and walked over to Evo.

BRENDA BROYALS

Why don't we enjoy ourselves here a while before we head back?

EVO KAPLAN<br>Sounds like a good idea.

VOICE OVER (FEMALE)

Evo Kaplan was feeling massive relief for the break Brenda was giving them. If he ever had any notion that Brenda wasn't one extremely tough woman, those notions were long gone. Evo Kaplan also had a growing respect for Brenda Broyals, knowing she was probably far more reliable in keeping them alive in the spy business than he ever estimated before.

Brenda Broyals wasn't super special, per say. She just knew the grim reality of what happens when an enemy gets ahold of a spy. The consequences were so terrifying that suicide was a better option unless you could avoid capture.

That's why Brenda Broyals decided she would get super tough because female spies captured usually go through an ordeal, quite different than men, because their brutal captors were usually rotten sons of bitches that did disgusting and inhumane treatment of captured female spies.

In ninety percent of all female spies captured by the Revolutionaries, death was soon deemed more desirable than receiving special treatment.

Female Revolutionary spies captured by the Dranzonian Empire were severely mistreated as well because the Secret Service had extensively experimented with psychoactive drugs to augment the brutality.

Evo was soon to discover Brenda Broyals felt he was just a mere puppy, and she would have her way with him. Brenda

Broyals knew her life could easily end tomorrow on the next mission.

Brenda Broyals sought sexual gratification from Evo Kaplan and since they were far from where anyone was expected to travel any time soon, she proceeded with her agenda.

Brenda Broyals approached Evo Kaplan who had no idea what Brenda would do. When she walked up and had her body close to him, Evo Kaplan starting thinking as a spy and was planning some evasive actions just in case.

Brenda softly reached up and grabbed Evo's head and pulled him closer and kissed him as best as she could, trained by the best kissing coaches in the spy business for her honeypot schemes, she had to do from time to time.

Evo Kaplan felt sudden electricity and the sweet scent Brenda had. He was emotionally invigorated and had not been with a woman in a long time, so Brenda's stimulation was quite extraordinary.

To Evo's great surprise, Brenda felt his manliness and squeezed it accelerating the erection then she did another act that utterly shocked Evo. Brenda got down on her knees and unzipped Evo Kaplan's trousers and pulled out his penis and started performing fellatio. Evo was now totally shocked by what his boss was doing to him.

Brenda wanted her own gratification and stopped before she jacked Evo Kaplan up to the point he would explode in her mouth and stood up and explained what she wanted.

BRENDA BROYALS

Come over to the tree so I can bend over. I want you to give it to me from behind.

Evo Kaplan didn't know what to do. He had no emotional connection with Brenda. Even though he had to do disgusting things in the past in clandestine coitus during a spy operation, he knew that if he must he could do a sexual act on any decently clean woman if he had too.

Brenda Broyals was exceptionally beautiful. It didn't take much to motivate Evo Kaplan, so he gladly obliged her. Brenda on the other hand thought she was using her puppy Evo Kaplan like a dish rag on her terms, grabbed the tree and bent over.

BRENDA BROYALS
Give it to me!


Evo Kaplan thought this was probably a one-shot deal and perhaps Brenda was testing him for her plans of using him in the spy business in a reverse honey pot scheme to seduce a female for nefarious purposes. Since this was likely a test, he would work for an A+.

Brenda in a while elucidated her physical reactions and wanted to feel Evo's release so he obliged and soon ended the copulation and put his manliness back inside his clothing.

Brenda did not offer any post orgasmic emotional outpour. Her pup gave her what she wanted and pulled her slacks back up and walked towards her Terrain Sportsters as if nothing extraordinary happened.

Brenda Broyals, now rarified by sexual gratification, hopped on her Terrain Sportster to get back to the training facility before C and others decided something had gone wrong and sent people out to investigate.

Finding them would be easy since each Terrain Sportster had a satellite tracker in it and live video capability to allow a drone pilot to remotely control it. Evo Kaplan, suffering now from sensory overload, transcended into a mental state that seemed rather synthetic. Because of his profession, nothing seemed real. The only thing that was real to him was, for a brief period after he was purged out of the Secret Service, he knew hunger for the first time in his life.

VOICE OVER (FEMALE)
(During Terrain Sportster ride back to the FIRM)
Evo Kaplan's ego had been shattered and he knew he had fallen down a long distance and was in no way his former self where he went on missions with full dignity and self-respect.

In just the past hour, between having a woman best him and then later use him like a cheap whore, made Evo Kaplan question his own being like never before. He had gone on dangerous missions long before being part of this spy operation on Sanctuary City while he was still working for the Dranzonian Secret Service.

But now Evo Kaplan slowly gravitated to the notion he was now in the employ of outlaws, gangsters, and foreign spies with no allegiance or morals. He also understood these vicious

animals would make him live up to the terms of his contract—
six years. It almost felt depressing.

Now Evo Kaplan had seen firsthand how such a climate created
by spy operations could turn a woman like Brenda into the type
of person she was. It was clear to Evo Kaplan that Brenda had
no limits. But what drove her? Why was she willing to take on
such huge risks? It didn't make sense.

Evo Kaplan was slowly realizing he met his match in Brenda
Broyals. Brenda Broyals would soon prove to Evo Kaplan she
in fact was one of the best spies in the galaxy who just happened
to be a woman.

As soon as Brenda Broyals determined Evo Kaplan had his
safety harness on and was ready to proceed, she pulled back out
on the narrow country road, heading back in the direction she
came. The speeds were moderate and comfortable. She was no
longer stressing Evo; for that he was grateful.

 Back out on the high-speed transport corridor, Brenda kept the
speed down to around one hundred and sixty miles per hour.
Even though she wasn't driving very fast, they covered the
distance rather quickly and before long exited the road that led
up to the mansion. They pulled up to the front entrance where a
security man stood to receive all possible guests.

BRENDA BROYALS

Please contact transportation services and have them service
these Terrain Sportsters. We are done with them for the day.

FRONT ENTRANCE
SECURITY GUARD
Right away, madam.

Brenda Broyals walked Evo to his living quarters. There was nobody around since
it was after dark. Brenda wanted Evo to understand a few things.

BRENDA BROYALS

I want you to know there is nothing between us. I have my
physical needs just like you do. It's been a while since I
had a chance to go somewhere private with a man to get the
gratification, I felt overdue.

EVO KAPLAN
Understand.

BRENDA BROYALS

Good. Get some rest. We will be doing quite a few things tomorrow to get ready for our mission. I suggest you get as much sleep as possible now because in a few more days, you will likely not get much.

EVO KAPLAN<br>All right.

Brenda walked away in a good mood. She was satisfied, and if she died tomorrow that's okay because she got great gratification by a man who is quite capable before it happened.

<u>INT.  EVO KAPLAN'S HIS LIVING QUARTERS AT THE REVOUTIONARY SPY CAMPUS - EVENING AFTER DARK</u>

VOICE OVER

Evo went inside his living quarters and the first thought on his mind was a nice hot bath to wash away the filth and grime Brenda gave him. She had taken him on an emotional rollercoaster ride. The peaks and valleys were high and low. *Perhaps she's conditioning me for future roles?*

Evo Kaplan maintained high morals. The Dranzonian Empire Ministry for State Security expected the Secret Service Branch to uphold strong moral values and loyalty.

Unfortunately, the same corruption at the top that triggered the Revolutionaries was the same corruption that purged him and ultimately dumped him into near starvation.

In a sense Evo Kaplan knew he was more than likely getting involved with an extremely dangerous organized crime syndicate, and the Secret Service would be very disappointed he didn't report it, like statutorily he was required, but then again, the son of a bitches threw me to the wolves, and I almost starved to death.

Any remorse he had suddenly dissipated with the anger that erupted as Evo Kaplan  contemplated his former disgusting supervisor Reginald Heiqishi who had damaged him so badly.

Perhaps one day he would make Reginald Heiqishi regret what they had done to him.

Evo Kaplan was soon in the bathtub relaxing and enjoying the soothing feeling of the warm water on his skin. After a while he got out of the tub, dried off, and put on his sleeping clothes and crawled between the sheets. It was slightly early, but he would enjoy the extra hours.

Unfortunately, Evo Kaplan forgot he had not eaten in a while, so he woke up hungry a couple hours before he had to. In due time he dressed and went to the cafeteria that was watching  the early arrivals. After a fortified meal Evo Kaplan was ready for the day's events.

More training on the mission occurred including their methods of transportation. They would not be going through normal entry facilities required at space ports where travelers from other worlds were required to be vetted.

They would be illegally dropped off near Wuxing right after their clandestine spaceship entered Stonue's atmosphere. Right after they were dropped off, the ship had to leave the planet because there was no doubt the

Stonue security apparatus located at Wuxing would be looking for the ship, and some illegal migrants that occurred now and then as smugglers were paid good money to move these pour souls to the planet where corrupt business owners paid for cheap employees recruited from off worlds that were accustomed to working harder for much smaller wages.

There was also another sinister reason for all the alien smuggling. Un beknowing a few of these aliens, they were organ donors. Organized crime got paid good money to find livers, kidneys, and in some cases heart/lung combined transplant unwilling donors. These cheerful immigrants would get out of the shuttles, and transported to safe houses where they would be shuttled away to unknown locations where they knew they would be indentured servants for a few years.

Unfortunately for a few of them, upon arrival to beautiful homes they thought was their destination working as maids or landscapers is where they were injected with knockout drugs and moved into makeshift operating rooms where they donated their livers, kidneys or whatever the market could bear. The human remains of the dead person who overdosed on opioids right after the surgery removing their vital organs was transported to individuals running a nefarious operation of converting that body and mixed as a protein supplement into animal feed sold to ranchers.

Within just a couple days, the training and preparations were complete, the team assembled.

<u>EXT. MANSION CIRCULAR DRIVEWAY – NIGHT</u>

The assassination team was soon loaded in a van-like vehicle and taken to a private hanger adjacent to the spaceport.

Because of all the organized crime and money laundering, shuttles were often seen arriving at such hangers where those people involved in nefarious activities got on and off coming to and from space at a mother ship that could not afford to land on the planet for fear of confiscation or embargo.

When it fit Zanziltar's purpose now and then, they would cooperate with the Dranzonian Empire Ministry for State Security and detain intergalactic organized crime figures involved in black marketing especially arms smuggling in the early years of the Revolution.

Other times Zanziltar officials would ignore requests and plead ignorance of such activities even though they knew damn well their bankers were cleaning up on the money laundering.

As expected, a shuttle pulled into the hanger beside the van and the doors shut for security.

The "FIRM" did not want any possibility of airport security photographing any of the team members even though they were all wearing masks to give them false identity.

<u>INT. ZANZILTAR SPACE PORT AIRCRAFT HANGER–NIGHT</u>

Once the doors were shut, the team members were escorted out of the van and into the shuttle where they stowed their gear and fastened their seatbelts for immediate departure.

EXT. CGI. SHUTTLE GETS READY TO LAUNCH NIGHT

One of the many Zanziltar spaceport aircraft hangars, doors opened and shortly the shuttle taxied to the launch runway.

The Revolutionary's shuttle needed almost three miles of runway because they utilized electric catapults to sling them up to twenty thousand feet where it was safe to activate their nuclear fusion powered cyclonic propulsion motors that could damage homes and business on the ground with their exhaust that exhaust vortex was probably worse than a tornado. Soon afterward the spies felt the G forces pushing them higher and it suddenly got dark looking out the windows as they were quickly in space.

<u>EXT. CGI. SHUTTLE AND HIGH-SPEED INTERGALACTIC TRANSPORT–SPACE</u>

In a brief period as expected the shuttle matted with the mother ship. After the shuttle was secured to the skin of the mothership, the access door in the bottom of the shuttle was opened and a ladder allowed the occupants to step down inside a compartment in the mothership.

<u>INT. HIGH SPEED INTERGALACTIC TRANSPORT-SPACE</u>

Soon crew members on the shuttle were handing them down all their equipment. The shuttle was essentially secured and tied down for the duration of the flight to the distant solar system where Stonue existed.

VOICE OVER
(During Transport to Stonue)

Team members were isolated from the crew members. There was no desire for socializing or intermixing.

The trip would take three days. During their voyage to Stonue, the team members were mostly quiet. It was all part of their culture.

Evo Kaplan glanced at Brenda Broyals a few times. She had that look on her face like she had during the joy ride on the Terrain Sportsters. Evo Kaplan speculated Brenda Broyals wanted sexual gratification, but due to the proximity to others in the close confines, it was not possible for her to even consider such acts, otherwise her "watchers" would report back she was unfit for duty.

Evo would learn over time Brenda was all business when it came to missions. He misread her facial features. Her poker faces were an enigma he would never crack.

As part of their training for the mission, they knew some of the greatest risks were associated with arriving on the planet. If they were spotted, the situation could turn ugly fast. The Stonue mission team members were advised that under such conditions they were expendable—sorry, but true. There was nothing the Zanziltar FIRM could do for them.

The other period of extreme vulnerability would be extraction. "C" and his planners were counting on the fact that Stonue's were seriously looking for a fleet approaching, whether it be the Revolutionaries or the Dranzonian Empire Fleet; either way could pose a problem for Chuo Wanpi, who was neither loyal to the Dranzonians nor cooperative with the Revolutionaries. Planet Stonue's strength was distance. If the Revolutionaries made a bold move on this planet, they would run the risk of being intercepted by the Dranzonians.

Likewise, if the Dranzonians arrived they knew the Revolutionaries were simply waiting for targets of opportunity. Even though Dranzonians had ample ship construction ability, the fact they lost so many seasoned and talented crew members put them in a situation where they could not risk many encounters because ship for ship, they were inferior due to manning issues. And since the leadership at Praxisvlasia wanted a sizeable force to always be there to defend the planet and the heart of the Dranzonian Empire, they could not deploy a crushing offensive armada.

EXT. CGI. SHUTTLE AND THE TRANSPORT – SPACE

The shuttle and the transport split apart, and the team flew down to the planet on the shuttle. Thus far, they had not been spotted or challenged.

EXT. CGI. SHUTTLE ABANDONED STONUE RUNWAY – NIGHT

The shuttle soon landed on an abandoned air strip that had been left behind when a newer modern space port was opened on the other side of Wuxing, the capital city of Stonue.

To the team's surprise, there were several Terrain Sportsters there. Behold transportation.

It only took the shuttle a few minutes to dislodge the passengers and their equipment and was soon heading for the runway to get off the planet and out harm's way.

The teams split apart and in pairs got on the Terrain Sportsters and soon headed toward Wuxing to their assigned safe houses. Now it was just to wait until it was time to go make the hit.

Brenda was with Evo. They were part of team Alpha. Two others were part of their team, and among the four they had two Terrain Sportsters.

INT. PLANET STONUE - SAFE HOUSE - NIGHT

The Alpha team arrived at the safe house fully stocked; everything they needed was available.

BRENDA BROYALS
I suggest we all get some rest and unwind and hopefully the
space lag will subside before we swing into action.

Brenda communicated in an authoritative manner. Each member had a private
room to rest. There were lookouts at the safe house for them and the Terrain
Sportsters were at the ready in case they had to bug out to emergency redoubts
that would not be so decent.

After they were all shown their rooms, Evo took to heart the suggestion and
soon was laying down resting peacefully. His mind was elsewhere. He would not
zone into the mission until they were launched via the Sportsters on their way.
His peaceful domain was suddenly shattered as he was abruptly awakened by
something he didn't expect.

Brenda must have had the look on her face he suspected because her she was. She
put her finger over Evo's lips.

BRENDA
Shhhh.

Brenda Broyals then did her magic, leaving Evo in a state of rarified transcendence
to an alternative state with her seemingly love making on top of Evo after she
inserted his manliness inside her. Because of space lag and slight sleep deprivation
from the crowded ship, Evo transpired and was soon cerebrally diminished into a
slumber. He didn't know how he managed, but he slept ten hours.

Evo Kaplan woke alert and alone. Brenda obviously did a hit and run and went
back to her own cave. Evo Kaplan got up. He didn't need to dress since he slept
with his clothes on in the event he had to suddenly bug out if they had been caught.

Evo Kaplan walked out of his berthing room and into the hallway and smelled
the unmistakable scent of a powerful aroma that added to his hunger. His nose
followed the scent, which took him into a cooking area where several people were
eating.

SAFE HOUSE STAFF MEMBER
Would you like something to eat?

PROCTOR PUGONG (a.k.a. EVO KAPLAN)
Sure.

SAFE HOUSE STAFF MEMBER
Please have a seat.

A cup of hot tea was placed before Evo Kaplan, a Stonue trait as the society on this planet was tea drinkers. And as advised in the spy business, when in Rome do as the Romans, Evo Kaplan drank the tea and was soon rewarded with a plate of tasty food items that was Wuxing-style cuisine.

The Wuxing cuisine was pleasingly delightful, filling, and tasty. The food was full of energy inducers, which might be needed later. This, of course, could be their last meal, as they were expected to get activated almost immediately.

VOICE OVER

Today was the day that Chuo Wanpi would be making his fateful journey to his lover's nest. His day would not end well. After eating everyone was directed to check their equipment and be ready to saddle up at any moment.

As expected, forty-five minutes later Brenda received the satellite message on her wrist phone that doubled as a chronometer: "*Qu sha yige biao zi de erzi*," which was the phrase in the operational order to commence the operation and carry out the hit.

EXT. SAFE HOUSE - DAY

The hit team exited the house into the garage and got on their Terrain Sportsters in pairs. The garage door was then opened by one of the staff members and they drove off.

EXT. ROAD NETWORK – DAY – HIT TEAM DRIVING SPORTSTERS

VOICE OVER

Chuo Wanpi picked his love nest for extreme privacy. Unfortunately, attributes bestowed upon Chuo Wanpi horrible principles of security. Chuo Wanpi gave up security for privacy, the fatal blunder he would soon wish he had not done. Also had he not compromised his morals and cheated on his wife, he would never have been able to be knocked off quite so easily.

Chuo Wanpi's routine was so flawless, and he was never spotted. He assumed his temporal paradise would last forever—at least until he was out of office and could no longer have the security detail provided to him to cover his bases.

To get Chuo Wanpi's spouse to the crime scene was easy. An operative approached her during one of her routine events and she was offered an exclusive chance to catch her husband's infidelity. Chuo Wanpi's spouse voluntarily left with the woman and went to the premises.

The Alpha Team arrived at their required position same time as the Bravo and Charlie teams. Bravo Team would approach the security detail to distract them so that Alpha could get in position to take them out. The silent killers did their work, leaving the two security guards with holes in their chests from the laser pistols. Bravo team members then moved the bodies to the side of the house, where they would be later repositioned and traces cleaned up, thwarting future forensic activity.

The house was unlocked, as Chuo Wanpi had no reason to fear anyone since he was protected by two lethal security detail members recruited out of Special Forces.

INT. CHUO WANPI MISTRESS HOME - DAY

Brenda and Evo Kaplan walked into the home, and they knew from training exactly where the bedroom was that Chuo Wanpi would be found. He was busy having sex with his mistress and did not notice when the two walked into the room and suddenly felt a searing pain starting in his back as the laser burned a hole through him and his heart. It was a clean shot and blood was suddenly pumped directly out onto his mistress, who started screaming until she too was silenced as the strong laser beam cut a hole into her cerebral cortex and further into her head, which suddenly stopped all her motor actions. They didn't have to do anything now but wait for the wife.

Chuo Wanpi's spouse soon arrived and was escorted into the house and into the bedroom where she saw the horror and before she could react also received a headshot. The laser pistol was quickly placed in her hand, which allowed a death grip it and they let her body fall to the ground as if it were a natural response to suicide.

EXT. ROAD NETWORK – DAY

Drone pilots using full remote control vectored A Team's Terrain Sportsters to the home, and Alpha and Bravo teams then departed, driving past Charlie team acting as rear guard who let them pass as planned.

After a brief delay to ensure they were not being followed, they headed to a new safe house like the others. The plan worked so smoothly because of the extreme privacy afforded Chuo Wanpi. Nobody wanted to initiate checking up on Chuo Wanpi's until it was obvious, he was well overdue back at his office with a big schedule for later in the day. Then and only then did his aid send a security detail out to check up on him when they found the bodies.

Thanks to the negligence of the staff and the initial reaction of a murder suicide by a jealous wife, the backup plan of arresting the suspects and taking them to Zuanshi-cheng to stand trial wasn't necessary.

## INT. CGI. SPACE SHUTTLE COUPLING WITH MOTHER SHIP - SPACE

The Chuo Wanpi hit team was on the shuttle and landing on the mothership before security detail arrived at the home of Chuo Wanpi's mistress. The mothership was soon heading out into deep space far away from any danger of Stonue forces on their way back to Zanziltar, where they would unwind for a few days and prepare for their next mission.

## INT. FIRM – EVO KAPLAN LIVING QUARTERS

VOICE OVER (MALE)

When Evo Kaplan returned to his living quarters at the FIRM campus, he quickly took a nice warm bath and  was soaking in his bath, relaxing, and trying to erase all his images and memories of the Chuo Wanpi mission. Evo Kaplan could not keep those reoccurring memories of killing all those people so quickly.

This mission took Evo Kaplan beyond being a spy. Now he was an assassin. He had just murdered a duly elected leader of a planet with over ten billion inhabitants. Five people in the span of a minute were wiped out because of his actions.

This mission took Evo Kaplan beyond being a spy. Now he was an assassin. He had just murdered a duly elected leader of a planet with over ten billion inhabitants. Five people in the span of a minute were wiped out

Evo Kaplan could not help but feel like a criminal. He also could not understand why Brenda Broyals used him the way she did. Was he insane or was this just all a dream? From on the verge of starvation to this in the span of a very short time.

Evo Kaplan also knew he was disposable. This criminal enterprise that now controlled all his moves will do so for almost another six years because of a contract he severely regretted ever signing would probably put him in a position soon to do something the people here at Zanziltar would disavow.

Evo Kaplan had killed before, but never sitting ducks like this. On several missions for the Dranzonian Empire Secret Service Branch of the Ministry for State Security, he had no choice but to kill or be killed. The Revolutionaries Evo Kaplan killed were actively trying to kill him, so it was self-defense and self-survival. It felt different than taking out the five people in what essentially was an ambush.

Evo Kaplan tried, but nothing worked. He had swirled and the combination of space lag and post-traumatic space disorder stress weighed heavily on his personal psychology.

Evo Kaplan felt alone.

Even though he was accustomed to this culture from his Secret Service days, he wished he wasn't alone now. Even if Brenda was going to do disgusting things with him again, at least she would be company.

INT. FIRM - CONRAD FANZUI'S OFFICE IN THE MANSION – DAY

Brenda was alone with Conrad Fanzui going over post mission analysis to glean any possible lessons learned. What Evo Kaplan didn't know was Brenda Broyals had body cameras and the Terrain Sportsters had video recording ability and satellite real-time tracking. The debriefing had all the facts and figures of what transpired. Conrad Fanzui was more than a perfectionist.

Conrad Fanzui was a detail man and observed the information very carefully. The mission reconstruction looked impressive and contained a lot of eye candy.

CONRAD FANZUI
What's your personal appraisal of Evo Kaplan's performance?

BRENDA BROYALS
It appears Evo Kaplan is an outstanding recruit. All we need to do is find out how he feels about working for the Revolution.

CONRAD FANZUI
That might be the key issue moving forward. We have no idea how he will react when we divulge who we are.

BRENDA BROYALS
If he remains positive after the disclosure, he will be a tremendous asset.

CONRAD FANZUI
Otherwise, we'll have to exterminate him.

BRENDA BROYALS
I hope it doesn't come down to that. I kind of like the guy.

CONRAD FANZUI
You of all people should know you can't get emotionally. tied
to anyone in this business. Either one of you can be killed
unexpectedly in upcoming missions.

BRENDA BROYALS
I understand that, but I can still like the guy. He has some
qualities I admire. He's cunning, powerful, objective, and
clearly an achiever.

CONRAD FANZUI
Yes, this video replay sure shows he has either considerable
bravery or complete lack of fear.

BRENDA BROYALS
How soon will we disclose to him who we are?

CONRAD FANZUI
I want a couple more missions under his belt first. We don't
know yet if we must disclose because the odds are fifty-fifty, he
could be killed in one of the next few missions we send him on.

BRENDA BROYALS
Will I go on those missions with him?

CONRAD FANZUI
You will not be able to go with him on his next mission. The
insertion and extraction are extremely problematic. We can
only deliver one person because the craft we must use to get
him to the target area only carries one person, and this is also
the first time we will have used it in a real mission.

BRENDA BROYALS
I assume it's been thoroughly tested.

CONRAD FANZUI
We are in the process of certifying it now.

BRENDA BROYALS
How's that working out?

CONRAD FANZUI
It's beneficial being in Zanziltar where we can operate without
a government, including our own, observing us. It allows us to
make mistakes, pick up the pieces, and try again.

BRENDA BROYALS
How's that working out?


CONRAD FANZUI
The Stratospheric Glider development took over five years to work out all the bugs, including the loss of four engineers working on the design. It was costly in terms of financial assets, but also the talent we lost in test flights were irreplaceable."


BRENDA BROYALS
How soon is this mission?


CONRAD FANZUI
We are going to give Evo Kaplan a few days to wind down, then we are going to transport him out to our secret base on Haiwangxing and train him for a few days in its operation.


BRENDA BROYALS
Will he be coming back here for more physical  fitness and martial arts training?


CONRAD FANZUI
No. He'll deploy from there to Praxisvlasia where he will use the Stratospheric Glider to get to Coy's Ridge where the Ultra Rich Industrialist Abniler Manther lives.


Brenda started thinking, *this mission will be the test to see if he will come back to us. We'll know then if he's a viable spy.*


BRENDA BROYALS
Is he going there to assassinate Abniler Manther?


CONRAD FANZUI
We have reasons to believe the technical details of the Dranzonian Empire's new Proton Gravity Disrupter Weapon is stored at Coy's Ridge. The Dranzonians plan going to full scale production of that weapon soon so they can equip their fleet with that weapon, they will have a qualitative edge over us and place our fleet in jeopardy.


BRENDA BROYALS
Is he going there to destroy the plans?


CONRAD FANZUI
No, we are sending him there to steal the plans.

BRENDA BROYALS
That sounds like a very dangerous mission.


The replay of all the video was over soon.


CONRAD FANZUI
Your report was very informative. I wish all missions were as successful as this one."


BRENDA BROYALS
It seemed like all the pieces fell into place. Part of it was luck, but part of it was Chuo Wanpi's personal conduct that placed him in an awkward position that allowed us to the apparent breakdown in security.


CONRAD FANZUI
The government at Wuxing is going though convulsions now as the population of Stonue has received some of the information on the lifestyle of Chuo Wanpi. Currently the public believes the wife killed everyone, but pragmatic individuals within the government are not believing this woman killed all those people then committed suicide.


BRENDA BROYALS
What are they doing about it?


CONRAD FANZUI
They are secretly investigating it as an assassination, and our reports from people inside the government your team left no clues.


BRENDA BROYALS
This will probably be a cold case forever and the public will always think the spouse killed Chuo Wanpi.


CONRAD FANZUI
Yes, that's what I think also.


BRENDA BROYALS
Is there anything I should tell Evo Kaplan?


CONRAD FANZUI
There is no reason to critique any of his actions. He performed flawlessly. About the only thing you can tell him is that his performance was excellent.

                              BRENDA BROYALS
                         Anything else you wish to discuss?


                              CONRAD FANZUI
             No. I think I have all I need. I will contact you if I need any
             other information.


                              BRENDA BROYALS
                        Why the extreme interest in Evo Kaplan?


                              CONRAD FANZUI
             Cornelius Xie de Hundan is personally interested in Evo Kaplan
             for a reason I cannot divulge to you.


Brenda Broyals knew not to ask any further questions. If Evo Kaplan was someone
of interest to the brutal dictator Cornelius Xie de Hundan, it was best she had no
personal knowledge of whatever it was.

Brenda Broyals shortly exited Conrad Fanzui's office and went back to her own
personal living quarters, where she would wind down and reflect upon herself and
her own circumstances.

COY'S RIDGE MISSION

INT. EVO KAPLAN'S LIVING QUARTERS – DAY


Evo Kaplan slept almost twelve hours. The space lag had affected him quite a lot
this time. When he found himself fully awake, he got up and dressed.

EXT. EVO KAPLAN WALKING TO CAFETERIA – DAY

Evo Kaplan, not thinking about much of anything, casually walked to the cafeteria
around 6:00 A.M. Evo Kaplan took a seat. One of the staff member waiters quickly
handed Evo Kaplan a menu, which he momentarily glanced at the menu.


                          STAFF MEMBER WAITER
                     Would you like something to drink, sir?


                              EVO KAPLAN
                          Yes, black tea please.


Before the waiter walked away Evo Kaplan knew what he wanted to eat.


                              EVO KAPLAN
                       I'll have Styrolian Sponges.

VOICE OVER
The staff member soon placed a cup of black tea on the table in front of Evo Kaplan. The voice analyzer of the cafeteria artificial intelligence immediately placed the order before the chef, who went about creating this highly desirable product for the guest.

The staff member walked behind the counter where he faced the terminal to look to make sure the automated process had kicked off correctly and the chef had verbally acknowledged the order in the other room, which had been recorded by the artificial intelligence to ensure efficient operation and validate the process.

The staff member looked at the order, which placed the name of the person on the order derived by facial recognition software. The person's name is Proctor Pugong. However, the staff member with a good memory remembered him as John Youling just a couple days ago. He knew this man probably just completed a mission.

Evo Kaplan's body language betrayed him. He almost appeared like a person who just went through a lot of stress. The staff members had seen quite a few spies coming and going and noticed a change in them, especially as they showed up with a new identity.

Within five minutes, Proctor Pugong (a.k.a. Evo Kaplan), was served his meal. The Styrolian Sponges were served on a bed of Zanziltar Shuidao, which was very much like rice on planet Earth or Vergentia Xiaomai, which looked and tasted about the same. The Styrolian Sponges were fried and slightly crunchy but amazingly tasted like black caviar.

The sauce put on the Styrolian Sponges to give it flavor also had energy inducers added with lots of vitamin B6 and B12, which was secretly prescribed by the medical staff as they integrated meals with the spy's development.

Mental inducers like Gingko Bilboa were also added to help them have a distinct advantage since the consequences of failure usually meant death and compromise of the mission.

The chef was also a pharmacist.

After a second cup of tea and the distinct pleasure of the meal, Evo Kaplan made his way back to his living quarters and changed into his exercise clothes. He knew one thing he could do to help himself overcome the trauma of realization of the blood he had on his hands killing all those people: a strenuous workout.

EXT. FIRM'S EXERCISE AREA OF THE SPY TRAINING CAMPUS - DAY

Evo Kaplan was the first one out of the field running laps around the track.

INT. BRENDA BROYALS IN HER OFFICE – DAY

VOICE OVER (FEMALE)
Brenda Broyals was sitting in her office contemplating her day and thinking about putting her exercise clothes on and looked at one of the surveillance videos she had access to showing the field and the track and quickly observed a runner. She immediately commanded artificial intelligence.

BRENDA BROYALS
Zoom in on the runner at the sports track.

VOICE OVER (FEMALE)
The artificial intelligence of operating Brenda Broyals computer system quickly complied and the numerous cameras all around the facility cycled the best cameras onto Evo Kaplan running. Automatically the system tracking Evo Kaplan compiled statistics.

BRENDA BROYALS
What is Evo Kaplan's pace?

ARTIFICIAL INTELLIGENCE
Evo Kaplan is currently running at eight and a half miles per hour.

BRENDA BROYALS
How does that compare to most people that work out here?

ARTIFICIAL INTELLIGENCE
The top joggers doing laps usually run at seven and a half miles per hour.

Brenda Broyals watched for a few minutes in fascination, then smiled, got up, and put on her exercise clothes and shoes.

EXT. EXERCISE AREA OF THE SPY TRAINING CAMPUS - DAY

Brenda Broyals headed out the door of the mansion and jogged over to the track and got in behind Evo Kaplan, trailing him about twenty meters. Evo Kaplan didn't see Brenda Broyals approach and didn't know she was behind him. She kicked into high gear and slowly closed the distance and was about two feet behind Evo Kaplan.

                    BRENDA BROYALS
                    Mind if I join you?

Evo quickly looked behind and spotted Brenda.

                    EVO KAPLAN
                    Sure.

The two of them ran together. Brenda enjoyed Evo Kaplan being a pacemaker. She had to struggle to keep up with his 8.5 miles per hour, but she knew she could do it and the five miles came quickly. In forty-five minutes after starting his run, Evo was ready to do stretches.

                    EVO KAPLAN
                    I'm going to pull over here and stretch a bit.

                    BRENDA BROYALS
                    Good idea.

The two of them entered the work out area that had mats, benches, and devices that people could use for their exercise they wanted to do. There were spray bottles of disinfectant and towels they could spray and wipe off the exercise-mats, so they didn't have to enjoy someone else's sweat and germs. Some of the spies there were germ freaks and demanded such. They were alone for quite a while and could thus have a conversation.

Brenda had warned Evo Kaplan the workout area was bugged and to be careful what he said there. They had to talk in personal code in ways others would not understand. Brenda had no desire to delve into her physical needs and demands, and Evo would be the last person to bring it up. They didn't have much to talk about and the small talk was rather irrelevant in most matters, discussing items.

                    BRENDA BROYALS
                    What did you have for breakfast?

                    EVO KAPLAN
                    I had Styrolian Sponges.

                          BRENDA BROYALS
                          How did you like it?


                           EVO KAPLAN
                      Good, cooked just the way I like it.


                          BRENDA BROYALS
            You look kind of frazzled, did you sleep well last night?


                           EVO KAPLAN
                  How should I feel after killing those people?


Brenda Broyals noted Evo Kaplan's remark and it raised a red flag she would have
to investigate and possibly bring in a psychiatrist to help Evo Kaplan resolve the
demons the mission caused him.


After stretching they did several different exercises to work on all their muscles.
As they were finishing up, Brenda had some comments.


                          BRENDA BROYALS
            Feedback from my superiors is that your performance was
            excellent. You did well.


                           EVO KAPLAN
            Thank you. A lot of it was due to your training. You did a good
            job preparing me.


                          BRENDA BROYALS
            That's what I'm here for. After martial arts training this
            afternoon, which is not mandatory, but you are invited if you
            wish— you will be taken to another facility to get some training
            for a future mission.


                           EVO KAPLAN
                              All right.


During the martial arts training, Evo Kaplan excelled. His instructors were
impressed with the stamina and the yearning Evo Kaplan demonstrated, as if
something was driving him. Evo Kaplan's intensity never diminished throughout
the entire session. As Evo left the martial arts area and the instructors were alone,
one of them commented.


                    MARTIAL ARTS INSTRUCTOR 1
            I wish our other students were that focused. and put that type of
            effort into the workout.

MARTIAL ARTS INSTRUCTOR 2
Something is evidently driving that man. He must be preparing
for something special.

MARTIAL ARTS INSTRUCTOR 1
Yes, probably that's the case.

After Evo Kaplan changed and put on his street clothes, his doorbell rang. He
went to the door and there was Brenda Broyals. Evo smiled.

EVO KAPLAN
Hello.

Evo Kaplan was kind of wishing Brenda Broyals was coming to say something
like, "Hey, can I come inside and hang out with you?" Unfortunately, Evo Kaplan
wish was suddenly shattered.

BRENDA BROYALS
We are going to another facility now so you can do specialized
training.

EVO KAPLAN
I guess I'm ready to go now.

BRENDA BROYALS
Good, follow me.

EXT. FIRM'S SPY TRAINING CAMPUS – DAY

Brenda led Evo Kaplan down the walkway toward the Zanziltar Operations
Planning Center. Evo assumed they were going for special briefings.

INT. ZANZILTAR OPERATIONS PLANNING CENTER – DAY

They went into the building past security, then they went down a hallway and to
a different section Evo had never been in, past another security station that they
were only allowed to pass because they had been pre-screened and scheduled
to take the elevator up to the top of the two-thousand-foot-tall hillside, which
covered most of the planning center complex. Evo had no idea where they were
going or why. Soon they went to an elevator. They both got in and soon it was
heading upward. Evo was surprised it was a long ride, one unlike he had ever
experienced before. Soon it stopped and they got out and were met by a couple of
security personnel.

SECURITY PERSONNEL
Please wait right here, your ride will be coming shortly.

EXT. CGI. MOUNTAIN TOP HELOCOPTER PAD – DAY  4-ENGINE VTOL CRAFT LANDS 15 SECONDS

A few minutes later they heard the craft come in. It was an odd-looking thing, apparently a VTOL aircraft with four jet engines that rotated a full 90 degrees on the ends of the wings pointing downward. As it got closer to the ground, the VTOL aircraft got noisier, and EVO KAPLAN could feel the wind gusts from the four jet engines as it slowly came down softly on the concrete landing pad.

Momentarily the jet engines shut down. The side of the craft suddenly had half the canopy open, and the side dropped down, which provided steps into the craft. Two men were inside. They were not pilots. This craft was fully automatic, and a drone pilot supervised it from a remote location via satellite links.

The two men looked well-armed. Indeed, they were as both had laser weapons and portable rocket launchers carried like an assault rifle with a strap on their backs that could take down just about any type of aircraft. None of them knew the craft had a barrel rocket launcher in the body of the craft with a magazine of eight missiles that had a wicket punch to them in case they had some strong opponents.

Evo Kaplan didn't bother asking where they were going, as he already figured out this would most likely be something to do with a future mission that very well could be right around the next few days.

Once everyone was settled down with their safety harness full attached and the interlocks closed, showing the remote drone operator it was safe to proceed, the engines started back up and after one minute were applying vast thrust and they lifted off the landing pad.

EXT. CGI. VTOL AIRCRAFT GOES AIRBORNE -DAY 20 SECONDS

As the VTOL craft got around one hundred feet above the landing pad, the jet engines started tilting to a horizontal position and the craft picked up velocity rapidly as it gained altitude. The VTOL was soon flying almost supersonic and quickly covered an area that appeared they were leaving plush green landscaped hills and valleys and suddenly they were in an almost desert-like area. In about ten minutes the craft tilted downward, and Evo Kaplan could see from the back seat a sprawling complex directly ahead.

The craft slowed as the air brakes kicked in and when it got down to around one thousand feet the jet engines rotated slowly to the vertical position. The craft softly touched down moments later and the jet engines shut down. The canopy split apart again and the four people exited the craft.

<u>EXT. SECRET REVOLUTIOINARY EMPIRE AIRBASE – DAY</u>

Waiting for them were several people in suits and lab coats.

BRENDA BROYALS

Doctor Buster, this is Proctor Pugong. He will be the person flying your Stratospheric Glider Mission.

DOCTOR BUSTER

Pleased to meet you, Proctor Pugong.

PROCTOR PUGONG (a.k.a. EVO KAPLAN)

Thank you.

DOCTOR BUSTER

Let's go over to the trailer we have set up so I can tell you what to expect.

PROCTOR PUGONG (a.k.a. EVO KAPLAN)

Sure, waiting to hear about it.

Evo Kaplan was in for a big surprise, and it came fast as they were inside the secure area. Inside the trailer was a scale model of the Stratospheric Glider. It looked rather advanced. Evo instinctively knew this craft was what they were talking about, and he somehow was going to fly in it.

DOCTOR BUSTER

This is a model of the Stratospheric Glider.

BRENDA BROYALS

It looks rather sleek.

DOCTOR BUSTER

It is, and it's quite compact. The Stratospheric Glider's truly revolutionary.

EVO KAPLAN

So, what will it do?

DOCTOR BUSTER

Later you will be given mission planning as far as what exactly you will use the Stratospheric Glider for, which we do not have a need to know.

EVO KAPLAN

I see.

DOCTOR BUSTER
Our job is to familiarize you with it and give you a few test
flights so you will become comfortable operating it before you
apply it to an actual real mission.


EVO KAPLAN
Interesting.


DOCTOR BUSTER
The Stratospheric Glider is designed to launch from a shuttle
and penetrate the atmosphere and land on a planet.


EVO KAPLAN
Why not just take the shuttle down to the planet?


DOCTOR BUSTER
A shuttle is too easy to observe and track. The Stratospheric
Glider is fully stealth and has a substantially smaller radar cross
section to avoid getting observed and tracked to enable you to
arrive unobserved.


EVO KAPLAN
Okay, I suppose I'm ready to try it out.


DOCTOR BUSTER
Good, let's go out and we are going to give you an introductory
ride today. In the next few days, you will take it through its
pace and practice getting down to a location like you will on
your mission.


EVO KAPLAN
Okay, let's have a look.


Doctor Buster led the group out of the trailer to a shuttle that just happened to be
parked next to the trailer, where technicians were doing final checkout. They all
walked up into the shuttle and to Evo's surprise, instead of having a bunch of seats
in the shuttle, it had another craft inside it. Also, what appeared to be unusual with
the shuttle is there was a bulkhead aft of the cockpit that was probably designed
to make the cockpit airtight.


DOCTOR BUSTER
You will enter the shuttle from the mothership at the point of
deploying the Stratospheric Glider, get inside the Stratospheric
Glider and the rear of the shuttle opens, and the Stratospheric
Glider is then jettisoned out of the Stratospheric Glider and
becomes an autonomous craft.

EVO KAPLAN
I assume that means the spacecraft would be deploying for a mission.

DOCTOR BUSTER
Yes, you will be in it. The purpose is for the, the Stratospheric Glider to deliver you to a planet.

EVO KAPLAN.
Interesting.

DOCTOR BUSTER
After you complete your assignment on the planet then you will get back into the Stratospheric Glider. At that time, you will then fly the Stratospheric Glider back into space to rendezvous with the Shuttle, and redock into it. The rear of the shuttle will then close, and seal and you will then fly back to the mothership that will return you back to Zanziltar.

EVO KAPLAN
Sounds kind of simple, but I bet it's not.

DOCTOR BUSTER
You are correct. Lots of points of vulnerability.

EVO KAPLAN
Do I need a space suit and equipment to fly this thing?

DOCTOR BUSTER
No. That is precisely why it's designed the way it is. You need to arrive in camouflaged clothing and equipment and be able to quickly depart the craft and get on with your business. You could be in street clothes if that's how you preferred to arrive.

EVO KAPLAN
I see, just like I'm dressed now if necessary?

DOCTOR BUSTER
That's correct.

EVO KAPLAN
Do I need to learn how to fly it?

DOCTOR BUSTER
No, it's all automatic and we have a drone controller as a backup if necessary.

EVO KAPLAN
Is it ready to fly now?

DOCTOR BUSTER
Yes, in fact, it's our intention to launch you now for your first
introductory flight.

EVO KAPLAN
Right this moment?

DOCTOR BUSTER
That's correct, it's ready to go now.

EVO KAPLAN
I guess I'm ready, since I don't know what I'm getting into, I
can't be scared yet.

DOCTOR BUSTER
Very well, let's show you how to get in and how to exit and
we'll indoctrinate you up on your first flight.


INT. SHUTTLE - DAY


VOICE OVER
The instructions were simple and intuitive. In thirty minutes,
everything they needed to explain to Evo Kaplan was done. All
the unnecessary people were removed from the shuttle and just
the pilot, mission specialist, and Evo were left in the shuttle as
it launched and went up into space to simulate a real mission.


EXT. CGI. SHUTTLE – DAY RUNWAY LAUNCH HEADING INTO SPACE
VIA ELECTRIC CATAPULT AND ROCKET ENGINES. ONE MINUTE


VOICE OVER
(During Stratospheric Glider launch)
Coy's Ridge where the Ultra Rich Industrialist Abniler
Manther's mansion exists was built on an escarpment that rose
over two thousand feet in the air. Access to Coy's Ridge was
extremely difficult and it only had one well-protected road with
full-time armed security personnel guarding it.

Abniler Manther picked this location because it could be well
defended and he had reason to fear the Revolutionaries would
attempt to get to him, since he was the sponsor and the brainchild
behind some of the Dranzonian Empire's latest GIZMOs.

The new Proton Gravity Disrupter Weapon was just one of many innovations Abniler Manther developed, which seemed to barely keep the Dranzonians one step ahead of the Revolutionaries.

The Proton Gravity Disrupter Weapon would give the Dranzonians a qualitative lead over Revolutionaries in weapons technology.

The plan centered around the idea if the Revolutionary Spy Network could steal the Proton Gravity Disrupter Weapon plans, the Revolutionary Empire could build the devices themselves to negate that apparent lead the development posed.

EXT. CGI. SHUTTLE - SPACE 15 SECONDS EXTERIOR SHOT OF SHUTTLE

The shuttle obtained orbit in space to launch profile coordinates.

INT. SHUTTLE - SPACE

                    MISSION SPECIALIST
Go ahead and get into the Stratospheric Glider. The canopy will automatically close just like you saw in the training video.

                    EVO KAPLAN
                    Alright.

By the way that Evo Kaplan responded, the Mission Specialist could tell Evo Kaplan didn't like laying down on his stomach in the Stratospheric Glider.

                    MISSION SPECIALIST
Laying on your stomach will give you the best observation, plus you will not be in that position very long. After your training, you will not view it as an issue.

INT. CGI. 30 SECONDS CANOPY CLOSES WITH EVO KAPLAN SECURED INSIDE THE STRATOSPHERIC GLIDER.

                STRATOSPHERIC GLIDER INTERCOM
                    (MISSION SPECIALIST)
                Evo Kaplan, are you all set to launch?

INT. SIDEVIEW OF EVO KAPLAN FACING THE STRATOSPHERIC GLIDER'S CONTROLS AND DISPLAYS

EVO KAPLAN
I suppose now is as good a time as any.


STRATOSPHERIC GLIDER INTERCOM
(MISSION SPECIALIST)
Very well, stand by.


<u>INT. SHUTTLE STRATOSPHERIC GLIDER BAY – SPACE</u>

The mission specialist went into the cockpit and shut and sealed the compartment with the access door mechanism.

The air inside the shuttle's *Stratospheric Glider Bay*, as it was referred to, was pumped down and below 5 PSI. The residual pressure was simply equalized overboard creating the complete vacuum of space.

Once the indicator in the cockpit indicated *Stratospheric Glider Bay*, equalization had occurred, the pilot engaged the switch that opened the rear access. The mission specialist then pressed the ARM button on the control panel that was an arming sequence, which checked all the interlocks to ensure a safe launch of the Stratospheric Glider. Artificial Intelligence (AI) computerized voice then started the verbal countdown.


STRATOSPHERIC GLIDER INTERCOM
(AI COMPUTERIZED VOICE)
Ready for launch, shuttle armed, interlocks closed.

Evo Kaplan watched indicators on his cockpit display panel. He then heard the launch sequence.


STRATOSPHERIC GLIDER'S INTERCOM
(AI COMPUTERIZED VOICE)
10, 9, 8....

At 3 seconds, AI performed a series of actions.


STRATOSPHERIC GLIDER'S INTERCOM
(AI COMPUTERIZED VOICE)
Standby to launch.


<u>EXT.  CGI.  SHUTTLE  REAR  GLIDER  LAUNCH  HATCH  OPENED.  15 SECONDS.</u>

Evo Kaplan didn't know it as it wasn't his concern now, but during the count down the shuttle hatch opened which the shuttle would be launched through. The countdown reached T-0. Suddenly the launch command initiated Stratospheric Glider launch.

The launching mechanism engaged, and the Stratospheric Glider was slowly shoved out of the shuttle by electromagnet arms. It wasn't anything abrupt. Evo Kaplan was surprised how smooth it felt.

<u>EXT. CGI. STRATOSPHERIC GLIDER LAUNCHES OUT OF THE SHUTTLE. ~15 SECONDS.</u>

The Stratospheric Glider slowly slid out of the shuttle. Momentarily the Stratospheric Glider was clear of the shuttle and after sensors tracking the Stratospheric Glider determined it was a safe distance away, the shuttle maneuvered to give the Stratospheric Glider ample room, then the Stratospheric Glider fired retro rockets, which greatly altered its flight path back to the planet Zanziltar for the test flight.

<u>EXT. CGI. STRAOSPHERIC GLIDER LEAVING BEHIND THE SHUTTLE. ~15 SECONDS.</u>

Evo Kaplan felt a strange sensation being alone as the Stratospheric Glider crept closer to the atmosphere, effectively going seventeen thousand miles per hour when it penetrated the ionosphere. Evo Kaplan was along for the ride. He watched all the displays, but there was nothing he could do about anything now. His life was in the hands of the engineers who figured it all out.

<u>EXT. CGI. STRAOSPHERIC GLIDER HEADING TOWARDS THE PLANET WINGLETS DEPLOY~15 SECONDS.</u>

Soon the Stratospheric Glider was in the atmosphere and the winglets were deployed, which gave it far more stability. From there it simply floated down to planet Zanziltar.

<u>EXT. CGI. STRAOSPHERIC GLIDER LANDING ON LANDING PAD~15 SECONDS.</u>

Twenty minutes after re-entry, the craft managed to slowly land on a landing pad.

<u>EXT. CGI. STRAOSPHERIC GLIDER CANOPY OPENS AND EVO</u>

<u>KAPLAN EXITS IT ~ 15 SECONDS.</u>

The hatch opened and Evo Kaplan got out of the Stratospheric Glider and stood next to it as the engineers approached and the shuttle landed next to him. Dr. Buster approached Evo Kaplan.

                              DR. BUSTER
                            How was the flight?


                             EVO KAPLAN
Even though the Stratospheric Glider is a little cramped, the
ride wasn't too bad.


                              DR. BUSTER
We recorded all the telemetry data on the Stratospheric Glider
during the flight and the results were all anomalous as we
expected. I think we are ready to proceed with the training
program.


                             EVO KAPLAN
                     Will we do any more flights today?


                              DR. BUSTER
No, this was just an introductory flight. Our scientists here
believe in the concept 'Nothing New After Two' and 'Don't
get it dirty after three thirty,' so we'll pick it up again tomorrow
morning.


                             EVO KAPLAN
         Are you taking me back to my living quarters this afternoon?


                              DR. BUSTER
No, we have some living quarters set up in some trailers right
over there.


Dr. Buster pointed to some other trailers.


                             EVO KAPLAN
                               All right.


                              DR. BUSTER
              That way we can get an early start in the morning.


                             EVO KAPLAN
                      Any place to eat around here?


                              DR. BUSTER
Yes, one of the trailers is a cafeteria. It might not be as good
as you are used to eating, but it will at least get you enough to
keep you going.

                    EVO KAPLAN
              It smells like something is cooking.


                    DR. BUSTER
Yes, the chefs' barbecue outside next to the cafeteria, which
some of the staff enjoy, and that's what you smell.


                    EVO KAPLAN
              It's starting to make me feel hungry.


                    DR. BUSTER
Let me take you to your quarters where you have a bedroom.


Dr. Buster led Evo Kaplan and Brenda Broyals to a trailer about one hundred
yards away. It had awnings along each side of it that stuck out twenty feet and
there was a tent-like structure above the trailer to keep the direct sunlight off the
trailer. Under the awning on one side of the trailer was some yard furniture that
gave the appearance that people could sit outside during the evenings and enjoy
the balmy weather and socialize.


A couple of well-armed guys standing beside the trailer as they approached it.
These were large trailers. Dr. Buster led Brenda and Evo into the trailer to show
them its features. It had air conditioning, probably set at seventy-two degrees, and
plenty of opulence.


INT. TEMPORARY QUARTERS – TRAILER – DAY


                    DR. BUSTER
There are bedrooms at each end of the trailer and double
bathrooms so that each occupant has their own privacy.


                    EVO KAPLAN
              Is this my trailer or is it for Brenda?


                    DR. BUSTER
You and Brenda will be staying together in this trailer.


Evo recalled a couple well-armed guys standing beside the trailer as they
approached it.


                    EVO KAPLAN
What are those guys with laser rifles doing outside our trailer?


                    DR. BUSTER
Those men are part of your security detail to make sure you are
safe, and nobody approaches this trailer. Only half of the staff is

cleared at the T4 level. They are not allowed to approach you or communicate with you in any manner.

EVO KAPLAN
Why did you put Brenda and me in the same trailer?

DR. BUSTER
She's assigned partial security to you while you are here to make sure you have privacy and to ensure people not T4 cleared get near you.

VOICE OVER
*They may not be sure I can defend myself,* Evo Kaplan thought. *Then he also surmised, there is strength in numbers. Brenda and I could probably put up a good fight together if we had weapons.*

After some small talk about the trailer's amenities, Evo Kaplan suddenly felt hungry from the smell of the barbecue meat cooking.

EVO KAPLAN
That aroma I smelled coming over here made me hungry. Let's go check out the cafeteria.

DR. BUSTER
Okay, I'll let you guys do your thing. I need to get back with my scientists. We are getting ready to critique the flight after the propulsion and heat shield sections go over the telemetry data.

EVO KAPLAN
All right, I guess we'll see you later.

Dr. Buster made his way to another trailer designed as a temporary office and Evo Kaplan and Brenda Broyals walked smartly in the direction of the slight smoke rising, which was probably the source of the smell that had a pleasing aroma to it. As they got up close enough to see what was going on, they noticed there was some animal being barbecued on a spit-like device.

BRENDA BROYALS
I hope that's not roasted dog.

EVO KAPLAN
Why would they roast a dog?

BRENDA BROYALS
It's a delicacy here on Zanziltar. Half the staff are Zanziltarians.

EVO KAPLAN
Well, let's go find out.

Brenda Broyals and Evo Kaplan walked up to the person in a chef's white uniform and cap who had a brush and was applying some type of coating over the carcass being barbecued as it was apparently slowly being turned by a mechanical device with an electric motor.

CHEF
Good evening, folks.

The chef continued to baste the carcass in the most dispassionate manner.

EVO KAPLAN
Hello.

Evo Kaplan looked closely at what the chef was barbecuing. It certainly did not look like a dog.

EVO KAPLAN
What is that you are barbecuing?

CHEF
I'm barbecuing a Gaoyang.

EVO KAPLAN
Is it a farm-raised animal?

CHEF
No, Gaoyangs are captured in the wild but fed for about a month at a farm to clear out their wild flora digestive content, which helps it taste better when we barbecue them. Plus, it puts on a few pounds and the meat gives it a fattier consistency so that it barbecues better.

EVO KAPLAN
Interesting. How soon will it be done?

CHEF
In about fifteen minutes if you like your meat rare, otherwise, thirty minutes if you want it well done.

EVO KAPLAN
That sounds good. I kind of like it medium rare.


CHEF
Have a seat and I'll serve you some in about fifteen minutes.


EVO KAPLAN
Thank you.


CHEF
You are welcome.


<u>EXT. OUTDOOR SETTING FOR A BARECUE MEAL – AFTERNOON.</u>


Evo and Brenda sat down at a table that was next to the cafeteria under an awning to give them shade. Near sundown the balmy weather was kind of nice. Because they were out in a desert area, there was low humidity, and near sundown the temperatures were subsiding as a breeze off the mountains was slowly flowing across the complex, which made it very pleasing.

The smell from the barbecue was very pleasing and added to the hunger pains. Staff members came out and set their table with all the necessary eating utensils, napkins, plates, dinner rolls, butter, and sauces to put on the barbecue if they wanted.

As Evo sat there taking it all in, his spy mode swung into action. He didn't analyze the compound up until now but sitting there with nothing to do afforded him the time to check it out. Immediately he spotted at a distance there was a chain link fence surrounding all the trailers and this work site.

Even more interesting was all the armed guards just inside the chain-link fence walking around, obviously sentries. Oddly they wore uniforms that could pass for the Dranzonian Empire or Revolutionary Guards. It struck him that it had to be one of the two.

Furthermore, as Evo Kaplan's training unfolded the true nature of his mission in the coming days, he realized it didn't take a rocket scientist to figure out the Dranzonian Empire didn't need to break in to one of their own arms designers to steal the plans.

Therefore, the firm had to be either an intergalactic organized crime syndicate as they indicated or worse yet, he was now in the employ of Revolutionary Empire Secret Service, a dicey position for him to be in.

Brenda Broyals had that interesting appearance on her poker face. *Why is she really here?*

This place seems secure enough. Then a thought occurred to Evo Kaplan. He knew Brenda Broyals was a spy and a ruthless killer.

*The only reason why she didn't shoot people on the mission to Wuxing, the capital city of Stonue to assassinate Chuo Wanpi, is she merely was there to evaluate my performance. But now the only reason why she would be here is to make sure I did not try to escape and make my way back to the Dranzonian Empire.*

Whether Brenda Broyals was truly simply part of an intergalactic organized crime syndicate called the FIRM or a member of the Revolutionary Empire Secret Service, his knowledge of what they had going on here at Zanziltar could be detrimental to their organization if he informed his former employer.

As he thought for one moment in doing so, he could use that knowledge to gain the confidence of his former administrators, he might be able to get Reginald Heiqishi, removed from his position. However, knowing how advanced this group was, it's doubtful he could safely make it back to Praxisvlasia alive, so there would be no point in attempting.

In a few minutes the chef came to their table with a plate of sliced Gaoyang and sat it down on their table.

CHEF
Here you go, I hope you like it.

EVO KAPLAN
Thanks.

Evo Kaplan, the perfect gentleman, gestured to Brenda Broyals.

EVO KAPLAN
Go ahead and take some.

BRENDA BROYALS
No, after you. I want to see how you like it first.

EVO KAPLAN
All right.

Evo Kaplan then took several nice large slices and placed it on his plate and grabbed his fork and knife and cut into it and started eating.

EVO KAPLAN
This is very good. Excellent.

The chef appeared proud of his barbecue satisfied the stranger.

Even though the site was compartmentalized, the chef knew the two had to be spooks, as they had never been seen before and they stuck out like a sore thumb not wearing lab coats or worker's uniforms everyone else wore.

 The Chef and all the staff were trained to never ask strangers any questions. Questions were not authorized except for questions pertaining to eating such as, "Would you like a second helping?" or "What can I get for you?"

The meal was very delightful. Instead of tea, they were served a special nectar, which was loaded in vitamin B6 and B12 and other additives to help their physiology. One of the side effects of those additives was it seemed to affect Evo Kaplan's libido and as he was thinking and pondering everything and feeling slightly lonely.

VOICE OVER (MALE)

Evo Kaplan hoped that tonight Brenda Broyals would once again engage in her disgusting and totally irrational conduct that he had recently enjoyed.

*Tonight, if she approaches me, I'm going to take command of the situation and put her in her place.* Evo Kaplan thought.

It's been a long time since Evo Kaplan had been with a woman on his terms and tonight, if the opportunity availed, he would make his prowess a factor in Brenda Broyals personal psyche going forward.

Men like to be in control of a situation with women. But most men have never been intimating with a powerful woman like Brenda Broyals.

Brenda Broyals experience level across the board in many areas eclipsed most men. Very few men except world leaders who had given orders to destroy their opponents had ever killed as many people as Brenda had done in cold blood.

*Note: shifted from MALE to FEMALE VOICEOVER in this sequence for effect.*

VOICE OVER (FEMALE)

It was not that Brenda Broyals enjoyed killing, she just enjoyed staying alive and sometimes when the chips were down, survival was predicated on taking that fatal laser shot and burning a hole in the chest of a victim of her very efficient application of her talents.

Brenda Broyals was making mental notes for her upcoming reports. One thing she could already state that was factual and clearly compelling is that Evo Kaplan strapped himself into the Stratospheric Glider exhibiting no fear or nervousness.

Evo Kaplan was all business and despite the fact he was riding a very complicated and risky device down to the planet that could easily kill him with just the slightest flaw, he went at it self-assured with no hesitation or regrets.

Evo Kaplan's post flight behavior was also quite extraordinary as he displayed no outward emotion. Those were very important attributes that added measurably to his portfolio.

Conrad Fanzui will be very pleased with the details of Brenda Broyals' report. And if Evo Kaplan makes it to Coy's Ridge and comes back with the plans for the new Proton Gravity Disrupter Weapon, that would be a feather in Brenda Broyals cap for the training and development of a tremendous asset that Evo Kaplan would prove to be.

These thoughts suddenly sent chills down Brenda's spine as she realized she suddenly had a very strong sexual attraction to Evo Kaplan.

VOICE OVER (FEMALE)

Am I losing control? Brenda Broyals asked herself.

Brenda Broyals suddenly felt her moistness and even though she sat there casually as a mere prop on the majestic stage of intergalactic espionage, possibly living on borrowed time, she knew she would enjoy the moment and relish the circumstances so auspiciously bestowed upon her by supporting this mission.

Brenda Broyals would be on the mothership and possibly the shuttle for the mission. She wanted to be able to assist Evo Kaplan and if necessary, help get him back if the mission hit a snag and he was suddenly confronted with an emergency extraction.

Dinner hit the spot. Evo Kaplan needed some time in the trailer as his digestive system was apparently very efficient and needed use of the facilities.

Brenda went into the trailer as well and took the opportunity to do her business and freshen up a bit. Brenda also a master at seduction, which she sometimes had to perform in espionage, and had special Haiwangxing perfumes that released unique pheromones that greatly helped facilitate the seduction and recruitment process when necessary. She dabbed it in a few spots on her body she suspected Evo Kaplan might later explore. She was ready to give him the biggest ride of his life and use that power over him to help control him if necessary.

VOICE OVER (FEMALE)

Brenda Broyals would not fall in love with Evo Kaplan because she had a heart of stone, but wanted to make sure she would always be in position to call all the shots, especially if they were deployed together and got into a dicey situation.

Sometimes when partners are involved in espionage, one of them must stay behind in a shootout so that at least one of them could get out alive.

Evo Kaplan thus would have a collateral duty as a bullet and laser magnet so she could get out alive. It wasn't necessarily a betrayal; it was just that in the spy business the number one priority is saving yourself.

Others sometimes must die for you. Evo Kaplan understood some of the sophistication of the FIRM in how they made such arrangements. Little did he know Brenda expected certain garments and objects to be available for her on training locations like they were now at.

Brenda had a very sexy negligee she quickly slipped into. They were alone in their trailer and since the guards were instructed to not let anyone approach the trailer or be a nuisance to them in any manner, Brenda knew it was safe to proceed as they had complete privacy.

As expected, Brenda observed Evo Caplan exiting his room into the center part of the trailer where a communal area was set up with furniture and an entertainment system, including video and audio. Brenda Broyals already put on some soft soothing music playing in the background that exemplified the ambience afforded to them.

When Evo Kaplan first glanced Brenda Broyals, he at first was taken back slightly as the negligee barely covered up much of Brenda's curvy body and was slightly transparent so he could see the essence of her nudity.

To Evo Kaplan's utter surprise, Brenda Broyals undid one button and her negligee dropped to the floor. She approached Evo, and when she got close to Evo Kaplan, she put her arms around him and began kissing him on his body and unbuttoned his shirt and kissed his chest. Evo was suddenly experiencing a whirlwind of emotions and had a psychological response that was transcendent and evocative.

Brenda Broyals then reached out and grabbed Evo Kaplan's hand. Brenda knew the pheromones were now starting to hit Evo and he would soon be under her spell. Brenda led Evo to her bedroom where there had been application of the same perfume on her bedsheets, which further clouded his air pathways and intermixed with his own personal enzymes, which released torrents of endorphins in his brain leading him to succumb to her desires.

Soon the two were passionately lovemaking, but this time Evo Kaplan carried out his plan which he managed to compartmentalize in his mind to ensure he would carry it out.

VOICE OVER (MALE)

Brenda never expected to ever get into this position. Up until now it was sex for sex. There were no emotions, no love, no spellbinding transcendence into that irrational state of mental attraction usually bestowed on a committed relationship where a person wished to never lose that mate the rest of their lives.

Evo, in his compartmentalized state, performed very aggressively. He was a tiger, a wild animal, full of vigor and enthusiasm. Evo's perseverance in his performance busted open a void in Brenda she never knew existed.

In this cat-and-mouse game of love, Brenda was no longer the cat, she was now the mouse. Her transcendence into a physical and emotional state she never experienced before left her slightly bewildered as she realized how much she feared losing control like this. Never in Brenda's life had she felt so utterly helpless.

Just like a mouse that gives up knowing the cat was about to eat it, Brenda too suddenly felt mentally incapacitated. Evo's vibrations and oscillations left her spellbound as she reacted to each one of his thrusts with splendid euphoria. Brenda's brain now released vast amounts of Dopamine, Oxytocin, Prolactin, and Serotonin. She never recalled ever having an orgasm quite this intense.

Brenda was thus raptured by Evo up until the moment he finally collapsed. His effort was no less than running ten miles at almost ten miles per hour. Their bodies were drenched in sweat and Brenda quivered in post-orgasmic tremors like she never experienced before in her life.

Regret soon swept over Brenda because she also knew the consequences of her actions. She had just failed as a spy. Her own vulnerabilities were penetrated and now she was helpless and realized for the first time in her life she was no longer in control of her own destiny.

Brenda Broyals wept for a few brief moments. Evo mistakenly assumed it was tears of joy that some women exhibit after such a transcendence into an ethereal-like state derived by an emotional explosion that can occur when a mental fusion from love occurs.

Evo Kaplan would be far more reflective if he knew the truth: Brenda Broyals wept because she knew she just failed as a spy.

Brenda's world was shattered. She would not be able to pick up the pieces and be the same person again. It wasn't that her confidence was shattered, nor would it preclude her burning a hole in an enemy's chest with her laser pistol; nevertheless, she knew a new reality existed and her future would not be as she expected.



They fell asleep in each other's arms and the peaceful night slowly allowed them to escape their world and their reality and reach a dream world filled with satisfaction and happiness.

The lovemaking modulated their dreams, and thus they both had a very pleasant sleep. Around five in the morning Evo was suddenly awake. He had an erection, not because of his lust for Brenda, but because he had to urinate severely.

Evo Kaplan had no choice but to get up and use the bathroom. He went into his own bathroom and took care of the business. During the S/S/S, he decided he would shower and clean up because there was no point in attempting any more sleep. Evo Kaplan had at least eight hours of good sleep, so he felt rejuvenated. He had a smile on his face because he felt he had turned the tide on Brenda Broyals and in doing so gave her some of her own business back to her.

After his Hollywood shower, Evo Kaplan dressed in clothes provided in one of the closets. He went into the combined area in the middle of the trailer and then decided to exit and go see if the cooks were making something for breakfast already.

Predictably there was an aroma in the air, and it contained the smell of a particular type of tea the Zanziltar people drank in the morning, which was heavy on caffeine. There was also the scent of something recently baked and the smell of fried sausages that permeated his scents and added to his hunger.

Evo Kaplan didn't realize it, but he wasn't too far ahead of Brenda. Soon she exited the trailer fully dressed and looking to impress. Evo said to himself, "My god she's pretty," as her luster was accentuated by her choice of clothing.

Some of the scientists such as Dr. Buster had wished Brenda didn't dress so pretty because whether she knew it or not, Brenda Broyals was now a distraction to some of his top scientists, making it harder to get things done.

Brenda Broyals approached Evo Kaplan then smiled. Her smile was beautiful and infectious.

Brenda Broyals
Good morning,


VOICE OVER (MALE)

Evo realized there was some kind of change in Brenda, but he couldn't quite figure it out.

What Evo didn't know was Brenda reconciled that even though she might have failed as a spy by allowing her emotions to get out of control, at least she knew that one time in her life, she had been with a man the captivated her heart like no other before.

Therefore, Brenda Broyals remained in a relatively cheerful mood and a sense of calmness descended upon all of them.

Dr. Buster didn't know what to expect from this couple that was paramount to their operations. In his past, whenever he got saddled with a couple prima donnas, there was a sense of brooding and discomfort they could bestow upon the staff.

Unfortunately, since they often interfaced with military prima donnas with huge egos and agendas, they were used to the abuse and had their rather clever ways of dealing with it.

For this couple the air was totally different. There were no displays of ego, and the level of cooperation was exemplary. These people were true professionals and yesterday alone, Evo Kaplan (a.k.a. Proctor Pugong), showed a level of bravery and dedication that was rare as Dr. Buster knew. He also knew that Proctor Pugong was fully aware his flight yesterday was extremely risky because they were just now starting to believe they had the bugs worked out.

VOICE OVER (MALE)

> The fact Brenda dressed extremely sexy and beautiful was a slight distraction, but it was enjoyable to the casual observer. After breakfast was over, the couple was taken to Operations and Planning, where they went over planning for the test flights scheduled today.
>
> Since the shuttle had three seats for pilot, mission specialist, and a rider, there was room for Brenda to go along, as she planned to go along during the mission in the shuttle. Once Evo Kaplan left the shuttle in the Stratospheric Glider, he was on his own.

EXT. SPACE SHUTTLE BOARDING – DAY

Evo Kaplan and Brenda Broyals were escorted to the Space Shuttle where they would soon be preparing for takeoff. They each had on street clothes because in a real mission Evo Kaplan would have to arrive disguised. There would not be enough time to change before accomplishing his mission.

EXT. CGI. SPACE SHUTTLE IS TOWED OVER TO THE ELECTRIC CATAPULT IN PREPARATION FOR LAUNCH.

When the catapult mechanism was fastened to the shuttle it was time to launch.

SHUTTLE PILOT

> We are getting ready to launch now. Everyone please remain seated with safety harness until we are out in space and ready to deploy the Stratospheric Glider.

INT. SHUTTLE COCKPIT PILOT SCENE - DAY

As soon as the pilot saw the indicator lit, he had permission to launch, he pressed the standby button that was covered by a protective cover to make sure it was not inadvertently pressed until an actual launch.

After pressing the STANDBY switch, it turned green which meant interlocks were closed and all conditions allowing launch were confirmed. The pilot turned and looked at the mission specialist.

SHUTTLE PILOT<br>
You ready?

MISSION SPECIALIST<br>
As ready as I will ever be.

The pilot lifted the protective cover over the launch button which immediately turned to a bright BLUE INDICATION. The pilot and the mission specialist did not want to see a RED INDICATION that would signal an abort situation and they would come to all stop immediately and safety checks would start.

The nature of the electric catapult was you felt a couple G force of pressure during the launch but at the end of the three-mile-long electric catapult that worked off the principals of maglev. The Space Shuttle started to slowly pitch up and in a minute was going vertical at supersonic speeds. Just as they passed 20,000 feet the nuclear fusion powered Cyclonic Rocket Engines kicked in.

The G forces were again felt strongly for a while until they reached MAX Q, the differential pressure between the ambient pressure of the air they were traveling in verses the pressures exerted on the hull of the space craft traveling at supersonic speeds to obtain orbit.

After reaching MAX Q with no tip over or unexpected unscheduled rapid disassembly, the scientists felt better about the likely outcome of the mission.

Once in orbit, they were ready launch the Stratospheric Glider out of the shuttle in accordance with ( IAW) mission guidelines. The shuttle flew right over the drop zone to deploy the Stratospheric Glider.

<u>INT. SPACE SHUTTLE - SPACE</u>

Evo Kaplan could not expect direct support except for an emergency extraction if it were possible. Today they went back out in space, but instead of landing back at the base on a landing pad, Evo would be going to an escarpment to simulate exact conditions he would have to contend with while landing on Coy's Ridge during the upcoming mission.

The mission specialist was there with Brenda Broyals observing Evo Kaplan get ready for the Stratospheric Glider deployment.

VOICE OVER
Once out in space at the desired location, Evo Kaplan got into the Stratospheric Glider by himself even though he was being coached because on the ground during the extraction phase it would be required.

As soon as Evo Kaplan was safe and secure in the Stratospheric Glider and the canopy automatically shut, system checks indicated all conditions were a go

Artificial Intelligence
Ready for Launch.

MISSION SPECIALIST
Evo Kaplan, All conditions satisfactory for launch. Standby for Stratospheric Glider launch.

EVO KAPLAN
Standing by. I'm ready.

C.U. EVO KAPLAN'S FACE 5 SECONDS

C.U. STRATOSPHERIC GLIDER DASHBOARD AND INSTRUMENT PANEL. 5 SECONDS.

The mission specialist and Brenda went into the cockpit, shutting the door and sealing it then sat down in their seats in the cockpit.

C.U. MISSION SPECIALIST.

SPOT ON SHUTTLE COCKPIT INSTRUMENT PANETL AND DASHBOARD.

C.U. BRENDA BROYALS

Just like before, the shuttle internal air pressure in the cargo hold was equalized and the rear hatch opened.

EXT. CGI. SPACE SHUTTLE DEPLOYING THE STRATOSPHERIC GLIDER 30 SECONDS - SPACE

Moments later the Stratospheric Glider slid out the back of the shuttle and quickly maneuvered toward Earth. In about twenty minutes the Stratospheric Glider was circling the landing zone, burning off speed and energy as it slowed.

EXT. CGI. STRATOSPHERIC GLIDER LANDING 30 SECONDS – ON THE ESCARPMENT

Note to the director: The Stratospheric Glider lands on a tripod landing gear mechanism like SPACE-X landings. A big difference is Stratospheric Glider has no flame exhaust and is relatively quiet. Skip ahead to the two-minute mark to see the *triple landing legs* deployed.

https://www.youtube.com/watch?v=ANv5UfZsvZQ

Down around two hundred feet above the escarpment, the Stratospheric Glider started shifting to an up angle that added more drag, slowing it even more. By the time the Stratospheric Glider was fifty feet above the escarpment, it was then vertical and started dropping slower as propulsion came online. The propulsion secretly designed to reduce noise and not give off any flame or sound to draw attention. And since the penetration was scheduled for night landing, it would be more important to not have any light producing items to expose the craft and put the mission in jeopardy.

The first Test fights occurred during daylight. However, they would break after lunch and come back in the evening and commence night flight testing.

EXT. CGI. SP STRATOSPHERIC GLIDER LANDING– ON THE ESCARPMENT 45 SECONDS

VOICE OVER
This will be the true test of Evo Kaplan. Going down in the dark, hoping sensors would work and he would arrive at the designated location. During the first night flight, as the craft got to an altitude of twenty thousand feet on its approach to the escarpment, prearranged lights were turned on, which were laid out exactly like satellite photographs indicated Coy's Ridge was illuminated. The infrared imaging equipment worked well off the lighting, and it turned out to be not much more difficult than a day landing.

Half the days were spent on mission planning and the other half night landings including coming down in the event of a power outage in total darkness. Dr. Buster had a backup plan for that as well. When the Stratospheric Glider reached two hundred feet in a total blackout, infrared lights would be turned on. Invisible to the naked eye, it would facilitate confirming the landing. The autopilot and the drone pilot could be overridden by Evo Kaplan.

Evo Kaplan could state commands such as "land a little further to the North," as an example, and the artificial intelligence in the craft would then start moving further north during the descent. Another possible command such as "You are coming down too fast," would then cause breaking action and a slower approach.

Under normal circumstances it's unlikely that Evo Kaplan would have to give verbal commands. He wouldn't unless something terribly went wrong, or the enemy started shooting weapons at him which could cause him to *bug out*.

Evo Kaplan would have to deal with all possible situations as necessary to reduce risk. The whole operation was mapped out and Evo Kaplan would be wearing an armband that extended from the palm of his hand in a glove like contraption that extended to about six inches away from his elbow. This allowed a communicator and display device that could be ordered on or off and set for low lighting, as would be the case in a black out scenario, even though Coy's Ridge would have ample lighting where he didn't need severe low lighting.

Evo Kaplan would also wear special glasses that had special filters and amplifiers, which gave him the ability to see better than humans. These special glasses gave him the ability to see better than practically any living animal on most planets.

Evo Kaplan's two ear buds gave him the audio channel to the mission commander and drone pilot flying his Stratospheric Glider for him, but also electronics in the arm strap had sensors that processed audio to enhance his psychoacoustics and hear better than any animal. There would also be warnings his body surveillance equipment monitored for things such as laser or energy beam weapon technology.

<u>INT. TRAILER BRIEFING CENTER – DAY</u>

VOICE OVER
Evo looked at all buildings that were mapped out and the secret storage was identified in one of the rooms of Abniler Manther's mansion he chose to lock up the plans to all his most secret and successful devices such as the new Proton Gravity Disrupter Weapon.

BRIEFING OFFICIAL
Abniler Manther's modus operendus is that only portions of the Proton Gravity Disrupter Weapon plans would only be parceled

out to various contractors who made components. That's why all the plans were stored in his mansion and not with the government.

                    EVO KAPLAN
How do his plans arrive at the manufacturing facility, maybe that's the place to steal them?


                  BRIFING OFFICIAL
Abniler Manther's own people deliver the plans then coordinate the assemblers and provide written and verbal instructions.


                    EVO KAPLAN
                 Why do they do that?


                  BRIFING OFFICIAL
Mainly to escape the clutches of the overreaching government officials who made their mark getting the plans or concessions out of contractors building such devices at much lower prices.


As the briefing ended Brenda Broyals gave Evo that strange look he knew meant she had some notions of engaging in celestial feasts. Evo Kaplan and Brenda Broyals had not been repeating performances on a theme from Paganini like their first night in the trailer, mainly due to timing and slight sleep deprivation they both suffered.

INT. TRAILER LIVING QUARTERS – NIGHT


                VOICE OVER (FEMALE)
The night before the mission, Brenda Broyals casually entered Evo Kaplan's bedroom, where she slid into the sheets while he was still sleeping. Brenda curled up next to Evo, savoring the moment and realizing tomorrow would be a very dangerous day and getting down to Coy's Ridge would be a heroic adventure because the Dranzonian Empire's defense force was on high alert.


Any craft coming into the atmosphere better have an invitation; otherwise, they would most likely destroy the craft for good measure. That in itself, was why the Stratospheric Glider was developed in the first place and the hope that the extremely small radar cross section would allow penetration of their defenses and carry off one of the most extravagant heists in Dranzonian Empire's history.

Evo Kaplan slept well, and his personal biology caused that erection because he needed to discharge body fluids. As he woke up feeling the pressure, he realized he had company and was soon aroused by the pheromones released in Brenda's perfume. He immediately went to action because the pressure wasn't that great to force his trip to the bathroom. However, he appreciated the biological function it bestowed upon him, as he was immediately ready to perform.

VOICE OVER (FEMALE)

Brenda Broyals was nude and ready to receive Evo Kaplan. She was still asleep when he started making love to her. It didn't take long for Brenda Broyals to reach a level of reality and discover it wasn't a splendid dream she was having; was the real deal!

When Brenda came to reality, she was virtually moments away from an orgasmic transcendence. Her entire psyche was elevated by the sudden surprise and as she soon felt the splendid euphoria, her gratification eclipsed almost all the other times she had ever experienced an encounter such as this.

By the time they finished their lovemaking it was already 5:00 A.M.

BRENDA BROYALS

Let's get up and shower and get ready.

EVO KAPLAN

Give me a minute I need to use the bathroom.

As soon as he flushed the toilet and opened the door, Brenda approached, and they both went into his shower together. There was enough room for both as they cleaned each other under the nice warm shower and kissed and hugged multiple times before they eventually had enough and got out and went about their business.

<u>INT. MEDICAL TRAILER - DAY</u>

VOICE OVER (MALE)

Just like all missions, due to lessons learned, they both went to a trailer set up as a medical clinic and that had a change room. After they disrobed and checked out by the doctor and given a medical clearance, their change of clothes was presented to them by the FIRM's support staff, and they dressed and went out the back door of the trailer to the waiting shuttle.

All their former attire and shoes were collected and disposed of. Evo Kaplan would arrive as a total spook, meaning he would carry with him absolutely no form of ID in the event he was captured.

Evo Kaplan realized the FIRM determined he would use his fake identity, but they all understood the Dranzonian Empire's Secret Service was methodical and within a few hours of capture they would have his identity through Secret Service records.

When or if Evo Kaplan was confronted at that time, there would be no point in further denial of who he was, as they would know and to obfuscate would be of no value. Plus, it might incur harsher treatment. Since he really didn't know where their headquarters was on Zanziltar, the Dranzonian Empire's Secret Service would still be in no position to locate them or do anything about it.

<u>EXT. CGI. SHUTTLE DEPARTS HEADING INTO SPACE TO MATE WITH MOTHERSHIP. SHUTTLE RIDES PIGGYBACK ATTACHED TO THE MOTHERSHIP 30 SECONDS.</u>

VOICE OVER (MALE)

Today they would take the shuttle up to a mothership and not come back, as that mothership would then transit to Praxisvlasia in the Dranzonian Empire and perform the Coy Ridge mission.

It took several days for the mothership to travel to Praxisvlasia. They would avoid the Dranzonian Empire World Fleets by not approaching too close to the planet. There was so much space junk and asteroids a distance away from the planet, they would arouse no interest staying at this distance.

The shuttle was relatively small and nowhere in the class of a military vessel so it would not garner much attention they hoped. On the way to the Dranzonian Empire World Praxisvlasia, Evo Kaplan spotted the look on Brenda's poker face that he now had come to realize he knew.

VOICE OVER (FEMALE)

Brenda's body language betrayed her enthusiasm for Evo Kaplan. But due to the cramped conditions on the segregated section of the ship to keep them away from the crew as much as possible, there was virtually no chance of conducting a physical embrace since the lack of privacy did not avail itself.

Brenda and Evo would, however, quietly exchange a few words on the shuttle. One of Brenda's failings as a spy by crossing over the line with one of her operatives now played out. Evo Kaplan was no longer expendable.

She could no longer objectively run this spy like she could before. It was now personal to her. She knew when she got back to Zanziltar she would have to have a meeting with Conrad Fanzui and confess her failure. They would then have to be split apart for operational security.

This would be their last mission together. But then again it might happen anyway because Evo Kaplan could be captured or killed on the mission. The mothership captain informed the shuttle mission crew they were now in position, and based on the timeline it was time for them to board the shuttle and commence the operation.

INT. MOVING FROM MOTHERSHIP TO SHUTTLE – SPACE 15 SECONDS

The shuttle pilot, mission specialist, Brenda, and Evo Kaplan all climbed up the ladder from the mothership into the shuttle and the mission specialist closed shuttle hatch. Crew members on the mothership closed the mothership hatch and soon the interlocks were closed that would allow launch of the shuttle that would take the Stratospheric Glider to the edge of the atmosphere and deploy it.

It took one-hour flight time for the shuttle to get into position. Brenda Broyals had remained with Evo Kaplan in the Stratospheric Glider Bay. The pilot and mission specialist remained in the cockpit where all their instrument packages existed.

INTERCOM – SHUTTLE PILOT
We are about five minutes away from the  deployment zone.
Recommend entering the  Stratospheric Glider.

VOICE OVER (FEMALE)
Brenda Broyals knew they were probably being video recorded,
but she didn't care since she would be doing a full confession
in about four days.

Brenda approached Evo Kaplan and put her arms around him
and whispered into his ear.

BRENDA BROYALS
I love you, Evo Kaplan

Because of the emotion, Evo Kaplan couldn't just leave Brenda Broyals without kissing her, so he did. She reciprocated and the embrace felt genuine and uplifting to both their egos.

EVO KAPLAN
To know someone like you creates a mystical quality.

The two separated from the kiss and looked into each other's eyes. Brenda's eyes watered slightly.

BRENDA BROYALS Good luck.

EVO KAPLAN
Thank you, I appreciate everything you did to help prepare me
for this trip. I feel confident I can get the job done.

BRENDA BROYALS
You are most welcome. Hopefully in a few hours we can have
a victory celebration.

Evo climbed into the Stratospheric Glider and shut the canopy by pressing the remote control that pulled the canopy down and locked it in place. Brenda went into the shuttle cockpit and locked the hatch shut to seal it because they would soon be equalizing the shuttle cargo bay with zero atmosphere of space.

EXT. CGI. STRATOSPHERIC GLIDER DEPLOYMENT – 30 SECONDS.

Once all the indications indicated the interlocks were closed, allowing them to proceed with the launch, the equalization started and soon the hatch was open. Just as they trained, the Stratospheric Glider was ejected out the back of the cargo bay through the rear door and it immediately maneuvered for planetary reentry at seventeen thousand miles per hour.

The inertial navigation system, which accurately tracked the Stratospheric Glider position and compared it with Praxisvlasia's global positioning system used by spaceships in near space within twenty thousand miles of the planet, insured the Stratospheric Glider would correctly reach Coy's Ridge very accurately.

All the flight algorithms worked flawlessly as the Stratospheric Glider made its way to the target area. Doing the night operations in the desert with the temporary lights turned on proved to be very useful, as Evo Kaplan easily recognized Coy Ridge due to the light configuration of the complex. The security configuration was to keep intruders out of the compound, which was the central theme. It never dawned on the designers the intruders would come from space vertically into the compound.

EXT. CGI. STATOSPHERIC GLIDER LANDING AT ABNILER MANTHER'S MANSION - 30 SECONDS.

Thanks to the congestion and opulence that a man like Abniler Manther could afford, the landing zone was on the other side of a bathhouse next to the Olympic-sized pool he swam laps in. The bathhouse was designed to accommodate the number of women that would be with him in a modified toga party.

At 2:00 A.M., thanks to the distance to the bathhouse from the mansion, there was enough of a gap so that people in the mansion would not hear the Stratospheric Glider touch down, as its radiated noise levels were not much greater than a large drone with multiple electric driven propellers. As soon as the Stratospheric Glider landed on its *tri-leg configuration*, Evo Kaplan swung into action.

With his special glasses, Evo Kaplan looked around and saw no activity. He knew, however, on the other side of the wall around the estate there were a couple dozen rovers and security staff working the night to prevent an attempted break-in. Since the security detail was not monitoring space, they didn't know the perpetrator already arrived.

The last person to go into the mansion from the swimming pool had left the door half open. This was a fantastic coup for Evo Kaplan because now he knew he could get inside without triggering any alarms as he entered the mansion.

INT. HALLWAY IN ABNILER MANTHER'S MANSION – NIGHT LOW LIGHTS

VOICE OVER (MALE)
Evo Kaplan's only fear was whether his descramblers would work on the intrusion alert systems on the archive room where Abniler Manther stored all systems plans.

Without some insider's help, they would never know which data cube to attempt stealing. But thanks to a Revolutionary sympathetic disenfranchised employee, the cube was identified, and all Evo had to do was get in the room and take it.

The plans were stored on a standard hypercube used by the Dranzonian Empire's military and industrialists who bid on government contracts.

The Revolutionary Empire Secret Service would have no issues reading the cube since they had their fair share of the loot found on numerous planets, they took over in the absence of government forces who either surrendered or defected.

The mansion was mostly empty. Some of the security guards were out front waiting for a van to arrive with supplies and the chef and maids who would start work in an hour.

Evo had to be completed and out of the mansion before they all returned inside the home.

The remainder of the security detail was upstairs in the hallway outside Abniler Manther's bedroom in position to protect him, and they had plenty of fire power. Evo Kaplan traversed through the mansion down a hallway he knew would take him past the archive records storage room.

VOICE OVER (MALE)
Thanks to Evo Kaplan's special acoustic processors, he could hear someone walking in the semi-dark hallway. He quickly entered a randomly selected room to get out of the hallway. Just a moment later his sonic detector registered the footsteps of the individual who walked on past. After the person was an estimated twenty feet away, Evo slowly opened the door of the room he was in and looked down the darken hallway. Whoever it was had walked toward the kitchen. Probably someone got hungry and went to go raid the refrigerator.

Evo knew he was close to the archive records storage room. It would be easy to find since it would be the only one with an intrusion alert system designed and programmed by the best security firm in the Dranzonian Empire that now had a Revolutionary mole inside working for it.

VOICE OVER (MALE)
Abniler Manther thought he paid for an alarm system that had a combination lock that could never be defeated since the code had one hundred and twenty-eight digits. Even a supercomputer would take weeks to break the code, but that would set off an alarm well before a person could capitalize on breaking the code.

Abniler Manther would be horrified to learn the lock also had a back door. The designer was lazy, and, in the event, they locked themselves out, he could simply use that eight-digit code and in the process render the lock useless, as its coding mechanism would be ruined and must be replaced.

Nobody would ever know it was simply an eight-digit code: 11166613.

Evo Kaplan discovered a couple doors down was the archives room. Now was the moment of truth. If the disgruntled employee was honest, the code should work. If the wrong code was entered, an alarm would go off and the best Evo could do then would be to shoot his way out and attempt to get to his Stratospheric Glider and airborne before he was killed.

One last check on the sonic detectors to see if any noise suggested someone approaching, then Evo Kaplan carefully entered the back-door number to allow entry into the archives room.

That intrusion alert system was thus turned off. They would not know until they went back into this room for whatever reason. Their first problem is the eight-digit back door code wrecked the locking mechanism. They would have to contact the lock company to get them out to open it up. And since the lock was ruined, the only way it was going to get opened would be drilling it out, which would take well over half a day with cobalt drill bits.

Time was of the essence. Evo Kaplan had to get the data cube and get out. He clicked on a display on his armband display, which showed the exhibit what he was looking for. Each data cube had a ten-digit number to identify it.

Without the cheat sheet, nobody could find it. It would be like looking for a needle in a haystack. Thanks to the organization skills of Abniler Manther's employees, all the data cubes were in serial number order.

Hence, within thirty seconds Evo Kaplan found the data cube. It was in a container he pulled off the shelf and had a standard lock on it, which took Evo, a master spy, fifteen seconds to pick and open. He removed the data cube and put it in a soft pouch that resembled a pistol shoulder harness to protect it. He closed the container and put it back on the shelf. In the moment when he left there would be no way back in. This had to be an exact transaction. They would never get another chance again. Evo Kaplan looked at the data cube one more time and read off the serial number, which matched his arm display, and then he put the data cube carefully into his carrying pouch.

Evo Kaplan walked over to the door and turned off the lights. He checked his sonic detector again and put it to maximum level. He detected no noise, so he then opened the door a crack and looked out. Again, the hallway was empty. While monitoring the sonic detector, he opened the door up enough to get out of the room and did a fast look around; again, there was no one coming.

Evo Kaplan then shut the door and repositioned the door lock mechanism to a neutral position. It locked and would not be opened again until the locksmiths drilled the mechanism out. Evo walked carefully and quietly to the outside door to egress to his Stratospheric Glider.

Evo Kaplan was almost home free when the sonic detector registered someone approaching. Whoever went in the kitchen a short while ago was coming his way.

Evo Kaplan had to step aside, let the person come through the door, and then disable him. The security man had been in the kitchen raiding the refrigerator.

The security man was all smug, he got away with eating some great food and since he was the only rover on the bottom floor now, there was no chance of someone catching him in the kitchen. As soon as the door shut behind the security man, he was hit with a Karate Chop by Evo Kaplan and knocked unconscious.

What to do with the body? Evo Kaplan remembered the room up ahead and dragged the body there and closed the door, and then made his way to the door leading to the swimming pool and patio area.

Evo's adrenalin was now rushing. Evo Kaplan was now in a very vulnerable state. As soon as Evo was outside, the sonic detectors registered someone coming. Adjacent to the pool was a hedge row for beautiful landscaping. Evo jumped over the hedge and got down low behind it as he now heard the footsteps coming his way along the swimming pool sidewalk. Another security guard was looking for someone.

EXT. ABNILER MANTHER SWIMMING POOL PATIO AREA WITH LOW LIGHTING - NIGHT

ABNILER MANTHER'S SECURITY GUARD
Aluezander, you out here?

The security guard heard or saw nothing and went back into the mansion through the same door Evo had just exited. Evo Kaplan carefully raised up and did a look around. He then elected to crawl quickly along the hedge row that would take him near the bathhouse. As soon as he got up near the bathhouse, he did a quick look around.

Evo Kaplan could hear some commotion out front of the mansion. No doubt it was the chef and the maids. Evo Kaplan had to get behind the bathhouse right away. There was no telling how soon they would be turning on the lights and his stealth would then be removed. Evo Kaplan had no choice: he jumped over the hedge and landed on the concrete of the swimming pool sidewalk, then quickly moved behind the bathhouse where the Stratospheric Glider remained unmolested.

VOICE OVER

Evo Kaplan quickly climbed into the Stratospheric Glider, shut the canopy, and started the preflight checks that would do a quick system check. There was more commotion in the house and as he feared the lights were coming on. He had to bug out right now.

EXT. CGI. STRATOSPHERIC GLIDER COCKPIT WITH EVO CAPLAN SIDE VIEW SHOWING INSTRUMENT PANEL AND THE RIGHT SIDE OF EVO'S HEAD THROUGH THIS SCENE SPACE -NIGHT

VOICE OVER (MALE)

Suddenly there was an alarm on the Stratospheric Glider status panel. It was do or die. Evo Kaplan had to ignore the alarm and get airborne while he could.

Otherwise, the Dranzonian Secret Service Agents would be beating his ass in a couple hours, making him wish he was dead as they extracted the poignant details out of him. Evo Kaplan bypassed the alarm and went airborne.

EXT. CGI. STRATOSPHERIC GLIDER LAUNCHING OUT INTO SPACE – 30 SECONDS - NIGHT

If nothing else, Evo Kaplan could fly a distance and check out the alarm far away from this facility so he would have time to cope. His other option was to tempt fate and simply get to the shuttle as damn quick as possible. The minute he went airborne, the Stratospheric Glider sent a burst message that would show up as noise on surveillance monitors, which was a prearranged signal that he was on his way. It also sent telemetry in the burst message concerning the alarm. His oxygen system had failed. He would not have long to live.

EXT. CGI. STRATOSPHERIC GLIDER COCKPIT WITH EVO CAPLAN SIDE VIEW SHOWING INSTRUMENT PANEL AND THE RIGHT SIDE OF EVO'S HEAD THROUGH THIS SCENE SPACE -NIGHT

The shuttle had to quickly recover his craft and re-pressurize the shuttle cargo bay in the minimal amount of time, otherwise Evo Kaplan might die of asphyxiation.

Brenda Broyals chose not to warn him what the alarm meant. As long as he stayed calm, the chances of recovering him alive were good. On the other hand, if he did something stupid and flew to the planet's surface, he would no doubt get caught and the mission fail.

Brenda Broyals training and the value of being a spy now showed her well developed competence as she put her emotions aside and suddenly, the successful completion of the mission was paramount. Brenda Broyals realized she might have to sacrifice her lover. That data cube was needed by the Revolution and was now more important than Evo Kaplan's life.

INT.  SHUTTLE COCKPIT -SPACE

Though Brenda Broyals knew deep down in her heart she would regret every day for the rest of her life if Evo Kaplan died. Based on the telemetry and the sensors on the Stratospheric Glider that gave five-minute reports in a burst, Evo Kaplan was now down to ten minutes of life left. It was going to be touch and go.

INT. STRATOSPHERIC GLIDER SPACE EVO KAPLAN'S EYES CLOSE 5 SECONDS

Evo's vision was blurred, and he didn't know for sure when he passed out, but soon he was unconscious. The telemetry reports indicated that as well.

Brenda looked at the mission specialist who knew Evo Kaplan was in serious trouble.

> BRENDA BROYALS
> Thank God there are no Dranzonian Empire Space warships out here to interfere with recovery actions.

> MISSION SPECIALIST
> The shuttle rear door is open; Stratospheric Glider is approaching.

EXT. CGI. SPACE. SIDE VIEW STRATOSPHERIC GLIDER ENTERING SHUTTLE'S GLIDER BAY. 20 SECONDS

The landing of the Stratospheric Glider inside the shuttle's Glider Bay happened flawlessly.

INT. SPACE. SHUTTLE COCKPIT AND LATER SHUTTLE BAY

> MISSION SPECIALIST
> Stratospheric Glider is aboard. Securing rear hatch.

> BRENDA BROYALS
> Hatch indicates secured.

MISSION SPECIALIST<br>
Pressurizing the Stratospheric Glider Bay.

Moments seemed to drag on, then finally the mission specialist looked at the indicator that just flashed on.

MISSION SPECIALIST

Fifteen-pound air test satisfactory. We can enter Stratospheric Glider Bay.

VOICE OVER (FEMALE)

Brenda opened the shuttle cockpit door leading into the Stratospheric Glider Bay and felt a slight amount of air as the cockpit had slightly more pressure than the cargo bay.

BRENDA BROYALS<br>
Good thing this damn door opened in the right direction.

Brenda swung into action and pressed controls on the exterior of the Stratospheric Glider in the right sequence and the canopy raised up, exposing Evo Kaplan's face now purple as he was near death.

BRENDA BROYALS<br>
Quick! Help me get him out of the glider!

Brenda and the mission specialist lifted Evo Kaplan out of the glider. He was not breathing or responding.

MISSION SPECIALIST<br>
Give him mouth-to-mouth resuscitation while I pump his heart.

Brenda put her fingers over Evo Kaplan's nose, closing it off, and breathed into him. His chest rose as she filled his lungs.

The mission specialist pumping on his chest to perform CPR helped to move the air out of Evo Kaplan lungs that were heavily saturated with carbon dioxide. This routine went on for fifteen minutes with no response. Brenda remembered in her training that sometimes shock helped. She didn't have a defibrillator or other machines handy, so she slapped his face hard a couple times. She then felt his pulse.

BRENDA BROYALS<br>
I feel a pulse!

Evo Kaplan had a near-death experience. He went into a mental state that has never been reconciled by mankind or any technologist, as it can never be proven what really happens.

EXT. UNKNOWN – OTHER DIMENSION

Evo met an old man in a white robe with gray hair. They had a lengthy conversation. Suddenly the man changed the subject.

LONG GRAY-HAIRED MAN
Evo Kaplan, I'm here to escort you to your next life.

EVO KAPLAN
I've never felt so good in my life.

Suddenly there was a change of light, vibration frequencies and other physical phenomenon surrounding Evo Kaplan.

LONG GRAY-HAIRED MAN
Evo Kaplan, we determined it is not time for you to go to a new life. You will now return to your prior life.

INT. SHUTTLE STRATOSPHERIC GLIDER BAY SPACE

It must have been the shock of Brenda slapping Evo Kaplan that coaxed him back to reality. First his pulse returned and a few moments later his breathing started on his own and he slowly came too. His head was swirling as he looked up and saw two familiar faces. As soon as he gathered enough strength, he asked the big question.

EVO KAPLAN
Am I alive?

BRENDA BROYALS
Yes, you are. You will be fine.

As the morning progressed, the activity at the Abniler Manther mansion intensified. The missing guard caused a minor uproar. When an inside mansion security person disappears in thin air, it creates quite a scenario.

Once Abniler Manther was awake, he was informed of the situation and thus ordered a search of the premises. There was absolutely no way the man could have left the compound because none of the security video showed anyone approaching or leaving until the maids and chef arrived and they were still here.

A room-by-room search began and eventually they found the security guard's body. The man was dead, and the autopsy would soon reveal he died from a broken neck.

The police soon arrived and started questioning everyone. Nobody thought to check the archives. It wasn't until a week later that a new data cube arrived for storage and the technicians quickly reported the one hundred twenty-eight-digit combination didn't work. After several more attempts it was a foregone conclusion the locking mechanism was damaged and not working.

That quickly set off the spectacle that possibly there had been an intrusion and the dead man was somehow connected. Perhaps he caught the intruders in the process of trying to break in? The police forensic activity went on for a while, then unexpectedly the police and Abniler Manther were surprised when the Dranzonian Empire Ministry for State Security Secret Service Branch arrived from their headquarters in Praxisvlasia.

None other than Reginald Heiqishi himself was there leading the investigation.

REGINALD HEIQISHI
The Secret Service is taking over this investigation and I'm in
charge. We will direct this inquiry.

If there was ever a case for Keystone cops, Reginald Heiqishi exemplified the best of them.

The police had been going down a pathway toward resolution, but when Reginald

Heiqishi inserted himself and his ideas, he only delayed matters by at least a week. By then the security breach was irreparable. In due time the lock company drilled out the control core, allowing the room to be opened until the lock was replaced. To their horror they found the intrusion alert system deactivated. Technicians were then brought in and did a check one by one to see if there were any missing data cubes. The next step would be to plug the data cubes into a terminal one at a time to validate the contents to make sure they had not been sabotaged.

INT. REVOLUTIONARY EMPIRE ZANZILTAR OPERATIONS CENTER-DAY

VOICE OVER
Evo Kaplan and Brenda Broyals were brought back to Zanziltar,
where they were soon taken back to the FIRM's Zanziltar
Operations Center.

Evo Kaplan still had not confirmed his real employer was the Revolutionaries, but he was now suspecting more and more likely.

Logically it made sense that Revolutionaries wanted what he stole from Abniler Manther. Who else would need the new Proton Gravity Disrupter Weapon?

Conrad Fanzui personally debriefed Evo Kaplan and Brenda Broyals.

Evo Kaplan had no way of knowing the data cube was well on its way to Zuanshicheng, the Revolutionary Empire home world and capital, where their best scientists would soon be analyzing the plans and the imbedded research all stored on the same data cube.

Despite all the secrecy the Dranzonian Empire attempted in hiding this new weapon and its extensive research, the Revolutionaries would be able to copy it and employ it ostensibly almost as quickly as their enemies. This created significant material damage to the security of the Dranzonian Empire.

Should the upper echelons of the Dranzonian Secret Service discover the spy involved in the heist was none other than Evo Kaplan, the person Reginald Heiqishi purged over a personal vendetta, Reginald Heiqishi would most likely fall victim to his own machinations.

Conrad Fanzui
I might want to discuss this mission again with you later after we finish all the data reduction in case events transpired, we do not know about. You may return to your living quarters and enjoy the rest of your day.

Evo Kaplan stood up and walked out of the briefing room and went back to his living quarters.

BRENDA BROYALS
Conrad, may I have a few minutes alone with you?

Brenda smiled at Evo Kaplan as he walked out of the room. He, of course, would be curious about what that private conversation entailed, but he knew Brenda would not share it with him, especially since she would be talking with Conrad Fanzui privately. As soon as Evo Kaplan was gone, the door shut and locked by automatic artificial intelligence programming.

CONRAD FANZUI
Okay, Brenda, what did you wish to discuss?


BRENDA BROYALS
Based on what I'm about to disclose, you very well may wish
to remove me for cause.


Conrad suddenly felt uncomfortable, because this was an extraordinary statement
made by one of the best spies in the Revolution.


CONRAD FANZUI
What made you come to this conclusion?


BRENDA BROYALS
I violated the covenants of a spy. I crossed over the line and
allowed me to get emotionally involved with a person of
interest.


CONRAD FANZUI
Please explain.


BRENDA BROYALS
In the preparation for the Coy Ridge operation, I allowed myself
to get involved with Evo Kaplan.


Conrad had a poker face just like Brenda. He was nevertheless quite intrigued
at what brought about this discussion. Brenda seemed to stall which prompted
Conrad Fanzui to get her disclosure to come out.


CONRAD FANZUI
Please continue. Tell me all about it, Brenda.


BRENDA BROYALS
A woman has her needs. Living on the edge of self-destruction
by operating in the field of espionage, I sometimes take men the
same way a lot of men take women.


I had my way with Evo Kaplan, virtually raping him in the
beginning. My ego was not contained and eventually as things
developed, I transcended at a moment when he turned it around
on me.


Instead of me using him, he used me and left indelible marks
in my psyche.

Conrad looking at Brenda, paused for a moment as he weighed the gravity of the situation.

CONRAD FANZUI
Is there anything else you want to tell me all this?

BRENDA BROYALS
In the spy business we cannot get emotionally attached to someone we may have to sacrifice during a mission, or we may cause the mission to fail with irreparable results. By the time we launched the Stratospheric Glider towards Praxisvlasia I was in love with Evo Kaplan.

The pain in Brenda's face was obvious. Conrad knew Brenda Broyals had reached a stress point and chose to remain silent and allowed Brenda to continue as best she could.

BRENDA BROYALS
I crossed over the line of common sense and the axioms of my training. I succumbed to my human need and discovered I had a weakness.

I could have put the mission in jeopardy by acting irrationally if a sequence of events occurred.

Simply put, I would have over-emphasized protecting Evo Kaplan's life, and by doing so I could have put the mission at risk.

CONRAD FANZUI
How do you feel about Evo Kaplan now?

BRENDA BROYALS
I will never be able to erase my emotions. Evo Kaplan's the first man to ever touch me and evoke me in the manner he did. I doubt no other man could ever to do my human psyche what he accomplished.

CONRAD FANZUI
Well, that does pose an interesting problem for us now, doesn't it?

BRENDA BROYALS
Sure, you have every right to remove me from my position. I screwed up. I'm not worthy to work for you like I have in the past.

Conrad Fanzui took to heart everything Brenda said and further reflected as he began speaking how he felt about the disclosure.

CONRAD FANZUI
The very most important attribute of a spy is his or her truthfulness to their handler. You know you are often under observation and just because we don't discuss it with you, doesn't mean we do not know what you did.

Brenda was now realizing Conrad had been spying on her the entire time. She felt so dumb and should have known better.

CONRAD FANZUI
The fact you came to me in full disclosure unclouds a lot of things. I wish it were this simple with other people, but it's not. Human relations are very complex and complicated at times, and when we throw in the spy business, we magnify that complexity because of the unique circumstances we discover ourselves in.

BRENDA BROYALS
I expected once I told you certain practices would change.

CONRAD FANZUI
You are right. I do have to make some structural changes because of your confession, but they will not affect you very much. I would not stand in the way of your relationship with Evo Kaplan if you kept it private among yourselves.

Brenda was feeling slightly better, but she knew the consequences were not yet fully understood. She waited patiently for the next foot to drop.

CONRAD FANZUI
We can't have your relationship with Evo Kaplan openly exposed here or it will add complications that would force me to transfer one of you.

BRENDA BROYALS
I understand.

CONRAD FANZUI
As far as future missions are concerned, because of the situation that exists between you and Evo Kaplan, it will not be possible for me to send you and him together on a team on another mission.

                    BRENDA BROYALS
            I would not expect you to do otherwise.


                    CONRAD FANZUI
I know it will not be convenient and it will mean you will see
less and less of each other. However, just as you pointed out,
you cannot operate objectively with him and therefore you will
not deploy in clandestine activities together unless there is some
compelling reason to send you two together on the same team.


                    BRENDA BROYALS
Thank you for your understanding and consideration.


                    CONRAD FANZUI
Go get some rest. You are probably suffering from acute space
lag.


                    BRENDA BROYALS
            All right. Thank you for your time.


Brenda stood up and walked out the door. As she walked back to her living
quarters, there was no sight of Evo Kaplan. He simply disappeared back to his
living quarters.


Revolutionary Empire Dictator Cornelius Xie de Hundan was soon notified of the
Coy Ridge mission by Conrad Fanzui.


                    CONRAD FANZUI
    We have obtained the holy grail of weapons technology.


                CORNELIUS XIE DE HUNDAN
                Who made this all possible?


                    CONRAD FANZUI
            Our recent recruit, Evo Kaplan.


                CORNELIUS XIE DE HUNDAN
        That's outstanding. Send him my warmest regards.


                    CONRAD FANZUI
I would also like to point out he came very close to death during
the mission.


                CORNELIUS XIE DE HUNDAN
                How did that happen?

CONRAD FANZUI

His oxygen system in the Stratospheric Glider failed upon launch back into space while he was carrying the stolen goods to the shuttle. When the team pulled him out of the glider, he was as near death as could be.


CORNELIUS XIE DE HUNDAN
How did this all happen?


CONRAD FANZUI

When he took off, he bypassed the alarm for the sake of completing the mission, knowing he was taking on a huge personal risk.


CORNELIUS XIE DE HUNDAN

Sounds like you need to send him on a vacation for a couple weeks before you send him on another mission to reward him for this excellent service.


CONRAD FANZUI
I agree, and I think I know just the person to send with him.


CORNELIUS XIE DE HUNDAN
All right, Conrad. Job well done. Keep me informed.


CONRAD FANZUI
Yes, sir.


VACATION


<u>INT. DRANZONIAN SECRET SERVICE SAFE HOUSE- ZANZILTAR – DAY</u>


VOICE OVER

Huaiyuansu Ka, a former Dranzonian Empire Secret Service agent who did a lot of logistics support and worked in the FIRM's mansion.


Huaiyuansu Ka, knew a lot about Evo Kaplan, but he would never divulge any of it because he took to heart his guidance from his superiors to never discuss FIRM's personnel under any circumstances.


That former colleague had been purged like Evo Kaplan and wished he had a way home and a way back into the in the

Dranzonian Empire Ministry for State Security Secret Service Branch.

When Evo Kaplan first arrived destitute and hungry from Praxisvlasia, Dranzonian Secret Service personnel initially traveled to Zanziltar to find Evo Kaplan out why he came and what he was doing in Sanctuary City.

Dranzonian Secret Service, of course, could not find Evo Kaplan, but by luck Huaiyuansu Ka encountered Evo Kaplan when he first arrived.

Evo Kaplan became a person of interest and was assumed he was working for organized crime or some other nefarious outfit.

A Dranzonian Secret Service Agent accidentally met Huaiyuansu Ka walking downtown in a red light district just after he left a strip club. This agent who had discovered Huaiyuansu Ka was working in Sanctuary City and most likely involved in some illegal activity, offered some incentives for assistance.

DRANZONIAN SECRET SERVICE AGENT
We are looking for Evo Kaplan. If you find out anything about his whereabouts, we have a nice reward for you if you contact us.

HUAIYUANSU KA
I don't want a reward. I want to go back into the secret service. I was purged for no good reason.

DRANZONIAN SECRET SERVICE AGENT
If you can provide an important tip that will result in a significant intelligence coup, the secret service is likely to reopen your case and reconsider why you were purged.

HUAIYUANSU KA
How will I get in touch with you?

DRANZONIAN SECRET SERVICE AGENT
Here's my business token. It scans with your communicator or most public communications booths.

HUAIYUANSU KA
All right.

VOICE OVER (MALE)

Huaiyuansu Ka (pronounced: *why you in sha ka*) separated from the Dranzonian Secret Service men and went home after he was dropped off in the center city red-light district.

Unlike the FIRM'S field operatives, the staff and logistics people lived in private residences around Zanziltar. Huaiyuansu Ka proceeded home from the red-light district on public transportation in case he was being observed.

Huaiyuansu Ka took the Secret Service man's business token and scanned it into a secret data cube that was encrypted well. Huaiyuansu Ka destroyed the business in an atomizer because he could ill afford to be caught with a link to Dranzonian Empire Secret Service personnel.

Weeks after the Coy's Ridge mission, Huaiyuansu Ka was tasked to make reservations for Evo Kaplan and Brenda Broyals to an off-world luxury vacation resort on the planet Shen de Huayuan (pronounced" shin da why you in).

Huaiyuansu Ka didn't know if this was a mission or a vacation, but he thought it would seem rather odd, a supervisor taking her employee to such a place thus assumed it probably could be a mission.

 Huaiyuansu Ka placed that information in the back of his mind and made all the reservations.

The next day, Brenda Broyals and Evo Kaplan were called into Conrad Fanzui's office for a private closed-door meeting.

CONRAD FANZUI

The reason why I called you here is to give you my decision on our plans and discuss a couple items with you.

Brenda and Evo observed Conrad closely as he proceeded to give them a rundown on policy and concerns. It has been brought to my attention that you two became lovers during the Coy's Ridge mission.

BRENDA BROYALS

Sir, I take full responsibility if there are any serious issues about my relationship with Evo Kaplan.

CONRAD FANZUI

Thank you, Brenda, but this poses a problem for us. You are both. excellent spies and professionals. But under the circumstances it would not be safe for us to send you two out together on missions unless there were compelling reasons to do so.

Brenda Broyals and Evo Kaplan looked at each other, realizing this was a major milestone in their lives.

CONRAD FANZUI

It's for your own protection, as well as eliminating that relationship from interfering with the conduct of the mission.

BRENDA BROYALS
Understand, sir.

Also, we can't allow fraternization between supervisors and employees; therefore, Evo will be transferred to a new group to end what appears to be a potential conflict of interest.

EVO KAPLAN
I'm sure I will do my best with the new assignment.

CONRAD FANZUI

Evo Kaplan, I do appreciate what you did, especially how you sacrificed yourself to complete this high priority mission which apparently is starting to appear like one of the most important accomplishments in the FIRM's history as an organization.

EVO KAPLAN
Thanks.

CONRAD FANZUI

The customer has voiced his gratification for your success in the mission and based on his recommendations, we are going to send the two of you away together on a two-week vacation off-planet.

BRENDA BROYALS
That's interesting. Where too?

CONRAD FANZUI

You will be taken to a resort on the planet *Shen de Huayuan* where we do not expect you to run into any other employees or enemies and can unwind and enjoy yourselves.

BRENDA BROYALS
When is this going to happen?


CONRAD FANZUI
Your reservations are completed, and you will leave on Intergalactic Passenger Transport tonight.


BRENDA BROYALS
How will we get to the space port?


CONRAD FANZUI
Just like going on a mission, you will go through a medical check and be given a change of clothes to eliminate any possibility you bring along any identifying information.


BRENDA BROYALS
Thank you, Conrad,


CONRAD FANZUI
When you get back from your vacation, we expect you to keep your relationship hidden or break up.


Both Brenda and Evo were silent and stared intensely at Conrad, carefully listening to every word he said.


CONRAD FANZUI
I personally would recommend the second option since you are both spies and the complexities of your lives will make maintaining a relationship almost impossible, especially since you will be always traveling in different locations.


EVO KAPLAN
Thank you for the gift and the consideration.


VOICE OVER
Evo didn't have much other to comment about. Somehow Conrad Fanzui figured out Evo Kaplan  probably didn't feel quite the emotion that Brenda Broyals had developed toward him. That's why he felt in a while the relationship would wane as Brenda also would figure out Evo Kaplan.


Conrad Fanzui needed to give Brenda Broyals time to adjust. But since Cornelius Xie de Hundan wanted to reward Evo Kaplan for his success, it seemed only fitting to give Evo

Kaplan two weeks with Brenda Broyals, to make these two weeks very enjoyable.

Then Evo Kaplan would be back to living hell, performing complex and risky missions, but without the extraordinary inspiration of Brenda Broyals.

That night a security man knocked on Evo's door to make sure he was going to be ready for his medical check, change of clothes, and transport to the space port.

Brenda Broyals was also given the same assistance. They had nothing to pack. Per procedures, someone else packed them out for security measures. Even though they were not actually going on a mission, it did not matter. There was always the possibility they could become embroiled in espionage against the Dranzonians even if they were on a vacation.

At the prescribed time Brenda and Evo arrived at the medical screening center. Both received a medical checkup and then were allowed to dress in their new clothes in preparation to be taken away to the space port.

Anticipation was gripping the couple as they were ferried away in the middle of the night to the space port. This was done to eliminate any exposure to other agents at the Zanziltar facility and to eliminate any possible appearance of fraternization by going on a lover's tryst with Evo Kaplan sneaking away with his supervisor Brenda Broyals.

The couple soon boarded and were on their way for two weeks of  heavenly paradise as a special award for exemplary performance behind enemy lines.

VOICE OVER (MALE)
Evo Kaplan was considered a new hire and a rookie by his peers who did not know his history at the Dranzonian Empire Ministry for State Security Secret Service. Evo Kaplan completed far more missions than Brenda Broyals or most of the people presently assigned to the FIRM's Zanziltar Operations.

The *Shen de Huayuan* planet was mildly primitive, but off-world travelers nicknamed it the Garden of the Gods planet. In many areas the rainfall was equivalent to the island of Kuai on the planet Earth on the extreme end of the Empire.

Places like Planet Earth were too far to travel, and the Empire only rarely sent survey ships there. Brenda advised Evo Kaplan to not be too intimate in public in case they were being followed by friendly spies or the enemy.

On the transport they were very quiet and reserved. Nobody would suspect they were two lovers going away on holiday.

It took several days to reach Shen de Huayuan in the heart of the Revolutionary Empire, where it would be unlikely the Dranzonian Empire would attack. Also, the logistics of placing any Dranzonian Empire Secret Service agents on the planet *Shen de Huayuan* was problematic and unlikely. The couple could really unwind. As they got closer to *Shen de Huayuan*, Brenda was acting a little strange.

Evo Kaplan didn't understand it then, but Brenda Broyals was just lacking the affection she needed and avoiding that public spectacle and potential exposure to prying eyes was taking its toll. As they were going through planetary re-entry and landing on *Shen de Huayuan*, her whole persona was changing because she knew gratification was right around the corner.

Conrad Fanzui had his logistics assistant Huaiyuansu Ka do all the preimmigration and customs proper forms, which were carried aboard the Intergalactic Passenger Transport spacecraft by the company who transported sealed records.

Evo Kaplan and Brenda Broyals boarding passes were thus stamped with the pre-customs certificate and when they exited the space craft with all the other travelers, they went through an accelerated line and were out on the curb of the transportation access passenger loading area.

VOICE OVER (FEMALE)
Within one minute. Momentarily their belongings were placed in the van-like vehicle, and they were off to their Lantiane Resort, also referred to as the Blue Swan, located on the beach.

Their Lantiane Resort room was prepaid. All they had to do was arrive at the customer service desk with their itinerary, which had the electronic reservation number, and they were handed their electronic room key.

All Brenda and Evo needed to do was to walk up to the bungalow door and the electronics would recognize their room key, whether it was in a purse or pocket, and unlock the door. The room was fresh and clean, and fresh flowers were in vases and a bottle of *Shen de Huayuan Champagne* was in a bucket of ice waiting for their arrival along with some snacks and a special cake.

No sooner than the two arrived in the room and set their luggage down on stands to unpack, Brenda walked up and put her arms around Evo and kissed his neck then his cheeks and then his lips. Evo kissed back and Brenda opened her mouth wide open to engulf him. There was no mystery to what Brenda wanted as Evo suddenly felt increased arousal. Evo's response animated Brenda even further as he embraced Brenda in a quite evocative manner.

Brenda led Evo to the bedside and slid out of her tourist clothes almost instantly, becoming fully nude. Evo followed suit and was guided by her into the realm she wanted as endorphins raced through Evo's brain intensifying the lust and desire.

All that pent-up emotion now poured out like a river. Brenda knew their special time together would become less and less. Because of the business they were in, either one of them could easily get killed.

Brenda is also quite aware that had she not been on the shuttle to revive Evo, the mission specialist might not have performed CPR at the vigor she otherwise did. Evo was only alive today because someone caring was near him at a time of need. In the future on dangerous assignments, Evo Kaplan would not have that same kind of backup, because this love affair separated them forever doing missions.

Splitting up into different teams meant Evo Kaplan's risk went up a few notches. It was good that they arrived at the Lantiane Resort late in the morning, otherwise they would not have had the chance to see much of the place on the first day due to their intense lovemaking. It took almost two hours for Evo to fully satisfy Brenda. She was afterwards purring like a kitten on his chest as they both drifted off into a nice nap that fortified them and gave them an edge to go out and explore this new world.

Pre-packed for Evo and Brenda was beachwear and a lot of casual clothes. There was no expectation of any formal events since they were traveling incognito. As they slowly regained their alertness and the drowsiness subsided, Brenda offered a suggestion.

BRENDA BROYALS<br>
Let's take a walk along the beach.

EVO KAPLAN<br>
Sounds good.

After a nice shower and change of clothes Brenda and Evo walked out the front of their bungalow along the beach where all the super expensive rooms were located just below the high-rise resort hotel. Twenty yards from their Bungalow was the splendid white sandy beach.

The sound of the gentle waves crashing ono the beach was southing as they walked holding hands down the beach. The aqua blue marine water that was shallow for some distance with the sunlight striking it at the perfect angle added to the majestic quality of the tropical paradise *Shen de Huayuan.*

                         EVO KAPLAN
          I have no doubt the reason why tourists call this lovely planet
          *Shen de Huayuan* the Garden of the Gods.


                         BRENDA BROYALS
          Shen de Huayuan truly is one of the most sought-after  vacation
          planet destinations for the Empire.


                         EVO KAPLAN
          Yes, but Shen de Huayuan is deep in the heart of the
          Revolutionary Empire. The Dranzonians no longer control this
          planet or this area of space.


                         BRENDA BROYALS
                    Is that so bad, really?


                         EVO KAPLAN
          Depends on if you have a Loyalist mindset.


Brenda Broyals stopped dead in her tracks and looked hard at Evo Kaplan.


                         BRENDA BROYALS
               Evo, do you have a Loyalist mind set?


                         EVO KAPLAN
          At one point in time, I was super patriotic. But suddenly I became
          a victim just like the many revolutionaries who turned on the
          corrupt government. I was placed in a disgusting situation and
          forced to live in squalor because of that corruption. I have no
          love for the Dranzonian Empire. I have no allegiance to anyone.


                         BRENDA BROYALS
          But you displayed a great deal of allegiance to the FIRM when
          you risked your life getting that data cube up to the shuttle.


                         EVO KAPLAN

I have a six-year contract with the FIRM. I'm an honorable person and will diligently carry out my assignments for those six years. But after that I want to settle down somewhere and avoid the complexities of the life of a spy.

BRENDA BROYALS
Evo, wouldn't you go back to the Dranzonian Secret Service if they invited you back?

EVO KAPLAN
No Brenda, the way they terminated me and threw me to the wolves with basically the shirt on my back proved to me they are not a worthy employer. Revolutionaries are right. There's a lot of corruption at the top. I just never believed they would ever destroy their own organization over a stupid hunch they had been penetrated by the Revolution.

BRENDA BROYALS
If the Revolution offered you a high position, would you turn it down?

EVO KAPLAN
As soon as my six-year contract is complete, I'm Hanging up my spurs. With the money I'm saving I will never be placed in a situation like before. I want to settle down, marry, have kids, and live a normal life.

BRENDA BROYALS
Who would you do that with?

EVO KAPLAN
Brenda, I hope it's someone like you.

Brenda reached Evo Kaplan and grabbed him and gave him an endearing hug.

BRENDA BROYALS
Evo, you are so sweet.

VOICE OVER (FEMALE)
But in the back of Brenda's mind, she knew she could never give up her spurs. Children were not going to be part of her universe. She didn't have religious beliefs and she wasn't going to have children. Her desires were to survive multiple spy operations and come back for more.

With Brenda Broyals mentor, Conrad Fanzui, she knew her possibilities were endless, though she also was pragmatic and knew she took on a lot of risks.

Perhaps that's why she had the strange behavior before she met Evo Kaplan? When would she decide to lay her cards down for Evo Kaplan?

Her deadline was in six years when his contract ended. Six years is better than none if she lasted that long. If Evo lasted that long as well. There was no way to know if Evo Kaplan would be alive in six years. Hopefully by then the Revolution would be over and the new government in place.

But could Brenda Broyals ever give up the spy business? Brenda knew firsthand that spies also worked in peace time since she was employed by Conrad Fanzui long before the insurrection started.

They continued their walk down the beach enjoying the lovely view and the tropical paradise when they both suddenly discovered they were getting hungry. As part of their package deal, their meals were all provided by the resort.

EVO KAPLAN<br>
I'm getting kind of hungry now.

BRENDA BROYALS<br>
I wonder if it's about time they start serving.

EVO KAPLAN<br>
Yes, it's probably about that time.

BRENDA BROYALS<br>
Let's go check it out.

<u>INT. RESORT BUFFETT – AFTERNOON</u>

VOICE OVER

Brenda and Evo made their way back to the hotel, and sure enough they had an extraordinary dinner buffet set up. At the very end of the food tables was a barbecued hog-like creature with its head and face still attached; it was fresh with very little carving done on it. A chef was there to carve out pieces of the barbecued hog as well as some of the other meats he had there to slice.

Everything available in the nearby galaxy was at the table, it seemed—including foods Evo had never seen before, as numerous types of aliens were staying in the Lantiane Resort. Brenda and Evo got themselves a plate of food and made their way to a small table that seated four people.

They arrived early ahead of the crowd and enjoyed the ambience of the view in the balmy weather under shade. While Evo was eating, he carefully examined Brenda. He was awe inspired at Brenda's splendid beauty.

BRENDA BROYALS
How's your food?

EVO KAPLAN

This meat tastes great, I might need have a second helping.

BRENDA BROYALS

You probably burned off excessive calories this morning pleasing me. You need the extra energy that meat will help give you.

EVO KAPLAN

I figured as well as I did this morning, you would give me a week off.

BRENDA BROYALS
No honey. That was just a warmup for the big game.

EVO KAPLAN
Championship game?

BRENDA BROYALS

The reward you will receive if you win will be the best I'm capable of.

 EVO KAPLAN You know I will put forth my best effort ever.

VOICE OVER

Brenda Broyals smiled and continued eating her meal giving Evo Kaplan a wicked smile.

She knew she was eye candy. Brenda's sexual prowess was second to none and she was an expert at arousing men. She had drugs and chemicals she could give a man to make him lose control or extend his performance a lot better than any prescribed medications.

Evo Kaplan was like the ever-ready battery; he didn't need any help at the present time but in the years to come if he did, Brenda Broyals was ready.

Brenda wondered what would happen six years from now when Evo Kaplan's contract ended. Would he simply walk out of her life, or would there be her tendrils in his heart Brenda could snag and always hold?

Some of the finer parts of life were always the ones that were often totally out of your control. As an example, when a spouse discovers their mate has pancreatic cancer or something that would take them quickly, there isn't much that can be done. Their fate is dealt with and that's reality.

Evo could have died the other day. Had they recovered the Stratospheric Glider just one minute later, Evo would be dead. Realizing what life could bestow upon them, Brenda was going to greatly enjoy these next two weeks just in case there wasn't a tomorrow.

VOICE OVER (FEMALE)

Brenda Broyals affection and conduct toward Evo Kaplan would be atypical of who she really was. This was not the kind of woman she was. But as she analyzed the situation, since Evo Kaplan was the first man to make her feel love, she would devote these two weeks to him to pay him back for something no man had ever done before.

Brenda Broyals feelings of love created transcendence in Evo Kaplan and her effervescent companionship. Brenda would mold Evo Kaplan like he never anticipated.

Brenda Broyals was a smart but a conniving woman and earned her promotion as a supervisor of spies by her success in the field.

Brenda Broyals harrowing adventures were second to none. Her numerous dances with death always ended the song with her survival. In essence Brenda earned her stature and recognition

·

as well as the power bequeathed upon her by her mentor Conrad
Fanzui. Conrad Fanzui was an old hand in the spy business.

Conrad Fanzui had worked with the best and had accomplished the most. His early
work in the Revolution earned his respect from powerful men in the Revolution
such as Glen Zhurenshuo, Head of Revolution Empire Section, Secret Service;
Cornelius Xie de Hundan, Revolutionary Empire Dictator; Revolutionary Guard
Force Commander General Guodu Jiaolu; as well as the five members of the
Committee for State Security.

The Revolution relied heavily upon Conrad Fanzui, and Conrad Fanzui now
relied heavily on Brenda Broyals.

Future requests and priorities would soon upset the fabric of Brenda's life as the
needs of the Revolution would rip Evo Kaplan out of Brenda Broyals arms and
send him places alone where she often worried about his safety.

VOICE OVER (FEMALE)

After dinner Brenda and Evo went back to their room where
they both felt the need to use the facilities and get comfortable.
Almost like newlyweds, they soon were soaping each other
up and offering tender caresses in the shower, which further
released more endorphins for their enjoyment.

They soon exited the shower, dried off, and put on their clothes
and talked about seeking some entertainment for the evening.
From the bungalow with the windows open allowing the sea
breeze to come in, they could hear music in the background.

EVO KAPLAN

Let's go listen that to music and see what's going on.

BRENDA BROYALS

Sounds like a good idea Evo. Maybe I can demonstrate the
Cerellian Twist for you.

Brenda was thinking she might need to captivate Evo's mind slightly more. It
wasn't hard finding the source of the music, one of the beachfront clubs at the
Lantiane Resort. They entered the establishment and quickly found a seat at a
small table with a direct beach view.

INT. LANTIANE RESORT BEACHFRONT CLUB – LATE AFTERNOON.
THE SONG *YOU CAN LIVE FOREVER* IS BEING SANG BY THE CABARET
SINGER.

.

The musicians were playing near the end of the bar in a small band, not overdoing it and producing invigorating modern cabaret music intermittently mixed in with tropical songs. Some of the songs were instrumental. Most of the songs were sung by a beautiful young cabaret singer with long black hair.

This female cabaret singer and member of the band, dressed very provocatively, and her face was very beautiful and inspired Evo. Evo wasn't a bad-looking man and because of his physical fitness and martial arts training, his body exemplified what some counter-culture women referred to as "stud.

Brenda recognized the body language suddenly exhibited by the singer. Some women like to take away from other women especial handsome men like Evo Kaplan. Brenda would have to stretch out her black widow nest to protect Evo Kaplan from this woman, whom she had no doubt would pursue him by the way she was focusing on Evo, Brenda knew the beautiful singer would do if given the opportunity.


It almost became plainly obvious to Brenda that the singer was singing to Evo. And her singing got better as if she was inspired, probably thinking she would one day have her way with this man.

But unfortunately, the singer had never met her match like Brenda, who knew how to take care of her if she got too close to Evo. Evo nevertheless enjoyed the music.

Anyone who has a glamorous woman singing at them would most likely respond in the same manner, as one's ego is twisted in the mind in complicated ways. Also, the beautiful singer's inspiration could spill over to Brenda as Evo's libido could be modulated by the transcendence from the singing.

The sound created by the singer's voice was unique and rare, blending in well with the exuberance of the musical instruments. The singer's voice influenced Evo's psychoacoustics and consequently his motivations. The music played on for a while and suddenly it was the break time for the band.

This was the calm before the storm as the singer approached Evo and Brenda's table and introduced herself.

SHERI
Hi, I'm Sheri. How are you guys doing this afternoon?


EVO KAPLAN
Hello, I'm Proctor and this is Betty. We are doing fine, thank
you.


*Betty* was Sheri's alias during this vacation.


SHERI
I hope you are enjoying the music.


EVO KAPLAN
Yes, it's lovely.


SHERI
Do you live here in Shen de Huayuan?


EVO KAPLAN
No, we are from Zanziltar.


VOICE OVER (FEMALE)
Sheri was immediately supercharged because she instantly
knew this was a rich dude, as all of them were from Zanziltar. *If
she could just get him away from that blonde bimbo for a brief
period and show him her stuff, he'd be dumping that woman
and moving onto this prime calling.*

Brenda wasn't too impressed with Sheri, wreaking of perfume
that was usually done by women to cover up some bad body
oder when parts of them were not up to great medical condition
caused by their reckless sexual behavior.


EVO KAPLAN
Would you like to sit down with us? Let me buy you a drink
Sheri.


SHERI
Thank you very much, I'm so thirsty.


They engaged in small talk, but Brenda was secretly upset with Evo for inviting
the singer to join them. *Is he toying with me?* In a while the band started playing
and Sheri had to go sing.

SHERI
Thank you very much for the drink, I must go back to work
again.


EVO KAPLAN
You are welcome.


BRENDA BROYALS
Don't give the kitten milk. It will come back for more.


VOICE OVER (FEMALE)
Sheri, on the other hand, got a close-up of Evo Kaplan. She
could see those muscles were real and he was in fantastic shape.
The kind of guy she liked, one who could be physical for an
extended time.


After a few more songs Brenda had enough of Sheri's flirting
overtly with Evo.


BRENDA BROYALS
Could we go back to the bungalow? I'm feeling space lag.


EVO KAPLAN
Sure.


Brenda beat Sheri in her own game. She left with the goods before Sheri could
figure out how to get her fingers in the cookie jar.


When they got back to the room and all the curtains closed so they could have
privacy, Brenda undressed and became nude and crawled in bed.


BRENDA BROYALS
Could you please turn out the light when you're ready?


Evo took the hint and expedited his metamorphism to nudity and crawled between
the sheets when Brenda dove beneath the covers and worked her magic to escalate
Evo's awareness of his libido's reaction. It did not take long for Evo to respond to
Brenda and the two soon were enjoying the horizontal tango and then afterwards
fell asleep into each other's arms.


<u>INT. THE FIRM'S ZANZILTAR REVOLUTIONARY MANSION - DAY</u>


VOICE OVER
Former Dranzonian Spy Huaiyuansu Ka had been brooding all
day, wondering what he should do. Every day Huaiyuansu Ka

wanted more and more to somehow be able to work his way back into the Dranzonian Empire Secret Service. Huaiyuansu Ka took to heart what the Dranzonian spy had said to him.

It was severely risky because if the Revolutionary Empire Zanziltar Operations ever detected Huaiyuansu Ka contacted the Dranzonians, it's quite possible they would quickly arrange for his demise.

But Huaiyuansu Ka was desperate. His family was still on Praxisvlasia, and he missed them terribly. He wanted to get back while he had a family, and the only way he could safely get back would be the Dranzonian Empire Secret Service would have to take him in and put him through some sort of witness protection program so he could exist and regain his family before it was too late.

Once his spouse hooked up with a better prospect, Huaiyuansu Ka would lose her and the kids. He knew better than to call the Dranzonians from home or on his personal communicator.

The number the Dranzonian Spy gave to Huaiyuansu Ka was a local number. He assumed there was a desk at the Dranzonian consulate in Zanziltar. Like all good diplomats, most of them doubled as spies with diplomatic immunity. All the country could do would be to expel them after seventy-two hours.

Making physical contact would also be tricky because there was ample opportunity for Revolutionary Empire Zanziltar operations personnel to discover Huaiyuansu Ka talking with the enemy.

Huaiyuansu Ka left work at the end of the day and reluctantly went into the heart of the city and to a restaurant that specialized in caffeinated drinks that had a phone booth.

Public phones were available less these days, but some people existed that could not afford a personal communicator or had no reason to have one most of the time. Huaiyuansu Ka went in the communicator booth and reluctantly made the call.

<u>INT. SPLIT SCREEN. ZANZILAR RESTAURANT TELEPHONE BOOTH AND DRANZONIAN CONSULATE – SECRET SERVICE DETACHMENT - DAY</u>

                    DRANZONIAN SPY
                         Hello?


                    HUAIYUANSU KA
            I would like to speak to a Mr. Nuvrean.


                    DRANZONIAN SPY
            He's not available. What's this about?


                    HUAIYUANSU KA
I'm a former Secret Service agent purged during the
reorganization, and Mr. Nuvrean informed me that if I came
up with an excellent tip that was actionable, it might help
toward reopening my case to get me possibly back in the Secret
Service."


                    DRANZONIAN SPY
                      You have a tip?


                    HUAIYUANSU KA
      Yes, but I would rather not say it here on the phone.


                    DRANZONIAN SPY
Where are you at? We can come to pick you up and take you to
a safe house where you can tell us your story.


                    HUAIYUANSU KA
      I'm at the Golden Dragon Restaurant  on Palm Avenue


                    DRANZONIAN SPY
                    What's your name?


            HUAIYUANSU KA Huaiyuansu Ka.
                    DRANZONIAN SPY


Someone will be there in ten minutes. He will know what you
look like because we'll pull up your records. He will enter the
restaurant and nod at you. Follow him outside and you will
have transportation.


<u>INT. GOLDEN DRAGON RESTAURANT  - PRAXISVLASIA – CENTER
CITY – DAY</u>


True to the Dranzonian spy's word, a man walked in approximately ten minutes
later and from a distance nodded at Huaiyuansu Ka before turning around and
walking out of the restaurant that was empty that time of day.

EXT. CURBSIDE – LIMO PRAXISVLASIA – CENTER CITY – DAY

Huaiyuansu Ka walked out the restaurant and there was a limousine waiting there
with the door open and the man standing beside it. He approached the car and the
man who then gestured for him to get in.

Huaiyuansu Ka got in the car, the man hopped in and shut the door, and they drove
off. They took a circuitous route out into the countryside where they could firmly
detect any possible surveillance trailers.

They eventually made their way to a safe house and drove into the garage and its
door was soon shut. Everyone got out of the car and walked into the safe house.

INT. SAFE HOUSE PRAXISVLASIA – SUBURB – DAY

> DRANZONIAN SPY
> Okay Huaiyuansu Ka, what do you got for us?

> HUAIYUANSU KA
> I provide logistics to an organized crime syndicate they call
> the FIRM that sometimes does jobs for the Revolution. They
> recently hired a former Secret Service agent that was purged
> about the same time I was and he's currently at the planet *Shen
> de Huayuan* on vacation with one of the FIRM's top spies who
> did a lot of projects for the Revolution and is most likely a
> sympathizer.

> DRANZONIAN SPY
> What's the woman's name?

> HUAIYUANSU KA
> Brenda Broyals.

> DRANZONIAN SPY
> And the other spy's name?

> HUAIYUANSU KA
> Evo Kaplan

> VOICE OVER
> The interviewer immediately knew the names. In the order of
> battle of spies, they targeted, Brenda Broyals was just about
> at the top of the list. And what Huaiyuansu Ka didn't know
> was the Dranzonian Empire Secret Service had a dossier on

Brenda Broyals that was very thick, and she was a major person of interest.

These Secret Service agents also would now investigate Evo Kaplan. This was a huge tip, as it just confirmed one of their former top agents was now probably working for the enemy.

This would get dicey. The interviewer asked several more questions but knew they could not keep Huaiyuansu Ka very long in the event he was under some sort of observation, which was highly likely.

They had to reposition Huaiyuansu Ka back in the heart of the city to give the appearance he had simply taken a limo somewhere for shopping or for entertainment.

Since Huaiyuansu Ka was picked up near the red-light district, that would be his cover story if his handlers ever pressed him for details.

An arrangement was made for future contact. It would not be initiated by phone calls that were easily tapped. Instead, one day of the week Huaiyuansu Ka would simply venture into a library if he wanted to contact the Dranzonian Secret Service.

Huaiyuansu Ka was given a list of highly desired information in case he came across any of it.

Huaiyuansu Ka would then betray his employer, and at the same time the Dranzonians promised they would reopen his case and use this most recent situation as a bargaining chip in his favor for the reviewers.

Huaiyuansu Ka, however, would have to earn his ticket home by playing the role of a double spy.

Huaiyuansu Ka's betrayal of Evo Kaplan and Brenda Broyals was very damaging, to say the least.

Huaiyuansu Ka was also playing a very dangerous game because if Conrad Fanzui discovered his treachery, he would discover his family wiped out just before the Revolutionaries informed him, he was to be executed in the most painful manner.

The Dranzonian Empire Secret Service didn't have sufficient time to get a team in place to either wipe out Evo Kaplan and Brenda Broyals during their honeymoon, but they at least needed to confirm the information that Huaiyuansu Ka provided.

In the spy business, no information is trusted until it is independently corroborated. The Dranzonians would expend great resources and risk to send a couple agents to the Shen de Huayuan planet and observe Evo Kaplan and Brenda Broyals and evaluate exactly what type of relationship existed. They might ostensibly offer to bring him back and, if the opportunity had arisen, even assassinate him if he refused to return.

INT. DRANZONIAN INTELLIGENCE HEADQUARTERS - PRAXISVLASIA - DAY

VOICE OVER
The scramble of picking agents to send to *Shen de Huayuan* was problematic, and now that the Abniler Manther investigation at Coy's Ridge was finalized as a dead-end open case, the star performer of that investigation, Reginald Heiqishi, was available and was tasked to go with another agent and bring back the details.

REGINALD HEIQISHI
You can't send me. Evo Kaplan will recognize me.

REGINALD HEIQISHI'S BOSS
You are the best man for the job. We'll do some cosmetic work on you.

REGINALD HEIQISHI
That crap only partially works. An agent as savvy as Evo Kaplan would spot me a mile away.

REGINALD HEIQISHI'S BOSS
That's not what you said in your report when you purged him.

REGINALD HEIQISHI
I stated a lot of things that were not flattering, because We had to get rid of him because he truly was an undesirable and we had no means to prove his loyalty.

REGINALD HEIQISHI'S BOSS
You said, and I quote in your evaluation of Evo Kaplan, 'He is a dumb son of a bitch and problematic controlling him in the field.'

REGINALD HEIQISHI
Well, that's true.


REGINALD HEIQISHI'S BOSS
If he's as you depicted him, why is he suddenly on a soiree at *Shen de Huayuan* with Brenda Broyals, one of the top spies working for the Revolution?


REGINALD HEIQISHI
Either she is desperate, or he got lucky.


REGINALD HEIQISHI'S BOSS
You know better than that. You purged him so you are now tasked to go find out what Evo Kaplan is doing at *Shen de Huayuan* with Brenda Broyals.


REGINALD HEIQISHI
It's kind of hard to figure out what a spy does for a living while on vacation.


REGINALD HEIQISHI'S BOSS
If you confirm the relationship he has with Brenda Broyals, that means he is working for the Revolution.

By the way, we just confirmed in your most recent investigation the vandals made off with the plans for our new Proton Gravity Disrupter Weapon. What if we discovered was Evo Kaplan involved in that heist?


REGINALD HEIQISHI
I think that's highly doubtful, but what if he was?


REGINALD HEIQISHI'S BOSS
That means your evaluation of him was totally inappropriate and probably due to a personal vendetta you took out on the guy.


REGINALD HEIQISHI
So what, I made have made a minor mistake.


REGINALD HEIQISHI'S BOSS
You may be responsible for handing the enemy one of our best spies. So, get your ass to Shen de Huayuan and report back what's going on between Evo Kaplan and Brenda Broyals.

When Reginald Heiqishi looked into his boss's eyes, he saw a mixture of rage and disqualifying emotions.

If they ever discovered Evo Kaplan made the heist of that Proton Gravity Disrupter Weapon and handed it over to the Revolution, Reginald Heiqishi's situation in the Dranzonian Empire Secret Service would become tenable if not downright unable to survive a purge of his own.

Reginald Heiqishi looked on the bright side, this might lead to an order to assassinate Evo Kaplan, which he would be most happy to perform and make him wish he had never crossed him and the Dranzonian Secret Service.

## INT. PLANET SHEN de HUAYUAN - LANTIANE RESORT- BUNGALO ROOM - DAY

On the next day after Evo Kaplan awoke and finished his morning routine, Brenda was quickly prepared and putting on tourist clothes and no makeup made the transition quite efficient.

It was so nice not living in fear or the stress of preparing for another mission. It had been a long time for either of them to go on a decent vacation. Evo went from continuous missions to the unemployment line, where his personal finances curtailed any notion of breaking away for such activity.

Brenda, on the other hand, was gripped by the outbreak of hostilities of the Revolution. She worked feverously on projects supporting the insurrection long before the shooting started. Brenda truly deserved a break and that's probably why Conrad Fanzui sent her and her lover boy to Shen de Huayuan.

They left the bungalow and the first thing on their minds was to find something to eat. There was an aroma in the air, and it came from the exact same place they ate last night, as the hotel had a beautiful breakfast buffet all set up and a few hotel guests were already there partaking in the sumptuous brunch. This was an expensive resort, so they could afford to let the champagne flow with brunch.

As Brenda and Evo approached the entrance, the artificial intelligence read their room keys and the terminal at the Maître d' podium identified the couple and cleared them for entry. The tall blonde maître d' with a short skirt and a beautiful smile greeted them.


Welcome to Brunch, please have a seat where you like. It's open seating.

The food was as good as expected at a resort of this stature. While they were eating, Evo contemplated his situation. *It wasn't that long ago I would never have dreamed I would be eating this well again.*

Brenda was just taking it all in, showing her beautiful transcendence into a melodious state where her personal vibrations had achieved a harmonious essence.

Brenda too reflected on her own situation. Just a few weeks ago she was raping poor Evo Kaplan. And here he was sitting right across from her, now the love of her life.

Evo Kaplan had reached out and touched Brenda Broyals soul and shifted her psyche and now her world was upside down. Brenda also had huge regrets, because it's usually when perfect love appears, tragedy was not far behind.

Brenda and Evo enjoyed a caffeinated drink that closely resembled coffee that grew on this planet. The average coffee drinker would not tell the difference.

On Evo's plate included some Shen de Huayuan sausages made from wild animals. Shen de Huayuan sausages tasted spicy and the aroma was out of this world.

Locally made, Shen de Huayuan sausages wetted Evo Kaplan's pallet quite well and the combination of duck eggs, breads, and pastries completed the wholesome meal without sacrificing quality.

EVO KAPLAN What do you want to do this morning?

BRENDA BROYALS
Let's go do some sightseeing and look this place over.

EVO KAPLAN
Good idea.

As a good spy Evo said to himself, *especially if we must find an evacuation corridor in case we come across trouble.*

Currently Evo Kaplan was unknown in the galactic spy world, as he had disappeared off the map shortly after being purged. However, if he were ever indicted for the Coy's Ridge, Abniler Manther's mansion break-in, and murder of the security guard, he would instantly be on the galactic watch list.

The Dranzonian Empire's Secret Service hunting would then hunt Evo Kaplan down, sparing nothing to snatch him. What he didn't know is that his betrayal by Huaiyuansu Ka would soon set the stage for such a future venture.

<u>EXT. PLANET SHEN de HUAYUAN - LANTIANE RESORT- ENTRANCE - DAY</u>

After they finished in the breakfast buffet, Evo and Brenda walked out to the front entrance of the Lantiane Resort. They immediately spotted several different types of transport lined up to take people to various destinations.

> EVO KAPLAN
> I have an idea. Let's take one of these cute vehicles and hire the driver to be a tourist guide and have him take us to all the sites.

> BRENDA BROYALS
> I like that idea; it might be a good way to discover what goes on around here.

Evo approached the first tri-wheeler driver.

> EVO KAPLAN
> Do you give private tours?

> THREE WHEEL DRIVER
> Yes sir, I would be most happy to give you a tour. How long do you want?

> EVO KAPLAN
> Half a day would be good.

> THREE WHEEL DRIVER
> That will be five credits.

Evo had several sets of credit tokens in the wallet his handlers provided him for this trip and pulled out one of the credit tokens.

> THREE WHEEL DRIVER
> Place the credit here.

The console had a credit reader. Five credits were immediately deducted off the bitcoin like device about the size of a credit card used on Earth.

                         THREE WHEEL DRIVER
                           Please hop on.


EXT. THREE-WHEELER -SIGHT SEEING TOUR- SHEN DE HUAYUAN –
DAY


Evo and Brenda hopped in the back seats of the three-wheeler, and it soon started
driving out of the circular driveway.

The driver in front had a single seat but the double wide seat in the back was
specially made for couples that were the mainstay of the Lantiane Resort patrons.

The driveway leading to the resort was decorated with flora that gave a pleasing
appearance and conveyed opulence. The landscape designer showed complete
genius in his application and strategic placement of various trees and plants. This
level of sophistication in landscaping was rare and Evo appreciated it greatly as it
gave an uplifting feeling.

They soon pulled out on a major thoroughfare that took them along the beach
community. The Tri-wheeler driver wore earphones and a microphone so that
he could better communicate with the occupants. The Tri-wheeler had speakers
mounted in the back so they could hear him better. The breeze coming through
the open car was nice.

The Tri-wheeler driver pointed out several good restaurants along the way and
a few attractions they might wander off and see. There was ample traffic on the
road, but not so much as an annoyance. The Tri-wheeler zipped along at a pretty
good pace. They soon came up to an area that had high rise buildings.


                         THREE WHEEL DRIVER
            This is the main business district. A lot of the economy comes
            from tourism, which remained strong through the Revolution.


                           BRENDA BROYALS
            Why is that? I would think with the harsh economic conditions
            that tourism would have dropped off significantly.


                         THREE WHEEL DRIVER
            Well ma'am, a lot of the tourists always come from Zanziltar
            where people seem to have a lot of wealth.


                           BRENDA BROYALS
                         That sounds plausible.


Soon the Tri-wheel passed some industrial buildings.

THREE WHEEL DRIVER
This is where a lot of tropical apparel is manufactured. People keep busy in this clothing district.

A few more blocks later, they saw more industrial buildings existed.

THREE WHEEL DRIVER
These buildings are where a lot of souvenirs are made.

The trip thus far wasn't all that inspiring, but then the driver asked about a side trip.

THREE WHEEL DRIVER
Would you like me to take a road up the side of the nearby mountains so you can see a good panoramic view?

EVO KAPLAN
Sure.

Evo soon to regret he agreed. The driver turned on a street and it headed directly toward the mountains. Soon they were snaking their way up the side of a mountain. They passed several points of viewing and they had climbed up the hill quite a way when Evo spotted the next turnoff to a viewing area.

EVO KAPLAN
Pull over here so we can look.

The Tri-wheeler pulled up to a two-foot-tall wall and everyone got out. The driver was surprised the couple didn't take a lot of pictures like most tourists do. But in the spy business the order of business is to never get your picture taken.

Brenda and Evo looked over at the scenery and the view. Evo looked around and observed how the road went up the side of the mountain. Way up above he could see a substantial platform. It was probably a main tourist attraction, so he figured they might as well continue and get up there and see what's going on.

BRENDA BROYALS
I think I've seen enough. Let's continue.

The three got back into the tri-wheeler and headed on up the mountain pass tourist road. It was windy and scary at times.

Evo Kaplan thought, *I probably didn't do good risk management doing this, but we've gone so far, I want to see what's up there.*

After a while it almost became annoying in the climb up the mountain. The tri-wheeler didn't have a lot of extra horsepower and it struggled at times.

EVO KAPLAN
Am I going to have to get out and push?

Eventually they made it to the top and there was a tourist platform that extended a good fifty feet off the cliff by a trestle-like structure that provided tourists with a very safe and sturdy platform to make observations and take pictures. This was a good experience for Evo Kaplan, as he was able to make a mental record of the area all along the beachfront and get ideas of places to visit. Brenda took it all in. Despite the laborious effort to get up here, now that they made it to the top, it all seemed worthwhile.

THREE WHEEL DRIVER
This building has a restaurant that specializes in mountain potatoes and  has an excellent gift shop.

BRENDA BROYALS.
Let's go in and look.

<u>INT.  PLANET SHEN de HUAYUAN – MOUNTAIN TOP GIFT SHOP - DAY</u>

They entered the gift shop. The driver remained with his Tri-wheeler, out of curtesy to the tourists. Inside there was a large area selling souvenirs, many of which looked very tempting, but as Evo and Brenda both knew, they would be tossed upon return to Zanziltar.

It was obvious that Conrad Fanzui would not want them to have mementoes of a place they went to that would confirm they had been there. Living in the artificial world of the spy business is either complicated or simplified in many issues.

It did not take long for the couple to figure out they didn't need any of the tourist junk. But it was apparent there were ample tourists filling their shopping carts. How's that going to fit in their four cubic feet on the Intergalactic Passenger Transport going home? They stopped by the restaurant.

BRENDA BROYALS
I'd like to order a small bowl of mountain potato soup to sample it.

EVO KAPLAN
We can share a bowl. I'm still feeling full from eating breakfast just a short while ago.

                              BRENDA BROYALS
                                Good idea.


Soon after placing their order and paying for it, they were served a small bowl of
mountain potato soup and two spoons.


                              BRENDA BROYALS
            This really tastes good. Perhaps we can come back and have a
            full meal here.


                               EVO KAPLAN
            Sounds like a good idea. I imagine the sunset here is rather
            spectacular, and this restaurant has such an incredible view.


The two then finished and went back outside and quickly spotted their driver and
the Tri-wheel.


                               EVO KAPLAN
            Okay, we are ready to head back down to the beach area.


                            THREE WHEEL DRIVER
            Hop on. Since we are going down the mountain, it might get
            dangerous. I recommend you put on your seatbelts, so you don't
            fall out of the vehicle.


                               EVO KAPLAN
                                  Sure


<u>EXT. THREE-WHEELER -SIGHT SEEING TOUR- SHEN DE HUAYUAN –
DRIVING DOWN THE MOUNTAIN ADVENTURE</u>


Recommendation for production staff:
            Chase car  & Drone filming the downhill adventure. Make it
            feel like a wild ride! Note the sound should be exciting (like a
            car commercial).


<u>EXT. SPLIT SCREEN - DRONE VIEW ON ONE SIDE AND CHASE CAR
IMAGES ON THE OTHER.</u>


Suggestion: a good place to film it: sunrise hiway mountains east of San Diego,
California that has nice curves.


<u>THREE-WHEELER  -SIGHT  SEEING  TOUR-  *SHEN  DE  HUAYUAN*  –
DRIVING DOWN THE MOUNTAIN ADVENTURE</u>

The driver observed the two passengers click their seat belts and then started the Tri-wheeler. In no time at all he was out of the parking lot and heading down the side of the mountain. The driver was going rather slowly, and Evo Kaplan wondered why, but discovered the answers soon enough. The driver was braking but didn't want to wear out his Tri-wheeler brakes, so he only gently braked, which allowed the tri-wheeler to gain momentum very rapidly. He did not brake hard until he had to.

By now the Tri-wheeler was no longer tourist transportation, it was now an amusement park ride going at extremely dangerous speeds!

It seemed to Evo kind of unfair he made it through a major espionage event to be killed simply by a three-wheel taxicab driver who showed little common sense. Evo Kaplan didn't know this driver had gone down this route many times before and he had it down to a science, though it would scare most of his passengers. It was good the curvy road had banking on the turns, otherwise they would have gone flying and in a few instances, they steadied out merely inches away from going over the side and tumbling down several thousand feet.

Brenda held on tightly to Evo as they continued down the sojourn on the mountain road in an odyssey that they would remember for a long time. A couple sharper turns and the stress level peaked.

EVO KAPLAN
Slow down!

The mountain adventure was now becoming too painful. The driver started braking more robustly, as he suddenly feared he would lose a tip. His brakes would have to take a little more wear and tear than he planned for.

As the Tri-wheeler slowed down, the ride became more enjoyable, and the passengers could take in the view instead of fretting about a possible road accident. Eventually they made it down to level ground. They would probably not be going back up there for mountain potato soup!

The tour still had a lot of time left and the driver continued along the waterfront, now heading north toward more beach communities. Unexpectedly there was some black smoke on the horizon. As soon as they got closer and could make out what they saw, they realized it was some type of machine driving on two metal rails adjacent to the road.

The driver eventually caught up to the machine and followed it until it stopped at a building that appeared to have people riding in carriages behind the black smoke-emitting machine. Evo Kaplan studied galactic history growing up and he recalled the obscure planet out on one of the branches of the galaxy spirals— the planet referred to as Earth— had used machines like this several centuries ago when they last surveyed the planet.

                         EVO KAPLAN
                 Pull over. I want to see that machine.


The driver pulled up to the building where the machine stopped. Evo hopped out and walked over near the machine so that he could take a good look. He walked up to one of the workers servicing the machine.

                         EVO KAPLAN
          Is this one of your transportation systems on this planet?


The worker looked astonished and soon responded after he recovered his wits.

              LOCOMOTIVE SERVICING EMPLOYEE
     No sir, this is a tourist ride. We leave here for a short trip once
     every thirty minutes.


                         EVO KAPLAN
     Tell me about this ride. Is it based on equipment this planet
     used?


              LOCOMOTIVE SERVICING EMPLOYEE
     We never used any of these machines on this planet. This one
     was imported a long time ago. Perhaps at one point in time they
     considered building a network using these machines, but it only
     came down to this tourist ride.


          EVO KAPLAN How long does the ride take?


     LOCOMOTIVE SERVICING EMPLOYEE
          We are usually back in thirty minutes.


                         EVO KAPLAN
                    Where can I buy a ticket?


     LOCOMOTIVE SERVICING EMPLOYEE
               In that building behind you.


                         EVO KAPLAN
          Do I have enough time to buy a ticket before you leave?

LOCOMOTIVE SERVICING EMPLOYEE We'll wait for you.


EVO KAPLAN
Okay, thanks.


Evo walked over to the The-wheel car driver.


EVO KAPLAN
We are going to take a ride on this machine. It will be back
in thirty minutes. Would you like to go with us? I'll buy your
ticket.


THREE WHEEL DRIVER
No, that will not be necessary. I prefer to wait.  here for you. I
have some things to read.


EVO KAPLAN
Okay.


Evo led Brenda Broyals to the building and purchased two tickets.


INT. THREE-WHEELER - - *SHEN DE HUAYUAN* – TRAIN RIDE


They were soon seated in one of the coaches and the machine made a strange
noise that sounded a lot like a boat whistle Evo recalled hearing when he was
a small boy out on the docks watching ships with his dad. The machine started
moving and it appeared to be going backward. It didn't go very fast. Evo guessed
they were traveling around ten miles per hour. After a while they sped up and were
doing maybe twenty miles per hour.


The tracks ran through a canyon, over a trestle, and through tunnels out past an
area that appeared to have farmers working in a field that strangely looked like a
Japanese tea farm. The ride was worth it to see the countryside. They never would
have seen all this on the Tri-wheel.


After traveling around fifteen minutes, the machine came to a stop. There was track
beyond where they stopped so Evo was curious as to why they stopped. Then the
train started moving in the opposite direction. Most likely it was simply heading
back to the building and the ride would soon be over. Going in this direction, they
could smell the acrid odder coming out of the machine, which burned a rocky
black substance. They must have been going downhill because the velocity picked
up pretty good and they were now doing probably thirty miles per hour or more.


The vibrations and sounds were significantly different too. There was an eerie
swaying of the carriage he was in. Evidently the tracks were not entirely level,

it seemed. The ride soon came to an end and Evo and Brenda exited and walked toward the tri-wheel and the driver who sat there smiling, earning thirty minutes of his fare reading and saving fuel costs!

<u>INT. THREE-WHEELER -SIGHT SEEING TOUR- *SHEN DE HUAYUAN* – COASTAL TOUR</u>

They were soon underway on the tri-wheel and, following a coastal road, went past several housing areas where Evo could see how people lived.

It seemed a lot less complicated than what Evo Kaplan was used to in Praxisvlasia, where some of the living spaces were so congested in parts of the world, the buildings were two miles tall. In the squalor heap Evo Kaplan had last lived in, the building was eight stories high and he had to walk up seven flights of steps to make it to his crappy apartment. At least he'll never have to go there again. And if he ever moved back to Praxisvlasia, he would be living in a fully furnished apartment in the Grazdang area.

The trees, sson and they would be detained. Security was tight in the Lantiane Resort, as it had to be with the clientele that stayed there. The couple had the option to put their valuables in a safe in the room, but the two spies knew sophisticated crooks could bust open those safes in a minute, just like Evo did the vault at Abniler Manther's mansion. Leaving their valuables behind in the room was not optional for them.

As soon as they sat down on the reclining seats, one of the resort staff walked up with a couple towels for them.

RESORT STAFF PERSON

Here's some towels. I'll be over at the counter next to the bar in
case you want any more towels or want to trade a wet one for
a dry one. You can just wave at me, and I'll come right away.

EVO KAPLAN<br>Thank you.

Brenda and Evo made themselves comfortable and with the umbrellas to provide shade, they didn't plan on getting sunburned. In a minute a waiter approached them

RESORT WAITER<br>Madam and Sir, would you like a drink?

EVO KAPLAN<br>Do you have a drink menu?

RESORT WAITER
Yes, sir.

The Resort Waiter handed Evo an electronic tablet that had scrolling drink pictures. Evo Kaplan had not been a boozer and in many of his missions, where clear-headedness predicated survival, alcohol was not optional. But in this vacation environment where no sources of trouble were present, he felt he could let his guard down a bit and when a drink he was familiar with scrolled down with two languages—standard Dranzonian, which even the Revolutionaries used out of necessity, and the *Shen de Huayuan* dialect— he ordered a drink.

EVO KAPLAN
I would like one of these Maotaijiuhe drinks.

RESORT WAITER
How about you, madam?

BRENDA BROYALS
I'll try what he is having.

The drinks were just like the food, and all the amenities were paid for as part of the package deal. Staying at the Lantiane Resort was great because a person didn't have to carry credits around and worry about prices or the budget since it was already taken care of. The drink Evo ordered was made from a pineapple-like plant that grew on trees and alcohol refined from a molasses-like substance. An Earthbound traveler would find a similar tasting drink at many island resorts.

Another staffer approached and asked Evo.

RESORT STAFFER
Sir, would you like to read the news?

Evo thought about it, and it might be a good source to check out what was happening around the Lantiane Resort for entertainment.

EVO KAPLAN
Sure.

The man handed Evo Kaplan a tablet like device that had 2D and 3D appearances on the video. The volume was turned down low so as not to disturb other guests, and most of the reports were in standard Dranzonian, the official language of the Empire and all its former planets that were once part of the proud expansive collection of civilizations. In the first few pages of information scrolled down, mostly local news was shown, which was all right with Evo, as he was inquisitive about the local situation.

After a few pages he discovered a lot of intergalactic news stories and some content devoted to the stalemate the Revolution found itself in.

Critics of Cornelius Xie de Hundan were blaming him for the erosion in the faith of the public. Evo Kaplan didn't expect those critics to be around much longer, as the brutal dictator would soon be dealing with them as the cloak and dagger tyranny slowly spread across the Revolution's Empire.

The op-ed called for the return of the five members of the Committee for State Security, who were currently spread across the galaxy doing fact-finding in the remote areas to return. The public believed Cornelius Xie de Hundan simply sent them away so that they would not interfere with his plans.

By all appearances, Cornelius Xie de Hundan was turning the Empire into a military industrial complex for the purpose of consolidating gains and eventually wrecking the remnants of the Dranzonian Empire so that he could create a new Empire and run things the way he wanted, including dealing with the malcontents who were part of the Revolution. The big purge in the Revolution was not too far away, and the purge of the Dranzonian Empire Secret Service would seem pale in comparison.

Evo Kaplan didn't want to spoil his vacation by creating negative psychology by reading all the negativity, and decided he didn't want to read any more.

BRENDA BROYALS

No, thank you, I don't want to think about work or the Empire
for the next couple of weeks. I want to enjoy myself and not
think about these things.

Just before Evo Kaplan put the tablet aside, he noticed an ad for a concert that night. *Perhaps Brenda might like going to this?*

EVO KAPLAN

Brenda, there is a concert tonight and it's in the city with a full
orchestra. Would you like to go?

BRENDA BROYALS

That sounds like fun.

EVO KAPLAN

Let me ask the hotel if there is a dress code. We might need
some clothes.

Evo raised his hand, and the staff member came to inquire about what the guest wanted. the Staff Member knew it was unlikely Evo needed a dry towel.

STAFF MEMBER
Yes, sir, what can I do for you?

EVO KAPLAN
We are thinking about going to this concert tonight. I was wondering if there was a dress code.

Evo showed the Staff Member the tablet image.

STAFF MEMBER
If you don't dress up for the concert, you will stand out. Men usually wear suits and women dresses.

EVO KAPLAN
Where can I get a suit and dress around here in time to go?

STAFF MEMBER
The Lantiane Resort prides itself on outfitting our guests with formal wear for such an occasion. If you would like to rent a suit and a dress for the young lady, we can have the outfitters send a fashion designer to you make some measurements and then deposit several suits and dresses in your suite to try it on after you go for a swim.

EVO KAPLAN
What about formal shoes?

STAFF MEMBER
If you want, we'll have them check your shoe sizes and bring suggested pairs and socks that will go with the apparel you pick.

EVO KAPLAN
That would be great.

STAFF MEMBER
Let me go contact them. I will be right back with some information.

EVO KAPLAN
All right. But how about reservations and tickets?

STAFF MEMBER
Sir, if you wish, we can make them right now for you. Give me the tablet and I will take it to my station and make those reservations for the two of you.

EVO KAPLAN
That would be fabulous, thank you.

The man left with the tablet and at a distance Evo could see he was working and talking apparently to all the above he mentioned. A few minutes later the man returned.

STAFF MEMBER
Sir, your reservations are completed. You should be there by 7:00 P.M. If you are going to take a taxi there, I suggest you leave here by 6:30 P.M. to ensure you are not late.

EVO KAPLAN
Thank you.

STAFF MEMBER
Also, in about two hours there will be a couple of clothing racks delivered to your bungalow with garments and shoes to match to try on. If they fit, you can just leave and go to the concert when you are ready.

EVO KAPLAN
What if the clothes do not fit?

STAFF MEMBER
If adjustments are required, then contact the hotel communicator from your bungalow and they will connect you to Guest Services to have a tailor and fashion designer sent to your room to make any adjustments necessary.

EVO KAPLAN
Thank you for your fast work.

STAFF MEMBER
You are quite welcome, sir. Is there anything else I can do for you?

EVO KAPLAN
No, that will be all that is necessary.

STAFF MEMBER
Raise your hand if you need anything, I'll come right over.

The Staff Member walked away.

BRENDA BROYALS
Evo, would you like to go swimming?

EVO KAPLAN
It probably would do me some good to swim a few laps.

BRENDA BROYALS
Me too.

There were several women at the pool's edge on very comfortable reclining chairs that had nice soft cushions on them that could be described by one word: Barracuda.

These rich Zanziltarian Barracudas were there for action and viewing such a lovely specimen like Evo Kaplan elevated their senses a bit. They knew he was apparently with that attractive looking woman, but at this resort it was well known a lot of men made themselves available when they discovered women with vast fortunes who needed a little attention.

The system worked well: they would inform the staffer to pass on to the man they were interested in him and sought a rendezvous. These were Barracuda with fangs and antennae. The fangs came out and the antennae went up when Evo walked close enough where they could get a good inspection. At first glance, his muscles were very compelling. Then they watched him get in the pool and swim.

Evo Kaplan had done missions on water worlds and had to be a good swimmer to carry out some of his past missions. He had gone through several swimming schools, trained by professional racers, and physical fitness trainers worked with him to improve his efficiency in swimming for endurance as required.

Evo Kaplan could maintain a 4.5- mile-per-hour pace walking, as well as almost maintain that pace swimming. Evo did a couple laps on the Olympic-sized pool, then got out and walked over to his reclining sun chair while Brenda went because they didn't want to leave their belongings unguarded.

One of the Zanziltarian Barracudas waited until Evo and Brenda left the pool area to go back to their bungalow and try on clothes before they gave their signal to the staffer, who had done a lot of work for them in the past, to send the message to this man.

STAFF MEMBER
What can I do for you Madam?

ZANZILTARIAN BARRACUDA

I would like to meet that man who was just swimming and left with the blonde woman sometime soon.

STAFF MEMBER

I will see what I can do for you Madam.

ZANZILTARIAN BARRACUDA

I will definitely make it worth your while.

As Evo and Brenda arrived at their bungalow, they discovered there were two racks of clothes and a dozen boxes of shoes waiting for them. The dresses on one rack were in line with the standards and the expectations for women at the symphony or a concert.

Likewise, the suits on the other rack would blend in well with the audience. After they showered and dried off, they tried out their clothes. These people were experts. They had already checked their clothes hanging in the closet for size and based on video from the swimming pool, calibrated the fitting so when Evo and Brenda tried on the clothes they fit perfectly.

It was just a matter of deciding which to wear. Brenda asked for Evo's opinion, which he gave, and she selected the most beautiful blue dress that complemented her looks very nicely.

Evo picked a black suit that fit him perfectly as well, and one of the shoes in a box was perfect match for the suit.

EVO KAPLAN

We probably need to get a snack now and dinner after the concert, or we'll be hungry during the concert.

BRENDA BROYALS

We can go to that place we went to yesterday where we listened to music. They had a menu and served food.

EVO KAPLAN

Okay, we'll eat then come back and dress for the concert.

The couple left their bungalow and went to the Lantiane Resort Beach Restaurant and Bar and sat down. Brenda and Evo immediately waited on and ordered a drink and simple meals, knowing they would have a full-course meal after the concert.

VOICE OVER (FEMALE)

The Cabaret Singer Sheri started singing her song, "YOU CAN LIVE FOREVER" about the time Evo Kaplan arrived.

*Was the song choice a coincidence a coincidence?* Brenda wondered.

Brenda and Evo had arrived at the beginning of happy hour, so the band was performing, and that female singer was back at it, giving Evo those *evocative looks*. It was almost as if Evo motivated Sheri, as her singing suddenly improved a notch or two. The band appreciated the fact Sheri went from doldrums to stardom performance instantaneously.

Evo ordered a sandwich and some fruit. Brenda ordered a dish that oddly looked like a quiche. The *Shen de Huayuan* sauce on Brenda's entrée made it all taste out of this world. It hit the spot!

Evo Kaplan was starting to look healthier every day. Evo's diet improved and medical technology used to improve his health and stamina for missions was clearly starting to influence his physique. Soon he would be back to his former glory when he was a proud member of a Dranzonian Empire Ministry for State Security Secret Service Branch.

Brenda and Evo could not stick around for the music since they had a concert to attend. Evo was happy to hear the entire "YOU CAN LIVE FOREVER" song before they left.

Brenda and Evo made their way back to their Lantiane Resort Bungalow and changed. Brenda went into the bathroom. Brenda was an expert in cosmetics application so she could put on masks and other concealment on missions in a frantic hurry, she did the same today and morphed into a living princess.

Brenda also decided to reward Evo by placing a double dose of her special pheromone laced perfume on, including applying it in areas Evo might chose to explore later that night after the concert.

Note to producers and director:

Paul D. Escudero's composition and lyrics for *"You can Live Forever"* will be included as part of the contract (4 songs will be provided under those terms). With a concert pianist like Yuja Wang playing the piano with orchestra backup and a singer like Jennie Kim, Ani Lorak, or Polina Gagarina singing the songs and playing the role of Sheri, those songs will be hits and add to the luster of the movie.

Brenda came out of the bathroom at 6:15. Evo was mildly stunned. Brenda's rapturous beauty, along with the pheromones Evo was suddenly breathing, elevated his heart rate at least fifteen beats per minute. Evo could easily have succumbed to Brenda's ecstasies right at that moment, but Brenda, mindful of the time, knew it was time to move them along.

BRENDA BROYALS
We need to get to the front entrance and get transportation or we'll be late.

EVO KAPLAN
I'm ready. Let's go.

The way to the front entrance went right past the Lantiane Resort Beach Restaurant and Bar that still had happy hour continuing for another hour or so, and the singer Sheri looked out of the open ports and watched the couple walk by. Sheri knew the couple had to have come from one of those expensive bungalows, and here they were all decked out and the dude looked exquisite. If Sheri could have her way with Evo Kaplan, she certainly would.

It only took them a couple minutes to walk to the front entrance. When the doormen and security representative saw they were formally dressed, they hailed a Lantiane Resort Limousine and had it pull up to pick them up and take them to the obvious location: the concert. After they were moving, the driver asked the obvious question through the intercom.

LIMOUSINE DRIVER
Are you going to the concert?

EVO KAPLAN
Yes.

LIMOUSINE DRIVER
Would you like me to pick you up after it's over?

EVO KAPLAN
That would be nice, thank you.

LIMOUSINE DRIVER
When the concert finishes, just walk out to the passenger-loading zone in front of the building. I'll be there to pick you up.

EVO KAPLAN
We appreciate that.

By 6:45 they were in front of the venue, and so were many other well-dressed people arriving to attend the concert. Evo had no way to know what to expect, but he assumed fine music had no intergalactic boundaries. Even though the Dranzonian Empire had not done a survey of Earth in many years, other worlds had visited and, in some cases, came away with examples of their music.

In one case, as they now knew, an enterprising entrepreneur managed to bring a steam engine back that wound up on the planet Shen de Huayuan. Earth classical music eventually mixed and augmented symphonic music developed across the Empire.

Tonight, the audience would be spoiled by the sounds inspired and copied from Brahms, Liszt, Mussorgsky, and Respighi. As Brenda and Evo got to the door, they followed everyone in. Tickets were not checked because the entrance scanner detected the tickets and validated them for entry. A person would be stopped if the artificial intelligence thought otherwise.

However, inside the venue as they approached the seating, there were ushers who asked for their tickets so they could escort them to their assigned seating.

This venue could easily hold four thousand people in the audience. It was huge and larger than any Evo had ever experienced. Because it was at the heart of the playgrounds for the rich, there were always packed houses, and few seats ever remained empty during the performance.

A two-hundred-member symphony sat in front of tiered seating for several hundred choir members. It did not take long for the ushers to get everyone seated and right on cue at 7:00 P.M. the conductor walked on stage, generating a high level of applause in the process. After several bows he turned and faced his orchestra.

With great precision and accuracy, the music began. The two-hundred-member orchestra created sounds that exemplified the genius of the best composers of the galaxy. Harps flutes, violins, cellos, oboe, other woodwinds, brass section, and percussion were expansive and created the greatest psychoacoustic transcendence any mere mortal could experience.

Earth-born people would contrast this orchestra and later the choir with Mozart's "Requiem." After one hour there was an intermission. The audience filed out into the lobby where drinks were served, including champagne and soft drinks. Evo Kaplan and Brenda went to the lobby where he obtained two glasses of champagne so they could toast each other. Brenda smiled and toasted.

BRENDA BROYALS
Here's to you, my love.


Evo Kaplan
Thank you for all the excitement.


VOICE OVER (FEMALE)
Brenda took one large gulp to feel the sensation of the alcohol, which would blend in with her other cosmic endorphin explosion from the emotions of the music sitting next to her lover boy Evo Kaplan.

Then Brenda Broyals almost went into a slight panic as she analyzed something she had been putting off and into the back of her mind.

Brenda had one more gigantic issue to resolve: Evo didn't know she was a Revolutionary. The day of reckoning was not too far off.

If Evo Kaplan remained a loyalist and became a runner (someone who escapes to the Dranzonian Empire Secret Service), he would have a price on his head and in no time would be assassinated. Killing Evo would be just as easy as breaking into Abniler Manther's mansion.

Poetic justice would be the FIRM send Brenda Broyals to kill Evo Kaplan. Would he suspect she was an assassin? If given the orders, she had no options but to comply.

Forced to kill Evo Kaplan would break her heart and most likely lead to her suicide.

Brenda wished she had not allowed herself to think such thoughts. She just spoiled her own evening. Would her body language betray that she was upset?


BRENDA BROYALS
Let's go back to our seats.


Brenda wanted to get away from the prying eyes of the public in the event she broke down and started sobbing. Brenda felt so bad she screwed up the perfect evening by bringing work into her special off time and vacation.

Brenda would struggle to refrain from doing so in the future, otherwise she would wreck their vacation, and she knew it!

In the second half of the performance, the choir participated not too dissimilar to Mozart and Beethoven's orchestral works for choirs. The incredible sound and oscillations created by the voices and the instruments blended into the psyche of Brenda and temporally healed her from her demons. *Hopefully the rest of the evening will continue along in such a fashion.*

A solid hour of the zeal put forth by the two-hundred-member orchestra and similar in size choir slowly erased those pent-up emotions and melancholy thoughts that this clandestine relationship manifested.

VOICE OVER
(FEMALE VOICE FOR
PSYCHOLOGICAL ENHANCEMENT)

Brenda knew, more than ever now, the day of reckoning with Evo Kaplan was around the corner. Brenda clearly understood waiting for a confrontation would eventually stress her to the point she would become dysfunctional.

Brenda needed to have another meeting with Conrad Fanzui and explain to him he should inform Evo Kaplan who his employers really were. Let the chips fall where they may. That way she could get on with her life and her mission and not have this distraction of thinking about the fate of her relationship with Evo Kaplan when the truth be known he was now a Revolution operative, working for *Revolution Espionage Elites*.

As soothing as the music was, Brenda was glad it was finally over; she wanted to be out of the public eye in case she suddenly had spasms of memories and thoughts of her pending personal emotional disaster by crossing over the line with a potential adversary. During the encore, Brenda whispered to Evo.

BRENDA BROYALS
Let's leave. I'm getting hungry.

EVO KAPLAN
Okay.

The two got up and since they had aisle seats, it made it easy to do while everyone was clapping and demanding an encore. Only a few people were leaving with them, and the lobby was almost deserted as they approached it and went out the front entrance to the loading zone directly ahead. As promised, there was the limousine, and the driver opened the door as they approached. After they started moving the driver inquired.

                              LIMOUSINE DRIVER
                        Is there any place else you wish to go?


                                 EVO KAPLAN
                       We would like to go to a nice restaurant.


                              LIMOUSINE DRIVER
                Right around the corner is a very nice restaurant, and it's perfect
                for what you are wearing. It's very formal dress there, as many
                concert goers stop in there.


                                 EVO KAPLAN
                           Okay, you can drop us off there.


The driver pulled up to the loading zone in front of the restaurant and got out and
opened the door, which allowed Brenda to get out first. When Evo was out, he
handed him a small black box.


                              LIMOUSINE DRIVER
                THIS is my pager.  Hold the red button down for about six
                seconds and the red button will light up, indicating I have been
                notified to come  pick  you  up.  I'll be five minutes away.


                                 EVO KAPLAN
                          Okay thanks, we appreciate this.


The limo driver got back in his vehicle and drove off. Evo and Brenda walked to
the front entrance of the restaurant and were met by the Maître d'.

<u>EXT./INT. NIGHT SEA SHORE & SANDS RESTAURANT</u>


                                 MAÎTRE D'
                Welcome to Sea Shore & Sands restaurant. Do you have a
                reservation?


                                 EVO KAPLAN
                                    No.


                                 MAÎTRE D'
                I think we have a few tables available. You made it just in time.
                As soon as the concert is over, there will be a line forming.


                                 EVO KAPLAN
                                  Oh great.

MAÎTRE D'<br>This way, please.

The Maître d' escorted them over to a table next to a window that had a great view of the city lights and slid the chair out for Brenda and assisted seating her, then copied the same actions for Evo before handing them both menus. They were truly a picturesque couple, showing youth and vitality, as well as success. The waitress in a short tuxedo with white shirt, bow tie, and dress that came within probably an inch of showing her crotch was very pretty and had a sweet disposition.

MARSHA

Hello, my name is Marsha. I'll be your waitress this evening. Would you like a drink or any appetizers?

BRENDA BROYALS

I would like a glass of water and give me a  minute about the drink.

EVO KAPLAN

I'll have a glass of water and a glass of Hongjiu.

Hongjiu was a wine-like substance made from Gribbits fruits that are like grapes. The taste is more pleasing than wine, but it did have 8% alcohol content.

VOICE OVER

A trained spy can detect a mood change. *Brenda is acting different*, Evo thought. It would not be surprising if she suffered from some space lag or a small case of PTSD (Post-Traumatic Space Disorder).

The lack of conversation piled up potential scenarios that might be lingering, and it was possible Brenda knew something Evo didn't that appeared to be unsettling. Perhaps she detected someone from the FIRM watching us?

Since Evo Kaplan adhered to the rule "When in Rome do as the Romans do," he ordered Shen de Huayuan cuisine via a sampler plate.

Brenda ordered a type of fish that was prevalent on this planet and exported to the Empire. It was a delicacy back in her home world, but it was a standard meal here. When Brenda picked at her food and didn't consume much, Evo knew something was troubling Brenda, but he wasn't going to press her for any information. He didn't want to add to her melancholy, as this was to be a great vacation. The dinner slowly came to an end and after Evo paid for the meal, he held down the red button on the pager.

EVO KAPLAN

Let's go out to the entrance. The limo should be arriving soon.

What started out as a joyous evening had slid into the abyss. Evo was glad it was just about over. They walked out front and just then the limo pulled up. The driver got out and opened the door for them, and they got in and he took them back to the Lantiane Resort. Brenda sure seemed to be in a sour mood, so as they were walking toward the bungalow Evo heard the music coming from the bar restaurant they were at earlier and said,

EVO KAPLAN

Why don't we stop here for a little while?

Brenda wasn't in the mood and wanted to be away from Evo for a while.

BRENDA BROYALS

Why don't you go listen to some music for a while. I'm going back to the room and get some sleep.

Evo took that as a hint to get lost for a while. Brenda was upset about something, and it was best he stayed away from her for a short while to give her a chance to get herself together. He knew the recent revelations and events were very troubling to her. He had walked into her life and shook the foundation to which she lived. They split apart and Brenda continued toward the bungalow.

<u>INT. PLANET SHEN de HUAYUAN - LANTIANE RESORT- BAR – NIGHT</u>

Evo went inside the Lantiane Resort Bar and Restaurant and not far from the band was an empty table. Evo went there and sat down.

Near Evo's table were four Barracuda, who saw him earlier today. They were taken back by his good looks and now he was dressed very handsomely, which added to their hunger pains. This portion of the bar smelled like a *house of ill repute* with all the Barracuda in one spot, waiting to latch onto their next victim.

Evo was already sleeping with the enemy, but this would be worse. They were all connected to powerful bankers, so discretion was paramount. The singer was elated to see Evo come in alone. The fact he looked better than ever added some to the mystique he brought with him. None of these women had ever slept with a true James Bond. If they did their lives would take on new meaning. Little did they know Evo Kaplan was a much bigger catch than they imagined.

Evo Kaplan was sipping on a concoction recommended by the waiter and getting into the music. Once again, the band noted Sheri the Cabaret Singer stepped up performance a few notches and were now starting to correlate it to every time that gentleman appeared, her singing got better. The song was soon finished, and she turned to the band leader to give him a song request.

SHERI
If you play "How to Mend a Broken Wing," now I promise to sing it better than you ever heard before.

BAND LEADER
Alright I want to see this.

Sheri lived up to her promise, which galvanized the band with her singing. It truly was a remarkable interpretation of the song with Sheri's great voice as she sang directly at Evo Kaplan.

VOICE OVER (FEMALE)
Some of the phrases in the Broken Wing song hit Evo Kaplan emotionally, as he thought Sheri's song was right on the mark especially if he soon discovered Brenda was a high-ranking spy for the Revolution.

Right at break time, the singer Sheri made a beeline to Evo's table and saved him from the Barracuda that were hot on his trail.

Sheri slipped into the chair in front of Evo probably two seconds before the first Barracuda would have struck. To say the table of Barracuda were upset with the singer was an understatement.

SINGER (SHERI)
You look well-dressed tonight.

EVO KAPLAN
I just came from the concert. I didn't bother changing since I came straight here.

SINGER (SHERI)
Where's your lady friend?

EVO KAPLAN
She's back in the room brooding.

SINGER (SHERI)
Did you upset her?

EVO KAPLAN
Not that I know of. Perhaps it's just the time of the month?

Sheri  burst out laughing.

SINGER (SHERI)
You are funny! What's your name?

EVO KAPLAN
Proctor.

Evo lied, but knew he had to use his alias.

PROCTOR (a.k.a. EVO KAPLAN)
How about you?

SINGER (SHERI)
I'm Sheri.

PROCTOR (a.k.a. EVO KAPLAN)
Nice name.

SHERI
Thank you. How long are you going to be staying at the
Lantiane Resort, Proctor?

PROCTOR (a.k.a. EVO KAPLAN)
A couple weeks.

SHERI
Wow, nice vacation.

EVO KAPLAN
Would you like a drink?

SHERI
Sure.

Soon they toasted a drink and Sheri became more infatuated with Evo. However, the Barracuda were quickly getting irritated because at least two of them wanted the seat Sheri was sitting in.

Lantiane Resort employees often referred to these women as Cougars. They were often noted as Cougars because they frequently observed with younger men.

Evo Kaplan could care less about the Barracudas. He was living on borrowed time, had a princess in his bungalow, and had no intentions of cheating on her, though talking with Sheri was a nice distraction from the tension in the air from whatever was troubling Brenda.

Finally, Sheri was called back up onto the stage so the band could commence playing. Evo Kaplan downed his drink, stood up, walked out of the bar, and made his way to the bungalow.

<u>INT.  PLANET SHEN DE HUAYUAN - LANTIANE RESORT- BUNGALO –
NIGHT</u>

The Lantiane Resort staff had removed the two clothing racks and extra boxes of shoes. They left behind two garment bags with a note to leave the borrowed suit and dress in the garment bags m and the maid would collect them in the morning.

Boxes for the shoes also remained. Brenda appeared to be sleeping, so Evo didn't want to disturb her. He undressed and carefully slid in between the sheets to avoid awakening her. The night was finally over. Was this the calm before the storm?

<u>INT. DRANZONIAN SECRET SERVICE ZANZILTAR SAFE HOUSE – DAY</u>

VOICE OVER
(MALE VOICE WITH EMPHASIS)
A voice similar to Sanctuay City Cinematic Trailer:
<u>Sanctuary City Book Trailer v2.mp4 (dropbox.com)</u>

Arrangements were made for the Dranzonian Secret Service Agents Reginald Heiqishi and his partner for this mission, Terrshey Wate. The two Secret Service Agents could not travel directly from Praxisvlasia to the planet *Shen de Huayuan*, deep in Revolution Empire territory. They would first travel to the planet Zanziltar with counterfeited credentials.

Reginald Heiqishi and Terrshey Wate were delayed traveling to Shen de Huayuan because the Dranzonian Empire Secret Service wanted them to interview Huaiyuansu Ka at Zanziltar before the final leg of the trip to Shen de Huayuan.

Huaiyuansu Ka was scheduled to visit the library to signal if he had a desire to meet and pass on information to the onsite Dranzonian Empire Secret Service which coincided with Reginald Heiqishi and Terrshey Wate's planned arrival at Zanziltar.

If Huaiyuansu Ka desired to meet Reginald Heiqishi and Terrshey Wate, he would be taken to a safe house. Reginald Heiqishi and Terrshey Wate could interview and question him to glean as much Evo Kaplan information as possible before they traveled to *Shen de Huayuan.*

Reginald Heiqishi and Terrshey Wate had two tasks to perform while at Shen de Huayuan.

The first was to confirm confirmed Evo Kaplan's relationship with Brenda Broyals.

The second Task was if the opportunity availed, request Evo Kaplan return with them to Praxisvlasia. Should Evo Kaplan refuse to return to Praxisvlasia, they would attempt assassination of Evo Kaplan.

If they could not kill Evo Kaplan at *Shen de Huayuan* due to extenuating circumstances, a plan would be put in place to assassinate Evo Kaplan when he returned to the *Sanctuary City Zanziltar*.

If Reginald Heiqishi and Terrshey Wate determined they were in position to carry out the assassination, they would do the killing on the same day they were schedule to depart the planet and return to Zanziltar and subsequent return to Praxisvlasia.

The assassination could only be done just before departure to escape a possible net the Revolution could put out, because if he were working for the Revolution, they would want to catch whoever was operating behind enemy territory.

Hari Nuvrean, the Dranzonian Empire Secret Service agent located in Zanziltar Consulate posing as a diplomat with full diplomatic immunity, waited patiently for Huaiyuansu Ka make contact in the library.

The mission could have gone without Huaiyuansu Ka's help, but if he had significant information to betray Evo Kaplan, it might help make Reginald Heiqishi's job a lot easier. Plus, Reginald Heiqishi wasn't fully satisfied with the cosmetic surgery. He felt there was enough of his former appearance where a trained spy like Evo Kaplan might be able to recognize him.

One flaw in the mission planning was they overlooked Reginald Heiqishi's voice. If Evo Kaplan caught Reginald Heiqishi talking, he might be able to recognize him despite his cosmetic surgery.

If Evo Kaplan was truly working for the Revolution, he would simply contact authorities and Reginald Heiqishi, along with Terrshey Wate, would be dealt with in similar manners as they had treated other spies caught behind enemy lines, wishing they were dead.

VOICE OVER (MALE)

The Revolution had developed interrogation techniques that were very effective. Most Dranzonian Empire Secret Service agents were given powerful pills to take for instant death if they felt they could not bear going through some advanced interrogation techniques the Revolutionaries had developed. The Revolution Interrogations went in phases.

The first phase was to rough them up. Most Dranzonian Empire Secret Service agents go through capture training and experience a terrible beating to prepare them for actual capture. Most of them could take it or swallow the pills.

For the next phase, the Revolutionaries put the captured spies in a large swimming pool. They were put into a wet suit, tied up like a mummy while they were unconscious through an injection, and then a special face mask was put on that provided fresh air and the ability to pump out vomit. The face mask was opaque and dark. Hence, all sensory inputs were sealed.

The captured spies were drugged and unconscious when they were first put into the water. The drugs were timed to have them in the water for almost eight hours before they woke up. Teams of Divers were in the water with them, constantly turning them in random fashion.

What usually woke them up was the nightmares they were starting to have as the drugs wore off and the effects of the loss of equilibrium and sensory inputs created neurological stimulus sometimes worse than LSD. By the third day they were almost insane and taken out of the pool and interrogated.

Half of the captured spies remained insane and never came back to reality; the other half who regained their mental abilities were very cooperative because they never wanted to go back in the pool again.

It was the most terrifying experience in their lifetime and most of the people vomited and let go of their bowels while in the pool, but the diaper and wet suit they wore kept the pool from being contaminated.

One out of one hundred people who went through this advanced interrogation technique could survive it and mentally control themselves to where it didn't break them. For the hardcore cases, they were taken to a crematorium. The Revolutionaries had a conveyor that normally was used to move bodies into the machine to be cremated.

Again, the people had their bodies wrapped up like a mummy and they were taken into the crematorium feet first. The handlers allowed their feet to get third degree burns and lots of pain to the point the person was going into shock. They were pulled out and water doused on their feet and given the opportunity to cooperate. Some did, some didn't. Even the ones who cooperated ended up in the crematorium furnace just like the ones who didn't. No evidence was ever left behind. The spook thus disappeared in a horrible death.

Dranzonian Empire Secret Service learned of these atrocities through defectors and prisoners.

Reginald Heiqishi and Terrshey Wate both knew if they were captured, they would end up in the pool or the crematorium thanks to the double spies that brought the information to the Dranzonian Empire Secret Service.

Reginald Heiqishi and Terrshey Wate elected to carry the pills with them in the event they were captured. They would simply swallow the pills after they bit their cheeks where they were implanted in a special non-soluble capsule, which would release the poison and kill them within probably thirty seconds. Right after they bit their cheeks, they would shoot their laser pistols at the enemy arresting them and most likely not feel the hole in the chest the laser pistols fired by the enemy created.

## INT. ZANZILTAR - PUBLIC LIBRARY - DAY

Hari Nuvrean sat at a table reading a book with a good view of the entrance. If necessary, he would wait all day long. Another agent would be there as well in the event he had to excuse himself for a bathroom break or some other reason, so they would know Huaiyuansu Ka had entered the library.

Even if Huaiyuansu Ka didn't want to give the secret semaphore signal, pulling three books out in a row and briefly looking at them, the fact he showed up meant he probably wanted a meeting. As he left the library, there would be a car there to nab him and take him to a safe house, with or without his desires. It has always been the case when someone shoved a laser pistol in someone's back and hit them with a low stun level, the message was clear get in the car or the next shot will put a hole through your chest.

Today, however, the timely arrival of Huaiyuansu Ka to the library just a couple days before Reginald Heiqishi and Terrshey Wate were due to arrive seemed rather auspicious. The Dranzonians were conducting a very loose surveillance on Huaiyuansu Ka. They could not get close in case the man was a double agent being used to expose their agents in a kill zone. One thing they were able to determine by his mannerisms and apparent grumpiness was he wasn't doing too well.

No doubt fear of getting caught betraying the FIRM was weighing heavily on Huaiyuansu Ka. Other factors included his spouse, and two children were still on Praxisvlasia, where he sent credits, but barely kept them above the poverty line.

Huaiyuansu Ka's spouse was smoking hot and losing patience with a man who, when they first met, had the financial resources to create that electricity between them. However, once he was purged and on the threshold of poverty, that lust and desire in her eyes quickly faded and the coldness transformed their former bubbly relationship into almost pure hell until he found ample employment.

Just like Evo Kaplan's recruitment, Mr. Catamountz discovered Huaiyuansu Ka while he was desperately looking for a job. His training period on Zanziltar was scheduled to be over six months ago, and his spouse was now openly calling him a liar and on the verge of asking for a divorce. The situation was getting dicey and Huaiyuansu Ka was getting desperate.

The Dranzonian Secret Service, at great risk, sent plumbers in to install surveillance sensors in Huaiyuansu Ka's apartment and knew the level of tension he exhibited, along with intercepting the few monthly communications to his spouse.

Long range communications were not real time. But people figured out how to do it. A person would send a series of statements that would get sent via a hyper-channel long distance to the other planet. It would take upward to a day for the person on the other end to receive it. They would respond and send back their replies in full video and audio.

Again, there was another day delay. To hold a simple conversation took over a week.

Hari Nuvrean was happy that Huaiyuansu Ka entered the library when he did because he was on the verge of needing a bathroom break. Huaiyuansu Ka walked in and toward a bookshelf where he knew Hari Nuvrean would observe him handle books. He pulled three out in a row, looking at each of them, and put them back in place, then turned toward Hari Nuvrean, who then nonchalantly dropped a writing stylus on the floor. The semaphore indicated a car was right out front and as prearranged, a man with a green cap would open the door to the car for him and they would drive off.

Hari NUVREAN bent over and picked up the writing stylus, acting like nothing really happened. He remained in his seat and Huaiyuansu Ka walked out of the library and immediately saw the man in the green cap he just put on who opened the door to the car.

<u>EXT. ZANZILTAR PUBLIC LIBRARY TO LIMOUSINE - DAY</u>

Huaiyuansu Ka got in the Limousine, and they drove off. Once in the safe house he was informed of the next meeting.

INT. ZANZILTAR DRANZONIAN SPY SAFEOUSE

HARI NUVREAN
Someone will be here in two days to talk with you. It's very important you make that meeting.

HUAIYUANSU KA
I'll try to make myself available.

Huaiyuansu Ka was then informed how they would pick him up because they could not risk Reginald Heiqishi and Terrshey Wate being discovered with Huaiyuansu Ka or they would never be able to travel to the planet Shen de Huayuan, deep behind enemy lines.

The Dranzonian spies then took Huaiyuansu Ka back into the city and dropped him off in a safe place where he walked home.

Because the risk was high and the needs so great, a surveillance team was set up to observe Huaiyuansu Ka to make sure nobody followed him home, meaning possible compromise. If it appeared spooks paid him a visit within the next forty-eight hours, that meant his cover was blown, and most likely the Revolution would either take him to the pool, the crematorium, or barbecue him on a spit then feed him to the hogs.

Two days later Reginald Heiqishi and Terrshey Wate arrived and through a series of elaborate transfers were deposited in a safe house, where they were fitted with masks that changed their appearance again. Huaiyuansu Ka would not see their cosmetic surgery modified faces. The mask built by 3D printing looked real and required very little makeup to blend the mask into the real skin. After just one hour, the change was rather spectacular. The men looked like Chuo Wanpi and Chin Wanpi, Chuo Wanpi's brother, who looked very similar to the deceased man.

INT. ZANZILTAR DRANZONIAN SPY SECOND SAFEOUSE

One hour before the meeting, Reginald Heiqishi and Terrshey Wate were moved again to a small house in the countryside that had a long access from either direction with no nearby neighbors. Roadblocks were set up several miles in each direction on the road, where very few amounts of traffic used this road. This area was almost abandoned as mudslides and forest fires were always problematic and hard to deal with because of rough terrain and numerous thirty-foot boulders and lots of brush.

INT.  ZANZILTAR - PUBLIC LIBRARY - DAY

Several hours later, coinciding with the end of the workday for Huaiyuansu Ka, he ended up in the city at the library. Hari Nuvrean had another semaphore because in the spy business the same one was never used twice. The library allowed drinks if they were in sealed containers that had a drink spout with a valve to prevent spillage. As planned, Huaiyuansu Ka came into the library, pulled a book off the shelf. Walked to an adjacent table and sat down and started to thumb through the pages. Hari Nuvrean picked up his drink, took a swallow, then set it down. Then he picked it up again and took a second swallow. Huaiyuansu Ka had been briefed by the two swallows to indicate he was not followed to the library and their agents outside monitoring the access detected no Revolutionaries, so it was safe to go out and get into the car.

EXT. ZANZILTAR PUBLIC LIBRARY TO LIMOUSINE - DAY

Today a man with a brown hat opened the door and Huaiyuansu Ka got in the car, and they drove off. They went to a safe house in a wealthy area where a lot of bankers lived, many who had their private air transportation.

EXT. ZANZILTAR MANSION/SAFEHOUSE - DAY

They walked into the mansion after the garage door was shut, walked through the home, and out the back door, where a VTOL craft sat with engines idling in the vertical position.

EXT. ZANZILTAR DRANZONIAN HELICOPTER - DAY

This would not be the first time nor the last time Huaiyuansu Ka would travel in such a craft, as the Dranzonian Empire Secret Service used them frequently, aside from this planet but many others. Within two minutes of arriving to the safe house, the craft was airborne and out of the grip of any possible Revolutionary intervention. It took less than ten minutes and the VTOL landed on the road in front of the small house, discharged its passengers, then took off.

<u>INT. ZANZILTAR DRANZONIAN SPY SECOND SAFEOUSE</u>

Huaiyuansu Ka was escorted into the house where he immediately encountered a person he thought and knew was Chuo Wanpi and a man who looked familiar, whom he couldn't place at the time but later figured out was Chin Wanpi, the brother of the man the FIRM had assassinated recently.

CHO WANPI (a.k.a. REGINALD HEIQISHI)
We understand you have some information concerning Evo Kaplan.

HUAIYUANSU KA
Yes, I'm a logistics man for the FIRM and I made Evo Kaplan's reservations at their resort in Shen de Huayuan.

CHO WANPI (a.k.a. REGINALD HEIQISHI)
Who did Evo Kaplan travel with?

HUAIYUANSU KA
Brenda Broyals.

CHO WANPI (a.k.a. REGINALD HEIQISHI)

Are you familiar with Brenda Broyals and her personal history?

HUAIYUANSU KA
Yes, she's a well-known traitor. The Dranzonian Secret Service almost captured her before she was able to escape to the Revolutionary Guard.

CHO WANPI (a.k.a. REGINALD HEIQISHI)
Do you know what she did before she defected?

HUAIYUANSU KA
According to information I found, Brenda Broyals was instrumental in deactivating a lot of sensors and defensive systems in time for their surprise attack on Praxisvlasia and our fleet anchorage at the Praxisvlasia Space Station.

CHO WANPI (a.k.a. REGINALD HEIQISHI)
So, you know Brenda Broyals was personally. responsible for us losing one half of our fleet.

HUAIYUANSU KA
Yes.

CHO WANPI (a.k.a. REGINALD HEIQISHI)
That was a terrible crime. Are you willing to help us nab her and take out Evo Kaplan if necessary.

HUAIYUANSU KA
Yes, I will help.

CHO WANPI (a.k.a. REGINALD HEIQISHI)
You will do it unconditionally, right?

HUAIYUANSU KA
No. As I told Mr. Nuvrean, I want my case reopened for my dismissal when all the agents were purged. I didn't deserve to be fired.

CHO WANPI (a.k.a. REGINALD HEIQISHI)
You are not willing to help us unconditionally unless we do you a favor.

HUAIYUANSU KA
I deserve that favor because I took on a lot of risk coming to you.

CHO WANPI (a.k.a. REGINALD HEIQISHI)
You realize it will require us to do an extraordinary extraction to bring you back.

HUAIYUANSU KA
Yes, I'm aware the Revolution will attempt to track me down and assassinate me. You will have to change my identity.

CHO WANPI (a.k.a. REGINALD HEIQISHI)
As well as your spouse and your kids.

HUAIYUANSU KA Yes, I realize that.

CHO WANPI (a.k.a. REGINALD HEIQISHI)
Is your spouse willing to disappear from all her relatives forever?

HUAIYUANSU KA

I would assume that after the fighting has ended and we sign a truce, things will be back to normal, and we can then re-surface.


CHO WANPI (a.k.a. REGINALD HEIQISHI)

Unfortunately, you are wrong. Either we must defeat the Revolution, or we'll be destroyed. It may take a long time and you will probably die of old age long before the civil war has ended.


HUAIYUANSU KA

I have no way of asking my wife if she is willing to disappear long distance without the risk of being turned.


CHO WANPI (a.k.a. REGINALD HEIQISHI)
Would you trust us to ask her for you?


HUAIYUANSU KA
Do I really have much of a choice?


CHO WANPI (a.k.a. REGINALD HEIQISHI)
What if she says no?


HUAIYUANSU KA

Then I still want to go back to Praxisvlasia and back to work for the Secret Service.


CHO WANPI (a.k.a. REGINALD HEIQISHI)

You have one little problem. You have been a traitor for over a year. Why should we bring you back?


HUAIYUANSU KA

You placed me in this situation by the purge. I'm willing to give you some good stuff if I'm brought back, my case reopened, and exonerated.


CHO WANPI (a.k.a. REGINALD HEIQISHI)

How do we reconcile you were a traitor for a year?


HUAIYUANSU KA

I really was a double spy for a year because I've been here collecting data that will be highly useful to you when you bring me in.

CHO WANPI (a.k.a. REGINALD HEIQISHI)
How is the data collected?


HUAIYUANSU KA
It's on a data cube stored at the FIRM. I'm the only person that knows it exists. The day you move me back to Praxisvlasia, I will bring the data cube and give it to you.


CHO WANPI (a.k.a. REGINALD HEIQISHI)
All right, this is what we are going to do. Someone will visit Evo Kaplan and ask him to come back to Praxisvlasia. If he agrees, he'll be coming back here on his way there. When he gets to Zanziltar, we'll take you and him back to Praxisvlasia.


HUAIYUANSU KA
My identity needs to be changed, how will that be handled?


CHO WANPI (a.k.a. REGINALD HEIQISHI)
You are right, your ID must be changed or the Revolution will track you down and kill you. We will wait until you are safely back at Praxisvlasia, and we will let you ask your spouse that important question.


HUAIYUANSU KA
What if she says no?


CHO WANPI (a.k.a. REGINALD HEIQISHI)
Regardless of her answer, your identity will be changing and if she doesn't agree and you go see her again for any reason, you will most likely become a target of the Revolution and we will no longer be able to help you.


HUAIYUANSU KA
What then?


CHO WANPI (a.k.a. REGINALD HEIQISHI)
If we place her off limits and you go see her, then you will be suspended again.


HUAIYUANSU KA
All right.


CHO WANPI (a.k.a. REGINALD HEIQISHI)
I have a few more questions about Evo Kaplan. Did he change his image through cosmetic surgery?

HUAIYUANSU KA

No, he looks the same. He's not been sent on any missions
that require his features to be changed to foil facial recognition
scanners.

CHO WANPI (a.k.a. REGINALD HEIQISHI)
Does Brenda Broyals look the same?

HUAIYUANSU KA
No, she's had extensive cosmetic surgery.

CHO WANPI (a.k.a. REGINALD HEIQISHI)
How would we identify her?

HUAIYUANSU KA
She's the only woman Evo Kaplan will be with  at the resort.

CHO WANPI (a.k.a. REGINALD HEIQISHI)
Why do you say that?

HUAIYUANSU KA
They became lovers on their last mission.

CHO WANPI (a.k.a. REGINALD HEIQISHI)
Isn't that sweet.

HUAIYUANSU KA
She has a reputation.

CHO WANPI (a.k.a. REGINALD HEIQISHI)
Any description of what she looks like now?

HUAIYUANSU KA
She's built about the same, one hundred twenty-five pounds
approximately, currently has blonde hair, and has a strong
resemblance to the entertainer Carly Lambragadi.

CHO WANPI (a.k.a. REGINALD HEIQISHI)
What is the name of the resort where they are staying?

HUAIYUANSU KA
Lantiane Resort.

Soon the interrogation was over. The weekly meetings would go on until Evo Kaplan returned. It was obvious what they had planned for Brenda. They might even do the same to Evo Kaplan if he didn't willingly come back with them.

Reginald Heiqishi was a coward and never went into harm's way on a mission unless the backup had overwhelming strength.

The nature of Reginald Heiqishi conduct would carry over to *Shen de Huayuan,* as he would direct Terrshey Wate to confront Evo Kaplan and give him some options he couldn't refuse. The bottom line is Brenda Broyals wasn't coming back and Evo Kaplan might not come back if he resisted.

The next day Reginald Heiqishi and Terrshey Wate were on their way to *Shen de Huayuan,* and they had reservations at the Lantiane Resort.

DEWALTRACEN GALLERY ADVENTURE.

The next morning Evo awoke mainly because Brenda was making too much noise. She shook the bed pretty good as she climbed out of bed. Then she went into the bathroom and without closing the door she urinated, giving off a sound that Evo—in his disturbed and mildly angry state for the abrupt wakeup when he wasn't ready—thought Brenda was peeing out of a garden hose it sounded so loud. Then she flushed the toilet, which had a high pressure flusher and made a lot of rackets as well.

Brenda Broyals then walked over and opened the blinds, letting direct sunlight in and brought bright daylight into the room, and opened the door so a fresh breeze would flow through. She then went back into the bathroom and hopped in the shower with the bathroom door open, making additional noise that killed any hopes for Evo to sleep any further.

When men first wake up, their kidneys have worked all night long and they need to urinate, especially if they had been at a bar drinking. Evo remembered some of his early days of training at the Secret Service Academy, where the trainers would come into the dormitory-style berthing and yell, "If you are going to hoot with the owls, then you will have to scream with the eagles the next day!"

Brenda was screaming with the eagles! If there ever were any chances of having Brenda as a spouse in the future, it all ended that morning as Evo realized this woman just might be a pain in the ass to live with.

Evo patiently waited for Brenda to end her Hollywood shower because he really needed to get up and go but didn't want to disturb her private time. Right around the fifteen-minute mark, the sound of the shower ended and a few minutes later Brenda left the bathroom with a towel around her and her hair up in a smaller towel.

Brenda put on fresh underwear as Evo got up and made a strategic flight to the bathroom, shut the door, flipped up the toilet seat, and let her rip. Oh God, does this feel good! Possession is nine tenths of the law. Evo thought.

Since Brenda finished her shower and is dressing, perhaps I can sneak in a quick shower? Soon he was showering, and it felt great. Evo didn't go Hollywood style because Brenda was acting strange, and he thought he should get out of the bathroom right away after the S/S/S. By the time he got out of the bathroom, Brenda was gone.

Evo dressed then looked outside to see if perhaps Brenda was just outside. The area was deserted. It was too early for the beach goers. As he walked back into the room, he noticed a piece of paper on the drawers in front of the bed. He walked over and saw Brenda had written a note: "I'm going to get a massage. I'll be back later." Evo sat down in a chair brooding, thinking. *Had she not woken me up, I could have slept for another couple hours!*

Evo turned on the entertainment and data terminal and selected a news channel to see what current events were going on in the area. The typical beach community was like just about anywhere else, all catering to the beach goers.

There were numerous advertisements concerning entertainment and venues and exhibits. Evo studied them because he apparently had a lot of time on his hands. If Brenda didn't come back soon, he might get on his swim trunks and go take a couple laps.

Brenda knew any good resort had a good massage parlor. All she had to do was walk up to a customer service kiosk and ask the question.

<u>INT. LANTIANE RESORT LOBBY - MORNING</u>

BRENDA BROYALS
Hello, can you give me directions to the  massage room?

RESORT EMPLOYEE
Yes madam, continue down this hallway and make a right at
the next door and you will see the sign about fifty feet ahead.
Would you like me to escort you there?

BRENDA BROYALS
No, that will not be necessary.


Brenda followed the instructions and found the massage room without any trouble and went inside.


MASSEUSE
Hello, may we help you?


BRENDA BROYALS
Yes, I would like a massage.


MASSEUSE
Do you want a massage in a private room, or do you want to be in the social message room?


BRENDA BROYALS
I think I'll go with the social massage.


MASSEUSE
This way, please.


A private massage was usually boring. The Masseuse was usually not very educated and usually lacked experiences worth of discussion. On the other hand, the public massage was fun because usually two or three or more women would talk about a lot of things in their lives and sometimes ask for advice, or brag about their husbands and boyfriends.

Sometimes the discussions got almost pornographic in detail. Today there were three women in the public room getting Nuru Massages. Several attractive men were working on them, and their bodies were covered with oils with different scents that seemed rather pleasant.

These were the three Barracudas from the swimming pool yesterday. The second they spotted Brenda; the Barracudas were immediately engulfed in inquisitiveness. They wanted to know who she was and who her boyfriend was. This message was going to be far more interesting than they planned.


BRENDA BROYALS
Hello, how is everyone?


BARRACUDA #1
Just great!


BARRACUDA #2
Feeling wonderful with those strong hands.

A female staff member walked up to Brenda and handed her a white cotton garment.

MASSEUSE
You can change into this so that we do not get oil on your clothes.

BRENDA BROYALS
Thanks.

MASSEUSE
The changing room is right over there, and you  can put your clothing articles and shoes in the shelves below the massage table.

Brenda noticed two of the women were nude with male masseuses working on them. She went into the changing room, took off her clothes and put on the white garment, and went back out to the social massage room.

MASSEUSE
Would you prefer a male or a female massage you?

BRENDA BROYALS
I'll go with a female since I have a male back in my Bungalow ready to take over where you leave off.

The Masseuse laughed.

MASSEUSE BRISTOL
Good, my name is Bristol, and I'll do the massage then.

BRENDA BROYALS Thanks.

MASSEUSE BRISTOL
Would you like the Nuru massage with the oil?

BRENDA BROYALS
I would not ask for anything less.

MASSEUSE BRISTOL
Please lay down on the massage table on your stomach. I'm going to disrobe you and put a towel across your buttocks to give you some privacy.

BRENDA BROYALS
All right.

VOICE OVER (FEMALE)

The woman was a pro and had Brenda nude in about a minute with a towel covering her rear end. The males were in front of her so there was no possibility of them observing her privates. Not that Brenda would care because she would never see them again and as a deadly spy, she could kill them faster than they could think.

The woman started applying oil and working her muscles. Brenda was very quickly transported to an ethereal domain as all her concerns and fears quickly left her mind that was feeling exquisite from the physical touch. The oil used was impregnated with certain drugs to add to the sensation.

Human bodies have opioid and cannabinoid receptors. The oil used endocannabinoids, also had opioids to help extend the sensation and improve the massage results, including the reduction of pain. The result of the muscle massage and the oils created a new mental state for Brenda. She enjoyed watching the other women react to the men touching them, and as the male hands messaged certain areas, it almost crossed the line of sexual arousal.

BARRACUDA #1
What's your name?

BRENDA BROYALS
I'm Brenda. What's your name?

BARRACUDA #1 MONICA
Theolonabatress von Surret. My friends call me Monica.

BRENDA BROYALS
That's an interesting name. It sounds familiar.

BARRACUDA #1 MONICA

My husband is Edgar von Surret, one of the central bankers on Zanziltar.

Brenda immediately remembered who the woman happened to be. She was the heiress to the Surret Estate. They got filthy rich from the suffering of many Revolutionaries. The Surret's play both sides, moreover, to reap huge profits, but also, they want to make sure they are aligned with the winning side, no matter who it is.

Brenda smiled because she knew the strategic plan. As soon as the Revolution took down the Dranzonian Empire, they would then send the fleet to Zanziltar, empty out their treasury, then settle old scores. She didn't know specifically what they had in store for the Surret coterie, but most likely they would get treatment like what was handed out to the spies. The Romanov family of Russia would be a good example of what was in store for Theolonabatress von Surret.

BARRACUDA #1 MONICA
Say, I saw you and a man at the pool yesterday.

BRENDA BROYALS
Yes, that's my partner.

BARRACUDA #1 MONICA
You mean spouse?

BRENDA BROYALS
No, we are not married yet.

BARRACUDA #1 MONICA
Is he single and available?

BRENDA BROYALS
If he walks out on me, I'll shoot him between the eyes with a laser pistol.

BARRACUDA #1 MONICA
So, you are the bossy type?

BRENDA BROYALS
No, but I own the guy. He's my personal property.

BARRACUDA #1 MONICA
Does he feel that way?

BRENDA BROYALS
It really doesn't matter. He's stuck with me now.

BARRACUDA #1 MONICA
What's his name?

BRENDA BROYALS
He's Proctor Pugong.

BARRACUDA #1 MONICA
He seemed like he could swim well.


BRENDA BROYALS
Yes, he competed in swimming events and won great honors.


Monica the Barracuda was already calculating how to get Proctor Pugong alone. Just knowing how easily he swam those laps meant he could perform for a long time. Theolonabatress von Surret (a.k.a. Monica) almost shivered as the combination of her massage and the thought of being alone with Proctor Pugong and enticing him to perform, which she knew she could do as every man had his price in credits. The ecstasy would outlive the temporal transcendence into her lavish and often perverted conquest of wonderful specimens of men.

Monica would soon relay a request to her special friend who was on the staff of the resort to get to Proctor Pugong to request a meeting. Oh, what men would do to get paid for an hour of work like she would pay! And it pays to be filthy rich!

Bristol worked over Brenda in the most professional and efficacious manner of the Nuru Message. The Nuru erotic message that has full body contact with the masseuse and client are nude and coated with a special *Shen de Huayuan Gel*, traditionally made from seaweed and in this application the added benefit of the opioids.

All Brenda's aches and pains and issues slowly went away. She felt much better and was clearer in evaluating her situation with Evo Kaplan. But no matter how good the massage felt, Brenda had that huge issue of the day of reckoning when Evo Kaplan was formally appraised of who his employers really are.

Brenda worst nightmare would be Evo Kaplan detested the Revolutionaries like some did and suddenly lost his zeal for the relationship with Brenda, and suddenly became an enemy and tried to do something stupid like become a runner.

Eventually the massage was over, and Brenda was covered by Bristol so that the male masseuses working on the Barracuda could not see her body. It was for Brenda's benefit only because the men had seen so many bodies in their occupation that another cute female made no difference. It had no effect on them.

The Nuru messages the Barracuda sometimes received in private included all their body—every inch was touched. And it happened often as these filthy rich women visited the resort at least a week or more a month.

Brenda was then led to a private bath area that had a Jacuzzi style bath.

BRISTOL

Would you like your hair shampooed while you take a hot bath? That comes with the message.

BRENDA BROYALS<br>Yes, please.

BRISTOL

Also, there is a hairdresser that can do your hair after your bath if you desire.

BRENDA BROYALS<br>It's nice you do all that with the massage.

BRISTOL

Yes, some women want their hair and nails done as well. It's one-stop shopping.

Brenda looked down at her nails. They were good for a spy who packed a gun and beat up male spies from time to time but didn't look too lady-like. She suddenly wanted to look like a gorgeous lady just like most women wanted.

BRENDA BROYALS

My boyfriend is probably mad I woke him up this morning the way I did. I was kind of mean. I was being a bad girl. I suppose I can go back to our bungalow looking good and reward him!

BRISTOL<br>That's what we like to hear.

BRENDA BROYALS

It's a shame I do not have any fancy clothes here with me to return in. I just have these tourist clothes I wore coming in.

BRISTOL

Once again you came to the right place. If you want, I will call up to our staff fashion designer and have her, bring down some garments for you to return in, and we'll send your clothes back with room service so that you can walk out of here as a glamorous woman.

BRENDA BROYALS<br>Yes, let's do that!

Bristol was the consummate professional. She knew how to please her customers, thinking about all the logistics and creative ways to help women leave here and go back to their husbands and boyfriends and command more respect and admiration from the transformation.

When the fantastic makeover by the resort staff was finally complete and Brenda dressed in her new dress, she walked to the exit about the same time as the three Barracudas, who were only partially satisfied with their masseuses who could not go the final step in the public setting. Though some would say the three Barracudas came as close to the line as anyone could without violating civil codes.

The three women were mildly astonished at Brenda's makeover and the exquisite beauty of the woman when she departed.They sadly knew the feasibility of influencing Proctor Pugong would be unlikely if he had the option of enjoying the caliber of beauty exhibited in front of them.

The resort benefitted too, because they loved to see exquisitely beautiful women walk out of a massage and through the resort showcasing what they were to offer, as Brenda certainly raised the ambience a few notches.

VOICE OVER (MALE)

Evo Kaplan didn't need much more motivation for attraction to Brenda. He had no idea how well she could clean up. After a couple hours he was starting to get worried. Brenda was acting kind of strange this morning, and the mere fact she was working for a very dangerous outfit presented numerous scenarios she possibly could have gotten herself into.

Brenda was a spy and in fact could have been sanctioned by some despicable activity.

*Perhaps I'm over analyzing what happened to her?* Evo wondered.

Evo was just about to go out looking for Brenda when suddenly she showed up. She was wearing a tropical dress, high heels, and a white sun hat.

Wowzer! Evo thought. Oh my God, she's beautiful!

EVO KAPLAN

You look very nice. What happened? Did some magical person find you and place a spell upon you?

Actually, he did, and his name is Evo Kaplan, whom I'm now
very fond of.

Evo suddenly felt like a jerk for being mad at the way Brenda woke him up and disappeared. He had no idea the profound beauty of his growing love Brenda exhibited until this moment. He now knew Brenda could clean up fabulously. Everything—from her hair, her fingernails, her skin tone, her makeup, her dress— was indescribable and put him into positive valence.

As much as Evo Kaplan pondered the genuine affection he had for Brenda, the shocking revelation of her ability to look extremely attractive engulfed his emotions and he felt slightly guilty of reacting with sexual arousal. Brenda was no different than the Barracuda and Cougars, as she had her physical and emotional stake in Evo Kaplan.

Brenda's number one anxiety driver was the future determination of how Evo Kaplan would deal with the conflict between the Revolution and the Loyalists.

Brothers were fighting brothers. Parents were fighting their children. The great divide created by such huge philosophical differences fell into the hands of the corrupt politicians on each side of the issue who knew how to exploit useful idiots.

Partisanship had no greater boundaries than the Dranzonian Empire Revolution.

While Brenda was gone, Evo Kaplan had looked through brochures and resort promotions for things to do. One thing he discovered was Shen de Huayuan had one of the best art galleries in the Empire.

Evo Kaplan realized that it is likely that he might never be able to come to this planet again the rest of his life and this was a rare opportunity. Evo wondered how Brenda would take the suggestion to go there, especially since she was already dressed for such a prestigious place.

Evo Kaplan's problem was his attire, but figured the resort could help him out again. Evo figured he better strike while the iron was hot and figured he had nothing to lose to suggest a quick trip to the art gallery.

EVO KAPLAN
Say, since you are already dressed up, the famous Dewaltracen
Gallery is only a few miles away and it opens in about an hour.
Would you like to go there?

BRENDA BROYALS
If that's what you want to do, sure.

Brenda did not sound convincingly, but she was putting her emotions behind, partially thanks to the massage and makeover, but Brenda decided there was no purpose in psychologically damaging herself by worrying about a future event that was out of her control.

                    EVO KAPLAN
     I'm not sure I have the proper clothes to go there. Let me call
     guest services and talk to them.

Brenda realized the Lantiane Resort, aside from being sophisticated, catered to the super rich and made absolutely everything available.

                    BRENDA BROYALS
     Call guest services and talk to them. I'm sure they can help you
     out.

Evo grabbed the guest phone near the bed and called guest services.

A nice female voice sounded on the other end.

                    GUEST SERVICES
     Hello, may I help you?

                    EVO KAPLAN
     I'm a resort guest and was thinking about going to the
     Dewaltracen Gallery and didn't bring a lot of formal clothes
     with me. What do you recommend and can guest services outfit
     me?

                    GUEST SERVICES
     Yes sir, we can outfit you. As you know the Dewaltracen Gallery
     has the reputation of having the greatest collection of the old
     masters of any known place in the Empire. As such they get a
     lot of special visitors and the decorum and is thus very upscale
     for most of the patrons.

                    EVO KAPLAN
     That's what I thought also.

                    GUEST SERVICES
     If you do not dress well, you will feel out of place. I highly
     recommend you do not go without the proper apparel.

                    EVO KAPLAN
     How soon can you bring me apparel you recommend?

GUEST SERVICES

We can send someone to your bungalow right away. Also, looking at the customer information sheet, Mr. Pugong, we already have your measurements, and the fashion designer will pick out several choices and bring them on a clothing rack.

EVO KAPLAN

That's great. I appreciate that. I'm ready so send them over now.

GUEST SERVICES

Yes sir. They are on the way and should be there in a few minutes.

It seemed to Evo that no sooner than he sat the communicator down on the desk than the bungalow doorbell rang. He went and answered it and there was a fashion designer with a cart and a tall enclosure on it.

EVO KAPLAN<br>Please come in.

FASHION DESIGNER<br>Thank you, sir.

The staff member rolled the cart into the room and Evo shut the door. The female fashion designer was exquisite but had some type of wild appearance. No doubt she practiced on herself to create such an exotic look.

EVO KAPLAN<br>What's your name?

FASHION DESIGNER - INCHALCHARY<br>I'm Inchalchary.

EVO KAPLAN<br>Is that a Shen de Huayuan name?

INCHALCHARY<br>Yes sir, I was born and raised on this planet.

EVO KAPLAN<br>Did you get your fashion design training here?

INCHALCHARY<br>No, my parents sent me to Zanziltar to learn my trade.

EVO KAPLAN
That must have been an expensive school.

INCHALCHARY
It was. My parents could not afford it, so I had to work as an apprentice and basically a slave to my master for seven years.

EVO KAPLAN
I bet that was tough.

INCHALCHARY
Yes. Madam Zraklevin checked me for my virginity; otherwise, she would not have accepted me.

EVO KAPLAN
That's amazing.

INCHALCHARY
I was not allowed any unescorted trips out of her Designer Taojo nor was I allowed alone with men the entire time I was there.

EVO KAPLAN
What was the training like?

INCHALCHARY
I worked as her personal slave for eight hours each day, then she trained me for several hours.

EVO KAPLAN
What kind of work did you do as a slave girl?

INCHALCHARY
I cut fabric, measured people, pressed garments, sewed garments, tried on garments so Madam Zraklevin could get a 3D view of the finished product, and assisted numerous customers.

EVO KAPLAN
Was it worthwhile?

INCHALCHARY
I'm certified by Madam Zraklevin in fashion design.

EVO KAPLAN
How does Madam Zraklevin' certification help you?

INCHALCHARY

Madam Zraklevin is considered the top designer in all Zanziltar.
Because of my credentials I can work in any world in the
Empire and earn good money. This resort is the best that exists
here at Shen de Huayuan.


EVO KAPLAN

Is it beneficial working at this resort?


INCHALCHARY

If you talk to people in the fashion industry, they will inform
you it's rather remarkable that a person from *Shen de Huayuan*
is able to be hired at this resort for a key position as one of its
top fashion designers.


EVO KAPLAN

Have you designed apparel for guests at this resort?


INCHALCHARY

Yes, I designed the dress she is wearing.


Inchalchary smiled and nodded at Brenda.


BRENDA BROYALS

Amazing! You really are good.


Inchalchary opened the doors on the side of the apparel carrier that was used
for two reasons: to protect the articles from possible rain, and to prevent anyone
to observe what it contained so that a guest could leave their bungalow or hotel
room with clothes nobody had yet seen or seen them wearing. There were at least
a dozen outfits to choose from and boxes of shoes to go with whatever he picked.
One suit in particular caught Evo Caplan's eye and


EVO KAPLAN

I would like to try this one on.


INCHALCHARY

Please undress, Mr. Pugong, so I can help you put it on and
make adjustments if necessary.


EVO KAPLAN

Sure.


Evo Kaplan took off his clothes and was standing almost nude in front of the two women as Inchalchary took pieces of the outfit, handed them to Evo, and then helped him put them on until he was completely dressed.

EVO KAPLAN
It fits perfectly.

INCHALCHARY
Yes, I have your sizes logged from the other day when we provided you with a suit.

EVO KAPLAN
This suit fits well too. What is this color?

INCHALCHARY
This is phthalocyanine blue. It is a bright, crystalline, synthetic blue pigment from the group of phthalocyanine dyes. Its brilliant blue is highly valued for irresistible properties such as light fractals and tint métier.

EVO KAPLAN
What do you recommend for shoes?

INCHALCHARY
For this outfit I recommend the chrome blue shoes in this box.

Inchalchary handed Evo Kaplan the shoe box.

EVO KAPLAN
These look good.

INCHALCHARY
Here's the matching socks.

Evo put on the socks and shoes, and then turned toward Brenda.

EVO KAPLAN
Brenda, how does this look?

BRENDA BROYALS
You look like you are ready to take me to the gallery.

INCHALCHARY

Mr. Pugong, if you are ready to leave now for your engagement, you can leave. The resort will take care of this. I recommend you take your personal ID with you and go out to the resort front entrance and get a lift from one of the limos.

                    EVO KAPLAN
            All right. I'm ready if you are, Brenda.


                  BRENDA BROYALS
                   Yes, I'm ready.


                   INCHALCHARY
        Have fun! When you get back this cart will be gone.


                    EVO KAPLAN
                Thanks for all your help.


                   INCHALCHARY
            You are welcome, Proctor Pugong.

<u>EXT. LANTIANE RESORT SWIMMING POOL – LATE MORNING</u>


                 VOICE OVER (FEMALE)
Evo Kaplan and Brenda Broyals left the bungalow and as they walked past the swimming pool, the three Barracuda were sitting on reclining chairs pool side and spotted the couple. Brenda was knockout gorgeous, which they had seen leaving the massage room. And here she was with her hunk as if she was showing him off.

All Evo Kaplan managed to do was increase the hunger pains of the three Barracudas, who were mesmerized by the glitter of the phthalocyanine blue dyes. Its reflective brilliance from the sunlight gave Evo Kaplan a stately image Brenda Broyals nor the three Barracudas would ever forget.

<u>EXT. LANTIANE RESORT FRONT ENTRANCE - MORNING</u>

Evo and Brenda walked out to the front of the resort, got into a limo.

<u>INT.  PLANET *SHEN de HUAYUAN - DEWALTRACEN GALLERY*- DAY</u>

Shortly after arriving, Brenda Broyals and Evo Kaplan gave the appearance of the best-looking couple walking around the Dewaltracen gallery and taking in all the artworks.

Some artworks stood twenty feet tall, majestically depicting another era. Other artworks were only a couple feet tall.

                    BRENDA BROYALS
Lord Dewaltracen expanded the size of the Empire more than any other Emperor.


                    EVO KAPLAN
As much as they do not like to dwell on it, art historians were aware that Lord Dewaltracen collected all these artworks as he plundered many planets and stole their precious artworks and treasuries.


                    BRENDA BROYALS
Sure, but that's how he paid for the expansion by taxation on the liberation since many of the conquered worlds were freed from evil dictators.


                    EVO KAPLAN
No matter how you look at it, some worlds still regard it as loot stolen from them and viewed Lord Dewaltracen as an evil miscegenation.


Brenda and Evo walked around the beautiful building radiating ambience exposing an environment seemingly surrounded by influence. No doubt many of the well-dressed patrons were bankers or wealthy individuals visiting from Zanziltar and were currently bored and seeking something to do in their spare time.

As Brenda and Evo stood before one of the most precious works in the gallery and perhaps in the galaxy—an incredible representation of raw brain power and imagination, from the long-deceased Mathematician Agstavar—a gentleman approached and politely and softly spoke.


                    STRANGER
It is said there are exactly one thousand one hundred and eleven objects in the artwork depicting all the demons in the afterlife.


                    EVO KAPLAN
Do you really believe such demons existed?


                    STRANGER
It doesn't matter what I believe. What matters is what the great Agstavar thought when he created it in one thousand one hundred and eleven days.

The gentleman appeared to be a retired wealthy senior citizen moping around like many other well-to-do hopelessly lost lacking things to do out of fear of failure or change, which they avoided.

Brenda thought she knew who this man was, as he was the chief of Revolutionary Security for *Shen de Huayuan*. They were far enough away from any other patrons in the exhibit where he felt he could say the few things he planned.

STRANGER

It took me a while to track you down Brenda. Conrad Fanzui contacted me and asked that I look you up and make sure everything was going all right for you.

Brenda suddenly recalled the stranger's name, Egor Pataslia, a high ranking official from the FIRM. It also meant they were being followed for their own protection. In some ways that gave her some deep satisfaction that at a period of one of the most precious times of her life, she was being looked after so she could let her guard down and relax a bit. Something she thought was impossible and precipitated the need for her massage earlier that day.

BRENDA BROYALS

Yes, please inform Conrad Fanzui that everything is fine, and we are enjoying our time here.

The man handed Brenda a business token.

STRANGER - EGOR PATASLIA

If you ever need my help in any way while you are here, use this to contact me.

BRENDA BROYALS<br>Thank you.

The gentleman (a.k.a. Egor Pataslia) turned and walked away. He obviously didn't want to give possible trailers the opportunity to connect him to Brenda, as it could put them both at risk.

Evo Kaplan knew he had seen that man sometime in the past. It was during one of those many missions he went on. He tried to place the man and thought hard. He suddenly recalled a time at a distant planet that was undergoing a Revolution insurgency. Was 1111 a code the two used as a semaphore? Evo was suddenly growing ill thinking he was discovering more and more each day that led him to believe Brenda might be part of the Revolution.

It would tear Evo Kaplan's heart apart to discover the woman he fell in love with was also his enemy.

BRENDA BROYALS
I'm getting hungry. Let's take a short walk and see if there are
some restaurants nearby.


EVO KAPLAN
Sure.


As Evo was walking near the entrance, an art curator had just finished taking to
one of the patrons and was suddenly alone, so Evo approached him.


EVO KAPLAN
Excuse me, sir, can you tell me if there are any restaurants
nearby that you would recommend?

The gentleman looked friendly and responded.


ART CURATOR
Yes, there are at least a dozen excellent restaurants nearby.
If you go out the entrance and to the street corner, you will
discover at least two restaurants within a block in any direction
you take.


EVO KAPLAN
Thank you for the information.


ART CURATOR
My pleasure, sir.


Noting the colloquialism the patron had, the curator suspected he had a Praxisvlasia
dialect and volunteered a special recommendation.


ART CURATOR
If you want to try some local cuisine at its finest, when you get
to the street corner, make a left and go down one block and you
will find a restaurant named Xingning Shizhe.


EVO KAPLAN
All right, thanks.


<u>INT.  PLANET *SHEN de HUAYUAN - Xingning Shizhe Restaurant*-  DAY</u>


MALE VOICE OVER
Brenda and Evo left the art museum and were soon they were
at the *Xingning Shizhe Restaurant* waiting for their meals while
Evo sat in awe. Evo Kaplan had just seen and tasted history like
he never imagined he ever would in his lifetime.

Evo Kaplan never believed he would ever get to see the Dewaltracen Gallery. But at the same time, he now realized a lot of issues facing the Empire today are the result of the way Lord Dewaltracen consolidated the Empire in the first place.

Lord Dewaltracen didn't create a lasting peace; what he created was lasting conflict and grievances.

CU. BRENDA BROYALS LOOKING INTO EVO KAPLAN'S EYES - *Xingning Shizhe Restaurant*

MALE VOICE OVER
Across from Evo Kaplan, elaborately painted for the day, was a temporal princess Brenda, who was most likely a Revolution Spy who had failed as a spy and fell in love with Evo Kaplan.

CU. EVO KAPLAN LOOKING INTO BRENDA BROYALS EYES - *XINGNING SHIZHE RESTAURANT*

VOICE OVER
But did Evo Kaplan fail as a spy as well?

The local cuisine tasted great, however, there was an eerie quiet during the meal. Nobody was talking. It was as if they both were contemplating their fate. It seemed they were each happy when they were done eating, acting if they wanted to leave and do something to take their minds off their predicament. They were each starting to realize they truly were enemies.

Though no overt discussion of that situation started as neither wanted to face it now. It would most likely turn into a heart-breaking episode when eventually they had to come to terms.

VOICE OVER (FEMALE)
Brenda took solace in that Evo Kaplan's former boss had ruined him over petty vindictiveness. So even if Evo Kaplan had a Loyalist mindset, he was most likely not jovial about helping the *Dranzonians*. Brenda thought, *Perhaps I can turn Evo Kaplan?*

BRENDA BROYALS
Shall we go back to the gallery and see more?

EVO KAPLAN
No, I think I saw the most important works. The Mathematician Agstavar artwork is so profoundly better than any other exhibit, the rest pales in comparison.

                          BRENDA BROYALS
I would like to take a VTOL sightseeing flight. The resort has
them.


                            EVO KAPLAN
                        Do we have enough time?


                          BRENDA BROYALS
Sure. We don't need to change our clothes. We'll just get back
to the resort and contact guest services.


                            EVO KAPLAN
            All right, I'm paging the limo now to take us back.


The pager gave global positioning coordinates to the limo driver. The limo
digital mapping and navigation system guided the driver to the *Xingning Shizhe
Restaurant* to pick up the couple.


In a short while they were back in their Lantiane Resort bungalow and Evo
contacted Guest Services.


                          GUEST SERVICES
                      Hello, how may I help you?


                            EVO KAPLAN
Hello, I'm resort guest Evo Kaplan. Can you arrange a VTOL
sightseeing tour for today?


                          GUEST SERVICES
            Sure Evo Kaplan. When would you like to go?


                            EVO KAPLAN
                          We are ready now.


                          GUEST SERVICES
    I'll call back in a few minutes with the schedule for you.


            PROCTOR PUGONG  (a.k.a. EVO KAPLAN)
                             Thanks.


Five minutes later the communicator rang.


            PROCTOR PUGONG (a.k.a. EVO KAPLAN)
                             Hello.

Mr. Pugong, the VTOL sightseeing van will be out in front of
the resort's main entrance in five minutes to take you to the
VTOL port and your flight will start as soon as you get there.

PROCTOR PUGONG  (a.k.a EVO KAPLAN)
Okay, thanks.

EXT. PLANET SHEN de HUAYUAN LANTIANE RESORT FRONT
ENTRANCE AFTERNOON

Evo and Brenda walked out to the front of the resort, got into , the VTOL
sightseeing van.

INT. PLANET *SHEN de HUAYUAN* – VTOL SIGHTSEEING VAN - DAY

Soon they were on their way about a mile away from where a private VTOL
Skybus operator had his aircraft.

INT. PLANET *SHEN de HUAYUAN* – *VTOL SKYBUS* - DAY

Brenda Broyals and Evo Kaplan got out of the van and were escorted to the VTOL
Skybus craft they boarded and soon had their seat belts on. There were several
other couples, as this craft could carry up to forty people along with the crew,
flight attendants, and tour guide.

EXT. CGI. PLANET SHEN de HUAYUAN – VTOL SKYBUS - DAY 30
SECONDS SKYBUS TAKING OFF AND GOING UP INTO THE SKY

Note to the CGI creators:

Iin the background the Lantiane Resort and the beach behind it. The
scene shifts as if it's being filmed from a drone circling it so to shift
the scene to passing city high rise buildings, they fly past and the
tropical paradise that soon shows as they fly out of the urban area.
Here is a video promotion that may give the CGI developers the
essence of a city flying past. In this case this is the Sanctuary City
Zanziltar.

Film technique: an actual drone flying along as the CGI screen shift
to give a nice 3D movement in the projection.

In moments the VTOL Skybus was airborne, flying over the countryside and being
schooled on points of interest. If Brenda Broyals and Evo Kaplan suddenly had
some issues with a potential hit team coming after them, knowing the countryside
would be good in case they had to bug out.

The VTOL Skybus could fly near the speed of sound so it covered distance quickly. They flew up the coastline and were soon away from all signs of urban activity and only small access roads appeared to exist.

Unexpectedly they slowed down and decreased altitude until they were only a few hundred feet over the water just off the coastline. What they observed was rather exotic looking flora, and soon they slowed and pulled over onto the beach where a concrete landing pad had been built. The VTOL Skybus settled down gently onto the landing pad, and the tour guide made the announcement:

SKY CAR TOUR GUIDE

Ladies and gentlemen, we are going to get leave the VTOL Skybus here so you can all observe the *Hupu Waterfalls*. Since it's a little walk back to the waterfall and we do not want to waste too much precious time, we have our tram next to the VTOL Skybus, which we want everyone to get on, and that will take us up to the waterfall and back promptly.

The tour guide led the group a short distance and they all got on a tram that had seats all orientated to one side. They would soon discover why.

INT.  PLANET SHEN de HUAYUAN – VTOL SKYBUS TOUR TRAM -  DAY

The Tour Tram Tracks went away and split into two tracks, one going along the side of a small river that emptied out into the ocean and another that crossed over a bridge and disappeared into a tunnel. The tram had cog wheels to ensure it did not lose traction going up the semi-steep hill of probably thirty-percent grade. Looking at half the customers on the tram, it was highly doubtful half of them could have made the climb.

The further the Tram traveled up the hillside, more lavish flora existed. There was a cacophony of sound coming from animals hidden from view they could hear from the open windows. The river and the tram abruptly curved and as they went a good distance around the curve, they discovered the hillside was obscuring the waterfall. The majestic waterfall came down the mountain side in a rather spectacular display of nature's finest natural resource.

BRENDA BROYALS
I wonder how tall that waterfall is.

EVO KAPLAN
It must be two thousand feet.

Moments later the tour guide made an announcement.

SKY CAR TOUR GUIDE
Ladies and gentlemen, one of the most frequently asked questions includes how high the Hupu Waterfall is. From the highest point you can see from the tram to the small lake below, it is two thousand five hundred feet.


EVO KAPLAN
There's your answer Brenda.


SKY CAR TOUR GUIDE
The next question often asked: how much water is dropping. Scientists have calculated that almost six acres fall in an hour.


Soon the tram went into a tunnel, and it got dark. As the tram curved, suddenly a large series of glass windows were exposed, and the angle of the light and the waterfall combined to produce a perpetual rainbow inside the protected cavity. The tram slowly curved around Hupu Waterfall so overall, the tourists were able to observe the waterfall for a full one hundred eighty degrees of turn around the U-curve. The best was yet to come. As soon as they straightened out and appeared to be heading for a tunnel up ahead, the tour guide made an announcement:


SKY CAR TOUR GUIDE
Ladies and gentlemen, coming up ahead is several families of Taro Tigers.


Everyone was in awe. These five hundred-pound monsters could grab a humanoid and probably eat him or her in a short period of time. They were terrifying, dangerous looking animals and only lived in a few discrete areas of the coastline, as they had been hunted almost out of existence. There were probably less than two hundred of them still living on the planet and they had never been seen on any other planet, so they were native to *Shen de Huayuan*.


Brenda's dress was perfect for the adventure; her numerous spectacular flowers on the dress print amazingly matched the flora they now observed in abundance.


Tour attendants were walking along the trams and offering drinks of various types. Brenda and Evo both accepted a domestic concoction that provided energy and acute awareness as indicated on the container.


BRENDA BROYALS
This drink tastes pretty good!


EVO KAPLAN
Yeah, it has a very pleasant taste to it.

The combination of the drink and being with the best-looking woman on the tram helped boost Evo Kaplan's ego a few notches. About that time the tram went into a tunnel, and it got dark. Evo felt Brenda give him a gentle hug and a caress. She was affected by the drink and the experience.

Brenda's energy level was where she loved it: nice and robust and ready for action.

 As the tram got closer to the tunnel opening it got lighter, and the very instant it hit the opening the light suddenly shifted brightly with direct glaring sunlight. Evo Kaplan turned toward Brenda and looked at her observing him. It was a moment that Evo Kaplan would always remember for the rest of his life.

Perhaps it was the drugs in the drink that gave them all the energy and acute awareness, or it was providence. He would never know for sure. But what Evo Kaplan did know was peering into Brenda Broyals eyes he read her soul and her mind.

Brenda Broyals was a grown, mature adult woman and at the same time a little girl. Evo Kaplan instinctively grasped this galactic class spy Brenda Broyals was fragile and on the cusp of the greatest challenges of her life.

Brenda Broyals positive valance flourished because she lived for today and for this moment. She didn't care about tomorrow, and she also knew the possibility she was facing a mortal enemy, and the day of reckoning was around the corner where the divide would tear her heart in half.

Brenda knew what Conrad Fanzui expected out of her. She was trained and she knew the rules of the road. Should Evo Kaplan not willingly join the Revolution and swear allegiance to his new masters, he would be sanctioned, and Conrad would do the most dramatic action that any spy master would do.

Conrad Fanzui would not be putting Evo Kaplan into the swimming pool to drive him insane, nor would he torture him with the crematorium. He would go one step above and have his lover kill him.

Brenda Broyles new if that happened, she would no doubt commit suicide immediately afterward, but the action and the history would be a benchmark for the future in dealing with weakness among the ranks.

The tram made its way across the bridge near the beach and came to a stop almost exactly where it started. The next group that rode the tram would first go across the bridge and go in the opposite direction, as the tram did not turn around.

INT.  PLANET *SHEN de HUAYUAN – VTOL SKYBUS* - DAY

In what seemed like a very short while, the tour guide and the attendants ushered the group back on the VTOL Skybus and they were airborne again.

The next stop about fifteen minutes later was a vineyard. Coming down from twenty thousand feet.

> SKY CAR TOUR GUIDE
> If you look out to the right side, you can see the vineyards stretch for miles and miles. One of the major exports from *Shen de Huayuan* is distillates from the fruits harvested in this area.

Just like on the beach, they landed on a concrete landing pad. No sooner than the VTOL Skybus propulsion shut down, bus-like ground transports pulled up on the landing pad and the tour guide announced:

> SKY CAR TOUR GUIDE
> Ladies and gentlemen, please exit the VTOL Skybus. and board the ground transport, as we are going to take you to a tasting saloon where you can sample the distillates as well as eat a snack that will be provided for you.

INT.  PLANET *SHEN de HUAYUAN – GROUND TRANSPORT/BUS* - DAY

The solar powered transports had a lot of torque in their drive systems, showing no hesitance in climbing a couple hills and circumnavigated a lakeshore that took them to a snazzy looking building that seemed mostly built of glass. The lake view and the multitudes of vineyards sprawling up the hillsides had a surreal effect, especially to city bound visitors used to living among concrete and steel.

The ground transports pulled into a circular driveway in front of the main entrance and stopped. Everyone meandered off the transport, meekly following the tour guide into the saloon that had a dozen bars and many tables so that clientele could sit, eat their snacks, and go up to one of the bars and get another sample to taste.

> EVO KAPLAN
> There were also boxes and crates full of bottles the tourists can purchase and take home with them. Maybe we can take some home with us.

> BRENDA BROYALS
> Honey don't forget we only have four cubic feet allowed on the Intergalactic Space Transport. That will not allow very many bottles if we intend on bringing home other items to Zanziltar.

EVO KAPLAN
Some enterprising individuals probably leave their clothes
behind because one bottle of Shen de Huayuan fermented
distillates could be sold and they would pay for several sets of
clothes.


BRENDA BROYALS
These Ferments are extremely rare on almost any planet other
than Zanziltar, which is why only Zanziltar has ample supplies
of it because all the rich industrialists who lived on Zanziltar
shipped the product home on return trips.


EVO KAPLAN
What brings the industrialists here? Vacations?


BRENDA BROYALS
Industrialists do trading with Shen de Huayuan for products
other worlds that have an appetite for many Empire products,
they lack from manufacturing deficits.


The ferments tasting went on for well over an hour, and indications were several
of the members in the group traveling were getting snockered. This was a well-
choreographed tour and right on cue the tour guide hustled everyone back on
the transports, headed back to the VTOL Skybus. The tourists were deposited
back aboard the VTOL Skybus in such an efficient manner, they were once again
airborne in less than ten minutes.

<u>INT.  PLANET *SHEN de HUAYUAN – VTOL SKYBUS* -  DAY</u>


Note to the director:


These couple of pages and a few that follow might not be necessary,
but they will add some interest to the audience. The font the publisher
used on the original Novel was small, so it was hard to gauge the
size and scope of this science fiction work. No doubt you will have
to cut a lot unless you want to invest in a 3-hour movie. Note this
screenplay only covers the first ½ of the Novel SANCTUARY
CITY. I probably should have broken it into 3 or 4 movies. We can
discuss that if you think such a rearrangement is necessary.


A second screenplay is being developed for the second half of the
original Novel. The first and second screenplays have substantial
action so it's not necessary to attempt putting it all in one screenplay.


A third and possibly fourth screenplay will be written for the sequel.

One of the crowning achievements *for Shen de Huayuan* was the Guilong Aquarium at Pangu Bay. Besides having the largest concentration of sea turtles on the planet, according to myth there once lived terrible creatures with a dragon appearance.

The VTOL Skybus arrived at Pangu Bay in less than twenty minutes and landed at a multiple landing pad area where there were a dozen VTOL Sky Buses already parked there, bringing groups in to tour the famed Guilong Aquarium. The aquarium was huge and covered over six hundred acres. The facility was so vast they provided electric carts for groups that would proceed down a "cart lanes" where tour guides provided quite an entertaining and educational description of all the sights.

At times they were traveling in a glass tunnel inside a huge aquarium. Observing the huge three-foot diameter sea turtles was quite an experience. A few of the turtles swam up to the glass tunnel and stared at the electric carts full of people. The only way they could show a lot of the sites to the public was on these guided tours on the carts that never stopped and clogged traffic. The event was a tranquil moment, and it allowed them to escape their world and all their problems for a brief period.

The large turtles were almost therapeutically endearing for Brenda, who struggled not to think about the future; this time, no serious thoughts clogged her thinking as she felt like a person loving fresh air after being cooped up on an intergalactic transport ship for weeks. This journey through this underwater menagerie had a transcendental effect on most of the individuals riding along in those electric carts observing as if they were underwater in the ocean without the inconvenience of actually being there.

The genius behind the Guilong Aquarium was to make it so huge, it gave the illusion a patron was in the ocean because the ocean was as far as they could see. As they traveled the distance in a horseshoe-like glass tunnel, it felt and seemed like you were in and part of the ocean environment.

 Schools of fish and predators such as the Fufen Ray glided along spectacularly, soaring the ocean as if it were some types of bird under water. The brochure given to all the guests as they boarded the electric carts gave a rundown of what possible ocean wildlife could be seen. The brochure also stated they had accumulated samples of almost every form of ocean wildlife that existed on the planet and ninety-five percent of them were represented in this massive underwater display.

The pilotless carts drove along without any steerage or control. Some people with technological backgrounds wondered how they did it. The cement roadway had wires imbedded in the concrete the carts drove over. Sensors in the carts detected the location of the wires directly below and steered the carts exactly following the trail it created. If one shined a flashlight down on the driveway.

A person could see tire marks had covered two areas where the wheels followed the invisible road markers very precisely.

An engineer involved in designing these electronic guided roads announced in the recorded tour:

GUILONG AQUARIUM ENGINEER
Accuracy and precision were the most important aspects of
what they were doing in designing the electric cart system.

About ten carts behind, some of the tourists were not sightseers. Egor Pataslia's men immediately went into surveillance mode of the Lantiane Resort in time for Evo Kaplan's arrival. Personnel at the resort were swapped out by the security men and the resort sent them home on paid leave, sighting a reward to employees who had done a very good job.

A couple of the Revolution Secret Service men were placed in guest services and filters were put on any transactions Evo Kaplan or Brenda Broyals made. If they made a reservation, the Revolution knew it immediately and were thus able to get agents in place promptly to follow them around. When Evo Kaplan and Brenda Broyals first boarded the VTOL Skybus, there was a couple agents who appeared as tourists ready to go with them on their adventure and be in position to intervene should something happen.

Because Evo and Brenda's preoccupation with each other and the psychological turmoil Brenda was facing, they collectively let their guard down, assuming everything was safe on this planet and they sincerely believed the Dranzonian Empire Secret Service would not attempt sending agents this far behind enemy lines.

It made no practical sense. However, this was not a normal situation. The fact one of the former Dranzonian Empire Secret Service best operatives was now ostensibly deeply involved with Brenda Broyals called upon them to take such extraordinary action.

If Terrshey Wate couldn't convince Evo Kaplan to return to Praxisvlasia, Reginald Heiqishi— who had enough plastic surgery to make him appear as a new agent, Blane Jiandie, as a cover—would kill Evo Kaplan through the means of sophisticated weapons, including a deadly aerosol, poisons, and if necessary, a new type of laser pistol manufactured to avoid detection in security scanners.

The only problem with the new type of laser pistol is that it came in pieces like a transformer and had to be put together. Once Reginald Heiqishi and Terrshey Wate got to their Lantiane Resort rooms and assembled their laser pistols they could be used after plugged it into a wall socket and charged it up in less than thirty minutes.

The lithium infused uranium batteries would be good enough for at least a dozen shots in case of a shootout or if Reginald Heiqishi missed the target a few times.

INT. LANTIANE RESORT DAY

While Evo and Brenda were traveling through the vast underwater complex, Reginald Heiqishi and Terrshey Wate checked into their Lantiane Resort rooms.

The Dranzonian Empire Secret Service had done extensive verification and had every reason to believe Evo Kaplan had never seen Terrshey Wate or knew he existed, as their compartmentalized cells were a great distance apart and they never took on missions in the same part of the galaxy. Reginald Heiqishi felt his facial features were so greatly changed, now appearing more like Blane Jiandie who was new and ostensibly never worked with Evo Kaplan, he would also escape detection.

Terrshey Wate and Reginald Heiqishi were quickly unpacked and ready for action.

                         TERRSHEY WATE
          Let's get something to eat and drink. I'm hungry. That space
          junk food didn't set well with me.

                         REGINALD HEIQISHI
          Not a bad idea. We might see Evo Kaplan or Brenda Broyals
          walking around.

Reginald Heiqishi and Terrshey Wate were not sure what to expect attempting in recognizing Brenda Broyals, but they knew based on intel reports from their operatives in Zanziltar that Evo had not changed his looks according to their man who betrayed him.

Reginald Heiqishi and Terrshey Wate left the resort room, took the elevator down, and walked toward the beach entrance where they figured they might find a bar restaurant. Their guess was good, and they were soon sitting at the bar, getting a drink, and looking over the menu.

IND. DAY LANTIANE RESORT BEACH RESTAURANT AND BAR.

The Lantiane Resort Beach Restaurant and Bar, typical of many resorts, had a nice mirror on the wall. The bartender left for a moment leaving the two alone at the bar.

REGINALD HEIQISHI

This is one of the main entrances to the beach area and those
expensive-looking bungalows and the pool. If Brenda Broyals
and Evo Kaplan are heading to the beach or the pool, we will
spot them.

TERRSHEY WATE

That nice mirror on the wall should allow us to look around to
spot people without tipping off we are doing surveillance.

As they sat there, happy hour commenced, and the band started playing some classic Shen de Huayuan songs. The music was slightly different, but very pleasing to the ears. The volume wasn't too loud, which allowed customers to talk with each other.

Sheri was singing again, as the management loved her voice and her looks.

REGINALD HEIQISHI
I like the way the singer looks and her voice.

TERRSHEY WATE

If we must suffer dead time on this stakeout to locate and
confront Evo Kaplan, at least we have some eye candy to look
at while we wait.

Soon the bartender returned, and men ordered some bar food that most likely tasted good and would take their minds off the horrible slop they had to eat on the Intergalactic Transports getting here.

BARTENDER
Have you gentlemen decided what you want to order?

REGINALD HEIQISHI
I'll have Turtle Steak.

TERRSHEY WATE
I'll go with the stuffed Peacock.

Turtle meat was scarce on a lot of planets due to scarcity and public opinion about killing such wonderful creatures.

Some turtles were very smart, and in Vergentia where Evo Kaplan spent his childhood, it was felt their turtles had gone through such evolution to where scientists claimed they were about twice as intelligent as dolphins and whale-like animals. Killing a turtle on Vergentia would create a very angry public if it became known. On the resort menu, there were interesting bar food suggestions such as turtle steaks, stuffed peacock, tiger steak, and roasted eagles, all of which were forbidden to be killed on numerous planets.

However, this was *Shen de Huayuan*, the playground of the super-rich and well connected. It was once said you can buy anything in *Shen de Huayuan*. They even sold husbands and wives. The better educated and prepared, the more they fetched which took human trafficking to a new level when businessmen had financial disasters due to their mismanagement. Daughters were often sold and sometimes beautiful wives, especially if the husband determined her reckless spending resulted in his bankruptcy.

Note to director:

During this segment of conversation, Sheri sings Paul D. Escudero's song: "You can Live Forever." Music and Lyrics will be provided upon contract.

While the two Dranzonian Empire Secret Service agents Reginald Heiqishi and Terrshey Wate were enjoying their turtle meat and stuffed Peacock meals hearing the lovely singer Sheri sing, Evo Kaplan and Brenda Broyals were still at the Guilong Aquarium.

INT. DAY. GUILONG AQUARIUM

The Guilong Aquarium was so huge the electric cart ride becomes extremely boring near the end of the ride, unless you were into ocean studies or a university professor.

Evo Kaplan was grateful he saw the exit coming up and exterior light creeping in at the final portion. When they got back aboard the VTOL Skybus, they were even more enthused after the tour guide said this was the last stop and they would be heading back to their temporary home base, Lantiane Resort.

There were other tours available, and they merely had to make an onsite reservation and this time of day, there was plenty of room for anyone wanting to go. In thirty minutes, they were flown to the resort. They were glad to be back. Evo was thinking it might be time to take a nap then prepare for dinner.

Before Evo could suggest anything, Brenda had her own plan.

                         BRENDA BROYALS
Evo, why don't you go to the bar, get a drink, and give me
fifteen minutes. I want to give you a surprise.


Evo Kaplan wondered what that was about.


                          EVO KAPLAN
                            Okay.


<u>INT. LANTIANE RESORT BEACH RESTAURANT BAR AND RESTAURANT</u>


Brenda Broyals continued to the bungalow while Evo Kaplan walked into the
restaurant bar and found a window seat in full view of the band. The waitress
shortly arrived.


         LANTIANE RESORT BEACH BAR WAITRESS What can I
                      get you to drink?


                          EVO KAPLAN
What do you have that has a touch of alcohol in it and an energy
inducer?


              LANTIANE RESORT BEACH BAR WAITRESS
The Huoshan Xingneng has alcohol and an energy inducer.


                          EVO KAPLAN
                       Does it taste good?


              LANTIANE RESORT BEACH BAR WAITRESS
Yes, it is a very pleasant drink. If you plan on being with a
woman tonight, it will give you added strength and performance.


                          EVO KAPLAN
                        Just what I need.


The waitress came back in a few minutes with Evo Kaplan's drink.


Had it not been for the distraction that Sheri and the band made, Evo might have
detected the surveillance from the bar.


The band soon had a break. As expected, Sheri made a beeline to Evo Kaplan.


                          EVO KAPLAN
                            Hello.

SHERI
Hi there, how have you been?

EVO KAPLAN
I'm doing okay. Thanks for asking. I hope you are doing great.


The small talk went on for a while with Reginald Heiqishi watching Evo Kaplan through the bar mirror. *Well, I'll be damned. There's lover boy.*

Reginald Heiqishi looked at the fancy blue suit, which on Praxisvlasia would be way more than anything Evo could afford to pay for. With that kind of luxury, he had to be a traitor, especially this far behind enemy lines.

As soon as Evo estimated  fifteen minutes transpired he needed to leave and go back to the bungalow.


EVO KAPLAN
It was nice talking with you, but I need to go change into something more casual and get ready for dinner.


SHERI
It was good seeing you again. Come back soon.


EVO KAPLAN
I will.


VOICE OVER
Shortly after, Evo walked out of the bar and headed back to the bungalow. Reginald Heiqishi watched Evo Kaplan through the mirror the best he could without creating any interest or possible compromise.

One thing Reginald Heiqishi evaluated and analyzed was that Evo Kaplan would only be walking toward the bungalows if that's the resort room where he was staying. That also conveyed more opulence and a lavish lifestyle.

Reginald Heiqishi no longer felt the slightest remorse in assassinating Evo Kaplan in the future. It was crystal clear to Reginald Heiqishi the opulent lifestyle Evo Kaplan now enjoyed, suggested he betrayed the Dranzonian Empire. From poverty to lavishness in such a short time. What a ride for Evo Kaplan!

Now it was just a matter of determining the best location to do the job. They didn't know for sure how long Evo Kaplan would be here. Hence the sooner they whacked Evo Kaplan the better. Reginald Heiqishi and Terrshey Wate finished their meal and were just about ready to leave the club when the band took another break.

The bar-restaurant was half empty despite happy hour, as many guests were away dressing for the evening. Sheri made her rounds talking with a few guests. She spotted Reginald Heiqishi and Terrshey Wate, who were dressed for the part.

Back on Praxisvlasia they could not afford these clothes and would never wear them except for a prop for a mission. Sheri assumed they were affluent men from Zanziltar and would have no qualms about developing them for possible future scenarios.

SHERI
Good evening, gentlemen. Are you enjoying your vacation?

REGINALD HEIQISHI
Definitely.

SHERI
Where are you from?

REGINALD HEIQISHI
We are from Zanziltar. How about you?

SHERI
I'm a local girl. I grew up here.

REGINALD HEIQISHI
That nice-looking man that was just here, is he your boyfriend?

SHERI
No, but I wish.

REGINALD HEIQISHI
If you like him, you should go for it.

SHERI
I would except he already has a lady friend.

REGINALD HEIQISHI
What is she like?

SHERI
You just missed her. She walked past here fifteen minutes ago.

REGINALD HEIQISHI
Really?

SHERI
That's too bad. She was wearing a flowery dress. She was very beautiful today.

REGINALD HEIQISHI
Maybe we'll see her some other time.

SHERI
She is usually here with Proctor at least once a day.

REGINALD HEIQISHI
That's his name?

SHERI
Yes.

Reginald Heiqishi noted the name and would file it in a report later.

<u>INT. BUNGALOW LANTIANE RESORT BUNGALOW – AFTERNOON</u>

VOICE OVER (FEMALE)
Evo Kaplan arrived back at the bungalow a short time later. He entered and approximately one minute later, Brenda walked out of the bathroom with a very sexy negligee on. She walked up to Evo and put her arms around him and gave him a brief hug, then transitioned into helping him undress before leading him over to the domain of celestial feasts and proceeded to make up for being so rude in the morning.

Whatever Brenda's strange behavior was that morning was soon overlooked as two people in great shape waltzed the horizontal tango on another theme from Paganini.

Time was encapsulated in a magical stream of never-ending tremors of joy and oscillations of sheer imagery as they both passed into a semi unconscious state after an explosion of splendid euphoria.

Brenda didn't know for sure what time it was as she first stirred as the vibrations from Evo's snoring aroused her. She slid out of bed and used the bathroom to take care of her business, then walked to the closet where her suitcase was laid flat inside on a stand so she could access her personal items. She was in the process of getting out some shorts and a top when she lifted some of the garments out of the way and discovered someone had placed a laser pistol and a note:

*We thought you might need this for your own protection. When you leave at the end of your vacation, give it to the limo driver, he works for us. Best wishes, EP.*

Brenda instantly knew this was a note from Egor Pataslia but was curious as to why exactly he would provide her with a laser pistol. In the murky world of espionage, one never knew for sure what scenarios were right around the corner. This brought back home the realization she really couldn't let her guard down.

Brenda Broyals looked down at the laser pistol and saw it was charged up. It was immediately ready to be used as a lethal weapon, and it was one of those streamlined models that would easily fit in her purse, which she now knew she must always carry with her.

Brenda Broyals also had some other self-defense items she carried, such as martial arts throwing stars and an exploding pen that could blind or incapacitate an individual long enough to get away from an attacker. Quite a bit of time had passed, and it was getting too late to go out to a restaurant to eat. Perhaps they could get something at a pastry shop when Evo woke up?

VOICE OVER (MALE)

Meanwhile Reginald Heiqishi and Terrshey Wate decided they had pumped Sheri for all the information on Evo Kaplan they could get out of her and after completing their last drink decided to take a walk down the beach and reconnoiter the beach to look for avenues of attack toward Evo Kaplan's bungalow.

Reginald Heiqishi and Terrshey Wate left the restaurant, went past the pool and onto the sidewalk that led almost all the way down to water's edge, and made a left turn that would take them in the general direction of the bungalows.

The two Dranzonian Spies Reginald Heiqishi and Terrshey Wate then walked past all the bungalows and looked at the strategic envelope and opportunistic admittance of the bungalows in general and signs of surveillance equipment that would have to be taken into consideration in whatever they employed for tactics.

As to avoid any possible detection or undue interest in them, they continued on down the beach a short distance of maybe one-half mile, giving a disinterested posture and an exhibit of just two tourists or resort guests just out getting a little exercise, which would not be out of the ordinary.

It was clear they would have to sanction Evo Kaplan on the last day as they were due to depart Shen de Huayuan on the return leg to Zanziltar. In the meantime, they would wait for Evo Kaplan to avail himself in an unpredictable fashion and snare him in a target of opportunity trap.

TERRSHEY WATE

Perhaps we can use Sheri to position him where we can meet and offer him a deal he couldn't refuse.

REGINALD HEIQISHI

The only problem with using a surrogate is we open up the plan to areas of vulnerability and third-party compromise.

TERRSHEY WATE

She's just a resort band singer. She doesn't have much going for herself, being stuck on a provincial world waiting to meet a Zanziltar banker.

REGINALD HEIQISHI

We need to get to know her a little better and find out what her price is and how far she would go.

TERRSHEY WATE

She might be loyal to the Revolution, and if she even thinks for one second, we are Loyalist a long way behind enemy lines, she could place us in jeopardy.

REGINALD HEIQISHI

We'll simply have to eliminate her after she accomplishes what we ask of her.

TERRSHEY WATE

What do we use to get her to cooperate and do something we need of her?

REGINALD HEIQISHI
We could simply tell her we are into voyeurism and want to watch her seduce Evo Kaplan and offer her a large number of credits to get him someplace where we can catch them carrying on and waste him then.


TERRSHEY WATE
We certainly have the credits.


REGINALD HEIQISHI
The Battle of Praxisvlasia outcome has certainly had a huge impact on the exchange rate between Empire Credits and Revolution Confederate Credits.


TERRSHEY WATE
Yes, our credits will go far on this planet. When we exchanged Empire Credits to Revolution Confederate Credits, we got a 10.8 exchange rate.


REGINALD HEIQISHI
Kind of nice since a year ago the exchange rate was around 1.05.


TERRSHEY WATE
Which means we are carrying with us more than enough credits to make her believe what we are offering is a bona fide offer.


The men continued their walk and made it back to the Lantiane Resort but did not see Evo Kaplan during the walk. They went back to their suite they shared with double bedrooms and eased into rest and relaxation in an attempt to get over their space lag now that they had decent food and drink.

Heiqishi and Terrshey Wate just missed Evo and Brenda leave for their bungalow.

Timing was everything. Tomorrow was another day, and they would enjoy being paid to hang out at the swimming pool to do surveillance and possible interdiction later.

The next day, after Brenda Broyals and Evo Kaplan finished their morning routines, they heard about a restaurant located up on a tall cliff a few miles away where they could enjoy a nice breakfast with a scenic view. They were soon dressed and out the door, heading for one of the tri-wheelers at the hotel entrance, all decked out in their tourist clothes.

Terrshey Wate had the morning watch. He was poolside on a reclining chair reading the local news provided to resort occupants every morning. For the most part the news was of little interest, but the ads giving tips on things to do was one of the reasons why many did look at them. Hanging out at the pool only took care of some of the time; other activities were required to get fulfillment of the time on the planet.

The sidewalk from the bungalows ran right past the pool and the reclining chair Terrshey Wate sat had an excellent view and spotted the couple leaving. He waited until they were out of site, and he sent a voice-encoded message to Reginald Heiqishi informing him the target just passed by. He would loosely trail them.

A loose trail required to not be spotted by the target. Due to the topography and the layout of the facility, that would be tough. Prior to this morning, they could have continued the surveillance without much concern. When the target is fully disarmed because they believe they are in a safe area, they are not paranoid or extra alert like they would be if they were surrounded by potential enemy agents.

That was the case until Brenda went to her luggage and discovered EP left her some protection. Her whole persona changed. In a way Brenda Broyals vacation was ruined; in another she was now safer because she had protection with her and she would be far more alert, just like she was on a mission.

Brenda Broyals would not disturb Evo's vacation and warn him to be on the alert for potential assassins. She would have to protect her love—and in an incredible twist, potentially also her enemy.

Terrshey Wate figured the couple was heading toward the main entrance for transportation somewhere. He timed his exposure to the Lantiane Resort entrance area until he figured they would be leaving. As he got out where he could observe the couple, they were leaving in a tri-wheel. He felt he was not spotted by his target. Unfortunately for Terrshey Wate, he was dealing with one of the Revolution's top spies. They had their protocols, rules of thumb, and experiences doing untold number of missions.

The axiom of counter surveillance is, if you see a person twice in a few minutes, consider it possible surveillance until proven otherwise. Brenda saw the man out of the corner of her eye, put her arm around Evo, and looked like she was giving Evo a hug and a kiss.

*How sweet*, Terrshey Wate said to himself in a pompous fashion.

What Terrshey Wate didn't realize was Brenda was simply performing a veiled movement to not alert the possible counter surveillance she was getting a closer look. If she saw the man a third time within the next few hours, that would confirm there was some surveillance going on. Was it one of the good guys or the bad guys?

The three-wheeler took them to the restaurant up on the cliff.

EVO KAPLAN
Could you come back in an hour and pick us up?

TRI-WHEEL DRIVER
No problem, sir.

The view was excellent from up on this tall cliff that appeared like the white cliffs of Dover along England's coastline.

There was a short wait as the restaurant prepared a table for them. This afforded Brenda an opportunity to place herself in line with approaching traffic outside the large glass window entrance to see if they were being followed. She was soon rewarded for her vigilance.

The man at the pool with the morning paper, later seen at the front entrance, moments later passed by in a tri-wheeler. That confirms the surveillance.

Now the big question: was it one of Egor Pataslia's men or the enemy? For her own protection she had no way of contacting Egor Pataslia at that moment. However, Brenda suspected Egor Pataslia's people were probably close at hand. As a trained spy, she rewound all her visuals over the past few days of possible surveillance and observation by Egor Pataslia. During the tour the day before, some of those people on the VTOL Skybus could easily have been working for Egor Pataslia.

Brenda Broyals would do her uncanny ability to filter future observations with memories of exposures to tourists she saw earlier. Evo and Brenda were soon seated and their breakfast with this incredible view started the morning out in a very pleasant aura.

EVO KAPLAN
I bet this place has an interesting sunset since it faces the west.

BRENDA BROYALS
Yes, we'll have to come back sometime for dinner to check it
out.

Evo was still somewhat in a psychophysical transcendence from the earlier morning intimacy. He had no situational awareness going on. He was lulled into that false sense of security, believing he was on a Revolutionary Empire planet deep behind enemy lines where no possibility of warring factions could possibly operate.

Evo Kaplan of all people, based on his five hundred plus missions with the Dranzonian Empire Secret Service, should have realized distance never stopped his former agency.

Brenda was not going to spoil Evo's surreal pleasure and turn on his spy persona. In case this was their last precious time together, she wanted him to have the time of his life and make great and fond memories.

For her sweet love, Brenda Broyals would reward Evo Kaplan with this quite significant generosity. No other spy or woman would be so accommodative. Brenda was a tough bitch and all the top people at the FIRM knew it. She knew she could take on the dickheads and deal with them if they threatened her or her special love.

Brenda was not going to live paranoidly, but she would be prepared and maintain her situational awareness and operate from then on as if they were on a mission together. In a sense they now were. Breakfast ended too soon. The ambience and the atmosphere felt idealistic. The service was superb and the food out of this world—and it really was since they were on a strange planet.

BRENDA BROYALS
I can see why the wealthy from Zanziltar like hanging out at
Shen de Huayuan.


EVO KAPLAN
Shen de Huayuan definitely has appeal.


BRENDA BROYALS
*What do you want to do now?*


EVO KAPLAN
You might think I'm crazy.


BRENDA BROYALS
What is it? Try me.


EVO KAPLAN

Okay, I was looking through some brochures in the room yesterday. I came across an advertisement for the Shen de Huayuan Quanqiu Museum. It's not far from where the Dewaltracen Gallery is.

Brenda thought about it and analyzed Quanqiu Museum would be a safe place to be, and if there was any surveillance on them that would be better detected.

BRENDA BROYALS
Sure, if that's where you want to go next.

The tri-wheeler was back an hour as he had agreed to pick them up.

TRI-WHEELER DRIVER
Where would you like to go?

EVO KAPLAN
Take us to the Quanqiu Museum.

TRI-WHEELER DRIVER
Certainly.

The tri-wheeler's passenger seat arrangement was to the side so that people can sight-see as they drive along.

BRENDA BROYALS
Evo, please sit in front.

Brenda wanted a clear view behind them. She had her suspicions they might be followed to the museum.

The tri-wheeler was off. At a distance another tri-wheeler was enjoying an expensive fare as the man asked him to wait at a distance away from the restaurant where he could observe a tri-wheeler or taxi arrive and pick up customers. The clothing attire Brenda was wearing with bright flashy colors was great for fashion but poor for avoiding reconnaissance.

Terrshey Wate had well-trained eyes. Part of learning surveillance in the field included techniques used in circumstances such as now to allow tracking a suspect without being counter detected.

Evo Kaplan and Brenda Broyals departed the passenger-loading zone of the Cliff Side restaurant, on the tri-wheeler.

TERRSHEY WATE
Follow that tri-wheeler.

TRI-WHEELER DRIVER
Yes sir.

The driver was now all smiles as he had been racking up a lot of credits and not wasting a lot of fuel. This was going to end up being one of his better days in a very long time.

Brenda had good eyes laser trimmed to allow her to see great precision at a longer distance. Where someone could see a lot of detail at one-quarter mile, Brenda could see the same resolution at one half mile.

The Tri-wheeler was moving along at regulated traffic speed. Brenda figured it was probably up to five miles to the museum and knew they had to slow down a bit to allow a potential trailer to get closer so she could definitively make it out. The odds that a random Tri-wheeler would follow them to the museum going a route that probably included several turns was unlikely unless they were doing surveillance. Without explaining to Evo because she didn't want to alarm him, she asked Evo to give the driver specific instructions.

BRENDA BROYALS
Could you please ask the driver to slow down a bit so I can do better sight-seeing?

EVO KAPLAN
Sure.

The tri-wheeler then slowed, and the driver of the following tri-wheeler had no specific orders to maintain a distance to the vehicle ahead of him, nor did Terrshey Wate realize his target had slowed until it was too late. He had clearly pulled close enough where Brenda's above average eyesight could see enough detail to figure out who was back there. It was the man from the swimming pool.

Brenda was now not quite at red alert, but she calmly initiated her spy protocols knowing someone was specifically interested in them. It was either one of Egor Pataslia's men or it was the enemy.

In the spy business, when you have a fifty-fifty coin toss, you always bet on the worst case scenario but hope for the best.

In a short distance the Tri-wheeler made a turn and appeared to be heading toward some high-rise buildings ahead, which was most likely the city center. Brenda knew in due time the second Tri-wheeler would change direction; it was a slam dunk they were being followed. The only part of the mystery they didn't know was who it was.

In a few more blocks the tri-wheeler turned again and drove down a few more blocks and had to stop at a red light. This was perfect. It forced the compression of distance furthermore. It also would force Terrshey Wate to either direct his driver to keep going past them when they turned momentarily or to also make that turn. Terrshey Wate was too complacent and having asked the tri-wheeler driver to follow the other tri-wheeler, he did not bark new orders until it was too late, and the driver made the turn following them to the passenger-loading zone at the Quanqiu Museum.

Realizing he just screwed up, Terrshey Wate directed the Tri-wheeler driver to drive on past the couple now getting out of the Tri-wheeler and approaching the Quanqiu Museum.

Brenda didn't have to turn and face the trailer. She could see it out of the corner of her eye and hear it as it drove past. She purposely looked straight forward to convey to the trailer she didn't detect him. In the spy business it's always best not to acknowledge the presence of someone trailing you because the unknown always works out in your favor.

Terrshey Wate watched the couple enter the building as they were getting further away and then told the driver to make a U-turn and go back to the museum. There he made his most fatal blunder in stopping and getting out and going into the Quanqiu Museum, telling the driver to come back in about twenty minutes to pick him up. Terrshey Wate would get a close-up of the two, then depart.

But in doing so he also would give Brenda an opportunity to get a close view of the spy Terrshey Wate, and as she was far too sophisticated to give any body language reaction to the presence of the other spy, she disarmed him. He was playing a dangerous game and just lost.

Brenda checkmated Terrshey Wate on the spot.

Curiosity killed the cat.

*Now who was the cat and who was the mouse?* Brenda Broyals felt good to have her laser pistol with her in the event something awful went down, but she realized that more than likely this person would most likely not take any paramilitary or clandestine assassin like action in public if he were the enemy.

Brenda thought, this person is probably not a Revolutionary following us because the trailing had become far too tight. *Friendlies would have radioed in backup and passed us off to another team and not get exposed like this man.* He had to trail us tight since he had no backup, which means this guy has to be a Dranzonian Empire Secret Service agent.

VOICE OVER (FEMALE)

Chills suddenly went up Brenda's spine. Why would they travel deep behind enemy territory? *They are probably here to kill Evo Kaplan. They must consider him a traitor and he probably knew too many active agents he could identify, as well as somewhat recent methods and sources, since he was only discharged from the Secret Service less than a year ago.*

Brenda would have to set a trap for these guys without tipping off Evo Kaplan. If he knew what was going through her mind, he would not act naturally. Part of the guise in defeating this group of hit men was to give the appearance nobody knew they were here and what they planned on doing.

Brenda had the ace, though she wished she could inform Egor Pataslia. She might need his help. She had Egor Pataslia's business token in her purse. She could not make that call in front of Evo without alarming him. She would have to wait until they got back to the bungalow and send Evo away for a while when she did.

Walking through the Quanqiu Museum, one could easily think it was a combination of the Louvre in Paris including ten-foot-tall paintings, the Hermitage in St. Petersburg glamorous furnishings and artwork, and the Smithsonian's array of contemporary exhibits. Brenda, being a little fussy internally about the whimsical request Evo made, suddenly was glad he picked this opportunity, as the same feelings and mental stimulation she felt at the Dewaltracen Gallery now affected her psyche in a similar fashion.

Brenda Broyals realized that, in all honesty, had she never met Evo Kaplan and had the experiences with him, she never on her own accord would have entertained a trip to this planet and seen these best kept secrets of the Empire.

Brenda Broyals and Evo Kaplan walked along as a couple would, communicating and sharing and enjoying each other's company. Because of some evocative statements between the two, great affection poured out and Brenda could not restrain herself and embraced Evo. It was a tender moment and the tendrils of love passed between them in this auspicious moment. Terrshey Wate, observing from a distance at the other end of a lengthy hallway sporting groups of ten-foot-tall oil paintings, detected the emotional bonding and made a mental note, *Evo Kaplan is deeply involved with Brenda Broyals, the enemy.*

VOICE OVER (MALE)

Terrshey Wate confirmed Brenda Broyals' identity, one of the most sought-after spies in the Revolution. Their orders were to bring Evo Kaplan back or sanction him. Now it appeared they would soon be in position to hit them both, taking out significant capability. On missions of this nature, they were to carry out their primary orders. However, if they were ever put in a position to strike a target of opportunity and inflict more collateral damage without being caught, they would.

Neither Terrshey Wate nor Reginald Heiqishi wanted to be the next spies sent to the swimming pool or the crematorium. This had to be a carefully coordinated attack to be conducted just prior to their exit flight back to Zanziltar. Terrshey Wate also knew neither one of them would be safe until they made it all the way back to Praxisvlasia. It was moments like this in the spy business that separated the neophytes from the Pros from Dover, who could extemporize and manifest a maneuver such as this and swim in an ocean of sharks without being eaten alive!

Terrshey Wate had seen enough. It was time to go, as his tri-wheeler was most likely outside now waiting. His most important task now was to get back to the resort and make the report to Reginald Heiqishi and start thinking about how they would go about the attempt to whack them both at the same time without getting caught.

Terrshey Wate left the Quanqiu Museum entrance and as predicted his tri-wheeler was in the loading zone, and it appeared a museum employee was compelling the driver to move his vehicle as Terrshey arrived just in time.

In a few minutes Terrshey was back at the Lantiane Resort and first went by the pool to see if Reginald Heiqishi was there before he went up to the room. As Terrshey Wate walked out the Lantiane Resort entrance facing the pool, he quickly spotted Reginald Heiqishi sitting in his swim trunks surrounded by three Barracuda who had seemingly shifted their focus to this semi-attractive man.

VOICE OVER

Terrshey Wate waited over in a shaded area for Reginald Heiqishi to make eye contact with him. The semaphore was a slight head shake left, which meant *meet you up in the room as soon as possible to discuss my surveillance.* A nod up and down would mean: *Nothing to report, enjoy yourself.* Reginald Heiqishi acknowledges the semaphore by scratching his head. In an emergency such as *we are being observed by the enemy,* Reginald Heiqishi would pick his nose.

Otherwise, he would disengage in whatever he was doing and make his way up to the hotel room for consultations.

Their portable communicators also had bug sniffers in them. Not knowing who possibly could have entered their room posing as hotel staff and cleaners, Terrshey Wate went up to the room and immediately did a bug sniff.

If there were any hits on it at all, he would simply say, "Let's take a walk on the beach," where they knew they had total privacy. Terrshey Wate walked around the room looking at his personal communicator sniffing all around. It was more difficult finding hidden video equipment, but his device would locate them as well, it just took longer.

By the time Reginald Heiqishi arrived at the resort room, the bug-sniffing and video locator checks were complete, and they could conduct business. However, they would say the least amount of work-related information and talk in a code-like fashion to prevent any advertent dissemination of their espionage information.

TERRSHEY WATE
Confirmed that lover boy is fully immersed in a relationship with the bitch.

Names were avoided, as they knew who they were talking about. Loverboy was their code word for Evo Kaplan. Bitch was the code word for Brenda Broyals.

REGINALD HEIQISHI

Yeah, I expect that.

TERRSHEY WATE

The Bitch is definitely in heat.

That was all Reginald Heiqishi needed to know. Evo Kaplan was sleeping with the enemy and Terrshey Wate had confirmed it was indeed the famed Brenda Broyals. This called for a major discussion they could not hold in the room for fear of compromise in case a hidden device was not found by the hand scanning.

REGINALD HEIQISHI
Let's go for a walk on the beach.

TERRSHEY WATE
Sure.

The men then exited the room and went down to the beach without getting spotted by the three Barracudas. Two of the three were not bad looking, but Reginald Heiqishi would never intend on taking any of them home to meet his mother! Out on the beach they began their strategic planning.

TERRSHEY WATE

We need to catch them and take them both out together.

REGINALD HEIQISHI

Our orders only pertain to Evo Kaplan. We don't want to screw that up by going after more than we should on this mission.

TERRSHEY WATE

If we can knock off Brenda Broyals at the same time, that will be a huge INTEL victory.

REGINALD HEIQISHI

Yes, but it's not essential or part of our planning.

TERRSHEY WATE

You of all people know we received the briefings to attempt sanction on any high-ranking Revolution Security Service member if the opportunity became possible. We will not be completing the intent of our guidelines if we fail to act on this additional target of opportunity.

REGINALD HEIQISHI

The Revolutionaries would not be quite as upset if we just sanction Evo Kaplan.

TERRSHEY WATE

Why the reluctance of killing Brenda Broyals?

REGINALD HEIQISHI

If we also take out a high-ranking official such as Brenda Broyals, we could force them to raise their *dander* a notch or two, possibly making it difficult to get off this planet alive.

Terrshey Wate knew Reginald Heiqishi was in tactical control of this mission as the onsite authority. He also knew Reginald Heiqishi could be a prick at times and might have a negative input on his fitness report if he tried to argue the case. But deep in his heart he knew taking out Brenda Broyals was probably a much bigger prize than Evo Kaplan, who was only being sanctioned over the threat of doing damage to the Empire.

Brenda Broyals had done damage to the Empire when she helped with the initial surprise attack that triggered the war and the incredible amount of damage the Revolution did to the Empire.

Terrshey Wate was mildly disgusted that Reginald Heiqishi was being a chickenshit and scared to go after the main prize. They would both get a serious promotion if they took out Brenda Broyals and made it back alive.

To Reginald Heiqishi the risk was well worth the reward, but it also would also place him in the history data cubes.

REGINALD HEIQISHI
Okay, I'm going back to the pool now. Continue your surveillance on our target. The plan we came up with is still in effect. We will do that on our last day and fly out of here immediately afterward.

The current plan subject to change based on developing awareness in-situ centered around employing Sheri to lure Evo Kaplan into the kill zone. They, of course, could not leave any witnesses behind. Sheri's betrayal would also cost her own life.

Moments later after the men separated and went in their own directions, Reginald Heiqishi was proceeding back at the pool and the center of attraction of the three Barracudas who were holding a peace conference over who got to get their digs into this man first.

THEOLONABATRESS VON SURRET<br>(A.K.A MONICA)
Glacy, you can have first shot at this guy, but I get first dibs on Proctor Pugong.

The third Barracuda Sparkles felt slightly rejected. knew that based on past experiences unless she lost some weight and got a good makeover, she would never be able to compete, and thus went along with the game plan in her somber yet very disappointed manner, knowing she was once again missing out.

Sparkles days of taking the leftovers had to end!

By the time Reginald Heiqishi made it back to his former reclining chair, the women were in full aggreement and ready for the next move. As a team they would help manifest and arrange Glancy's lover's tryst with Blane Jiandie (a.k.a. Reginald Heiqishi.).

Just like the rumors had floated around and Evo Kaplan had made jokes about that got him into serious trouble with Reginald Heiqishi, his subordinate Terrshey Wate was out working his ass off on surveillance while Reginald Heiqishi enjoyed the attention of the ladies, who seemed to be creating a scenario that played right into his motives.

It didn't take long for the Barracuda Glacy to coax Blane Jiandie (a.k.a. Reginald Heiqishi) up to her penthouse suite, which included a butler and a maid, to look at her butterfly collection. After Glacy and Blane Jiandie were gone the other two women couldn't help but giggle at the butterfly line, which she had used numerous times, but it got the job done.

Reginald Heiqishi wasn't quite used to such exquisitely extravagant furnishings that would even make Napoleon blush. The woman asked the butler to make Reginald Heiqishi a drink while she changed her clothes. The maid and the butler were her personal staff she traveled with from Sanctuary City.

With exclusively. They were also both experts in martial arts and provided her security. They knew her husband well and knew he was off to the "Orgy Planet" and started this whole persona by leaving the woman shamefully neglected. His only reason for not divorcing was a wealthy man of his stature could not afford the public personification that such proceedings might generate.

In a few minutes when Glacy came out of her dressing room in a very sexy negligee that covered little and exposed practically everything, the drugs she knew her butler would put in Reginald Heiqishi's drink was like ten shots of Viagra. There were also sexual arousal and stimulation drugs in a highly concentrated dosage perfected for her purposes.

Glacy knew not to pursue matters until Blane Jiandie had downed most of the drink. She was a patient woman, and the wait was worth it, for her own drugs would slowly take affect and soon the two ragingly horny people would be mating that could last upwards to several hours.

As if on cue Glacy informed the butler and the maid they were dismissed. They took their leave and walked down a long hallway the five thousand square foot penthouse could afford. Right after the last door closed and they were alone, Glacy could see Blane Jiandie had downed most of his drink and the effects would be momentarily.

GLACY<br>
Come Blane, let me show you my butterfly collection.

Glacy smiled and held out her hand.

Reginald Heiqishi was more than ready, not realizing he had been drugged and lubricated for this moment and took her hand and waltzed into her bedroom with Glacy.

Glacy closed the door and turned the dead bolt, giving them complete privacy. She turned around facing Reginald Heiqishi and with just undoing one button allowed her extremely sexy and alluring negligee to drop to the floor, then approached Reginald Heiqishi and began to help him disrobe.

Moments later they were going at it. Reginald, totally engulfed in the narcotic effects of the concoctions he just ingested, was in a state of mind he had never experienced before. He had no reason to think or understand why this woman turned him on so much. His lust was tremendous, his passion was exploding, and his cognitive control was quickly short circuited by the chemical equilibrium along with the pheromone explosion from her extremely expensive perfume that made Glacy smell better than any woman he had ever been with.

Glacy's numerous cosmetic surgeries rendered her looking twenty years younger than her real age. In a way Glacy was helping Brenda because Reginald Heiqishi would now be distracted for the remainder of the mission, as his little head was doing all his thinking instead of his big head.

Glacy received gratification repeatedly as Reginald Heiqishi's body was not used to the drugs and responded as well as could be expected by the design of them. For the first time in his life Reginald Heiqishi had been seduced and used like a cheap whore.

The shoe was now on the other foot as Glacy was in the driver's seat and knew that she would enjoy this man for the remainder of his vacation, and probably by then she would be looking for her next victim.

Terrshey Wate lost surveillance on Evo Kaplan when he returned to the Lantiane Resort. If he tried going back to the Quanqiu Museum he would most likely discover Evo Kaplan and Brenda Broyals were already gone, or risk running directly into them and creating more exposure to physical appearance.

If Terrshey Wate kept popping up into their view, they might equate him with espionage and look deeper into who he was. Therefore, he went to the pool and found a nicely cushioned reclining chair and sat down with some reading material.

With Glacy already preoccupied, the other two Barracudas eyeballed Terrshey Wate. Since one of them already planned to manifest a soiree with Proctor Pugong, she left this big fish for her friend to catch.

MONICA (BARRACUDA #1)
You should go over there and introduce yourself.


SPARKLES (BARRACUDA #3)
Do you think he would want to be with a woman like me? He
certainly appears quite a bit younger.


MONICA (Barracuda #1)
He probably likes the Cougars. You need to go find out.


This third female Barracuda the others nicknamed *Sparkles* because she was the richest in the group and always wore more elaborate jewelry and sparkled all the time. Her only problem was pushing herself away from the dinner table too late and was packing quite a few more pounds than what men ideally sought in women, so she thought.

Terrshey Wate was more of a curves man. He loved curvy women. Women that starved themselves to look one hundred twenty pounds didn't give Terrshey Wate much enthusiasm, as he wasn't in the crowd of men who liked women with anorexic builds. Skinny women turned him off.

In a while Barracuda number one Monica convinced Barracuda number three Sparkles to approach the man.

With sheer reluctance Sparkles stood up and walked toward Terrshey Wate, who was more interested in surveillance on Evo Kaplan and Brenda Broyals. The woman was nothing more than a distraction to him, which he didn't care at the time because in his reclining chair he had a full panoramic view of all the access ways to the bungalows.

When Evo Kaplan and Brenda Broyals returned, they would have to walk directly in Terrshey Wate's view. He would note the time and their disposition and be poised to follow them again in case they had a pattern they could exploit.

The pool was semi-empty. There were a lot of people off doing other things, taking tours, and seeing the sights. One could almost have a private conversation now due to the lack of people.

Terrshey Wate acted like he was consuming his reading materials. In reality. the reading materials were nothing more than a prop. There was very little reading comprehension going on and Terrshey Wate seldom turned pages.


SPARKLES
Hello, how are you doing, sir?

Sparkles broke Terrshey Wate's concentration for a few minutes. She bent over and held out her hand in a greeting. She was exposing a lot of cleavage, which Terrshey always enjoyed as he fantasized about what else was available.

TERRSHEY WATE
I'm doing okay, thank you.

SPARKLES
May I join you?

TERRSHEY WATE
I don't see why not.

The woman sat down on the reclining chair next to him, which was a good position because if Terrshey Wate turned to talk to her, he would still catch Evo Kaplan in his peripheral vision should he walk past.

SPARKLES
I'm Sparkles.

TERRSHEY WATE
Is that your real name?

SPARKLES
It's the name I go by. All my friends call me Sparkles.

TERRSHEY WATE
Okay.

SPARKLES
What's your name?

This mission sprung so quickly the Dranzonian Empire Secret Service didn't have enough time to give Terrshey Wate a fake identity. Since he became an agent after the Revolution started, it was felt the Revolutionaries did not have any identifying information on Terrshey Wate, so for this mission he would keep his current identity and change it after they returned.

TERRSHEY WATE
I'm Terrshey Wate.

SPARKLES
I'm pleased to meet you Terrshey Wate.

                           TERRSHEY WATE
                              Likewise.


                              SPARKLES
                     Are you enjoying your vacation?


                           TERRSHEY WATE
                             Definitely.


                              SPARKLES
                       Did you come with someone?


                           TERRSHEY WATE
                     Yes, my buddy, Blane Jiandie.


Terrshey Wate looked a lot like Chin Wanpi, who was Chuo Wanpi's brother the
Revolution had assassinated.

Sparkles thought Terrshey Wate appeared a lot like someone she recently read
about in the news as word circulated that Chuo Wanpi had been assassinated.

That odd physical appearance gave the woman slightly more attraction to his
partner Blane Jiandie than she might otherwise had. She had watched the pro
Glacy seduce his partner Blane Jiandie with her Butterfly Collection. She knew
she couldn't outright lie like that, but she had another idea. She did have one
hell of a gem collection with her, as she had more expensive precious gems and
jewelry that any other woman at the Lantiane Resort.

That would be her line: show him her gem collection.

The fact Sparkles lived on the very top penthouse with the best view didn't hurt
either. Her husband was currently away on a business trip and her own well-paid
spies gave her daily reports of the man carrying on with his mistress, which upset
her more and led to her eating more than she should and putting on the extra
weight.

Sparkles noticed the woman at the massage parlor had a makeover that was
spectacular. Perhaps she should try that too?


                              SPARKLES
                       Are you reading a book?


                           TERRSHEY WATE
              Yes, I'm reading it for inspiration and to expand my mind.

SPARKLES
Interesting. Will you be here long at the pool today?

TERRSHEY WATE
Probably another hour or two reading my book.

SPARKLES
Good. I'm going to go get a massage. If you are here when I get
back, I would like to take you to an exclusive  restaurant, which
is invitation only.

TERRSHEY WATE
I suppose I could go.

In two hours, it would be Reginald Heiqishi's shift to maintain all possible
surveillance on Evo Kaplan.

SPARKLES
Hope to see you soon.

TERRSHEY WATE
All right.

Sparkles stood up and went directly to the massage room and arranged for a
private massage. She asked for Bristol, who made that woman look glamorous
yesterday. Sparkles then informed Bristol what she wanted.

I want you to give me a makeover just like you did that beautiful woman yesterday
morning.

BRISTOL (MASSEUSE)
I will try my best.

SPARKLES
That's all I can ask of you.

Sparkles went to work and thought now would be the time to try a new drug on
the woman that was designed for such a purpose.

BRISTOL (MASSEUSE)
Sparkles, if you agree to the injections, we can make it appear
like you lost fifteen pounds, and this condition will remain for
at least twelve hours and most likely the rest of the day.

SPARKLES
Any side effects or mixing with other substances dangerous?

BRISTOL (MASSEUSE)
No, if you take sexual enhancers, it has no effect.

That made Sparkles' Day, as she wanted both worlds: to instantly look better at the same time be poised to enjoy her new love toy to the fullest.

Just like Sparkles promised, by the time the fashion designer arrived the drugs had done their magic, giving the appearance of fat shrinking. She did have to use the bathroom a couple times, because as the fat cells ejected half their contents it flushed out of her body. Unfortunately, the fat cells were still alive and would be rejuvenated after time and a few good meals.

Bristol informed the fashion designer Inchalchary of the injections and treatments.

BRISTOL (MASSEUSE)
I gave Sparkles an injection of Chaofei Jiansuji.

The fashion designer then cautioned Sparkles.

INCHALCHARY
I will fit you and make you look beautiful, but you must be out of these clothes in about twelve hours before the effect of the drug wears off. Otherwise, I will be forced to cut these clothes off you since you will not be able to remove them.

SPARKLES
Not a problem. If I don't make the deadline, I'll just buy the clothes outright.

INCHALCHARY
That's your prerogative, madam, and these clothes are available for your purchase.

Inchalchary was quite aware that Sparkles was a super-rich woman could buy the clothes without blinking an eye. But her biggest surprise would be the following day and it would be painful to cut them off if Sparkles didn't heed the advice.

One hour to the mark, Sparkles was finished. The staff at the Lantiane Resort had done their magic just like they did with Brenda. The woman had gone through a metamorphism like few others. When she looked in the mirror she almost started crying, and Bristol caught her fast enough to warn her.

BRISTOL (MASSEUSE)
Sparkles, if you cry, you will screw up your makeup and it will
take another half an hour to fix it. Please restrain yourself.

It worked and Sparkles barely maintained her composure, but she did and as
she marched proudly out of the massage rooms in her new identity, it was quite
clear she had an appeal to her. Makeup, drugs, and of course the massage totally
revamped her spirits and set her on a new pathway to enlightenment.

When Sparkles approached the pool, Monica (a.k.a. Theolonabatress von Surret)
didn't even know who the hell she was!

SPARKLES
Hello Monica.

Monica was the name given to her by the other two women who got tired of
saying Theolonabatress. The voice had not changed and without the voice Monica
would have taken a while to figure it out.

MONICA
Sparkles, what happened to you?

SPARKLES
I decided I would clean up a bit to go out to dinner with that
gentleman.

MONICA
Dang, you are pretty. Wow!

SPARKLES
Bristol and Inchalchary did such a superb effort in preparing me
during the massage.

MONICA
No kidding. It's fabulous. I'm impressed.

SPARKLES
Okay, I need to go talk with my new friend. Wish me luck!

MONICA
As beautiful as you are now, you do not need luck!

Monica was so happy Sparkles had blossomed so much. This was one of her
happiest days at the Lantiane Resort watching her friend transform by almost a

miracle. Now if only she was able to complete the task at hand and seduce the fine young gentleman, she would earn the Cougar of The Year Award.

Sparkles approached Terrshey Wate, who at first did not recognize her.

SPARKLES
Hello again.

Terrshey Wate looked up at the woman standing there, who had a beautiful appearance. Her fashion designer clothed her in a way to accentuate the best part of her body, which happened to be her boobs, and scaled down the part that was in obvious need of maintenance, her rear end.

The genius of the designer was apparent, as the outcome was unexpected and quite extraordinary. A plain Jane, older woman just went back twenty years in time and now had a luster that gave Terrshey Wate a quite satisfying account, since he knew this woman had approached him, which at a resort usually signified they wanted some kind of action.

SPARKLES
Are you ready to go?

TERRSHEY WATE
Just about, but I do need to take care of a few personal items first.

SPARKLES
Okay.

Shortly afterward up in Glacy's penthouse, Reginald Heiqishi, who appeared like he had been ridden hard and put away wet, begged forgiveness.

REGINALD HEIQISHI (a.k.a. Blane Jiandie)

I must go meet with my friend, but I'll meet you down at the Resort Bar and Restaurant by the pool in about an hour.

Glacy was fully satisfied. Her gratification tipped the scales. She no longer needed Blane Jiandie for her lust and desires but wouldn't mind the company.

GLACY (Barracuda #2)
Sure, I'll meet you down there.

Reginald Heiqishi (a.k.a. Blane Jiandie) made his way down to the beach entrance to the Lantiane Resort and walked at a spot where he knew Terrshey Wate would see him give their secret semaphore. No meeting was required, but Terrshey Wate needed to get up to his room and change his clothes.

TERRSHEY WATE

I need to go up to my room and change my clothes. I'll be back in a short while if you are still interested in going somewhere.

Sparkles, now enthused about her new conquest, was more than happy to wait.

SPARKLES
Sure, I'll wait here for you. I'm going to go talk with my friend
while you are gone.

TERRSHEY WATE
All right. See you soon.

By the time Terrshey Wate left the pool, Reginald Heiqishi was already showering and changing into his evening clothes, as he was due to take over the stakeout and glean information that would help them figure out the best way to either convince Evo Kaplan to go back to Praxisvlasia or, if necessary, terminate him.

Terrshey Wate arrived just about the time Reginald Heiqishi was ready to leave the resort room.

REGINALD HEIQISHI
Is everything going, okay?

TERRSHEY WATE
Yes, I followed them to a restaurant and to the museum but was
not able to regain contact with them again until a short while
ago when they went to their bungalow after a day out on the
town.

REGINALD HEIQISHI
They are probably going to get cleaned up for enjoying a night
out on the town.

TERRSHEY WATE
I suppose so.

REGINALD HEIQISHI
I'll be down at the bar waiting for them.

TERRSHEY WATE
I'm going out with that woman from the pool to a restaurant she
wants to take me to.

                    REGINALD HEIQISHI
                 Okay, stay safe and good luck.

                      TERRSHEY WATE
                        Certainly.

Reginald Heiqishi then left the room and went back down and to the bar restaurant, which was slightly early and still happy hour, but he wanted a good seat where he could observe Evo Kaplan's coming and going.

CRUISING AND REMEMBRANCES

The band was performing, and Reginald Heiqishi ordered a drink. As he was keeping an eye out for Evo Kaplan, the band came up at break time and Sheri came over to talk with him since the place was empty and the other customers were unknown and ones she had never seen before.

                    REGINALD HEIQISHI
                 Hello, how have you been?

                         SHERI
                   Doing fine, thank you.

                    REGINALD HEIQISHI
              Did you hook up with your lover boy today?

                         SHERI
                 No, but I certainly wanted to.

<u>INT. EVENING. LANTIANE RESORT BUNGALO ROOM</u>

Evo Kaplan had dressed, and Brenda Broyals was taking a lot of time. He knew this might take a while.

                       EVO KAPLAN
        I'm going over to the bar by the pool and have a drink. Come
        over there when you are ready.

                     BRENDA BROYALS
                     Okay, sweetheart.

Those words caught Evo Kaplan by surprise. He had an emotional bond to Brenda, but she had never uttered such words like *sweetheart* before. *Perhaps this means we are at a new level in our relationship*?

On his way out, Evo grabbed a couple more brochures to read through at the bar for tomorrow's plans.

INT. EVENING. LANTIANE RESORT BEACH RESTAURANT AND BAR

The timing was good because the band was taking a break and he arrived halfway through it and found his usual table, where he had an unobstructed view of them. As soon as he sat down, the waitress was there to take his order. Sheri smiled at Reginald Heiqishi, then walked over to Evo Kaplan.

SHERI
May I join you?

EVO KAPLAN
Sure, have a seat.

Sheri's attire was more revealing tonight, and her top didn't do a very good job of hiding her breasts. Evo could not help but notice the glaring deficiency. Where he came from, she would not have been allowed to perform in a bar so thinly covered. But it did add to the allure. Evo had the brochures out on the table and one in particular was a two-day cruise along the coast.

SHERI
Are you getting ready to take a trip?

EVO KAPLAN
Yeah, I'm thinking about taking this cruise tomorrow.

SHERI
Can I go along?

EVO KAPLAN
I would sure like you to tag along, but I doubt my girlfriend would allow us to spend any time together.

SHERI
The story of my life. I always miss out on the good guys.

EVO KAPLAN
You will find a good guy one of these days.

SHERI
How about dumping your girlfriend and take me!

EVO KAPLAN
I can't do that. I might have fallen in love with her.

About that time the drummer in the band made a few noises that gave Sheri the message to get back up on the short stage.

SHERI
I'm sorry, I must go back to work. Perhaps we can have a secret rendezvous before you leave *Shen de Huayuan*.

Evo just smiled. He knew either a positive or negative response would get him into trouble.

Reginald Heiqishi heard what he needed to hear. Evo Kaplan would be going on that cruise tomorrow. Lantiane Resort patrons had priority on cruise bookings because the resort paid out big credits to keep their clientele happy.

This was the perfect setup. They would talk to Evo Kaplan on the ship and if he gave a negative response, they would throw him overboard. They would then take an Intergalactic Passenger Transport  Spaceship back to Zanziltar the next day, either with Evo Kaplan in tow or without him because he fell overboard.

When they got on the ship, the first order of battle would be to find blind spots in the security monitoring system where they could do the dirty work if required and not be spotted.

<u>INT. EVENING. LANTIANE RESORT BUNGALO ROOM</u>

While Evo Kaplan was out, Brenda couldn't make herself look attractive in her mind, so she called guest services and told them her problem. They promptly sent a makeup artist, hairdresser, and the fashion designer, Inchalchary, who had a helper bring her cart to the bungalow with a dozen garments she thought would make Brenda attractive.

Brenda knew she was stressing Evo Kaplan by making him wait at the bar. But it wouldn't be the first or the last time he had to wait for results if he wanted to go out with a pretty girl.

Brenda had also looked at some brochures and discovered *Shen de Huayuan* had several dance halls that had professional dancers performing and teaching but also dancing for the public. Dinner and drinks were provided at the venue. It sounded like a lot of fun, like she hadn't done since she was a lot younger.

Inchalchary knowing the venue and type of entertainment they would ostensibly participate in, her fashion designer expertise understood which local fashions would accentuate her ability to radiate her beauty.

Inchalchary therefore suggested one of the three dresses of that type included with all the garments she brought, plus shoes that would lend themselves to dancing.

Brenda explained the situation that Evo was waiting at the bar, and it didn't have to be perfect, but it had to be quick.

The team worked with what they had. There was no time to shampoo the hair and prepare it for the design work, but that was okay. The hair designer had a special hair spray that was a neutrality benefactor, allowing the hair to assume a neutral lay where she could then apply her magic and mold it into something beautiful and unforgettable.

Likewise, the makeup artist had some interesting products. She took swipes all over Brenda's face, getting off all dirt, debris, and any accumulation of previous makeup. With the clean skin, it was much easier for the new materials to adhere to.

The fantastic team, working like Indy Racers pit crew, hit their target. Brenda, now dressed to "wowzah" Evo Kaplan.

BRENDA BROYALS

I think this dress was a little on the short side. While I'm dancing strangers might see more than they should.

Inchalchary explained to Brenda.

INCHALCHARY

If some stranger sees your panties a time or two, it makes no difference. You will probably never see that person again, especially since you live on another planet. But if you want to turn on your boyfriend while you are dancing, let it show. You will be rewarded for your artwork.

BRENDA BROYALS

I suddenly feel more confident with your inside knowledge, and I do appreciate you Inchalchary for schooling me on dress dynamics in how to influence my lover.

INCHALCHARY

My pleasure Brenda, and you do look beautiful tonight.

Brenda Broyals left the Bungalow exit exactly in thirty minutes.

<u>INT. EVENING. LANTIANE RESORT BEACH RESTAURANT AND BAR</u>

One thing that was perfectly clear: Brenda Broyals had stressed Evo by taking so much time to get ready, the band had performed a set and Sheri was back at his table like a lap dog wanting to be petted.

Reginald Heiqishi had not seen Brenda Broyals in almost five years before her treachery, and certainly not this close. He was astonished: she looked younger! And now he could see why Evo Kaplan had interest in her.

C.U. REGINALD HEIQISHI DURING VOICE OVER

VOICE OVER
(Reginald Heiqishi)
Brenda Broyals dress is so short it almost shows off her ass and exemplified the notion of perfect legs. The geometry was quite compelling.

Evo Kaplan was suddenly glad he waited for the extra time. Brenda made it all worthwhile.

Sheri, on the other hand, felt slightly bewildered because this put the nail in the coffin on her ever being able to entice Proctor Pugong to ever make an assertive move on her.

BRENDA BROYALS
Are you ready to go?

EVO KAPLAN
Yes, more than ready.

Evo Kaplan stood up smiling at Brenda Broyals, liking her fashion statement as well and were soon out of the bar and a distance away.

EVO KAPLAN
Did you decide where you want to go?

BRENDA BROYALS
Yes, I would like to go try out the *Banma Julebu.*

EVO KAPLAN
All right.

Evo Kaplan barely looked like he fit with his date, but it was too late for him to call guest services for a male makeover. He would have to go with what he had on. Plus, in another week or so these people would never see him again, so it really didn't matter.

As they approached the customer-loading zone, the resort limo coordinator saw the gorgeous lady with the gentleman and knew they had to go in a nice car to wherever they were going and told the driver of the parked limo at the loading zone,

LIMO COORDINATOR
Take these passengers.

The driver nodded, walked over, and opened the right-side passenger door, and gestured to Evo and Brenda to get in, which they did. As they were driving off, the driver up front inquired.

LIMO DRIVER
Where may I take you tonight?

BRENDA BROYALS
We want to go to *Banma Julebu.* Do you think that's a good place to go?

LIMO DRIVER
Yes madam, it is perhaps the most exciting nightclub in the city. Being that the *Banma Julebu* is on the top of the building, you can see a long distance and all the city lights.

BRENDA BROYALS
How is the food served there?

LIMO DRIVER
*Banma Julebu* is hailed as one of the best restaurants in town and most of the best-looking women like going there to meet dates because a lot of Zanziltar businessmen like visiting there.

BRENDA BROYALS
Do any tourists from elsewhere go there?

LIMO DRIVER
Yes, and the flight crews for all the Intergalactic Passenger Transport companies stay in hotels in and around that building.

Brenda gave Evo a funny look which conveyed, *don't get out of line with any of the young honeys.* In a short period of time the limo pulled up to the passenger-loading zone in front of the very tall building where Banma Julebu existed on the top floor.

A security man dressed in a tuxedo-like suit opened the door and Brenda got out first. The man had seen a lot of legs in his time and noted this pair was very nice-looking as he cracked a sneak peek. Then he quickly walked around to the other side and opened Evo's door.

The two went into the building entrance and to the elevators. As expected, there was a small crowd forming, but the elevators were large enough to take most of them. Brenda got some looks in the elevator. The limo driver drove back to the resort and as soon as he pulled over, a man appeared.

REGINALD HEIQISHI

I saw you take my friends off to a nightclub. In a bit I'm going to take my girlfriend there after she gets ready, and I want you to take us there.

LIMO DRIVER

Sure, no problem. I took them to the *Banma Julebu*. But you had better go soon or it will be too crowded to get in.

REGINALD HEIQISHI
Can guest services reserve me a table?

LIMO DRIVER

I'm not sure. It's getting late for reservations, but there is a guest services phone right over at the podium.

The man pointed to about twenty feet away.

Reginald Heiqishi walked over and grabbed the phone, which automatically rang guest services.

GUEST SERVICES
How, may I help you?

BLANE JIANDIE (a.k.a REGINALD HEIQISHI)

Yes, I'm Blane Jiandie, a guest here at the resort. I'm currently out front at the front entrance at the guest phone. Say, can you make me a reservation for a table at Banma Julebu?

GUEST SERVICES
I'm not sure. Let me put you on hold and see what I can do.

BLANE JIANDIE (a.k.a REGINALD HEIQISHI)
Sure.

Moments later guest services came back on the phone.

GUEST SERVICES
You are lucky they can make a reservation, but it's going to cost one hundred credits.

BLANE JIANDIE (a.k.a REGINALD HEIQISHI)
That's kind of expensive.

GUEST SERVICES
It is, but you should have made your reservation earlier; it gets tight about now. The restaurants are good at jacking up the prices for reservations this time of day.

BLANE JIANDIE (a.k.a REGINALD HEIQISHI)
I understand. I guess I don't have any choice. I have a hot date and she wants to go so badly.

GUEST SERVICES
Should I make the reservation for you?

BLANE JIANDIE (a.k.a REGINALD HEIQISHI)
Yes, charge it to my room.

GUEST SERVICES
One moment please.

BLANE JIANDIE (a.k.a REGINALD HEIQISHI)
Okay.

A moment later the guest service man confirmed the reservation.

GUEST SERVICES
Mr. Jiandie, you have reservations for one hour from now.

BLANE JIANDIE (a.k.a REGINALD HEIQISHI)
Fantastic.

GUEST SERVICES
Anything else we can help you with?

BLANE JIANDIE (a.k.a REGINALD HEIQISHI)

No, now all I need to do is round up my girlfriend and go. That hour gives me some flexibility for her to get ready.

GUEST SERVICES Have a nice evening.

BLANE JIANDIE (a.k.a REGINALD HEIQISHI)
Thank you.

Reginald Heiqishi hung up the phone and beat feet to the bar, hoping the Barracuda Glacy would quickly show.

INT. LANTIANE RESORT POOL RESTAURANT-BAR

Just like Brenda and Sparkles, Glacy wasn't ready to go out in public the way she was dressed when she met Blane Jiandie at the pool restaurant-bar.

Reginald Heiqishi could go the way he was dressed, which was gentlemanly like.

BLANE JIANDIE (a.k.a REGINALD HEIQISHI)
We are going to the Banma Julebu, I have reservations.

GLACY
I'm not dressed to go to that place.

BLANE JIANDIE (a.k.a REGINALD HEIQISHI)
Could you go to your room and change into something you would feel comfortable wearing there?

GLACY
Yes, but it will take a little while.

BLANE JIANDIE (a.k.a REGINALD HEIQISHI)
That's okay, our reservation is not for another hour.

GLACY
Okay dear, I'll go change.

Reginald Heiqishi was in over his head with Glacy the Barracuda. He didn't know he would be her boy toy for a while until she dumped him for someone else. But if her intergalactic banker husband ever found out about it, worrying about the Revolutionaries would be the last thing on Reginald Heiqishi's mind. He was now playing a double dangerous game and didn't know it.

INT. LANTIANE RESORT GLACY'S PENTOUHOUSE SUITE - EVENING

Glacy went back to her penthouse suite unexpectedly and the maid and the butler, thinking they might have a few hours alone, were almost in the pre-coitus state.

Had Glacy taken another five minutes to get there she would have caught them fully engaged in it and fired them both on the spot for violating her rules. Under no circumstances was the staff to do any hanky-panky anywhere near her residence.

PENTHOUSE MAID
Glacy, you are not going out tonight?

GLACY
Yes, I am, but I'm dressed horribly for the *Banma Julebu*. Call guest services and have them bring some couture for me to wear. I only have thirty to forty-five minutes to get dressed and out of here.

PENTHOUSE MAID
Right away, madam. Do you want nails and hair too?

GLACY
Sure, if they can get something done that quick.

PENTHOUSE MAID
I'm sure they can.

In five minutes Inchalchary the fashion designer along with a hairdresser, nails person, and makeup artist were at the door.

INCHALCHARY
We understand this is a rush job. We'll do the best we can.

GLACY
Thanks, I appreciate that.

While the staff was at work on Glacy's hair, makeup, and fingernails, the fashion designer Inchalchary showed her some of the couture that would work well for the *Banma Julebu*. A stunningly beautiful purple dress was on the rack she brought.

GLACY
I love the look of this one.

INCHALCHARY
In a minute you can try it on. The hairdresser and makeup person are almost done.

In a brief amount of time, she tried it on and looked in the mirror and saw how beautiful they had made her hair and makeup and knew on the spot she would have to give them a fabulous tip.

GLACY
What about my nails?


INCHALCHARY
Five more minutes, Madam. When she finishes your nails, we'll
put on the shoes for you we think you should wear so you can
dance in them.


At first Glacy was taken back but started thinking, Dancing might be fun tonight,
so high heels will not be good. Again, all in just one evening, Inchalchary had
pulled off the impossible with three highly strung women.


Even though the fashion designer Inchalchary had many bitter memories of
Madam Zraklevin who trained her, it was apparent to her that the only reason why
she could pull of these miracle transformations was the incredible job Madam
Zraklevin did while teaching her.


Now Inchalchary was starting to realize her slavery was nothing more than high
pressure conditioning for moments like this.


INT. *BANMA JULEBU* RESTAUANT NIGHT CLUB - EVENING


Most of Glacy's ordeals occurred while Evo Kaplan and Brenda were getting
settled in at the restaurant. It took some time for the elevator to get the heavy load
all the way up to the top of the building, where it opened into a lobby where a
Maître-d stood asking for reservations. Most of them did not have reservations.


BRENDA BROYALS
I have a reservation.


The Maître-d' looked at the sizzling lady.


MAÎTRE-D'
What is the name under, madam?


BRENDA BROYALS
Betty (a.k.a. Brenda Broyals).


MAÎTRE-D'
One moment please.


Looking down at the reservation, the Maître-d' saw it came from guest services at
Lantiane Resort. And yes, the first name was Brenda. He knew this was most likely

a very powerful and rich woman, not too different than many of the Barracuda and Cougars that roamed the premises late in the evening looking for action.

MAÎTRE-D'
Follow me please.

The rest of the people waiting were slightly taken back as one of the Bourgeoisie types just got ahead of the line privileges. This was deep in Revolution territory where sentiments still raged high, and if it were not for the fact the economy would crumble if Zanziltar businessmen were not here all the time spending like drunken sailors on Lavish and frequent vacations. The only ones that didn't come were off to places like "Orgy Island" with their political cronies and mistresses.

The red booths seemed to come from a different era. There was a stage in the very middle of the establishment and there was a live band currently playing dinner music. Brenda figured after dinner hours there would be the changing of the guard and a different type of music would sit in.

Brenda's reservation put them in an exclusive booth next to a huge glass window where they had an incredible unobstructed view. The ambience was compelling. The music wasn't bad for dinner music. The small orchestra performing apparently played local *Shen de Huayuan* classics that had a strange pleasantness to them. Brenda had never heard any of this music ever performed on the one hundred or more planets she had been on.

Evo Kaplan, in a similar manner, was foreign to the music as well, but appreciated it greatly. Going from penniless, broke, and hungry to this extravaganza had quite an uplifting to his personal psychology. Every man had his price.

Is a sexy woman like Brenda Broyals and the living standards that radically improved worth compromising his allegiance to his people, his planet, and his Empire? He didn't have confirmation the FIRM was the Revolution, but as time passed, Evo Kaplan couldn't help but guess that was the ultimate reason for being here: to give him an incentive to defect.

Was Brenda acting or was her physical and emotional drama legitimate? The multiple course meal and desserts were all designed around the palates of *Shen de Huayuan's* but also enjoyed by the Zanziltar business clientele who frequented the restaurant.

A good comparison between *Shen de Huayuan* verses Zanziltar and Planet earth would be like comparing British cooking with Italian or Chinese. The composition and techniques were extraordinarily different, all of which can be enjoyable to vast numbers of travelers. After the waiter cleared off the table after desserts.

                              WAITER
                   Are you staying for entertainment?


                         BRENDA BROYALS
                           Yes, definitely.


                              WAITER
         Would it be okay for me to close out your bill because it's the
         end of my shift?


                           EVO KAPLAN
                            Certainly.


              A few minutes later the waiter came up to them.


                              WAITER
         Your bill has been closed out and your new waiter will be
         arriving shortly to take your order for drink selections.


                         BRENDA BROYALS
                    How did my bill get closed out?


         See the elderly gentleman at the bar with the goatee beard?


         Brenda looked at the bar and saw no other than Egor Pataslia
         sitting there.


                              WAITER
                     He took care of everything.


         Brenda smiled at the waiter.


                         BRENDA BROYALS
            Could you please tell the gentleman, 'Thank You,' for me?


                              WAITER
                         Yes madam, I will.


The waiter walked over to the bar where twenty bar stools stood and were packed
with people, as well as others standing next to the bar, as the after-dinner crowd
coming in for dancing was slowly appearing. The waiter delivered the message
and at that time Egor Pataslia turned back and nodded at Brenda.


Brenda Broyals She would seek Egor Pataslia later and let him know they had
surveillance on them in case it wasn't one of his guys.

Brenda Broyals now had Egor Pataslia's communications token in her purse, she carried with her along with her laser pistol, but was reluctant to call him. This opportune moment was going to work out well. She was able to see if Egor Pataslia was in the process of leaving so she could catch him on the way out if necessary.


                              BRENDA BROYALS
                       What do you want to do tomorrow?


                               EVO KAPLAN
                  I was looking at brochures. Here's one on a cruise. Would you
                  like to go on it?


Brenda took the small brochure out of Evo's hand and scanned it. It had been a long time since she had been on any type of ship, and she had never taken a cruise with a lover. In fact, she had not had many lovers, as she could count them all on a couple fingers. All her previous lovers were dead, killed in the line of duty. The Revolution had taken its toll.

Evo Kaplan was the only person in over four years Brenda Broyals opened her heart and body too. Brenda gave it reluctantly and soon she hoped she didn't have to go through gut-wrenching heart-breaking events with Evo Kaplan. But then again, she realized that it might not be Evo Kaplan; it could be her, simply killed in during a mission in the nasty spy business.

That also saddened her, and she struggled to hold back the tears knowing it would tear Evo's heart out if he suddenly lost her. His compassionate lovemaking and sweet words during delicate moments transcended time and space and elevated her feelings and emotions unlike ever before.

Brenda Broyals female intuition clarified the truthfulness and sincerity in every word Evo Kaplan uttered.


                              BRENDA BROYALS
                  If you want to go on this cruise, I would love to go with you.


                               EVO KAPLAN
                  Okay, I'll contact Guest Services back at the Lantiane Resort.


A new waiter came and took their order for drinks. They both ordered from the drink menu that had some fruity mixtures.

INT. LANTIANE RESORT- EVENING.

When Glacy was finally ready to go about forty-five minutes on the dot, she hastily took the elevator down and made a prompt appearance at the resort swimming pool bar/restaurant.

There patiently waiting for Glacy was the man she had rode hard and put away wet earlier. Reginald Heiqishi was almost taken back when he saw Glacy arrive. It truly was an incredible transformation, and it proved the theory that rich women could look good any time they wanted if they had a reasonable diet.

GLACY SPENCER<br>
Are you ready to go?

REGINALD HEIQISHI<br>
Yes, shall we?

This also did not go unnoticed by Sheri, as she too was mildly stunned to see how the Barracuda in the span of forty-five minutes turned into a princess quality beauty. The limo driver was waiting for them, knowing they were going to *Banma Julebu*. As soon as they got near the limo, the door was opened.

LIMO DRIVER<br>
This way, sir.

Glacy Spencer and Reginald Heiqishi were seated and comfortable, the limo pulled out and was on its way to the *Banma Julebu* where they would have fun tonight. Reginald Heiqishi's main purpose was to observe his target in action and quantify the relationship Evo Kaplan had with Brenda Broyals.

When they got to the passenger-loading zone of the restaurant building, there was a long line waiting to get to the elevator and several security personnel keep the crowd under control. It looked ugly, but Reginald Heiqishi had dealt with similar situations before and knew he could handle it, so he tugged Glacy along with him up to what appeared like the head security person.

BLANE JIANDIE (a.k.a REGINALD HEIQISHI)<br>
Excuse me, sir, we have reservations for this time.

SECURITY PERSON<br>
Give me a minute.

The security man then called the Maître-d'

SECURITY PERSON<br>
A couple with a reservation was out front with a big line formed.

MAÎTRE-D'<br>
What's his name?

SECURITY PERSON
Excuse me, sir, what is the name of the reservation under?

BLANE JIANDIE (a.k.a REGINALD HEIQISHI)
Blane Jiandie.

SECURITY PERSON
One minute, sir.

The Maître-d' responded to the name, knowing he received a one hundred-credit bribe.

MAÎTRE-D'
Please escort Mr. Jiandie to the elevator and put him on the next
one up.

SECURITY PERSON
Right away, sir.

The security person looked at Blane Jiandie (a.k.a Reginald Heiqishi) and then instructed.

SECURITY PERSON
Mr. Jiandie will you and your party please follow me.

Reginald Heiqishi followed the security officer to the elevator, getting some nasty looks and a few low-level curses. People don't like other people cutting ahead in lines, and half the line would not make it up to the restaurant tonight.

In five minutes, Reginald Heiqishi and Glacy Spencer were taken to the reserved table that had only been cleared off two minutes prior, as an elderly couple finished their dinner and had no desire to hang around for the dancing music that was just starting. The fact they were arriving late and would now start dinner, which was served at the restaurant past midnight, would give Reginald Heiqishi a chance to observe Evo Kaplan and Brenda Broyals and not be distracted by dancing and other activities of the club.

It was only natural for people to observe dancers, so Reginald Heiqishi watching Evo Kaplan and Brenda Broyals would not elevate any concern or anything out of the ordinary. In no time the dance music started. Some of it was exotic, to say the least, and people with professional dancing skills were on the dance floor showing off as usual.

Early in the night, the dance floor was generally half empty, so the showoffs could do the radical dance maneuvers and impress themselves and the audience. As the night wore on and the dance floor got crowded, they would no longer be able to show off.

At about the tenth song, Reginald Heiqishi was rewarded for his patience as Brenda Broyals convinced Evo Kaplan to dance with her and they were now exhibiting a rarified glimpse into passion and extravaganza.

Reginald Heiqishi was quite surprised at how short Brenda's dress was and the fact she was showing off her ass. Whatever was her motive, it seemed to be captivating Evo Kaplan as he started getting braver and more physical the more of a spectacle Brenda Broyals put on. It also influenced other women, who seemed to want to get up and strut their stuff as well. After the third dance that Brenda Broyals and Evo Broyals had danced, the dance floor was now packed.

The club manager was happy, as it appeared this was going to be an excellent night as he observed some extremely beautiful and well-dressed women. Little did he know one of them was wearing an outfit that cost more than his yearly salary.

After about ten songs Evo Kaplan wanted to sit down.

EVO KAPLAN
I'm getting tired and thirsty. I want to sit down for a few minutes.

BRENDA BROYALS
No problem.

Brenda led Evo Kaplan off the dance floor back to their booth where they polished off their drink and ordered another.

Unexpectedly, the gentleman with the goatee, whom Evo Kaplan recalled seeing at the Dewaltracen Gallery while observing the famous artwork of Mathematician Agstavar, got up he approached Evo Kaplan.

EGOR PATASLIA
Good evening, sir. I don't know if you remember me, we met
at the Dewaltracen Gallery. I would like your permission to ask
Brenda for this dance.

Evo Kaplan remembered the man and wondered how he knew Brenda's name. He then recalled this man also picked up their dinner tab. The plot thickened. Evo Kaplan responded in a positive manner.

EVO KAPLAN
Yes, you may.

After all they were not married, and Brenda Broyals was still a free spirit. This also gave Evo Kaplan to assess the situation, and he quickly concluded Egor Pataslia was likely a FIRM operative meaning he was probably a Revolution Spy.

The music slowed down a bit so couples could dance closer together, which allowed Brenda and Egor Pataslia to exchange some operational concerns.

EGOR PATASLIA
You look stunningly beautiful.

BRENDA BROYALS
Why thank you.

EGOR PATASLIA
Is everything going, okay?

BRENDA BROYALS
I have some concerns that someone is doing surveillance on us.

EGOR PATASLIA
Well, our men are following you around.

BRENDA BROYALS
There are a couple Lantiane Resort guests that are doing the surveillance on us and one of them is in the restaurant sitting right behind you with the woman in the beautiful expensive purple dress.

EGOR PATASLIA
Okay, we'll investigate it.

BRENDA BROYALS
Also, we are going on a cruise tomorrow. Can you have a couple guys on the ship with us?

EGOR PATASLIA
Absolutely.

BRENDA BROYALS
Thank you. I appreciate your assistance.

EGOR PATASLIA
You should have called me sooner. I gave you my communicator token.

BRENDA BROYALS
I never had it with me when I needed to call you. But I take it with me now wherever I go.

EGOR PATASLIA
Good plan.


BRENDA BROYALS
Also, thank you for leaving me the gift in my bungalow room
at the Lantiane Resort.


EGOR PATASLIA
Think I should bring another for Evo Kaplan?


BRENDA BROYALS
That might be a good idea.


EGOR PATASLIA
As soon as you get back from the cruise, you will find more
gifts.


BRENDA BROYALS Thank you, I appreciate that.


EGOR PATASLIA
Good. I better let you go back to your boyfriend. I wouldn't
want to make him jealous.


BRENDA BROYALS
Indeed.


The waitress arrived with Evo Kaplan and Brenda Broyals drinks. Evo ordered a
*Huoshan Xingneng* Drink slightly fortified with alcohol. Brenda had one of her
fruit drinks, also slightly spiked.


Egor Pataslia, sitting at his bar stool next to his bodyguard, alerted him.


EGOR PATASLIA
See the man with the lady in the purple dress?


EGOR'S BODYGUARD
Yes?
EGOR PATASLIA
Put a tail on him. He might be a Dranzonian Empire Secret
Service agent.


The bodyguard got off his bar stool as if he were going to the restroom. He made
eye contact with another agent who worked for Egor Pataslia and gave the signal
to follow him.


In the restroom after they were alone for a brief period, Egor Pataslia's bodyguard
directed the other man.

Put a team together to follow the man with the woman that has on the fancy purple dress. Find out everything about the man you can. Also find out who the woman is.

By morning Egor Pataslia would have a bargaining chip with the man, whoever he was, because he was screwing around with a powerful man's wife. All he had to do was send Glacy Spencer's husband a few pictures and he would not have to get his hands dirty with the business that would occur later

A beautiful slow dance song played next. Evo Kaplan had never heard it before, but it certainly captured his imagination as the melody seemed to modulate his emotions along with the Huoshan Xingneng drink. Brenda was also feeling the effects of her drink enhanced the song and wanted to suddenly be held in Evo Kaplan's arms and dance to this tune.

BRENDA BROYALS
I really like this song.

EVO KAPLAN
Would you like to dance?

BRENDA BROYALS
Definitely.

Brenda stood up and held her hand out to Evo, who took her out to the dance floor where they had that embrace only afforded to slow dancing.

VOICE OVER
Reginald Heiqishi observing saw the couple do a couple kisses as the dance floor was darken and crowded to provide people some privacy.

The female singer almost slashed through Brenda's heart in the most exotic melody and words combining to unlock her emotions like she never felt before. The way she kissed Evo Kaplan left no doubt in Reginald Heiqishi's mind the great affection exhibited between the two.

It was crystal clear now to Reginald Heiqishi how far Evo Kaplan had gone. The likelihood Evo Kaplan would agree to go back with them to Praxisvlasia seemed quite remote.

Reginald Heiqishi realized this was slowly turning into an assassination, as any other remedy was probably not feasible as it appeared Evo Kaplan had reached the point of no return with Brenda Broyals.

In a sense, Reginald Heiqishi didn't relish assassinating a man he sent on five hundred or more missions in the past. Had he not caused Reginald Heiqishi so much grief in their work environment, it would not have had to come down to this where he first ruined his life and now, he was going to kill him.

As the high caloric meal slowly transformed Reginald Heiqishi thinking, and looking at his beautiful date, he was easily able to clear his mind of all those nasty thoughts surrounding Evo Kaplan.

It is what it is, and tomorrow is another day where they could deal with all of it. For the rest of the night, the case was closed with Evo Kaplan. Glacy, knowing Blane Jiandie was probably seriously tired from their sexual tryst earlier that day and wanted to at least get a few dances in was also familiar with the Huoshan Xingneng drink and its restorative properties, suggested they each have one and quietly told the waiter to have the bartender give Blane an extra shot in his drink because he was tired.

By the time Blane Jiandie finished half his Huoshan Xingneng drink, he was ready to comply with Glacy's desires on the dance floor. Plus, she wanted to strut her dress, which nobody in the club ever saw before since it was an exclusive couture garment.

Just as soon as Glacy Spencer's thought Blane Jiandie was ready to dance, she asked.

GLACY SPENCER
Would you like to dance to this song?

BLANE JIANDIE (a.k.a REGINALD HEIQISHI)
I would be delighted.

Blane Jiandie knew he had to blend in, so he accepted and danced in a mildly conservative fashion so as not to draw too much attention on himself.

Glacy Spencer was very happy because she had discovered an elegant man whom she could go out on the town with.

It had been a long time since a line formed for the club that went around the block. The manager was ecstatic. Better yet, the Maître d' was even happier as he made off with the one hundred credits for a reservation.

After a dozen dances, Glacy realized Blane looked tired. She also felt tired, and the drinks did not help.

GLACY SPENCER

It's getting late and I'm tired. Let's go back  to the Lantiane Resort.

BLANE JIANDIE (a.k.a REGINALD HEIQISHI)

Good idea. We need to get some rest. Pick it up again tomorrow.

Blane Jiandie then felt the pager the limo driver gave him and turned it on, signaling they wanted a ride back to the Lantiane Resort.

The two stood up and walked out of the club as Evo and Beverly were dancing one more time. Security was set up and as the couple departed and went to the loading zone waiting for the limo to pull up. They didn't have to wait long. The limo driver was a couple blocks away finishing up his meal in a modest all-night restaurant.

The couple only had to wait two minutes for the Limousine, and they were on their way back to the Lantiane Resort. So was Egor Pataslia's security detail following them. Reginald Heiqishi would be tailed for the rest of his mission if he survived.

Terrshey Wate had a nice evening with Sparkles. Sparkles took him to an invite-only restaurant. One entrée cost more than his monthly salary.

Note to the cinematographer:

> The action depicted during the VOICE OVER should show the events occurring such as drinking the coffee, looking at the gems for 15 seconds, undressing and copulating, Terrshey Wate dressing and leaving, etc.

<u>INT. LANTIANE RESORT SPARKLES PENTHOUSE.</u>

VOICE OVER (FEMALE)

After dinner, Sparkles was in a hurry to do two things: get out of her clothes before the drugs wore off that caused all her fat cells to shrink temporarily. Also, she had a lot of pent-up emotion and lack of gratification.

Sparkles had not been with a man in quite some time, as her filthy rich husband would rather spend his time on Orgy Island with some prominent politician who enjoyed the human trafficking of young helpless women brought in from planets where their desperate families sold them into bondage and indentured servitude, where they might possibly have a chance in life later.

When Terrshey Wate arrived at Sparkles' Penthouse for coffee, Sparkles was still four to six hours away from blowing up like a blimp.

Sparkles wanted to have romantic intercourse with Terrshey Wate before she started the inevitable metamorphism. Sparkles wanted Terrshey Wate's memories of her to be like they were now. In due time she might try to slim down a bit legitimately if Terrshey Wate could somehow make himself more available in the future. Unfortunately, Sparkles didn't know that was not in the works for her.

Tonight, Sparkles would be Cinderella, except she would later turn into the pumpkin. Sparkles had her personal chef who traveled with her, make Terrshey Wate the special coffee. The chef knew exactly what to put in the drink: performance enhancers. Sparkles knew the chef also provided her with some as well.

NOTE to the director:

> The scene should show the Chef drugging the coffee before the drinks were delivered to Sparkles and Terrshey Wate. The film should show the Chef spiking the coffee. 5 seconds

VOICE OVER (FEMALE)

Sparkles' exotic *Romla de Verla* perfume costs one hundred thousand credits per ounce. That alone should do the trick with a pheromone explosion, but the additives in the coffee created psychophysical responses that a good Barracuda would want applied to her victim.

Their age difference made Sparkles' a Cougar tonight, which she didn't mind at all. Sparkles led Terrshey Wate into her private area so that she could show him some of her gem collections. Then she showed him some other things as well and they soon were eagerly engaging their bodies in tangled copulation as the effects of the performance drugs caused them to transcend beyond their senses and engage in reckless splendid coitus on a Theme from Paganini.

Two hours later, covered in sweat neither Sparkles nor Terrshey Wate had any energy left. Terrshey Wate didn't have to be enticed to leave. He knew he was on a mission and in a few hours, he would have to be prepared to do mission objectives.

Terrshey Wate did a clever escape with Sparkles' full sympathy
because she didn't want him to see the metamorphism that
would start any time.

The mutual parting was pleasant, and Sparkles started thinking
maybe in a couple days when she felt up to it she would
encourage the young buck to once again glide down that avenue
of splendid moorings.

Terrshey Wate only had to ride the elevator down a dozen floors to get back to his
room, but he needed some sleep right away. The suite he and Reginald Heiqishi
shared had two bedrooms, two bathrooms, a living room, and a small kitchen. It
essentially was an apartment.

Terrshey Wate brushed his teeth, took a quick shower, and was soon sound asleep
and did not hear Reginald Heiqishi come in and simply plop into bed because he
also was exhausted.

Evo Kaplan had a good assessment of Reginald Heiqishi damaged their mission
and put it at risk because he was too arrogant and trailed one of the galaxy's best
spies too closely.

Reginald Heiqishi was a rookie and a neophyte compared to Brenda, who didn't
have to work too hard to detect him. And now that Egor Pataslia's group was on to
Reginald Heiqishi, he also now had added trouble he never counted on.

Brenda and Evo were not far behind arriving at the Lantiane Resort and were
soon also sleeping and deferred the affectionate embrace until the morning just
before they got up to prepare for their cruise they would board around noon. In
the morning after a wonderful sleep Brenda was lying in bed fully awake, staring
at Evo Kaplan looking for signs he was waking up. She didn't want to disturb his
sleep. Eventually his eyes opened out of a dream and looking face to face with
Brenda saw her smile.

Within a moment they had an endearing kiss. Brenda then took action and Evo
was soon engulfed into a sea of tranquility as he transcended to a super-stimulated
mental state as his ample male hood touched Brenda's erogenous zone to propel
her into a state of ecstasy. The splendid euphoria lasted an endless amount of time
until they both collapsed into a tranquil state.

Brenda the task master intuitively knew they could not lay around all morning in
bed, especially if they were going on a cruise. Brenda broke the silence.

BRENADA BROYALS

Since we are only going out overnight, we don't need to pack
many things. Let's pick a change of clothes and essentials and
put it into one of our luggage pieces.

                              EVO KAPLAN
                                 Okay.


Evo Kaplan stood up and put on his cotton briefs and picked up the guest
communicator and called guest services.


                             Guest Services.
                  Guest Services, hello, how may I help you?


                   PROCTOR PUGONG (a.k.a. EVO KAPLAN)
              Good morning. This is Proctor Pugong, a resort guest. I would
              like to book the cruise for me and my partner you offer in one
              of your brochures that leaves today around noon and returns
              tomorrow at about the same time.


                              GUEST SERVICES
              Sure, no problem Mr. Pugong. Give me a minute to book it and
              confirm it. Please hold.


Brenda watched Evo in anticipation. Shortly, the guest services lady came back
online.


                              GUEST SERVICES
              Mr. Pugong, your reservation is confirmed. There will be a
              VTOL Skybus arriving around noon at the passenger-loading
              zone in front of the Lantiane Resort. The VTOL Skybus will
              take you directly to the ship. Your reservation is just your last
              name, party of two.


                              EVO KAPLAN
                              Okay, thanks.


                              GUEST SERVICES
                  Anything else I can be of assistance?


                              EVO KAPLAN
                  No, that will just about cover it.


The two did their morning business and dressed in tourist clothes. Soon they felt
the hunger pains.


                             BRENDA BROYALS
                  Would you like to go out and get some breakfast?

                              EVO KAPLAN
                       Like the resort breakfast buffet?


                           BRENDA BROYALS
           No, how about we go back to the restaurant up on the cliff?


Brenda had a hunch and wanted to check it out.


                              EVO KAPLAN
                             Sure, why not?


The couple made their way to the Lantiane Resort front entrance to the passenger-
loading zone and asked for a Tri-wheeler. The security man signaled the next tri-
wheeler in line to come forward for the passengers, and as soon as he stopped in
front of Evo and Brenda, they hopped on and the driver who they had used before
was happy to see them again.


                          TRI-WHEELER DRIVER
                  Good morning. Where would you like to go?


Evo Kaplan remembered this was the driver who drove them to the restaurant on
the cliff once before.


                              EVO KAPLAN
                  Take us to that restaurant up on the cliff.


The driver instinctively knew exactly where they wanted to go.


                          TRI-WHEELER DRIVER
                                 Yes, sir.


It did not take long to drive to the *Cliff Restaurant* situate with a great view up on
the cliff. Brenda and Evo were soon at the *Cliff Restaurant's* lobby that has a large
glass front window area where they had an outstanding view of the road that led
up to the restaurant, where they were immediately greeted.


                              MAÎTRE D'
                             Table for two?


                           BRENDA BROYALS
                             Yes, please.


                              MAÎTRE D'
            We'll have your table ready in about five minutes.

Cinematographers film the scene as described in the following paragraph.




The restaurant appeared busy. That was fine with Brenda Broyals, as it afforded her the opportunity to do surveillance on the road. Just as Brenda predicted, another Tri-wheeler drove past and went up the road.

In a short period as Brenda predicted, a third Tri-wheeler suddenly appeared, but instead of following the other Tri-wheeler, it stopped in front of the restaurant. Two men got out.

Brenda Broyals had somewhat of a photographic memory. It helped her greatly in the spy business for espionage as well as survival skills.

As the two men entered the restaurant, she recalled seeing these men at the nightclub the night before. One of them, Brenda Broyals observed talking with Egor Pataslia. She knew this was probably security and surveillance that Egor Pataslia initiated based on her conversation with him at the *Banma Julebu* restaurant dance club.

The men ignored Brenda and Evo as they should and were soon met by the Maître d' who took their reservation and promised a table in less than ten minutes. Brenda and Evo were subsequently seated at a nice table by the window with an excellent view. The edge of the cliff was a mere ten feet away and the foundation the restaurant stood on was at least ten feet tall on this side, which gave the customers a view of almost directly down on the beach several hundred feet below.

As they were eating and almost finished, Evo spotted a high-speed ship at a distance that appeared to be approaching land.


EVO KAPLAN
There's a ship coming in.


BRENDA BROYALS
I wonder if that's the cruise liner we'll take for the cruise.


EVO KAPLAN
It could be.

When the ship arrived closer to land, Evo Kaplan could distinguish it as a cruise liner as it slowed and dropped down into the water from its hydrofoils. Prior to slowing the cruise liner doing well one hundred knots, then slowed down as it lowered down on the surface.

The large wake the hydrofoils left behind and the sea spray were suddenly gone, so it was harder to observe. The ship now slowly approached land and at this time was probably several miles offshore.

The Cruise liner slowing coincided with the end of their meal and the time Evo Kaplan had asked the Tri-wheeler driver to come back and pick them up.

Evo Kaplan and all tourists visiting *Shen de Huayuan* paid for their meals when they ordered them, which includes the tip, because there was no currency; it was all electronic credits. Hence, they simply only had to leave. There was no need to wait for a waiter and a check.

Brenda followed Evo out of the restaurant and the happy Tri-wheeler driver was there patiently waiting for them. He didn't have to drive far because he spent the hour up the road at a *Shen de Huayuan* local-cuisine roadside tavern he frequented while waiting on passengers who went to the *Cliff Restaurant*.

Terrshey Wate had also stopped at the roadside tavern and invited his driver in for a free meal. The two drivers knew each other and as they sat at the bar eating, they had a friendly discourse. When the first driver left to go pick up Evo, the Tri-wheeler driver, beholden to Terrshey Wate for the free meal, knew he was following the couple and offered the appropriate report.

TRI-WHEELER DRIVER

That driver is going back to the *Cliff Restaurant* to pick up that couple and take them back to the resort.

TERRSHEY WATE

Okay, let's go.

Even though only half of their food had been eaten, Terrshey Wate left the roadside tavern and just as they came in view of the restaurant, they spotted Evo and Brenda leaving. Terrshey Wate regretted not having his laser pistol with him; otherwise, he would simply take out Evo Kaplan and complete the mission and get the hell off the planet before they got caught.

However, Reginald Heiqishi had his own idea of how to handle it and with the auspicious moment at the Lantiane Resort Beach Restaurant and Bar, he wanted to confront Evo Kaplan on the cruise ship, which would be far more convenient to dispose of the body if necessary. Terrshey Wate didn't like the plan, but he knew not to rock the boat because he knew Reginald Heiqishi was a vindictive prick and would have him removed from the Secret Service if he didn't carry out his orders.

Several minutes later as Terrshey Wate rode past the Cliff Restaurant, Egor Pataslia's two agents exited the restaurant and observed the tri-wheeler fly by chasing Evo and Brenda. Their own Tri-wheeler was stopped there waiting for them to board and were soon on their way chasing the other two Tri-wheelers back to the resort. Terrshey Wate had not developed as a spy well enough to recognize he was under surveillance. He simply followed Evo and Brenda back to the resort and as they went to their bungalow to make the final preparations for their trip.

Terrshey Wate simply went into the pool bar-restaurant, which afforded an excellent view of the access to all the bungalows.

Egor Pataslia's agents also placed themselves in position to intervene, if necessary, should Terrshey Wate attempt assassination or any other clandestine action. If it were any other time, they simply would have bagged Terrshey Wate, but Egor Pataslia wanted to confirm who the individuals were working for, though he surmised they were Loyalist agents out to sanction a defector.

Moments later Reginald Heiqishi came to the bar.

REGINALD HEIQISHI

In about thirty minutes they should be walking to the Skybus
that will take us to the cruise liner. I'm going up to our room to
grab the suitcase we got packed.

Inside the suitcase were weapons and technological devices to help them find all the hidden cameras on the ship to find a blind spot to do the sanction if required. When Reginald Heiqishi arrived at his room, the guest phone rang. It was Glacy.

GLACY SPENCER

Hello dear, what are you doing today?

REGINALD HEIQISHI

I'm getting ready to go on the Cruise in about thirty minutes. I
will be back tomorrow.

GLACY SPENCER

Oh really? That sounds fun.

REGINALD HEIQISHI

Yep, my partner booked the cruise, and I was curious as to how
it was, so I want to try it.

GLACY SPENCER
You will love it. It will be excellent.

REGINALD HEIQISHI
Okay, I need to get ready now, I'll see you when I get back.

GLACY SPENCER
All right, honey.

After Reginald Heiqishi hung up, Glacy called guest services.

GUEST SERVICES
Hello, this is guest services. How can I help you?

GLACY SPENCER
This is Glacy Spencer. Is it too late to book the  cruise ship for today?

GUEST SERVICES
There should be room on board for you. I know they have not been sailing full lately.

The Revolution had cut back on tourism, and Shen de Huayuan was not immune to the economic paralysis now starting to grip the outer regions of the Empire as the economic collapse spread throughout the Revolutionary held territory.

After a brief delay, the guest services representative informed Glacy of her reservations.

GUEST SERVICES
Madam Glacy Spencer, you have been booked on the cruise for today.

GLACY SPENCER
Thank you.

GUEST SERVICES
Anything else I can do for you?

GLACY SPENCER
I probably look like a pig. This is all so unexpected. Can you send a fashion designer and some cosmetic technicians up to help me prepare?

GUEST SERVICES
Absolutely.


GLACY SPENCER
One question, though. When I'm on the ship, what types of help
can I get there?


GUEST SERVICES
We are affiliated with the cruise line. Our company owns that
ship. So, anything you get or expect here you will get on the
ship.


GLACY SPENCER
That's marvelous, thank you.


In five minutes, Glacy's maid was ushering the fashion designer Inchalchary and
her group of magicians into the penthouse, where they promptly went to work on
her and having been informed, she was going on the cruise, they knew they had to
hustle to make it. Just like the day before, Inchalchary did her magic and beautiful
dress, and the makeup and hair design quickly converted her into that splendid
image that would captivate lesser mere mortals. Just as soon as they put on the
final touches, they announced they were done.


INCHALCHARY
You can now leave for the cruise.


GLACY SPENCER
I wonder what I need to take with me.


INCHALCHARY
Nothing. The cruise liner will take care of everything.


GLACY SPENCR
What about my ID and travel documents?


INCHALCHARY
You were booked through the Lantiane Resort. Your facial
recognition file is wired to the ship as part of your reservation.
They know who you are and everything you purchase or require
will be automatically accounted for.


GLACY SPENCER
That's nice. So, I can just leave as I am?

INCHALCHARY
Correct.

Glacy felt happy and would be even further pleased when she got to the ship and escorted to her sea cabin, which was reserved, just like her Lantiane Resort booking, as a penthouse. Many people would just about die to have the chance to sail the ocean in one of these exclusive ship's penthouses, where pampering is expected.

Glacy went to the Lantiane Resort entrance and noticed a Skybus parked in front.

<u>EXT. DAY. LANTIANE RESORT FRONT ENTRRANCE</u>

GLACY SPENCER
Is this the Skybus to the cruise liner?

SKYBUS STAFF
Yes madam, please go aboard now. We are almost ready to leave.

Sitting halfway back in the Skybus, Reginald Heiqishi barely recognized Glacy. Her new image was an outstanding achievement for the makeup artist and the fashion designer Inchalchary. Glacy's couture outfit was so beautiful and colors so unreal, she made just about every other woman on the SKYBUS jealous.

Brenda had enough time to get a massage and a makeover before leaving the Lantiane Resort. She too wowed the male libidos on the Skybus.

Just those two women alone made all the males glad they booked the cruise, even though they earlier regretted going and only did so because of their nagging spouses. The automatic system knew all reservations had boarded the Skybus and the door shut, propulsion engaged, and the VTOL Skybus went vertical, giving off a little bit of annoying racket just momentarily as it exited the space near the Lantiane Resort. Within seconds the VTOL Skybus was flying over the beach and out toward the ocean.

Parked a couple miles offshore was the cruise liner hydrofoil equipped ship, they didn't have to fly far to reach their destination. The VTOL Skybus landed on a landing pad near the stern of the cruise liner. Once they got out to sea and away from land, this landing pad was turned into a tennis court where registered guests could reserve court time and play underway after the ship slowed down from its high speed run up the coast. Even though they had automatic nets that went up about twenty feet, they still ended up losing a lot of tennis balls over the side.

EXT. GCI. DAY. HYDROFOIL CRUISE LINER.

As the passengers disembarked the VTOL Skybus, onto the ship's landing pad area, they were met by escorts carrying electronic tablets with them, which had built-in cameras to do the facial recognition. They were then escorted to their cabins by crew members and receptionists. For the prior hour and half, dozens of VTOL Skybus trips had delivered all the second- and third-class passengers arriving from multiple originations of various hotels and resorts along the coastline.

This last VTOL Skybus was all first-class passengers, mostly all staying in penthouses way above the waterline in what appeared to be a super streamlined hull section. There was nobody on deck. All the doors to the outside areas except for this Skycar access were currently locked for high-speed transit. That door was secured as soon as the last Skybus departed from the landing pad and made its way back to land at the hotel.

<u>INT. DAY. HYDROFOIL CRUISE LINER</u>

Everyone was taken to their quarters and informed that due to the high velocity, wind speeds were lethal, and the ship would be sealed until they slowed down in several hours near their destination, where they would cruise at slower speeds for everyone to enjoy the unique coastline in this area. They would also make one port call and tie up to a pier where the passengers could get off the ship for a few hours and do shopping.

The main reason for this stopover was to transfer cargo and take on supplies. Then they would be off again cruising until early in the morning, when they would shift back on the hydrofoils and go high speed back to their home base. There was a beautiful casino, many restaurants, a movie theater, and clubs and bars to go unwind during the highspeed transit. Some chose to simply take a nap and had a wakeup call for when the ship slowed to cruise along the coastline.

There was an announcement from the ship's intercom system.

> SHIP'S CAPTAIN via INTERCOM
> Ladies and gentlemen, this is the captain speaking. We will be starting our high-speed run in a few minutes. You will experience some slight vibrations as this occurs. There is nothing to be concerned about.

On the bridge of the cruise liner, the captain put down the microphone and turned to the First Officer.

SHIP'S CAPTAIN All ahead FULL.
The First Officer repeated the order.

FIRST OFFICER All ahead FULL, Captain Aye.

The artificial intelligence on the bridge voyage navigation system encoded the orders and there was a flashing icon on the display the first officer had to acknowledge, confirming the order. He touched the finger on glass icon and shortly felt the results.

Under the ship, huge hydrofoils lowered that almost looked like aircraft wings. All the interlocks indicated locking pins in place and hydrofoils extended for high-speed running.

The huge turbines of the propulsion power plant spun the propulsion generators at 25,000 RPM producing megawatts of power. Separate generators were used for electricity. Super conductors in the electric motors driving the water pumps started streaming a thrust that everyone could feel as the acceleration was linear yet powerful.

The Ocean Liner crew had to be careful not to jerk to a start or passengers could fall. Hence, acceleration took a while. It took a lot of energy to get the ship up on the hydrofoils, but once the hull broke free of the water and only the computer-controlled hydrofoils were left submerged, the drag on the ship's hull ended and it took considerably less energy to maintain hydrofoil operations.

At about 70 knots, the great hull slowly rose up out of the water. As more hull area was exposed in the rise, less drag existed allowing sustained speed increase. It took longer to go from 60 knots per hour than it took to go from 70 to 140 knots per hour.

The sea was calm this time of year with only three-foot swells, which got nowhere near the hull now riding almost fifty feet above the surface. All Shen de Huayuan ships that went beyond five miles of the coastline had to be registered and include installed transponders, which were tracked by satellite.

High speed hydrofoils had legal right of way unless there were two of them approaching; then the transportation department regulators staff would give one of the two right of way and direct the other to take a course to prevent collisions.

All other ships in front of the cruise liner were shown on the hydrofoil navigation system displays and an automatic system-controlled course to keep them from running into each other.

C.U. FIRST OFFICER OBSERVING NAVIGATION SYSTEM DISPLAYS.

C.U. CAPTAIN OBSERVING AI GENERATED SAFETY SWEEP DISPLAYS AND COLLISION AVOIDANCE DISPLAYS. LONG DISTANCE NAVIGATION HAZZARDS HIGHLIGHTED ON DISPLAY WITH AUTOMATED RUDDER CONTROLS POSTING ADJUSTMENTS FOR COLLISION AVOIDANCE.

Note to director/producers:

This is a futuristic scenario while traveling at 140 knots on hydrofoil requires artificial intelligence to maneuver the ship. Human response is too slow.

Artificial intelligence is designed to not overwhelm the helmsman with alerts that happen frequently. Only during essential events is audio alerts given not to direct the helmsman to take action, but instead to inform the purpose of the radical course change to avoid collisions.

The three-dimensional display of the sea ahead automatically places trackers on ships or fishing boats in an arch of travel ahead of the cruise liner.

Photonic and Radar overlays have the tracker symbols on the animated trackers showing a miniature scale model of the ship that resides in the area of the traveling arch. To keep the big picture that's all the Captain monitors until they get out into deep ocean away from most ships and fishing boats.

In most cases due to the velocity they traveled, a one- or two-degree course change was always sufficient to navigate around any possible hazards.

At 140 knots, they covered their distance rather quickly and two hours later the captain again stated over the intercom,

CAPTAIN
Ladies and gentlemen, this is the captain speaking. We will commence slowing down momentarily. After reaching safe speeds, all doors and access to the main deck will be restored.

The captain turned to the first officer who anticipated the order.

CAPTAIN
Slow to cruise speed and retract the hydrofoils.

The first officer touched the acknowledge icon on the glass panel, which immediately started the automated process. No matter how much sound silencing they attempted, pushing a large ship on hydrofoils at 140 knots produced background vibration and audible oscillations. The ship could not instantly slow, or passengers would be thrown forward and possibly injured.

The automated system slowed the ship over a period and the vibration, and the audible oscillations changed pitch as a result.

If you were on a boat nearby observing, you could hear the harmonic resonance and sound change as the hull slowed down and went into cruise mode.

Right around 70 knots, the hydrofoil could no longer hold up the hull as it slowly slid down upon the water. The passengers and the crew could feel the slowing as the hull dug deeper into the water. The sea spray off the hull rose exponentially about this time and if you were close observing you would probably be drenched from the rooster tail the ship now put up.

The automated system put a slight up angle on the ship so that engineering spaces hit the water first. That would help prevent a sudden stop as the drag from the ships cruise propellers water jets added further slowing.

By the time the rear of the hull was fully submerged down to the waterline, the bow of the ship was coming down as the automated hydrofoils did a great job of slowly putting the bow down to prevent any hard landings that would upset the passengers. With propulsion reduced, the water jets and the hydrofoils created quite a bit of drag so slowing from 30 knots down to barely having a headway didn't take long.

Once the ship was in the correct profile at slow speed, the hydrofoils were retracted into the ship's hull, where they would not run the risk of getting damaged in potentially shallow water near the shorelines if their navigation had an error.

While the ship was stopped, raising its hydrofoils, the doors were unlocked, and passengers started streaming on deck. Glacy made a beeline to the main deck in hopes of contacting Reginald Heiqishi. She was almost panting in lust for her prince charming.

It did not take long for Glacy to spot Reginald Heiqishi since he was already out on deck as soon as the doors were opened with Terrshey Wate, looking for all the video cameras to stake out their location of operation where they would deal with

Evo Kaplan and, if necessary, throw him overboard if he didn't cooperate.

Reginald Heiqishi knew Glacy was aboard the cruise liner as he had spotted her all dolled up on the VTOL Skybus. He knew it would be almost impossible to avoid her, which would complicate matters greatly. He would have to rely more on Terrshey Wate, whom he was starting to feel was a loose cannon.

Things could get dicey, because Reginald Heiqishi also had to make sure he isolated Brenda Broyals, who could be a formidable opponent with her martial arts skills. Plus, they would have no idea what kinds of toys she brought with her for self-defense.

The plan would only work if they could get Evo Kaplan alone in one of the dark zones. Walking around the main deck, they soon realized most of the cameras were out in the open and easy to spot. The ship's video monitor system was not set up for espionage or sabotage; it was more set up for insurance policies and to observe, via automated video processes.

Someone falling overboard would immediately slow the ship down so they could turn around and ostensibly send divers over the side to save the victim if it was not too late and the person could swim for a few minutes.

But if a passenger went overboard, they would likely die in these shark-infested waters.

Rumors were some of the three-foot-wide sea turtles considered humans a delicacy.

Reginald Heiqishi was surveying the deck area for cameras when he met up with Glacy and they exchanged greetings.

REGINALD HEIQISHI

I was taking a walk around the deck for some exercise. Would
you like to go for a walk with me?

GLACY

I would love to.

With *WELCOME TO SANCTUARY CITY* Theme Song playing in the background:

VOICE OVER

Glacy curled her arm around Reginald Heiqishi's arm as the two
strolled down the length of the thousand-foot-long hydrofoil
ship. They dabbled in small talk. There was not a great lot

of neurological exchange happening, as Reginald Heiqishi was more interested in making a mental note of all the easily identifiable video cameras. The video cameras were obviously designed for ease of installation and maintenance, Reginald Heiqishi speculated.

When the hydrofoil cruise liner was built a few years before the Revolution, there was no anticipated war. So, it stands to reason ship owners would only be concerned about ease of installation and maintenance to provide measures to the insurance companies they could account for all deaths associated with falling overboard.

If the person was committing suicide and caught on camera, the company would be released from all liability. Ninety-five-percent, of deaths attributed from drowning while falling off a cruise ship was confirmed as suicide. The other five percent were murderers also caught on video.

<delay VOICE OVER for EFFECT>
Lovers' disputes sometimes resulted in unpredictable actions of passengers. Jealousy, unwanted pregnancies, divorces, and several other reasons led to such murders, which sometimes also incurred a murder-suicide as the perpetrator jumped overboard after killing the other person.

Glacy was in a temporal haze, and compartmentalizing her life from her cheating husband, who was no doubt at *Orgy Island* with a politician. But Glacy was now finally getting her sweet revenge as she planned on carrying out her romantic tryst with Blane Jiandie on this overnight quick cruise. As they walked along the starboard (right) side of the ship that faced the shoreline, they stopped and took the time to gaze upon the splendid flora abounding a mere half mile away.

The water depth dropped off quickly here and the ship was following the hundred-fathom curve with their automated fathometer and GPS working with integrated. ship's radar for collision avoidance. This would not be the only cruise liner that traveled these waters this day.

The fresh sea breeze fortified their breathing. This peaceful and tranquil moment was like the calm before the storm. If they did, in fact, mange to sanction Evo Kaplan that evening, they would be scrambling to get off Shen de Huayuan and back to Zanziltar to catch a direct flight back to Praxisvlasia. That's how it worked in the spy business.

One peaceful moment like this quickly erupted into panic and fear as the wheels of motion started turning on the event. After observing Evo Kaplan confirming he had a significant relationship with Brenda Broyals, Reginald Heiqishi felt no remorse over killing his former subordinate, whom he trained and sent on over five hundred missions. *If Evo Kaplan had not diminished my character and slandered me, I would not have fired him and came here to kill him.*

Evo Kaplan brought this to himself.

To Reginald Heiqishi, the ends justify the means. Evo Kaplan was a traitor and the Empire needed to deal with his defection to the enemy. He knew that Brenda Broyals was the big fish and would put several feathers in his cap if he took her out, but Reginald Heiqishi instinctively knew if something happened to Brenda Broyals behind enemy lines, they would spare nothing in locating her killers to make an example of them.

It would not be the first time the Revolution sent video tapes of them driving people mad in the pool or burning them alive cussing in the crematorium. Reginald Heiqishi didn't want to be that person. That's why he wasn't going to allow Terrshey Wate to kill Brenda Broyals even if he had an easy target.

The Revolution would not waste much energy tracking a traitor's killers. And since his orders to sanction only Evo Kaplan if required was all that was necessary, then that's all that they would do and nothing more.

After a couple laps around the ship's main deck, Reginald Heiqishi thought he needed to excuse himself and go find Terrshey Wate and confer over the pending sanction later that day, either in broad daylight or dark if necessary.

Unfortunately, Reginald Heiqishi discovered the cameras had 360-degree coverage. There were no dark spots. But since they knew where the cameras all were, almost forty of them, he figured he only had to disable a couple along an area of the port side that would be facing out to sea where fewer passengers would be hanging out since the sights were all on the starboard side viewing toward landfall.

Reginald Heiqishi looked at his chronometer. He had planned a meeting in about fifteen minutes from now. Reginald Heiqishi had to temporarily separate from

Glacy, go do that planning meeting, then meet up with her again so that she would not be bird-dogging him and possibly interfere with his business.

Later that day after some copious lovemaking he would drug Glacy and put her out for a few hours so that he could have the free time he needed to conduct affairs.

REGINALD HEIQISHI
I need to go back to my cabin for a short while. I can meet you in, say, thirty minutes.

GLACY
Okay, honey.

REGINALD HEIQISHI
What cabin are you in?

GLACY
I'm in 4C. You can't get access to the area unless I give security your authorization. I'll do that now so they will let you in the penthouse suites.

REGINALD HEIQISHI
All right.

GLACY
See you soon.

Reginald Heiqishi gave Glacy a hug and a kiss on the cheek and turned and walked away heading to his first-class cabin suite he booked with Terrshey Wate. Their sea cabin was laid out like their resort rooms. Two bedrooms, an open area, and two bathrooms. No kitchen was available, as the ship provided all the food in their dining rooms and special restaurants.

RECONNAISSANCE AND PLANNING

Terrshey Wate had done his own reconnoitering, and as they compared notes, they concluded they had both sited all the cameras.

TERRSHEY WATE
It will be problematic disabling some of the video cameras.

REGINALD HEIQISHI
A couple of cameras could disable temporarily, do the hit if necessary, then turn them back on without getting caught.

TERRSHEY WATE
Wouldn't that cause some concern and alarm?


REGINALD HEIQISHI
Most ships that have material conditions, repairs are often deferred until return to port for several reasons. First and foremost, they do not want passengers to know something serious is broken.


TERRSHEY WATE
You think they would temporarily ignore it?


REGINALD HEIQISHI
The company would later think it was just an anomaly until someone reported Evo Kaplan missing, provided he didn't agree to come back to the Dranzonian Empire with us.


Reginald Heiqishi and Terrshey Wate would have no way of knowing the surveillance they had on them, because Brenda had informed Egor Pataslia they were taking the cruise today. As a result, he had four agents on board keeping an eye on the couple but maintaining a discrete distance to not tip them off they were under surveillance.


INT. CRUISE LINER CAPTAIN'S STATEROOM


Since planet *Shen de Huayuan* was under Revolutionary Empire direct control, the captain was informed by one of the secret service agents.


SECRET SERVICE AGENT
We have a total of four agents on board and will be monitoring several passengers.


SHIP'S CAPTAIN
What's their names?


SECRET SERVICE AGENT
Evo Kaplan, Brenda Broyals, Reginald Heiqishi, and Terrshey Wate identified as persons of interest. Evo Kaplan and Brenda Broyals were under our protection and the other two are suspects. We do not desire nor require any interference on the part of the crew. We plan on catching them in action and will deal with them.


<u>INT. BRENDA BROYALS and EVO KAPLAN CRUISE LINER CABINAFTERNOON – AT SEA.</u>

EVO KAPLAN
Brenda, why are you always carrying that purse with you everywhere you go?

BRENDA BROYALS
I have my toys in here.

EVO KAPLAN
Toys?

BRENDA BROYALS
Laser pistol, secret communicator, and a few other essentials in case I need them.

EVO KAPLAN
We are deep in Revolution territory. I would not expect any dangerous activity that would affect you here.

BRENDA BROYALS
One never knows when trouble will find them. I like to be prepared just in case.

VOICE OVER (FEMALE)
Brenda Broyals noticed Evo Kaplan's slip up that suggested he knew she was part of the revolution. He didn't seem overly concerned about it, which means his allegiance to the Dranzonians was most likely ended.

This in itself immediately reduced a lot of stress on Brenda Broyals. She would of course have to report this to Conrad Fanzui as a most positive development for her.

INT. REGINALD HEIQISHI AND TERRSHEY WATE CRUISE LINE CABIN-AFTERNOON – AT SEA.

and Terrshey Wate

REGINALD HEIQISHI
We will deactivate those two cameras on the port side after we leave the port the ship will soon pull into.

TERRSHEY WATE
How will we attempt to locate Evo Kaplan and coax him out on the main deck port side under the dead camera area to give him the ultimatum?

REGINALD HEIQISHI
On short cruises like this, passengers didn't stay long in their cabins. They were up on deck, in the casino, or at one of the many fine places to eat, which turns into dance clubs later in the evening after dining hours.


TERRSHEY WATE
Perhaps we can meet him at one of these locations and invite him out for a talk and if he refuses, deal with him then.


REGINALD HEIQISHI
That's most likely how it will have to be done.


Reginald Heiqishi then made his way to the elevator to go up to the penthouses.

INT. CRUISE LINER ELEVATOR AFTERNOON – AT SEA.

As Reginald Heiqishi approached the elevator, the security man observing his computer display saw the message to admit Blane Jiandie. His facial recognition picture and certification filed aboard the ship instantly identified him and gave the semaphore of admittance. The security man pressed the elevator button and when it opened, he gestured with his hand.


ELEVATOR SECURITY MAN
You may proceed, sir.
The elevator artificial intelligence knew Blane Jiandie was destined for cabin 4C, and as he was leaving the elevator, the computerized voice made an announcement.


ELEVATOR ARTIFICIAL INTELLIGENCE
COMPUTERIZED VOICE
Blane Jiandie, 4C is to your left, four doors down.


Just like the computer voice said, there was 4C. Reginald Heiqishi pressed the doorbell, and the butler answered the door and invited him in.


LUXURY ACCOMMODATIONS
CABIN 4C BUTLER


Blane Jiandie, please come in. Would you like a drink, sir?


BLANE JIANDIE
(a.k.a. REGINALD HEIQISHI)
Certainly.

LUXURY ACCOMMODATIONS
CABIN 4C BUTLER
Any preferences?


BLANE JIANDIE
(a.k.a. REGINALD HEIQISHI)
Yes, I've kind of taken a liking to a Huoshan Xingneng drink.
Can you make one of them?


LUXURY ACCOMMODATIONS
CABIN 4C BUTLER
You will have it momentarily, sir.


The butler went into the other room. There he contacted guest services ordering the drink to be placed on the small vertical conveyor dumbwaiter that serviced the suite. Within less than three minutes the drink arrived up the dumbwaiter on a small tray covered with a thin cardboard paper top to ensure no debris accidentally fell into the drink.

Per Glacy's instructions, who desired rip-roaring high-energy sex, she previously directed the butler to spike Blane Jiandie's drinks with one of the dozen small vials she gave the butler, which included an exotic drug about ten times more powerful than Viagra to help get him in the mood.

The butler took the paper cover off the top of the drink, poured the contents of one of the vials into the strong-tasting drink, stirred it with a stirrer, placed the paper cover back on then left his pantry and walked to the front room and served Blane Jiandie.


LUXURY ACCOMMODATIONS
CABIN 4C BUTLER
Here is your drink, sir. I hope you enjoy it.


VOICE OVER (FEMALE)
Glacy also placed her one hundred thousand credits per ounce *Romla de Verla* perfume that was loaded with pheromones on her breasts and along the curvature of her genitalia in case Blane wanted to explore. Just like at the Lantiane Resort, a cruise liner fashion designer had just been to the room, providing Glacy with the most provocative negligee. Glacy was ready. The sweet moment of a romantic cruise was just now manifesting. *Just wait until I tell the girls about this*, Glacy thought.


The Butler knocked on Glacy's bedroom door.

LUXURY ACCOMMODATIONS
CABIN 4C BUTLER
Madam, your guest has arrived.

Glacy
Thank you, Charles. That will be all for now.

Butler etiquette demanded that Charles return to his private cabin in the suite and remain there until summoned or discretely sent away, which sometimes happened when women who had a habit of being screamers during sex wanted privacy. Every butler assigned to the cruise liner penthouses was given the name Charles so that repeat passengers would not get confused. Their real names were something else.

Glacy waited a moment until she heard Charles's door close, and the green butler light lit, indicating he was available in his room for duties, before she left her bedroom, as she didn't want the butler to see her almost nudity. This delay also gave time for Blane Jiandie to finish most of his drink and have the drugs start to have their effect.

Today Reginald Heiqishi was slightly thirsty, so he polished off the drink rather abruptly. He was starting to wonder where the butler went and if he could get another drink as he felt thirsty when unexpectedly he started to feel arousal. He was also thinking about Glacy, who had a knock-out body, beautiful scent, teeth, and everything about her was exquisite.

Then suddenly Glacy appeared, and Reginald Heiqishi quickly forgot about his thirst as his lust soon overcame any other notions. Glacy held out her hand.

GLACY
Please come with me, darling.

Glacy led Blane Jiandie (a.k.a Reginald Heiqishi) into her bedroom that was very plush, had a king-sized bed, and lots of pillows. This suite was no doubt made for royalty. Glacy closed the door and locked it behind her, then walked up to Reginald Heiqishi, and put her arms around him.

GLACY
I want you now, Blaine. Can you take care of me please?

The negligee was designed so that one button at the top completely released it and it fell to the floor, exposing Glacy's nudity. Glacy then started helping Reginald Heiqishi undress and kissed him several times while she was assisting. Between looking at her body and the psycho-effective nature of the drugs in the drink,

Reginald Heiqishi was poised for this moment, but his lust and desires were multiplied, making him want Glacy as much as she wanted him.

The mutual attraction was magnetic, and their mental valence orbited each other's desires with incredible energy. In the matter of minutes, they were copulating and taking each other to succeeding higher plateaus as the splendid euphoria raged significantly longer than any normal person would ever experience. The two lost total track of time and collapsed into each other's arms as the lovemaking succumbed to the physical realities of their endurance.

VOICE OVER (FEMALE)

> Even though the drugs gave them the mental stimulus to continue copulating, their bodies could no longer respond so they lay there in each other's arms savoring the moment. Glacy had thoughts of her husband down at Orgy Island with the distinguished politician and smiled and said to herself and thought, **two** *can play this game.*

Despite the odds of their mental stimulation allowing it, they both fell into a slight coma, sleeping restfully and gratified to the maximum. Their tranquil period was eventually interrupted by the loud ship's whistle and the intercom.

SHIP'S CAPTAIN

> This is the captain speaking. We are now mooring at *Shenhuaban de Baozang.* We expect to be here about two hours to give passengers time to explore the nearby area and buy gifts while we exchange cargo and take on supplies. Organized tours are arranged and all you must do is go to the kiosk at the main entrance or call guest services. There will probably be a lot of people calling guest services, so I highly recommend you go to the kiosk where crewmembers will be there to assist you.

Glacy and her lover boy were soon making quick plans, and at the same time Evo Kaplan and Brenda Broyals were soon on their way to the kiosk area where a dozen terminals and a dozen crew members were helping guests get assigned to the various tours mostly designed by the locals, where they would be in position to offload a few credits from the passengers to support the local economy.

Evo Kaplan and Brenda were soon boarding the top of a triple-level bus that provided an hour and a half tour and would get the passengers back to the ship in plenty of time to accommodate the sail time.

The bus was soon underway and packed. All four of Egor Pataslia's agents were on the bus.

Coincidently Reginald Heiqishi and his new flame Glacy were also seated on the bus in the mid-level under observation by two of Egor Pataslia's agents. Thanks to hidden cameras, Egor Pataslia would have a considerable amount of video to share with Glacy's husband when the time came.

Glacy was unaware Egor Pataslia's agents had a long talk with Charles while Glacy was on deck talking to Reginald Heiqishi before their lover's tryst and she had already been filmed in a compromising position.

The tour guide began orating the information and all the passengers eagerly waited.

TOUR GUIDE

*Shenhuaban de Baozang* started out as a fishing village. As the coastal population slowly increased, arts and craftsmen descended upon *Shenhuaban de Baozang,* and a new culture emerged. Because of the nearby forests, large trees were felled, as they were needed to construct business and homes. Early history of the community is there were no roads in and out of *Shenhuaban de Baozang.* All transportation was by sea.

The tour guide gave everyone a chance to look at the countryside before continuing.

TOUR GUIDE

Eventually *Shenhuaban de Baozang* became a stopover for the traveling public going up and down the coast. Small hotels, bed and breakfasts, restaurants and taverns opened. Roads slowly came about and three hundred years ago, the Coastal Highway was completed, linking *Shenhuaban de Baozang* to the rest of the continent.

TOUR GUIDE

*Shenhuaban de Baozang* maintains its flair as an artist's community and as we drive along, we will make a few stops so that you will have opportunity to purchase souvenirs and art objects ranging from paintings to sculptures, 3D puzzles, and local craftsmanship you will not find anywhere else.

The tour guide didn't say much for a couple minutes then made an announcement. Evo Kaplan was looking over the landscape as the triple decker bus drove along.

TOUR GUIDE

If you look to the right, you will see hides tanning. The leatherwork is from certain wild animals that live in abundance in the hills and valleys east of the beach community. A lot of products you buy come from the wild. We only hunt enough to control the wildlife population so it does not over produce, which would lead up to damage to the forest and encroachment upon nearby family farms. Some of Leather also comes from domestic animals.

VOICE OVER (FEMALE)

The first stop was a short distance later. People piled off the triple decker tour bus off the front and rear entrances as well as a circular staircase at the end of the bus. Evo and Beverly walked through the exhibits, just enjoying looking at the products, mostly handmade with ingenious tapestry and geometry.

Unlike many planets that advanced technologically before confronted by alien beings, *Shen de Huayuan* was a backward planet without any knowledge of aliens when the Empire first visited almost three hundred years ago. To say the people were startled was a good assessment.

Because of the consequence of primitive means, there were still many establishments in the outward lying areas, barely using electrical power and lighting when Dranzonian super sophisticated spacecraft first landed that were operated by super computers.

This *Shen de Huayuan* primitive society would normally not develop for a thousand years from that first Dranzonian Empire visit. People enjoying the tour recognized the primitiveness in many of these handmade souvenirs.

Even though Evo would like to purchase something. for himself and Brenda, the reality is that once he got back to Zanziltar, those items would quickly be disposed of when he made subsequent missions. The sad fact was, until his six-year contract was complete, he couldn't accumulate anything.

Conceivably, Evo Kaplan might not last six years with the types of ongoing danger he experienced. Brenda Broyals appeared engrossed in the various items she observed. Brenda's life as a spy over the past five years removed her from society. Her artificial world had no room for trivial matters.

This was the first time in five years Brenda Broyals had a vacation where she could unwind and enjoy simple things like these trinkets, arts, and crafts.

Brenda Broyals and Evo Kaplan worked their way over to oil paintings  and sculptures and silently enjoyed observing them. Some of the artwork appeared existentially primitive in nature. Perhaps it was Dranzonian Empire aliens arriving at this planet before *Shen de Huayuan's* had developed technology that created the notion, and it was apparent that *Shen de Huayuan's* existence preceded essence.

Just about the time Brenda and Evo finished observing the last oil painting with great curiosity, the tour guide was calling everyone to return to the bus.

The tour guide was an experienced professional in this business and as soon as the head count matched the manifest, the triple-decker bus was traveling along continuing the tour.

TOUR GUIDE

*Shen de Huayuan's* The first generator used a reciprocating steam engine powering dynamos and a large flywheel with a regulator on it for smooth operation.

Ladies and gentlemen, if you look to the right, you will see a waterwheel spinning. That is a museum relic on display and was the first hydro-electric installation  providing this community electricity.

Unfortunately, the waterwheel only had enough volume of water to work nine months out of the year. During the dry summer months, the town was void of electricity until the first oil burning generator was brought in.

One of the most often asked questions about the first generator installed is: What kind of engine burned the oil?

Ladies and gentlemen, if you look to the right, you will see a small building with a smokestack. That was the first original generator installed in that building and is preserved by the National Historic Society.

Evo Kaplan noticed Brenda Broyals appeared to be enjoying herself quite immensely. Just what the doctor ordered. Just a few days of downtime had rejuvenated Brenda into almost a new person. When Evo first met Brenda, she was slowly declining into a state of haggardness. Perhaps Conrad Fanzui realized Brenda was reaching the state of exhaustion and mental breakdown?

Brenda was all smiles, full of life, loving, giving, and accommodative. What Evo didn't realize her state of ease was only manifested by the knowledge she had her laser pistol and she observed at least two of Egor Pataslia's men get on the bus with them. Brenda Broyals could be happy knowing she had some protection even though the possibility existed there was another enemy agent aboard the bus with his wealthy-looking lady friend.

Glacy (known as Lady Spencer back in Zanziltar) was also going through a period of surreal satisfaction. Turning into a Barracuda and sometimes a Cougar because her cheating husband made those frequent trips to Orgy Island with his politician friend, Glacy had accidently discovered a man who was quite affectionate and had one heck of a body on him that could perform. She had no idea she was sleeping with a deadly spy.

Reginald Heiqishi's physical fitness was only at peak performance as such because of his extensive training over the past few months, getting him prepared for this mission as well as several others.

Since Reginald Heiqishi's department thinned out with the massive expulsions, management had to suddenly do the yeoman's duty of intergalactic espionage since a large percentage of their field operatives either defected to the Revolution or were purged just like Evo Kaplan.

Since Glacy was shielded from the knowledge of who she was fooling around with, she had no concern. But one thing was certain, if she kept seeing Reginald Heiqishi, she would eventually hire a private detective to find out everything about him to protect herself.

The tour bus made a few more stops along the way, including a fresh fruit stand with juicers that had special ingredients that were on the contraband list passengers normally would not be allowed to access.

More artwork, a religious temple, and a few notables' homes who had discovered this community and retired here. One author in particular had a life story like the Earth person Hemingway.

Eventually the triple decker bus went back to the dock and the tourists re-boarded the ship.

The ship's purser was given a complete check of the sailing list of passengers thanks to the marvelous facial recognizing capability of the ship's computers. Everyone who left the ship was accounted for, so the ship could get underway.

One loud blast of the ship's whistle and the side thrusters pushed the ship away from the dock, and the water jets helped move it around and point it in the right direction to transit out into the deep ocean along coastal waters.

<u>EXT. VIEW OF SHIP FROM A DRONE SHOWING THE SHIP AND THE
COASTLINE - DAY.</u>

There was a couple more hours of sunlight left so the ship continued hugging
the coast at the one hundred-fathom curve to allow fewer course changes and go
in a more straight line passage. Occasionally the cruise liner would pass a boat
or another cruise liner, but for the most part there just wasn't a lot of ship traffic
in this area. The ship continued close to shore until sunset, then it veered on a
course of 270 degrees (West) out toward the open ocean and ostensibly where
there would be less traffic and threat of collision.

<u>INT. CRUISE LINER BRIDGE AREA WHERE THE NAVIGATOR PEERED
OVER ELECTONIC NAVIGATION CHARTS.</u>

The cruise liner slowly moved past the coastal shipping lanes set up on electronic
charts, which all ships used. The shipping lanes had north-bound traffic and south-
bound traffic lanes, each several miles wide to give separation and account for
potential navigation errors, which were slowly becoming less and less thanks to
satellite navigation. After the ship got a safe distance away from the shoreline and
the shipping lanes, it turned south in the direction it would go back to home base
and let off most of these passengers on a streaming flight of VTOL Sky-buses.

Glacy invited Reginald Heiqishi to her penthouse, which he did not agree with
because he had something to do.

REGINALD HEIQISHI
I want to go check in with my partner to make sure he knows
I'm aboard.

While Reginald Heiqishi was away doing his business, Glacy arrived at her
penthouse and was immediately met by her butler Charles.

CHARLES
Good evening, madam. May I please have the honor to inform
you that your presence has been requested at the captain's table
for dinner tonight.

GLACY
Oh my, I never planned for such an occasion. What do I do?

The butler Charles, who was an integral component to the penthouse, had dealt
with numerous scenarios over the years and offered a suggestion.

BUTLER CHARLES
If you are concerned about how to dress, why not have Guest
Services send a fashion designer and take care of that for you?

GLACY
Great idea, I should have thought about that.


CHARLES
Would you like me to call guest services for you?


GLACY
Oh Charles, that would be so wonderful, thank you.


A few moments later Charles reported back.


CHARLES
Madam, guest services have a lot of requests this evening. If you are going to utilize a fashion designer, they would need to come now with the hairdresser, makeup artist, et cetera.


GLACY
I suppose I have no choice. Send them here.


CHARLES
Right away, Madam Spencer.


GLACY SPENCER One other thing, please.


CHARLES
Yes, Madam?


GLACY SPENCER
Could you contact the ship's operator and have them send a message to Blane Jiandie and tell him I will be delayed getting dressed for dinner at the captain's table. Also contact reservations and tell them I needed to be seated with my friend Blane Jiandie at the captain's table or I would not be able to make it.


CHARLES
Madam, this is an extraordinary opportunity. The list of invitees has probably been thoroughly vetted. It may be impossible at this late hour.


GLACY
Well, I can't go to the captain's table for dinner without Blane.


CHARLES
I'll see what I can do.

About that time the fashion designer and the group arrived ready to work over Glacy. Blane Jiandie (a.k.a. Reginald Heiqishi) received the message from the ship's operator and sat there wondering how it would affect his evening. It might even work out better if she's out of my hair so I can supervise the Evo Kaplan mission.

The butler Charles was very elegant and savvy man. He knew that at this late hour he would have to take this seating issue to the first officer or even the captain himself if necessary. He started with the first officer, calling him on a private company line that only few knew the code to ring his office.

FIRST OFFICER
Hello, first officer speaking."

CHARLES
Sir, this is Charles Xianfeng. I'm the Butler for the penthouse 4C.

FIRST OFFICER
What can I do for you, Charles?

The first officer knew this was probably going to be a complicated request.

CHARLES
Sir, our deluxe passenger, Lady Glacy Spencer, is on the list of passengers invited to dine with the captain tonight. It turns out her secret lover is also on this ship, a Mr. Blane Jiandie. She wants to be seated next to him, or she will not be able to attend at the captain's table.

FIRST OFFICER
Charles, you should know, this time of day it's almost impossible to change that list without offending someone.

CHARLES
Yes sir, I'm aware that some of our distinguished passengers would be highly irritated to be kicked off the list of the captain's table.

FIRST OFFICER
There is nothing I can do about it now. The captain has already approved the list.

CHARLES
Would it be possible for me to talk with the captain about this matter?

FIRST OFFICER

Sure Charles, I'll transfer this call to the captain. I understand the delicate situation you are in, but I doubt he will be willing to make any changes this close to dinner hour.

CHARLES

I appreciate your help, sir.

FIRST OFFICER

No problem, Charles. Please standby, I'm going to put you on hold.

The First Officer picked up another phone, which was a private line between him and the captain and informed the captain of the situation. The captain had access to that phone line and touched the button that gave him access to the call.

SHIP'S CAPTAIN

Charles, this is the captain. I understand your situation with Mrs. Spencer.

The captain was thinking out loud.

SHIP'S CAPTAIN

Looking at the list of names, we are only seating twelve people. The table provides seating for fourteen people. They take up the extra room with extra flowers and such. I'll have the first officer add one more guest to the table and move the people around as necessary.

CHARLES

Thank you, sir. That solves a lot of issues.

SHIP'S CAPTAIN

You are quite welcome, Charles. I often get trans-galactic messages from vacationers off other worlds that speak very highly of you. Your professionalism is outstanding.

CHARLES

Thank you for your kind words, captain.

The captain then looked over his report provided to him as a curtesy of Egor Pataslia's men about the suspected Loyalist spy Blane Jiandie (a.k.a. Reginald Heiqishi). It was going to be an amusing moment: the captain of a cruise ship dining and entertaining an enemy of the state.

Speculating on how Glacy Spencer fit into all this also added an interesting twist to it. *I wonder how Mr. Spencer feels about his wife screwing around with an enemy spy?*


Moments later, Blane Jiandie (a.k.a. Reginald Heiqishi) received a call from the cruise ship guest services.

GUEST SERVICES.
Mr. Blane Jiandie, you will be seated at the captain's table with Lady Spencer, and you are requested to arrive at 7:00 P.M.

BLANE JIANDIE (A.K.A. REGINALD HEIQISHI)
Sounds interesting.

GUEST SERVICES.
Formal attire is required. If you did not bring formal attire with you, we will send a fashion designer who will fit you.

BLANE JIANDIE (A.K.A. REGINALD HEIQISHI)
Okay, when can they be here?

GUEST SERVICES.
Due to our high volume, they will have to come to your cabin now.

BLANE JIANDIE (A.K.A. REGINALD HEIQISHI)
Send them up.

Blane Jiandie (a.k.a. Reginald Heiqishi) was in for a big surprise.

Glacy who was currently getting her hair shampooed and, in a tub, getting a special splashdown that would give her effervescence and remove the essence of too much sexual activity done earlier in the day. After the two girls rinsed Glacy's hair, she was urged to exit the tub, which they immediately started draining, and they dried her off. They put a towel around Glacy's head.

FASHION STAFFER
The designer will have to measure you nude to properly fit you in the couture gown.

GLACY
I understand, I get a lot of makeovers.

As Glacy walked into the other room there was the fashion designer and others such as the makeup artist. The door was shut, giving them privacy and Charles was at his station in his private cabin reading a book, listening to music and waiting for his green light to come on that would be triggered via voice reorganization.

The couture designer had an eye for a body. She knew what type of garments to put on a woman based on her age, her size, her weight, and the essence of who she was.

A person would look out of place if they were not dressed for the lineage of who they were.

Good intel is always important for a couture clothing designer. On her way up to Penthouse 4C, the designer queried databases to discover exactly who Glacy Spencer was.

It became instantly clear that Glacy Spencer was the wife of a flamboyant wealthy banker who could wear just about anything she wanted because she could afford any couture the fashion designer had available.

The intel the designer got off several sources was the recent notoriety of the banker flying his political friend to Orgy Island, where the caretakers participated into human trafficking of young girls. The banker was obviously a creep and had now corrupted his wife, who had turned into a Barracuda and sometimes a Cougar, living a separate and equally sinful lives.

With the fashion designer's knowledge Madam Glacy Spencer would be entertained by the captain at his special table with a dozen other socially mobile people, sitting across from her male concubine, meant she needed to look like *a knockout beautiful bitch in heat.*

Looking at Glacy's body, she wasn't bad for a woman of her age. Glacy apparently got a lot of exercise doing the horizontal tango or other physical activity. There were numerous glamorous gowns the fashion designer could fit on this woman would be a great advertisement for her.

If Glacy was photographed and splashed on sordid contemporary periodicals that qualify for the title of yellow journalism, it would also propel the fashion designer's notoriety. Yes, she would make this woman look like an irresistible woman with an extravagant garment that would be extremely rare and costly.

The first startling revelation the fashion designer made to Glacy seemed shocking.

FASHION DESIGNER
You cannot wear underwear or a bra with this couture dress I'm going to fit you with. Also, during dinner try not to eat much or it might spoil the image.

GLACY What if I get hungry?

FASHION DESIGNER
After the captain leaves and the group melts away, come back to your room and change into something more casual and go to a restaurant and eat.

Glacy
I would rather use room service.

FASHION DESIGNER
Remember, this is all for your image, which you must protect as the beautiful woman that you are to make yourself alluring to other individuals that you might want to meet in the future.

The hint was well received, as Glacy allowed the fashion designers to proceed. The hair designer, makeup designer, nails makeover, and her toenails were soon showing works of effervescent beauty. Sooner than she realized they were all done and took her to the mirror, which captivated her in what she saw.

FASHION DESIGNER
You are now ready to go see the captain, Madam Spencer.

GLACY
You did such an incredible job. I'm almost shocked. I look twenty years younger.

FASHION DESIGNER
You were always twenty years younger and didn't know it!

Just as Glacy was about to whale up, the makeup designer admonished her.

MAKEUP DESIGNER ARTIST
Don't get emotional now. You will screw up your makeup and it
will take us another fifteen minutes to fix it. Be strong!

Glacy had the inner glow that gave her the confidence and the reserve she needed
to avoid that emotional outburst she felt so compelled to erupt.

The designers and helpers were slowly filing out of the cruise liner penthouse.
Looking at the clock, Charles, who saw the group depart on his security scanner,
went into the front room where Glacy stood in awe of her new image.


CHARLES
Madam Spencer, it's getting close to time to proceed to your
dinner. Would you like me to contact Mr. Jiandie and let him
know you are ready?


GLACY
Yes, could you ask him to come to the penthouse and escort me
from here?


CHARLES
Right away, Madam Spencer.


Charles reached Blane Jiandie just as his own fashion designers were exiting his
first class cabin.


CHARLES
Hello Mr. Jiandie?


BLANE JIANDIE (A.K.A. REGINALD HEIQISHI) Yes


CHARLES
Mr. Jiandie, this is Charles, the butler at Glacy's penthouse. She
asked me to contact you to inform you that she is ready and
would like you to come here and escort her to the first-class
dining hall.


BLANE JIANDIE (A.K.A. REGINALD HEIQISHI)
Charles, please inform Glacy I'll be right there.


CHARLES
Mr. Jiandie, I shall inform Glacy you are on your way.


After Reginald Heiqishi hung up the phone, he turned towards Terrshey Wate to
lay out the plan for this evening.

REGINALD HEIQISHI

Evo Kaplan and Brenda Broyals will most likely be in the first-class dining hall. When you think you can get access to Evo Kaplan, ask him to go outside in the dark zone and give him the ultimatum. If he turns you down, we'll figure out how to deal with him after that.


Terrshey Wate<br>All right.


VOICE OVER

Terrshey Wate was already decided how he would handle Evo Kaplan's assassination. He was going to perform an independent operation. He would kill Evo Kaplan and throw the body over the side and get this mission over with. That is exactly what Reginald Heiqishi didn't want him to do because he felt it would blow the mission.

Any time Evo Kaplan and Brenda Broyals left their sea cabin, Egor Pataslia's men were close by. With the captain's permission they installed a surveillance camera in the hallway and were in a cabin nearby to intervene if some nefarious activity started.

Evo and Brenda left the cabin and proceeded to the first-class dining room where they would be seated with another couple.

Evo hoped they were not nosey people asking too many questions. They had their cover story, but it was getting a little annoying having to tell the lie over and repeatedly.

Evo and Brenda were seated somewhat in the corner, which was terrific because Evo could look over the entire room and see all the guests. At the end of the dining room was a glass wall with a dining table on the other side of it. The person sitting at the end of that elevated dining table could observe the entire room. Evo instinctively knew that was the captain's table.

The thick glass wall was a special material, making it bullet proof in case there was a crazed assassin who suddenly appeared. The access to the captain's table was through a door that had two cruise line officers in dress uniforms standing at a podium with an electronic tablet, which contained the list of names invited to dine with the Ship's Captain with their most recent updated picture taken by surveillance video and processed by facial recognition technology.

For a while Evo and Brenda were at the table by themselves. During this time several people walked up to the ship's officers and were escorted to the captain's table. Moments later Blane Jiandie led Glacy Spencer up to the podium with the two officers.

Artificial Intelligence had already alerted the two officers the invited couple was arriving showing their latest pictures, thanks to facial recognition technology used throughout the ship. Glacy Spencer appeared fabulously gorgeous and exotic.

Glacy Spencer appeared to be the most beautiful woman in the dining hall this evening. Even Brenda greatly respected Glacy for her appearance and instantly knew who she was and who was with her, a Loyalist operative who created curiosity as to why he was here and seemed to always show up where Evo Kaplan went.

It was becoming crystal clear: Evo—and maybe even herself— were their targets. On the other side of the room two men were seated. It wasn't uncommon for men to travel together making business deals, but also making themselves available for Barracudas and Cougars that roamed these ships to reduce stress getting over activities their rich husbands were doing on far off planets.

Brenda recognized the two men as Egor Pataslia's men, probably sitting there to provide protection and keep an eye on the man with the wealthy woman. Most everyone in the dining hall knew they had to be there at 7:00 sharp if they wanted to hear the captain's comments and his toast to all the diners.

By 7:00 the dining hall was three quarters full. The background music, which was light and fresh, was suddenly interrupted. A military march that sounded like the MARCH portion of the Franz von Suppe "Light Calvary Overture" was played by the small orchestra that sat in the area in front of the tall glass wall, and the captain and two military escorts in dress uniforms marched down the long corridor and stopped just before the orchestra and large glass window.

Note to the cinematographer:

    The "Light Calvary Overture" March that should be played for the Ship's Captain entrance starts at the 2:22 mark and again the 5:14 mark on this YouTube video:

    https://www.youtube.com/watch?v=aF5nhMIyeqI

The Ship's Captain and his escorts did an "about face" and turned around, facing the diners. The music tailed off to a quiet room that had been previously loud and engaged in numerous conversations. In the quietness the captain began his speech.

SHIP'S CAPTAIN
On behalf of me and my crew I would like to thank you all for choosing this cruise ship and I hope you have a good experience while we are here. The weather report is good, and we expect to have calm seas tonight to make it a very enjoyable evening. We shall be arriving at noon tomorrow at your demarcation point. I hope you all have a safe and glorious evening.

Just like on cue from the side, a steward walked up to the captain and his two escorts with a glass of champagne on a velvet-covered tray and presented the glass to the captain.

SHIPS CAPTAIN
I would like to toast to all of you and hope your evening is filled with joy and happiness.

The captain tipped his glass and consumed the contents.

SHIPS CAPTAIN
Don't rush to eat, because in three hours this room turns into a dance hall, and you are all invited to stay and take part. For those of you with the desire to try your luck at gambling, our casino is next door, just aft of the dining hall, with access through the door behind you as well as from the main deck on the port and starboard sides.

Then on cue the orchestra began playing another portion of the "Light Calvary Overture" military march music and continued as he walked past the two ships officers by the podium and entrance to the captain's table behind the glass wall.

As the Ship's Captain arrived at the end of the table, he bowed and sat down. The march music played by the orchestra faded and soon they were playing light music again with violin, cello, and other wonderful instruments and combinations.

With the large glass window between the captain's table and the main first-class dining room, the noise level in the captain's dining area was considerably less. Sound-absorbing tiles in the ceiling and the opposite wall did a great job of quieting and isolating the sound from the casino next door.

The Ship's Captain was highly curious to hear from Blane Jiandie. He knew that whatever Blane had to say was fabricated, but he wanted to hear it, nevertheless.

To the captain, who was quite sophisticated, being former military and a shipping company captain who traveled the oceans and the stars in his distant past, was astonished to discover the wealthy banker's wife was fooling around with this alleged spy who was so poorly trained he didn't recognize his own cover was blown. Nor did he know Egor Pataslia had a novel way of getting rid of him.

Word was already on the way to Mr. Spencer about what his wife was doing. The banker didn't mind what Glacy did as long as she didn't take it public. By her scandalous action on this cruise liner and probably elsewhere, Glacy Spencer created huge embarrassment to Randolph Spencer. If she couldn't keep her affairs private, Randolph would have to set an example for her.

Unlike in the dining hall where the individuals ordered off a menu that was rather diverse and superb, the diners at the captain's table all received the same servings. That simplified everything and made it far more efficient. The captain figured out this method because he would rather spend time talking with the guests than them talking to waiters. Between courses, the banter existed in some cases joking, laughing, smiling, the discussion was light, and the captain was a master at keeping people off topics like religion, politics, and other divisive, sensitive topics.

The captain handled the people at the dinner table as well as he handled his ship and the employees that ran it. The ever-present Ship's Captain slept four hours a day while the ship was underway, which was at least five days a week. The remainder of his time he spent with his precious dog Scotty going on walks.

While the captain was away, he put his neighbor in charge of Scotty. Scotty loved the neighbor, but when the captain arrived home, he and Scotty clicked. There was no doubt who was the man's best friend.

Brenda and Evo waited to order dinner until the couple sharing the table arrived, out of respect and decorum. After they made their introductions and scaled each other down well, the atmosphere warmed a bit as the couple discovered Evo and Brenda were a handsome couple and quite sweet and demure, though they had no awareness that Brenda could erupt into a killer real fast if someone threatened her or her lover Evo Kaplan.

If the couple sitting across from them had any notion of what Evo had done at Stonue to Chuo Wanpi and others, they would be standing up and running for the exits. It was better for the public if they didn't know these things.

The other couple was from an outlying solar system, and both could speak standard Dranzonian so they could effectively communicate. The husband was a businessman and the wife a schoolteacher.

Evo and Brenda's cover story was boring so there wasn't much to get into. They ordered their dinners and soon were delighted at the expertise of the chefs. The drama began when after dessert when a man in a tuxedo approached Evo Kaplan and asked, "Sir, may I have a moment of your time? I need to talk to you about a pressing matter.

Evo looked at the man and was curious and said, "Okay."

On the way to the dining hall, Evo Kaplan almost demanded Brenda take her purse back to the sea cabin, but she outright refused and also would not explain why. Evo was suddenly glad she didn't comply with his wishes.

Brenda overheard part of the conversation and thought there was some resemblance to the man she had seen before. What she didn't know was Terrshey Wate was an expert at putting on temporary masks and often put on disguises.

Terrshey Wate and the Dranzonian Empire Secret Service were quite aware of the explosion of facial recognition technology and the massive databases that existed that had just about every living person in the Empire recorded.

Evo wanted to know what this was all about and followed the man outside, which from his seat was really a short distance. From the captain's table, Reginald Heiqishi knew the operation was underway and hoped Evo Kaplan would come to his senses and not force them to go the extra mile that would end up unpleasant to all of them. Evo was being led a short distance to a prepared dark zone. Once there the man turned around and looked at Evo.

TERRSHEY WATE

Evo Kaplan, we don't have much time so I need to get this message to you as fast and as careful as I can. You need to pay attention and realize that you must do as I direct or else something bad may happen to you.

EVO KAPLAN<br>What is it you want me to do?

TERRSHEY WATE<br>We want you to return to Praxisvlasia with us tomorrow.

EVO KAPLAN<br>Why would I want to do that?

TERRSHEY WATE

You are with a Revolution Spy, Brenda Broyals. She's on our top ten kill list at all costs.

EVO KAPLAN
I don't believe you.

TERRSHEY WATE
Listen, Evo Kaplan, we don't have time to argue about this. You are cozying around with a female Revolution agent who killed a lot of our people. You need to come back with us tomorrow, or bad things will happen to you.

EVO KAPLAN
I'm not going back with you. Remember, you guys threw me out and to the wolves. I was almost starving to death when the FIRM picked me up.

TERRSHEY WATE
You mean the Revolution.

EVO KAPLAN
I don't know that.

TERRSHEY WATE
I can't waste any more time with you. Are you coming back with me tomorrow?

EVO KAPLAN
No, I'm not going anywhere with you.

Terrshey Wate lost control. His arrogance overruled his common sense and out of ego and false sense of power because he carried a laser pistol with him and he was a top expert in martial arts decided to do exactly what Reginald Heiqishi implored him not to do: he pulled out his laser pistol.

Evo was about six feet away–a safe distance where Evo had no chance to defend himself.

Terrshey Wate pointed the laser pistol at Evo's head and one half second before he started to pull the trigger with a high-power shot that would send a sharp needle point through the center of Evo's head and kill him instantly. Just at that moment Terrshey Wate suddenly felt a pain in his side.

Terrshey Wate's intestines were cooking as Brenda's laser pistol was cutting deep into him. His natural response of turning and recognizing the pain—which, due to its location—was intense.

This delay gave Evo Kaplan enough time to grab Terrshey Wate's arm and the pistol and dragged it down as hard as he could on his knee, snapping Terrshey Wate's wrist.

Egor Pataslia's men had quickly following Brenda Broyals out of the dining hall and arrived right about the time Brenda fired her laser pistol and Evo broke Terrshey Wate's wrist and kicked the gun overboard through the railings. When Terrshey Wate turned toward Brenda with that incredible look on his face, Brenda Broyals raised her aim and hit Terrshey Wate between his eyeballs. He fell, instantly dead.

Egor Pataslia's two men knew Terrshey Wate was dead and grabbed the body and picked it up and walked to the railing and tossed the body into the ocean with about five thousand fathoms of water below them. That simplified everything. Nobody would be looking for him since he was a spook and his boss just disavowed him.

Terrshey Wate became another casualty of the ongoing fratricidal Revolution and civil war. The scuffle hardly affected any of their appearances and they went back to their dinner as if nothing happened.

Reginald Heiqishi looked out from time to time to try and spot Terrshey Wate and saw Evo Kaplan and Brenda Broyals sitting at their dinner table as if nothing happened.

After dinner Evo Kaplan and Brenda Broyals went back to their ocean liner cabin and soon there was a knock on the door. Through the peep hole, Evo could see it was one of the guys who tossed the enemy over the side. Evo opened the door and invited him in. Brenda stood up, knowing this was one of Egor Pataslia's men.

EGOR PATASLIA'S AGENT<br>
I want you two to stay in your cabin until we return to port.

EVO KAPLAN<br>
Sure, no problem.

EGOR PATASLIA'S AGENT
I have orders from Egor Pataslia to escort you to the spaceport as soon as we arrive back at Lantiane Resort. You have reservations to Zanziltar on the next Intergalactic Transport leaving *Shen de Huayuan.*

Brenda Broyals felt sad their vacation was cut short. But it was for their own good to get off the planet in case there was an inquiry and surveillance video connected them somehow to the disappearance of the Loyalist.

Egor Pataslia knew that Brenda and Evo would become suspects after all the video was analyzed. Since both were spooks and Brenda was due for a name change and Evo had traveled under an alias, they would re-invent themselves in the weeks to come.

Tracking them back to Zanziltar would help create another dead end. As morning arrived, they were looking forward to going back to Zanziltar.

The ship had traveled slowly and quietly during the night so everyone could sleep. After breakfast the high-speed running would commence. Breakfast was provided by room service arranged by Egor Pataslia's men. Coincidently, no sooner than the dishes were taken away by guest services, the captain began his announcement over the ship's intercom.

SHIP'S CAPTAIN

> Ladies and gentlemen, we are in the process of locking the ship
> down. Everyone on deck is being escorted inside the ship and
> all outside doors are being locked for passengers' safety. We
> will start our high-speed running in approximately five minutes.

Just like before, the captain ordered the hydroplanes lowered and locked in place. When reports indicated all doors were locked and a final deck sweep found nobody left outside the hull on deck, the orders to accelerate to high speed were given.

The thousand-foot-long ship, very well streamlined, increased speed, and as expected at 70 knots the hull broke the grip of the water on the hull and it rose its hydrofoil profile fifty feet into the air. After a while they were up to 140 knots per hour, cruise speed.

Design specifications indicated the hydrofoil cruise liner could easily operate at 170 knots per hour, but 140 knots gave it far better margin of safety for not only stress on the hydrofoils but also collision avoidance. The closure rate of two similar hydrofoil ships closing each other on reciprocal headings meant very little reaction time.

Time passed seemingly quickly during the high-speed operation and after a couple hours the Ship's Captain made an announcement.

SHIP'S CAPTAIN
The ship will be slowing.

A brief time later after they had slowed down to around 5 knots pointing shore, the first of a wave of VTOL Skybus's came down on the ship and landed. The richest were the last on and the first off.

Evo Kaplan and Brenda Broyals were on the first off, the cruise liner ship in a VTOL Skybus.

As soon as the Skybus landed near the front entrance of the resort in a landing pad area that had wind deflectors to prevent the huge blasts from the four jet engines from hitting pedestrians and vehicles nearby. Two of Egor Pataslia's men were in the VTOL Skybus and when the passengers disembarked, a limo pulled up and one of these two men notified Brenda and Evo this was their vehicle.

EGOR PATASLIA'S OPERATIVE

This is your ride to the spaceport. You will be leaving in about an hour. All your travel documents and personal items are in the trunk of the car.

VOICE OVER

Reginald Heiqishi never saw Terrshey Wate again, nor any sign of what happened to him. The fact he disappeared after taking Evo Kaplan out of the first-class dining hall suggested that foul play was involved.

Reginald Heiqishi didn't observe Brenda leave the dining hall when she left and returned because he was temporarily distracted by Glacy talking to him and the captain.

The two men sitting at the end of the dining hall were innocuous and didn't stand out. Reginald Heiqishi had no reason to observe them and didn't spot their departure and return.

As far as Reginald Heiqishi was concerned the only person possibly involved in Terrshey Wate's disappearance was Evo Kaplan. That also meant Evo Kaplan refused to go back to Praxisvlasia. Terrshey Wate probably got himself killed doing exactly what Reginald Heiqishi directed him not to do.

In a way Reginald Heiqishi felt guilty because he should have leveled with Terrshey Wate and explained he had Evo Kaplan removed on a personal vendetta, but the fact was he truly is a deadly spy, and you are in peril if you tango with him. Terrshey Wate was really facing four deadly spies. He had no chance his arrogance and Reginald Heiqishi's extremely poor leadership got him killed.

Now Reginald Heiqishi was in a bind himself: he had to leave right away or explain the disappearance of Terrshey Wate, making himself a suspect. He absolutely could not make a report to the authorities because his identity could possibly be discovered, and he certainly didn't want to visit the swimming pool or the crematorium for which the Revolution was famous.

Reginald Heiqishi got off the cruise liner and went back to the resort. He immediately made reservations. He missed the flight leaving in fifteen minutes. His next opportunity was a flight around midnight. Since he was effectively running from the law, he didn't bother checking out of the resort. He only took what he needed, as he had already thrown overboard the ship all his spy craft he no longer needed as soon as he figured his partner had screwed up.

No incriminating evidence was left in their hotel suite. He was essentially leaving the resort with little more than the shirt on his back and some fond memories of Glacy Spencer. Since Reginald Heiqishi wasn't carrying much and had time to kill, he took a Tri-wheeler to the heart of the city and walked around for a few hours, taking in all the sights. A couple hours prior to his flight to Zanziltar, Reginald Heiqishi took another tri-wheeler to the space port and was eventually boarded and traveled to Zanziltar.

Reginald Heiqishi was picked up by Hari Nuvrean, the Dranzonian Empire Secret Service agent located in Zanziltar Consulate and driven to a safe house.

Hari Nuvrean debriefed Reginald Heiqishi and since nobody could track him down from his alias Blane Jiandie, who was also the name of a real Secret Service operative on Praxisvlasia, he was in the clear.

Before Reginald Heiqishi traveled back to Praxisvlasia, he was going to receive cosmetic surgery on Zanziltar and go through another identity change and alias. Egor Pataslia had set up Reginald Heiqishi, who made the fatal blunder of going into the city with his Blane Jiandie appearance.

Glacy Spencer's husband was notified that Glacy's secret lover was now at the Sanctuary City, at planet Zanziltar, probably to continue with the scandal he didn't want going anywhere.

Guns for hire who heard rumors of contracts available were on the lookout. They would be paid handsomely for information on Blane Jiandie's whereabouts.

One such desperate soul who was overdue payment to his bookie spotted Blane Jiandie walking in the central business area of the sanctuary city the day before the cosmetic surgery despite repeated warnings to Reginald Heiqishi to stay at the safe house.

<u>INT. DAY. SANCTUARY CITY ORGANIZED CRIME ASSOCIATE MEETING UNDISCLOSED LOCATION</u>

The Informant was paid for his information.

INFORMANT
Can I get the contract to do the contract killing?

We don't want to kill him. We just wanted to find him. Our customer has his own killers.

The customer knew the killers were professionals he knew would never be discovered. He knew the organization by the name FIRM.

Conrad Fanzui called Evo Kaplan into his office for a little talk.

CONRAD FANZUI
Hello, Evo.

EVO KAPLAN
Hello, Conrad.

CONRAD FANZUI
Sorry your vacation didn't turn out as well as you planned.

EVO KAPLAN
That's okay. It was fun while it lasted.

CONRAD FANZUI
I have two new jobs for you.

EVO KAPLAN
What's the nature of the jobs?

CONRAD FANZUI
You should know we have a lot of sources of information you wouldn't realize.

EVO KAPLAN
I assume you do.

CONRAD FANZUI
Your old boss, Reginald Heiqishi, is here on Zanziltar.

EVO KAPLAN
Do you know why he's here?

CONRAD FANZUI

He's due to get plastic surgery tomorrow before they ship him
back to Praxisvlasia.

EVO KAPLAN

Why did they ship him here for plastic surgery, the Dranzonian
Secret Service is quite capable of doing it on Praxisvlasia.

CONRAD FANZUI

We know how he ruined you. Did you know he was on that ship
with you and with the assassin who tried to kill you?

EVO KAPLAN

No, I was unaware. That's interesting.

CONRAD FANZUI

He was with that beautiful woman in the purple dress at the
night club *Banma Julebu* sitting near you. You didn't spot him
because he had changed his identity with cosmetic surgery.

EVO KAPLAN
Okay.

CONRAD FANZUI
I'm going to give you the opportunity to kill him.

EVO KAPLAN
When?

CONRAD FANZUI
Today, in probably an hour.

EVO KAPLAN
Where at?

CONRAD FANZUI
You will be taken to him.

EVO KAPLAN
How am I to kill him?

CONRAD FANZUI

You can either beat him to death using your martial arts or just
shoot him with a laser pistol. It's entirely up to you.

EVO KAPLAN
You said two jobs.


CONRAD FANZUI
As soon as you kill your old boss, I'm going to send you to a
planet called Arzon, where we need to know what's going on
the planet. You will receive a special briefing over the next few
days before you go there.


EVO KAPLAN
How am I going to get there?


CONRAD FANZUI
You will travel to Praxisvlasia on a blockade runner that will
make a quick stop to pick up additional passengers for Arzon
and it will then continue on Arzon.


EVO KAPLA
When can I see Brenda again?


CONRAD FANZUI
After the Arzon mission.


EVO KAPLAN
How long do you anticipate the Arzon mission will last?


CONRAD FANZUI
It could be several weeks or several months.


EVO KAPLAN
What do you expect me to find there?


CONRAD FANZUI
We do not know much about their military buildup. That's why
we are sending you. To find out what their military situation
is and how prepared they are and report back via special
communications we'll set up for you.


EVO KAPLAN
Anything else?


CONRAD FANZUI
No. Go out to the front entrance. There will be a vehicle there
to take you someplace to go visit your old boss.

VOICE OVER

Evo knew he was in over his head. He was not going to be a permanent Revolutionary, and since they had Reginald Heiqishi in their custody, he was a dead man anyway.

The least Evo Kaplan could do is quickly put Reginald Heiqishi out of his misery. Evo Kaplan knew that Reginald Heiqishi and his assistant came really close to killing him and that he was sent out to do the job.

Reginald Heiqishi knew the rules of the game. Had he listened to Hari Nuvrean and stayed in the safe house until after his facial change surgery he would not be facing death. Eventually his arrogance caught up with him and now he had the opportunity to face the man he ruined in a way he never would have imagined.

If a spy gets caught, they are usually dead men. Evo Kaplan would never be able to go back to Praxisvlasia after doing what he had to do. He instinctively knew he had to do it just to stay alive.

This killing ritual was simply a test put on Evo Kaplan to validate his reliability and to show no remorse for killing a Dranzonian Empire Secret Service Agent, who also happened to be his former boss who mistreated him and came close to killing him as it was.

In a way it felt evil killing Reginald Heiqishi but doing it also meant Evo Kaplan got to stay alive an additional day. Killing a dead man, one already slated to be killed by the Revolution, had no bearing on the outcome of the war or anything else. It was more humane because Evo Kaplan would shoot him in the right spot to ensure he was instantly dead and not feel much pain.

The vehicle drove to the countryside to another shack that had been abandoned some time ago because of the chemical works nearby often emitting large plumes of chemicals, making it intolerable to live there. When the car came to a halt in front of the building, a man opened the car door and Evo got out and followed him into the abandoned house.

There in front of him was a man who looked like someone else. In fact, it was an ingenious disguise making him look like another Dranzonian Empire Secret Service agent. But Evo Kaplan knew the Revolutionaries had already verified his identity through DNA analysis, palm prints, and retina scans, since the Revolution had captured all the demographic information on most of their enemies' spies in data breaches.

EVO KAPLAN

Looks like they did a good job of cosmetic surgery on you, Reginald Heiqishi.

Reginald Heiqishi didn't answer and had some bruises from being worked over. One of the benefits of being a spy is when you captured the enemy you got the opportunity to knock out a couple teeth or do some real sadistic things like you did to their men.

EVO KAPLAN

Had you not fooled around with that rich guy's wife, you wouldn't be here now. Apparently, the banker hired the FIRM to make you regret touching his wife.

REGINALD HEIQISHI
Go to hell.

Any other spy would have smashed Reginald Heiqishi about then, but Evo Kaplan knew it would be a waste of energy since he was going to kill him in a few minutes anyway.

EVO KAPLAN

I just want to know one thing. Why did you purge me and throw me out to the wolves to starve to death?

REGINALD HEIQISHI

You're a filthy punk. You embarrassed me in front of my supervisors.

EVO KAPLAN

Well, now, if you were not so incredibly incompetent, I would not have had to embarrass you. You almost got me killed on numerous occasions because you didn't do your job correctly.

REGINALD HEIQISHI

I feel good I threw you to the wolves and now you will never be able to step foot in the Dranzonian Empire for the rest of your life.

EVO KAPLAN

Okay, boss. Now I have something for you too. You will never be able to step foot in the Dranzonian Empire again as well.

Evo raised his laser pistol, and the strong beam of light went right through the middle of Reginald Heiqishi's head. The spy died instantly and felt no pain. Evo

Kaplan did him a favor because he was going to the swimming pool if Evo didn't pull the trigger. Conrad Fanzui, who soon watched the video recording of the event a short while later, no longer had any concern about Evo Kaplan. He would never swear an oath to the Revolution. He had a higher calling: surviving as a spy and beating his opponents.

<u>Arzon Mission</u>

VOICE OVER (FEMALE)

Things were not going well in Arzon. This once highly developed civilization thought it was immune to most galactic strife. Its fleet had been highly developed and second to none. It ranged the galaxy, much for exploration as the Arzon's had very little appetite for imperialistic spreading like many other civilizations, as their wise men understood the consequences of expanding an Empire too far and wide.

Arzon itself was the by-product of the overambitious spreading of civilization beyond manageable distances. In the great divide that occurred, they were cut off from the Dranzonian Empire and suddenly found themselves isolated and existing in a vast distance that would require travel through the aggressive Revolutionary sectors of space.

It did not take long before the Arzon's discovered they were permanently cut off from all other Loyalist forces.

Life continued and, thanks to great distance and seemingly lack of excessive resources, revolutionaries had no incentives to travel to the barren region that had been a drain on the Dranzonian Empire and had not learned to stand on their own two feet, since obtaining all they needed from the Dranzonian Empire was easy to accomplish as they traded intellectual properties with all the resources they needed delivered over vast distances.

When the sudden realization existed, that Arzon was cut off from the Dranzonian Empire, the Arzon's suddenly were thrust into picking up the pieces and began self-sufficiency. No doubt it was rough at first, but thanks to the ample brain power they developed over the years due to the emphasis they placed on education, they slowly engineered their way out of their circumstances and, quite sooner than anyone predicted, built, and designed systems that provided self-sufficiency.

The Arzon's were alone in their solar system. The nearest inhabited solar system existed beyond seven other solar systems, where the Revolutionary Empire had consolidated much of the infrastructure and political systems. Plagued with continuous attrition from war with the Dranzonian Empire, venturing out toward Arzon was neither desirable nor required.

The Arzon's simply were forgotten, and since after learning the mistakes of travel toward Loyalist planets the Arzon's never attempted, it made it much easier for the Dranzonian Empire to forget Arzon existed.

Since the Arzon's were free to develop and would have received the Revolutionary Empire Fleet peacefully, because they had chosen to not arm themselves; they would be treated humanely had that visit occurred, but it did not.

There would never have been any Arzon spacecraft except for the need to get precious materials off nearby mining planets to support life. Hence, the Arzon Space Fleet really began as simply commercial transport for bauxite, iron ore, petroleum distillates that were refined on the mining planets, and vast other natural resources.

The few remaining Dranzonian Empire spacecraft that had made their way to Arzon but could never safely traverse the vast region of Revolutionary Empire space, served a couple useful purposes.

These Dranzonian spacecraft provided the basic essential transportation to the outward lying planets in the Arzon solar system, but they could never be reverse engineered.

Normally such reverse engineering would not be permitted as the Dranzonian Empire was strict about manufacturing all spacecraft at the home planets to prevent proliferation of technology into rebel areas, which ultimately happened without their consent.

Faced with the need to import a vast amounts of resources from nearby planets and since they were conceivably cut off forever from the Dranzonian Empire, the Arzon's selected a couple of the most useful class of transports for disassembly and reverse engineering.

Re-engineering progress took almost three years, but in due time the Arzon's achieved the impossible: they succeeded at copying and building a standard fleet transport that could also be reconfigured with armaments for self-protection.

Because of several intrusions into Arzon space by Revolutionary Empire assets, fear suddenly drove the Arzon's to do what they detested the most: build warships.

Hence the genesis of a powerful fleet began for that one day in the future when they feared they may be forced to defend the planet from Revolutionary forces.

Arzon cities were built at great expense before the Dranzonian Empire fell apart. Arzon was considered a future provincial capital, which would be the stop over for another finger of expansion of the Dranzonian Empire in their direction.

Thanks to the nearby nebula and other astronomical findings, they certainly were on the path to expansion, as people on Earth would think, the great Silk Road to the universe.

The consensus is that if the Revolutionary Empire only sent a modest fleet, the Arzon's might be able to defend their planet. However, if they arrived with a large invasion fleet, the outcome would seem rather bleak. Another good reason to avoid travel through Revolutionary Empire space.

Unfortunately, a diverse society such as the Dranzonian Empire before the breach and breakup left families separated. People made every effort to get home to see their families again. It resulted in travel that ostensibly was restricted, nevertheless.

The five members of the Committee for State Security that formed in the Revolutionary Empire sector called all the shots. They held routine meetings to decide the faith of the New Empire and they subsequently renamed the Revolutionary Empire.

The Revolutionary Empire suddenly discovered interest in Arzon as it lay in the pathway of future expansion. Soon followed high level meetings to discuss the plan forward.

REVOLUTIONARY EMPIRE<br>
LEADER NUMBER ONE<br>
We can infiltrate Arzon with our spies.

REVOLUTIONARY EMPIRE
LEADER NUMBER TWO
Not a bad idea since it's almost mandatory that we do and find
out what is really going on there.


REVOLUTIONARY EMPIRE
LEADER NUMBER ONE
When is the next blockade runner scheduled to go there?


REVOLUTIONARY EMPIRE
LEADER NUMBER TWO
According to intel sources, a hyperspace runner is clandestinely
taking reservations now, due to depart in a couple weeks from
Zanziltar and stop at Praxisvlasia to pick up all the Arzon-
bound passengers. We could put a spy on that ship before it
leaves Zanziltar.


REVOLUTIONARY EMPIRE
LEADER NUMBE ONE
We need to let the ship pass through our zone so that we can get
our spy planted on Arzon.


REVOLUTIONARY EMPIRE
LEADER NUMBER TWO
Certainly. We will have exact times and dates within two weeks.


One could equate the Committee for State Security to what occurred on Earth
during Napoleon's rise to power. Ultimately the Revolutionary Empire would
make the same mistake as the French did, as they were now in the process of
anointing Cornelius Xie de Hundan.

The future events the Revolutionaries would experience had amazing parallels to
the French in the early 1800s.

A reckless leader led the Revolutionaries down the path of self-destruction when
they could simply have consolidated their gains and carved out a new existence in
the former crossroads to the Empire.

Immediately upon his coronation, Cornelius Xie de Hundan dispersed the five
members of the Committee for State Security to the four corners of the new
Empire on fact-finding trips to discover the strength and weaknesses that may pose
a threat if the remnants of the Dranzonian Empire they now occupied attempted
to recover their vast lost territories. During the Revolution, surprisingly, a lot of
military personnel joined in with the Revolutionaries. More spectacular was the
number of intelligence operatives who also switched allegiances.

As soon as it became apparent a mutiny occurred in the fleet and over half of all space assets ended up in the hands of the Revolution's Committee for State Security, the foregone conclusion was rather apparent.

One could describe the process similar to rats jumping off a sinking ship back in the wood ship sailing days. Hence Cornelius Xie de Hundan ended up with one of the largest spy networks in the galaxy.

In due time Cornelius Xie de Hundan had meetings with his spy masters and got his reports.

Your excellency, the transport is leaving Praxisvlasia in the very near future heading to Arzon.

Good, make sure we let it sneak through to Arzon.

Our forces will be instructed to not interfere with its progress even though we know it will be traveling through an area we could easily jump it and commandeer the ship.

I'm more concerned about getting a spy to Arzon so we can get an update what they are up to.

One of our spies will be on the ship. He'll get the bottom line for us.

What's his name?

Sir, it's best you do not know. We do not disclose our spies' identities to anyone. They are very easy to compromise if people outside our control can identify the individual.

How will we manage to get a spy into Praxisvlasia and then on to Arzon?

We recruited him at Praxisvlasia and trained him at our Zanziltar facility. He's been tested on a few missions. He was part of the Secret Sanctuary City Service establishment prior to the revolution. Once he altered his allegiance to our cause, we asked him to go to Arzon to be ableto be useful to us and report the situation there.

So, he'll be a deep cover operative.

Yes, sir.

The black market was alive and well on Arzon. This activity was overlooked because the Arzon's were so desperate for materials, the government looked the other way.

Ships originating at Zanziltar would arrive via Praxisvlasia or some other Dranzonian Empire port loaded with people and trans-shipments to Arzon.

The outlaws that run this operation often described it as the "Pigs and People Run," and the pilots of those ships were called "Hoggers" since there were many cases of livestock shipped in the cargo holds.

Those animals, of course, had to be sedated the entire trip; otherwise, they would injure themselves in the cargo bay of the ship and lose their value to the black marketers who sold such animals to settlers starting up new agriculture activities or simply a restaurant business that wanted to provide some extremely rare meats and poultry, until the world became more civilized.

<u>INT. DAY. SECRET SERVICE BRANCH OF THE MINISTRY FOR STATE SECURITY, DRANZONIAN EMPIRE PRAXISVLASIA HEADQUARTERS</u>

VOICE OVER

The Secret Service branch of the Ministry for State Security in the Dranzonian Empire headquarters in Praxisvlasia had heads up of Evo Kaplan's mission that had already been compromised by Huaiyuansu Ka's recent report to Hari Nuvrean in a safe house Zanziltar.

This mission was deemed so important to the Dranzonian Secret Service that a Department Head summoned a hand-picked person to handle it and deal with Evo Kaplan.

This spy deemed to be one of their premier operatives was none other than the real Blane Jiandie. This would be a dangerous assignment because Reginald Heiqishi had used Blane Jiandie's identity.

Blane Jiandie was dismayed that his long-awaited vacation just got canceled.

Blane Jiandie arrived at room 40 of the Revolutionary Empire Dranzonian code breakers annex. Dranzonian code breakers were hard at work in nearby rooms decrypting and discovering the contents of Revolutionaries communications. This room was selected for this briefing because of its extra security and graphics capabilities.

BLANE JIANDIE
Sir, do you wish to see me?

SECRET SERVICE DEPARTMENT HEAD
Yes, shut the door and come on in and have a seat.

VOICE OVER
The Secret Service Department Head knew the conversation was not going to be a pleasant one.

The real Blane Jiandie knew people didn't get summoned to see a Secret Service Department Head unless it was an important issue.

Timing was not pleasing because Blane Jiandie anticipated he would soon depart on his vacation he had planned for a while to unwind and drink copious amounts of drug-fortified alcoholic beverages on Fantasy Island, the ultimate tourist destination for single men who were poised to meet a nice woman.

If Blane Jiandie was not able to meet a nice-looking woman, Fantasy Island management would fly in to the resort appropriate hostess with impeccable credentials of a pleasure provider as good as anywhere in the galaxy. Fantasy Island operates just like a Japanese Love Hotel.

Blane Jiandie assumed he would meet a very nice lady to spend some quality time and felt secure enough to know he would not be needing the second alternative. But he also knew very few of those single men that arrived would be in fantastic shape like he was, because as part of his requirements for the spy business was twenty hours of hard work out per week to maintain top physical condition.

Once a month Blane Jiandie went on one hundred-mile hikes to measure his ability to self-relocate under arduous conditions, which was often the case in the spy business when one had to bug out when their cover was blown.

Blane Jiandie thoughts of meeting that mysterious woman was brutally interrupted by that unpredictable phone call, several hours prior, just the day after he signed out for leave and would not be back for three weeks, on a Praxisvlasia calendar.

Blane Jiandie knew what type of man the department head was, because people didn't get promoted in this business to a department head level without some extraordinary politics or connections.

No doubt, the department head had been involved in some of the most wicked experiences bestowed on such mortals during the revolution, when it was not clear who was the enemy and who was a friend. Behind that poker face of the department head wore a mask of steel and a heart of Krypton.

This department head was the type of person who would send his own mother to hell if he thought it would help him get ahead in some way. No dirty task was too much to ask of him.

The department head helped to sift out most of the moles and no doubt killed quite a few innocents just because their loyalty could not be proven beyond a shadow of doubt. In the Secret Service, the post revolution days were a period of cleansing unlike anyone could ever imagine.

The fratricidal event slowly carved the cancer out of the organization and loyalty was a premium. Without loyalty, you would not be allowed to remain in the Secret Service, where nobody got fired— they simply disappeared in ways nobody could ever trace. Since they were part of the secret service, their murders were easily explained to their families: *We are very sorry, but your husband was killed in the line of duty fighting the revolutionaries.*

SECRET SERVICE DEPARTMENT HEAD

You probably weren't expecting to be called back to work today.

BLANE JIANDIE

I already made arrangements and signed out on leave.

SECRET SERVICE DEPARTMENT HEAD

Yes, I'm aware of that, but something has come up.

BLANE JIANDIE

I just spent two months-pay for my reservations and transportation.

SECRET SERVICE DEPARTMENT HEAD

I'm aware of that, and you will provide receipts and you will be reimbursed for the loss of the use of those reservations.

BLANE JIANDIE

I realize there is a lot of unsettled business still going on, but we established some relative calm last year and the Revolutionary

Empire, or whatever they wish to call themselves, have not spread in this direction and appear to have calmed down quite a bit. I've been working hard for a long time without a break.

SECRET SERVICE DEPARTMENT HEAD
The assignment you will receive will give you plenty of time to unwind, and your disguise will be traveling as a tourist, so to speak, so you will be able to have plenty of down time and enjoy yourself as you carry out your tasks.

BLANE JIANDIE
What exactly will I be doing?

The department head turned on a two-way computer terminal designed so that he could be looking at one screen simultaneously while a guest was looking at another screen on the opposite side so they could share information and discuss matters. Suddenly a picture of a man popped up.

DEPARTMENT HEAD
This is your new assignment."

BLANE JIANDIE
He vaguely looks familiar.

DEPARTMENT HEAD
He should. He is currently hiding out on the planet Zanziltar. You might have seen him out and about. He was a very social person, goes to clubs and entertainment centers routinely.

BLANE JIANDIE
What's his story?

DEPARTMENT HEAD
The man's name is Evo Kaplan. He's a Revolutionary Empire operative.

BLANE JIANDIE
Working for the Revolution?

DEPARTMENT HEAD
That's what we believe.

BLANE JIANDIE
What is my task with this man?

Blane Jiandie started thinking he would possibly be sent as an assassin.

DEPARTMENT HEAD
Intel has reported Evo Kaplan has sought and was granted passage on *Toutoumomo de Hundan*, a blockade runner that has a destination to Arzon.

BLANE JIANDIE
Why is he going to Arzon?

DEPARTMENT HEAD
That's where you come in.

BLANE JIANDIE
To find out what Evo Kaplan is doing on Arzon.

DEPARTMENT HEAD
Precisely.

BLANE JIANDIE
That could take a while. How will I get back?

DEPARTMENT HEAD
We understand the logistics involved will be rough. All we can do at this point is promise you we'll find a way to get you home.

BLANE JIANDIE
The last thing in the world I would want is to be caught by the Revolutionaries. We already know what the sick bastards do to spies they capture.

The department head handed Blane a small pouch.

DEPARTMENT HEAD
There are some fast-acting pills in there that you can take, which will kill you in a few seconds, so you don't have to worry about suffering. If you take one of these pills you will immediately become unconscious and by the time you fall on the floor you would already be dead and feel no pain.

Blane took the pouch and put it in his suit coat pocket with sheer reluctance. But he knew some of the sick bastard traitors now working for the Revolutionary Empire's Committee for State Security secret police loved to engage in torture and other cruel and inhumane acts. He knew that if members of the Revolutionary Empire's secret police arrested him in a short period of time, he would have wished he had those fast-acting pills with him.

BLANE JIANDIE

When I get to Arzon, how would I communicate with the home office? The Revolutionaries have cut off all the relay stations, and the last I heard, we have not regained communication with the planet?

DEPARTMENT HEAD

When you get off the transport at Arzon, your old flame Loraine will observe your arrival. She has been briefed on your itinerary and when you check into one of the safe houses, she will contact you.

BLANE JIANDIE

If communications are cut, how did you contact Loraine?

DEPARTMENT HEAD

We have several methods of communicating. Some are slow and some are ultra-fast depending on the urgency. I can't disclose to you how we do it in the event you get captured and tortured to reveal the process.

BLANE JIANDIE

You mentioned I have an itinerary?

DEPARTMENT HEAD

Yes, when you leave my office, you will report down to section Q3, who will outfit you with special gizmos you will take with you and be given your itinerary as well as critical information and egress plans in the event the inevitable happens and we must extract you.

BLANE JIANDIE

When precisely will I be leaving?

DEPARTMENT HEAD

Your departure date and time have not been fixed. The blockade runner is not going to leave until all the seats have been sold or the prices so extreme that he doesn't need to fill all the seats.

BLANE JIANDIE

Will it be a day, a week, or a month?

DEPARTMENT HEAD

Since we can't lock in an exact departure time and date, I suggest you start your vacation that has already been prepaid, which we will reimburse you for, and be ready to deploy within twelve hours' notice.


BLANE JIANDIE

What if I meet a pretty lady and need to stay longer?


DEPARTMENT HEAD

You know you will be on that transport, whether you arrive awake or unconscious.


BLANE JIANDIE

Anything else you wish to tell me about Evo Kaplan?


DEPARTMENT HEAD

Evo Kaplan had been a rather successful Secret Service agent. His character flaw that went unnoticed for a period was his sympathies toward the Revolutionaries. We believe he was recently recruited and has been seen on a couple planets and we believe he conducted missions for the Revolutionary forces.


BLANE JIANDIE

What other information about Evo Kaplan do you have?


DEPARTMENT HEAD

Okay, let's look at this presentation.


The department head started a dossier review presentation that suddenly started streaming on the display in front of Blane. Evo Kaplan's photographs and factoids streamed sideways across the 24-inch 3D screen, which had a narrator discussing the finer points and elucidating the essence of Evo Kaplan.


(VOICE OVER)
NARRATOR FOR PRESENTATION

Since Evo Kaplan had worked for the Ministry for State Security in the Dranzonian Empire, there were many data points recorded prior to him changing his personal identity and obtained new credentials allowing him to stay on the planet Zanziltar.

We believe that after Evo Kaplan's recruitment by Revolution forces, he performed various nefarious activities there and may

have gone to the resort planet Shen de Huayuan where one of
our agents went missing.

The Department Head didn't think it was wise to tell Blane
Jiandie that Reginald Heiqishi, who came up missing on
Zanziltar, had used his identity, including cosmetic surgery
to acquire his facial features he had prior to Blane's recent
cosmetic surgery.

Otherwise, Evo Kaplan would think he was the same person if they came in
contact. Blane had the advantage: he now knew Evo Kaplan's appearance, but Evo
had never seen Blane with his new identity he would soon have: Cap Zapatero.

Based on Reginald Heiqishi's debriefing prior to his reckless venture in the heart
of the city that ultimately got him killed on a contract to the FIRM by an angry
banker. The FIRM, aka Revolutionary Secret Service, required a lot of funds
they acquired by performing services such as assassination, racketeering, and the
operation of red-light districts. They justified their criminal enterprise as a means
of funding all the intel operations they performed against the Dranzonian Empire.

The Revolutionary Empire Zanziltar Operations survived and flourished
operating in the Sanctuary City. An element of the Dranzonian Empire Secret
Service operating as diplomats out of the Zanziltar Consulate also had an element
of success; however, the Dranzonians and the Revolutionaries were never able to
go after each other in Zanziltar without being kicked off the planet.

Only those extremely rare moments when they conducted operations such as
seizing Reginald Heiqishi while he was drifting around the business district of
the city and disappeared in thin air, were there actual casualties in the feud on this
planet. More importantly, they were both excellent practitioners of concealment
and disinformation and if necessary, the purveyors of lethal actions.

Why Conrad Fanzui disallowed Evo Kaplan from seeing Brenda Broyals again
prior to his deployment to Arzon was a mystery. However, Brenda knew why
since she was already on her way to another planet on another mission unrelated
to the Arzon operation.

Conrad also believed it would be best for the FIRM to keep Brenda Broyals
and Evo Kaplan apart as much as possible in the future because they were now
fugitives of the Dranzonian Empire with a large price on their heads.

By keeping Brenda Broyals and Evo Kaplan apart, it would force the Dranzonians
to expend far more resources to trap and kill them independently than if they were
together and a sitting duck target.

Evo Kaplan had his last chance to come home when he was on the cruise ship. From now on his only way home would be in a body bag, and most likely the Dranzonians wouldn't waste the time and effort doing that and would simply put him in a crematorium, disappearing forever if he were captured.

<u>EXT. DAY. FIRM SAFEHOUSE</u>

Immediately after Reginald Heiqishi was eliminated, a VTOL craft came down on the road in front of the abandoned house. The body was carried out and placed aboard and it immediately took off to some undisclosed location where no doubt they had a novel way of disposing of the body. After the body was stripped, it was dropped in the middle of a very large hog farm, where the semi-wild animals had razor sharp teeth and, after smelling the corpse and sampling a few limbs, immediately started fighting over the carcass.

It was about sundown and the farmer was almost a mile away in his farmhouse, listening to the local news on his videoscope and because of his hard hearing was not in a position to hear or see the VTOL craft drop the body. By the time the hogs finished up, there wasn't much left, as the bones were scattered over several acres and the skull was carried off into brush where another type of wild animal finished what the hogs didn't get accomplished.

Due to the large amount of brush surrounding the hog farm, the remains of the skull would most likely not be discovered for hundreds of years. The mystery of Reginald Heiqishi's disappearance would never be solved, though the banker had satisfaction his credits were well spent while his wife simply thought Reginald Heiqishi had simply just enjoyed her briefly and departed.

No matter how hard Glacy Spencer tried to discover Blane Jiandie's (a.k.a. Reginald Heiqishi) whereabouts, there was never any leads including dead ends from the Lantiane Resort, where staff was more than happy to assist finding him for a lot of credits, and they tried unsuccessfully and eventually gave up because he left without a trace. Even transportation records at the space port, which could be purchased by large bribes, rendered no information.

Eventually Glacy Spencer figured out Reginald Heiqishi wasn't the person she thought he was. In fact, she had no idea what he was doing other than the fond memories of what transpired between them while her husband was off with the politician to Orgy Island.

After the VTOL carrying Reginald Heiqishi's body was about out of sight, a vehicle pulled up and one member of the FIRM got out and approached Evo Kaplan.

Give us your laser pistol. We can't afford to have you captured
with a weapon on your way back to the FIRM.

Evo handed him the laser pistol quickly, wondering if that was a smart move to
do since they could kill him just as easily as he had just done Reginald Heiqishi.

As soon as the Firm Agent took the pistol, he opened the door to the vehicle.

FIRM AGENT
Get in the vehicle Evo. These guys will take you back to the
FIRM.

Evo got in the vehicle, which immediately drove off. There were a couple other
vehicles suddenly there. No doubt they were there to sanitize the house to make
sure there was no traces left behind.

They too would be gone soon. Traveling down the high-speed corridor placed
them back at the FIRM in a short time. The car pulled up front and a security man
opened the door for Evo Kaplan, who then got out. He was then escorted to his
living quarters on the compound and was soon met by a doctor and a couple of
other people.

DOCTOR
We are going to give you an injection.

EVO KAPLAN
Why?

DOCTOR
Because you are most likely suffering from space lag and you
will be deployed really soon.

EVO KAPLAN
What does the injection do for me?

A FIRM agent took over the conversation from the Doctor.

FIRM AGENT
This will put you to a deep sleep, almost a coma, and we will
wake you up in about twenty-four hours.

EVO KAPLAN
Then what?

FIRM AGENT

You will be fully rested and given a physical checkup and taken to the space port, where you will be put aboard the Toutoumomo de Hundan, which will be making a stop at Praxisvlasia.


EVO KAPLAN

Is there something I'm going to be doing on Praxisvlasia?


FIRM AGENT

No, this is just a stopover for the transport to pick up more passengers. Do not try to get off the ship at Praxisvlasia. If you do, the Dranzonian Secret Service could possibly capture you and your life will be cut short.


EVO KAPLAN

Why should I be concerned?


IRM AGENT

Evo Kaplan, you have a price on your head, and you are a Dranzonian Secret Service person of interest in the disappearance of Reginald Heiqishi and Terrshey Wate. You, being a former Dranzonian Empire Secret Service agent, should know how they will treat you if you are captured.


EVO KAPLAN

Shouldn't I eat something before I get this injection?


DOCTOR

No. It's better that you do not, so that your bowels are not full of material. Since you'll be unconscious, you will not have any hunger pains.


EVO KAPLAN

You want to inject me now?


FIRM AGENT

Correct.


EVO KAPLAN

Okay, what do you want me to do?


DOCTOR

Sit down on the side of the bed, take your shoes off, and then we'll inject you.

As the doctor prepared the syringe, Evo noticed two large guys suddenly standing on each side of him.

EVO KAPLAN
What's these guys doing?

DOCTOR
When you get your injection, you will collapse within ten seconds. They are here to make sure you do not fall and get injured.

Evo watched the female doctor fill up the syringe with a crystal blue liquid from a dispenser bottle. She then directed Evo Kaplan.

DOCTOR
Okay, hold out your right arm and let me see if I can find a good vein. Make a fist and squeeze.

Evo complied and immediately felt the sting of a needle piercing his arm just like he was getting a blood sample drawn. In about five seconds, the room suddenly started getting darker. At seven seconds the room was all dark except for a small white circle directly in front of him that slowly closed, and it all went black.

The men grabbed Evo as he was collapsing and laid him softly down on the bed. Within a minute, one of the big men walked over to the door and opened it. Several people pushing carts went into the room. These people were advanced cosmetic surgeons. They had advanced techniques where a rich woman could walk into their office and come out the same day looking like someone else.

Thanks to advanced drug therapy and new robotic surgical techniques including three dimensional (3D) biological printing, a new face could be put on and when the patient woke up twenty-four hours later, they would be someone else. They did not tell Evo in advance they were changing his face because it would be better for his psychology to simply wake up as a different person.

Evo Kaplan was gone forever. Just like his enemy Blane Jiandie, whom he would be facing soon, his identity also changed. All the preparations beforehand were now useless since neither party would know who the other appeared to be. Nobody in the galaxy would see Evo Kaplan's new identity until he arrived at the space port forty-eight hours later. Evo had one of the strangest dreams he ever had.

Evo Kaplan was indeed hallucinating but didn't know it as he was unconscious and almost in a coma from the powerful drugs given him. The beautiful aspect of the knockout drugs was that when they gave him the antidote, he would awake and be awake and alert in fifteen minutes.

The success of this mission hinged on whether they were able to plant a spy on the *Toutoumomo de Hundan* without detection or attracting any undue attention. Evo Kaplan's new disguise was lifted off a black marketer whom the Dranzonian Empire Secret Service knew about, as well as Arzon officials who allowed them to operate since without them, no Loyalist could go between Arzon and the Dranzonian Empire.

The black marketer Krawz Almarip, who was given great privileges on Zanziltar, was rather flamboyant and disappeared for days at a time while engaged in various contemptible activities. The fact he disappeared then reappeared getting on the spaceship raised no concern since that was his typical behavior. He also had the tendency to not do a lot of talking and usually ignored people outright and only spoke when he wanted something from another party.

The Intergalactic Passenger Transport would have several black marketers onboard who mistrusted each other. The others steered away from Krawz Almarip. They knew he would feel no remorse if he slit their throats if they got in his way.

Krawz Almarip's reputation as a gun slinger was legendary. Part of his finesse with his laser pistol resulted from artificial intelligence that reconciled at a microsecond the target and as he positioned his hand to shoot sliding up and down usually in twenty milliseconds from the don shin position to killing his opponent. His blaster was linked to his AI holster that had several sensors and cameras on it to facilitate that deadly fast attack.

Since the real Krawz Almarip worked out as much as any Revolutionary guard, Secret Service, or FIRM personnel, he could carry and manipulate a laser pistol blaster weighing over twice as much as the standard models, which only had enough stored energy for ten shots. His blaster could shoot over twenty shots, meaning he wasn't going to run out of options in a dog fight.

Twenty-four hours later as Evo Kaplan—now disguised as Krawz Almarip—was awakened with chemicals to neutralize the sleep-inducing chemicals in his body, he slowly looked around and saw several medical people smiling.

MEDICAL STAFF PERSON

> In a few minutes as you wake up you will start to feel some
> hunger and pain and we have a meal prepared for you, but
> before you eat, Conrad Fanzui wants a few words with you.
> He'll be here momentarily.

True to the notification, a moment later Conrad Fanzui walked in the room carrying a small mirror that one would attribute to a woman putting on makeup. He nodded to the medical staff, who understood they needed to leave the room because they were not authorized to hear what transpired over the next few minutes.

CONRAD FANZUI
Evo, how do you feel?


EVO KAPLAN
They warned me I would develop hunger pains. I'm starting to get them now.


CONRAD FANZUI
Not a problem. They will soon serve you breakfast in bed.


EVO KAPLAN
Any way I can get it.


CONRAD FANZUI
We didn't want to alarm you about the preparations we felt we needed to make for your own safety. Your mission will be dangerous enough as it is, and we felt we could not allow you to travel to Arzon with Evo Kaplan's appearance. I know you will probably be upset for a while concerning what we did, but it will provide you with a lot more security.


EVO KAPLAN
What did you do?


CONRAD FANZUI
We gave you the identity of a black marketer named Krawz Almarip who often travels to Arzon. That way you will not stick out. We have studied him and know who he contacts on Arzon and anyone you might encounter; we think we have them identified and how they fit into his smuggling operations. Conrad Fanzui handed Evo Kaplan the mirror, which he instinctively grabbed and looked at.

Evo Kaplan strangely felt the surgery improved his looks. He looked far more urbane and masculine.


CONRAD FANZUI
The doctors informed me the surgery is already seventy-five percent healed and the exponentiators they fed your blood stream with the IV still connected to your arm will fully heal the cosmetic surgery over the next twenty-four hours.


VOICE OVER
Evo Kaplan was now realizing his life had a new direction. He's always been a spy in his adult life and now he has new masters that will determine his future.

CONRAD FANZUI

As you heal over the next twenty-four hours, you will be given briefings and see images of all his contacts and what they do. Your voice is not too different than his, so we felt no need to alter it.


EVO KAPLAN

I probably can never be Evo Kaplan again, I suppose.


CONRAD FANZUI

Evo Kaplan is now on the Dranzonian Empire Secret Service top ten list of enemy agents to kill on site. If you want to survive, you must leave Evo Kaplan behind forever.


EVO KAPLAN

Since I don't have much of a family, there probably isn't much of a reason to keep my original identity.


CONRAD FANZUI

If you stay alive and stay in the spy business, you will no doubt have cosmetic surgery a few more times.


EVO KAPLAN

Interestingly, I do not feel any pain.


CONRAD FANZUI

There are painkillers in your IV, but in twenty-four hours you will no longer require any.


EVO KAPLAN

Did you ever go through this procedure?


CONRAD FANZUI

Yes, several times. I was number one of the Dranzonian Empire Secret Service lists to kill on sight. If I leave the planet for a mission, I will get an identity change.


EVO KAPLAN

What happens to the person when you take their identity?


CONRAD FANZUI

We must make sure their identity can never interfere with what we do. They must be exterminated, much along the lines of what you did to Reginald Heiqishi and Terrshey Wate.

Evo Kaplan looked in the mirror again.

EVO KAPLAN

Will Brenda Broyals get cosmetic surgery?

CONRAD FANZUI

You will never see Brenda Broyals again. She has already changed into another person.

EVO KAPLAN

So, is it possible we may pass each other or be involved on a mission and not know the other person is someone we know?

CONRAD FANZUI

I know you care a lot about Brenda. You will not go on missions together, but you will have to trust me. When it's possible to send you both on a vacation together sometime in the future, I will bring you together. You will then discover her new looks.

EVO KAPLAN

How did her surgery work out?

CONRAD FANZUI

She thinks she is far more beautiful than before. We intentionally improved her looks for her pending mission to help her penetrate and exploit her contact on the planet she is now involved in.

EVO KAPLAN

Does that mean exploit with all her resources?

CONRAD FANZUI

A good spy uses all their resources for exploitation if necessary. A good analogy is a lawyer doesn't have to tell the truth; all he has to do is advise his client so they win the case.

EVO KAPLAN

When exactly do I leave?

CONRAD FANZUI

We have no control over that. The operator will not launch the ship until he has either filled all the seats or extracted enough fees to cover the empty seats.

EVO KAPLAN

How will we know how soon that is?

CONRAD FANZUI
If he doesn't fill the seats in forty-eight hours, we'll buy the remaining seats and tell him to go. We have something important to get from Praxisvlasia, the stop over to Arzon.

EVO KAPLAN
Are you sending important materials?

CONRAD FANZUI
We are shipping contraband for your utilization.

EVO KAPLAN
What is the purpose of the contraband?

CONRAD FANZUI
To bribe officials or to use as barter.

EVO KAPLAN
Wouldn't that make me stand out?

CONRAD FANZUI
Remember, we gave you the identity of a smuggler. They expect you to do it and after you finish eating, trainers will come in and help you start preparing as they school you on a few matters and the personalities you might run into or those you need to look up, and about Krawz Almarip's prior relationship with them.

EVO KAPLAN
How do you know all this?

CONRAD FANZUI
We get a lot of information from the individual that you have his identity.

EVO KAPLAN
Is this person still alive?

CONRAD FANZUI
Yes, we'll keep him alive until your mission is complete in case we have to get essential information out of him or place his body conveniently in some place to help insure you get out alive.

EVO KAPLAN
He cooperates?

CONRAD FANZUI

After we gave him a couple samples of our advanced interrogation techniques, he would much rather enjoy the good food, wine, and women we supply him than to get back in the swimming pool or the crematorium.


VOICE OVER

Evo Kaplan wondered: *did Conrad Fanzui say this as a warning to me a clue what could happen to me if he crossed him?*


Conrad Fanzui looked at Evo Kaplan (his identity would stay as Krawz Almarip until the mission was completed).


CONRAD FANZUI

Do you feel you are ready to go on the mission?


EVO KAPLAN

I kind of wish I could have a few good workouts before I leave on the mission.


CONRAD FANZUI

Since we probably have a couple days, you can go out to the workout area tomorrow incrementally between your training sessions. I'll tell your trainers to give you three or four workout periods during the day and I'll have some martial artists there for you to practice with.


EVO KAPLAN

That's good, I want to work on my timing.


CONRAD FANZUI

Your timing was pretty good on Coy's Ridge.


EVO KAPLAN

Yes, but I've done a lot of travel and had too many good meals since then.


CONRAD FANZUI

The medical staff will be back momentarily. See you when you get back.


Conrad Fanzui turned and walked out of the room. A moment later the medical people returned and brought with them a covered cart that brought with it an aroma. Evo Kaplan's hunger suddenly intensified.

Nobody woke Evo the next day. He awoke on his own and evidently had received a good sleep medication the night before because he did not feel them remove the IV needle in his arm. All that equipment was gone, and he was alone. Evo got up, did his morning routine S/S/S, then put on gym clothes that were in their usual spot in the closet and running shoes. He dressed and was out the door several minutes later. He started doing his laps, putting his heart into it, knowing he would be on a long space ride soon and better get the maximum workout now.

Evo Kaplan felt he had a lot of energy and no hunger. It was as if he were gliding on air and had never run so easy in his life. The drugs that were still in his body to enhance the healing for the cosmetic surgery had a huge effect on his muscle tissue and prevented the buildup of lactic acid.

After several laps that he usually did, he went over to the workout area and did stretches then some calisthenics and special exercises his trainers taught him. Several women were now running laps as well and by the time he completed his workout they were over to the workout area doing similar calisthenics and special exercises like Evo Kaplan had done.

Evo Kaplan was just about to go back to his quarters, shower, put on his street clothes, and get ready for training, when unexpectedly one of his martial arts instructors appeared.

MARTIAL ARTS INSTRUCTOR
Hello Krawz Almarip.

The martial arts instructor evidently had been briefed on his current name. He knew better than to ask if he remembered him as Evo Kaplan. He could tell by their reaction the women had overheard the name. He had no idea who they were or what they did, but they definitely looked healthy.

MARTIAL ARTS INSTRUCTOR
Okay, let's go through the standard forms!

The forms, which built up the muscle memory and speed, were scientifically designed by ancient elders. Evo broke the man's neck at Coy Ridge with just one chop to the neck in less than one second. It was efficient and it was quiet but may not be the technique he needed the next time, so he had to practice them all.

Going through the martial arts forms burns up energy twice as fast as actual fighting. Most fights last less than three minutes and often use only half the body's energy.

Going through the twenty standard forms, some of which have one hundred and eleven moves, burns up eighty percent of the body's energy in the same amount of time. Evo Kaplan practiced moves from kicking to jumping to punching to twisting and simulated blocks occurred contiguously with no pause until that form was complete. Evo would stop for a moment, announce the next form, and then continue.

Martial arts instructors observe students every day. They see the very best and they also see the not so good as well. They are compelled to help someone because if they do a crummy job on the forms, they might get killed in the line of duty. There was a strong correlation to survival rate with the forms performance. People who had the best forms generally came back alive from missions alive more often.

The instructor knew this and tried his best to convince the practitioners of their fate. Due to scanners and technology, there were many times when you could not carry a laser pistol with you into harm's way. That also goes for the enemy. Hence in 50 percent of all the desperate fights that occur and was in fact a life-or-death manner, it came down to the person knowing martial arts surviving.

In some cases, even though the opponent had a laser pistol, a martial arts expert survived because he was able to disable the enemy before they got a good shot with the laser weapon. Evo knew he was a little rusty because of his recent travel.

The instructor seemed like a pest having him repeat some forms four or five times until he performed them at the level of perfection the instructor required.

At the end of the twenty forms, the instructor knew any further activity would not result in improvement. Evo needed a rest, plus he was advised that about now he needed to shower, clean up, and start receiving his indoctrination for his pending travel.

Evo should have figured by now he was under surveillance all the time and had no privacy. As soon as he was dressed and cleaned up, the doorbell rang. Outside were several people with a cart.

STAFF MEMBER

You will be eating your meal in your room so that you can receive training while you eat.

EVO KAPLAN
All right.

The staff brought in the cart that doubled as an improvised dinner table. They took one of his chairs and set it next to the improvised table, removed the hood, and exposed an elaborate meal prepared for him.

EVO KAPLAN
The food looks good and smells good.

It's designed to further help your healing and training. Please sit
down and we will start your training while you eat.

Another cart rolled in had a screen on it that was covered up until they rolled it about ten feet away from Evo. As soon as the covering material was removed, revealing the display technology under it, one of the technicians pressed a button and it started playing. The narrator to the training started discussing Krawz Almarip.

Within thirty minutes, Evo knew Krawz Almarip's life story, his former girlfriends, and the high points in his life.

The video then started showing all the people he met in Arzon, some of which he would have to seek out to barter and trade for benefits or privileges. Some of the information was only derived a week ago when the real Krawz Almarip got a taste of the crematorium because the Revolutionaries discovered some information he withheld. As one wise person a long ago said, *"Trust but verify."*

The meal Evo Kaplan ate was highly digestible and the drink he had included energy and alertness formulas. After two hours of training, the staff member made an announcement.

STAFF MEMBER
We are going to take a break now so that you can go work out
more, and the doctors will be here momentarily to give you a
quick checkup.

EVO KAPLAN
Okay.

The training crew left the room and the medical people came in immediately after the last trainers departed.

DOCTOR
How are you feeling today, Krawz Almarip?

KRAWZ ALMARIP (a.k.a. EVO KAPLAN)
Pretty good. I felt very strong and fresh when I was running
this morning.

DOCTOR
We expected you would, as the drugs wore off that we gave you
in the IV to promote healing and sleep.

KRAWZ ALMARIP (a.k.a. EVO KAPLAN)
It was one of my better workouts even though I was probably a little out of shape.

DOCTOR
Would you please take off your shirt so we can look at your neck and shoulders.

Evo complied and the doctors began pawing all over Evo Kaplan's neck and head.

DOCTOR
Looks like you are healing well. All the scar tissue is healed.

KRAWZ ALMARIP (a.k.a. EVO KAPLAN)
Feels good and I think I look better as well.

DOCTOR
You have no scars. It would be impossible for anyone to know you had cosmetic surgery.

KRAWZ ALMARIP (a.k.a. EVO KAPLAN)
Evo Kaplan grabbed the mirror that Conrad Fanzui had left him still sitting on his bed. He picked it up and looked again. I'd say I'm probably ninety-five percent healed now.

DOCTOR #2
Krawz Almarip, you are at least ninety-eight percent healed. We'll be back later this afternoon to look at you one more time. So far it looks like the procedure went well. We'll visit you again to check you before you go on a mission.

KRAWZ ALMARIP (a.k.a. EVO KAPLAN)
See you then.

<u>EXT. "FIRM" CAMPUS WORKOUT AREA.</u>

Evo Kaplan then put his workout clothes back on and went out to the track and started running a couple laps. This time it wasn't quite as easy. *Those drugs must be wearing off now.* After a couple laps, he went to stretch and do more calisthenics. Just as if someone was watching him and timing it, the martial arts instructor suddenly appeared again.

MARTIAL ARTS INSTRUCTOR
Krawz Almarip, are you ready to do some more forms now?

KRAWZ ALMARIP (a.k.a. EVO KAPLAN)
Yes, but I may not be as good as I was this morning.

MARTIAL ARTS INSTRUCTOR
Okay Krawz Almarip, let's begin.

MONTAGE. MARTIAL ARTS WORKOUT.

Note to the cinematographer:

> During the next voice over sequence, a stunt man dressed up like
> Evo Kaplan in workout clothes performs some elaborate Karate
> Kata's. The voiceover should last approximately one minute. The
> shoot on the Karate Katas can be a montage of an actual blackbelt
> performing Katas wearing a mask to look like Evo Kaplan.

VOICE OVER
Evo Kaplan started standard-form number one. It had a strange
name given to it by the inventor at some obscure planet such as
"Shishido no y ni Tatakai, Taka no y ni Korosu" (Fight Like a
Lion, Kill Like an Eagle).

During his martial arts training, Evo Kaplan needed to know
how to make each move precisely. He also had to know the
definition and pronounce it in the language it originated for
promotion through the ranks.

Based on his experience running, Evo Kaplan realized he would
probably run out of gas around form number fifteen, which was
a very intense movement form that lasted five minutes. It was
one of the longest and demanding forms including jumping and
landing in a cat stance.

If there was any form that best portrayed a Japanese ninja, it
was form number fifteen with one hundred and eleven moves.
One hundred and eleven is also known as the magic number.
The form number fifteen was referred to as translated from an
ancient civilization: Xiong Yu Yi bai Yishiyi Emo Zhandou
(Bears Fighting 111 Demons).

Just before Evo started form number fifteen, the martial arts
instructor stopped Evo Kaplan.

MARTIAL ARTS INSTRUCTOR
Let's stop for a moment. I want you to do form fifteen well, so
before you start, I want you to drink an energy drink.

Everything at the FIRM was scripted beyond belief. No sooner than the martial
arts instructor muttered these words, a staff member came walking out with a small
bag strapped across his shoulder. He walked up, took the bag off, and handed it to
the martial arts instructor, who unzipped the top and grabbed a canned drink that
was chilled nicely.

MARTIAL ARTS INSTRUCTOR
Here, drink this.

The martial arts instructor handed the energy drink to Evo, who popped the top
and took a nice gulp.

KRAWZ ALMARIP (a.k.a. EVO KAPLAN)
This drink tastes pretty good.

MARTIAL ARTS INSTRUCTOR
It was developed for special forces for moments of extreme
stress. We took delivery of a certain amount to help accelerate
our training.

<u>MONTAGE. MARTIAL ARTS WORKOUT.</u>

Note to the cinematographer:

During the next voice over sequence, a stunt man dressed up like
Evo Kaplan in workout clothes performs some elaborate Karate
Kata's. The voiceover should last approximately one minute and
five seconds. The shoot on the Karate Katas can be a montage
of an actual blackbelt performing Elaborate Karate Katas. Most
Americans have never observed a blackbelt Kata.

You might consider hiring Hanshi Miki who has a Dojo in Carlsbad
California as a technical advisor for these Kata's. He probably has
some blackbelts to recommend to perform them. With a mask
or makeup you can probably make the Karate Ka appear as *Evo
Kaplan* in this sequence.

<u>Shito Ryu Grand Master Minobu Miki in San Diego County — Japan
Karate-Do organization (jko.com)</u>

<u>Hanshi Miki Minobu - San Diego Iaido - America Tosa Jikiden
Shigetsukai (アメリカ土佐直傳士月会)</u>

Evo took his time drinking the energy drink, savoring it. The instructor wasn't annoyed and was glad Evo wasn't drinking it too fast, that way it would have more impact on the outcome of the coming form-fifteen demonstration: Xiong Yu Yi bai Yishiyi Emo Zhandou.

Evo Kaplan finished the contents of the can and sat it down on one of the picnic tables there that allowed trainees to sit, drink, and rest between sets of exercises. He walked out in the middle of a padded mat where a person could do martial arts training and avoid falling hard and getting injuries. He then started his fiveminute Xiong Yu Yi bai Yishiyi Emo Zhandou martial arts form routine.

Evo Kaplan felt amazingly refreshed just as if he had been totally rested. He had more energy, concentration, and emotionally he hung on a plateau that invigorated his ever being. It was as if he knew he could easily pull this off. He suddenly had the psychological advantage, and his spirits were lifted, empowering him to do all one hundred and eleven individual movements in great precision.

The martial arts instructor observed quietly and intently. He had eagle eyes. Just as if Evo Kaplan was operating in a combination of intermittent suspended animation and time lapsed periods, the instructor cogently spotted the quality of each movement and in the back of his head could later recall any criticism he had to give. Since he felt it was a life-or-death matter based on statistics, he would not be cutting Evo Kaplan any slack.

The martial arts instructor would inform Krawz Almarip (a.k.a. Evo Kaplan) in as much precision as he could muster a full critique of his performance. Evo Kaplan continued the form-fifteen without the slightest care in the world for the full five minutes performing the one hundred and eleven moves. Some of the moves are repeated four times for quadrants on the compass. The base one hundred and eleven moves morphed into close to four hundred total moves.

The five different jumps in the routine expended a lot of energy and when the practitioner landed on all fours just like a cat, they had to hold it a brief period solid and not wiggle. Just like in the animal world, a wiggle or movement could betray him.

As Evo Kaplan was near the last ten moves, he felt marvelously refreshed. The energy drink was doing its magic. The instructor predicted the outcome with the drink and based on experience gave it to Evo Kaplan because when you do a poor job in practice, you end up doing a poor job in real combat.

All the exercises and running were video recorded by several video cameras strategically located around the track and workout area. This Xiong Yu Yi bai Yishiyi Emo Zhandou forms routine would be replayed later by the instructor several times at a slower speed to verify his analysis was done correctly and in a future workout, concentrate on the weak areas to improve execution of the forms.

When an operative was killed, part of the investigation went into pulling their workout video and observe how well and competently they were training. They had a team grade their workouts. When they compared to survivors, one thing was crystal clear: the ones who trained more effectively survived at a much higher rate.

Management was thus moved and embraced the notion of installing more quality control into the process. At the end of form number fifteen, the instructor spoke.

MARTIAL ARTS INSTRUCTOR

How do you feel? Can you go full force with number sixteen, all the way?

KRAWZ ALMARIP (a.k.a. EVO KAPLAN)<br>Yes. I feel great. I think I can do it just fine.

The eighty-nine moves associated with form number sixteen wasn't a challenge. Even though Evo Kaplan was now sweating profusely, his movements and techniques were precise, and his timing was impeccable. At the end of number sixteen the instructor stopped Krawz Almarip (a.k.a. Evo Kaplan).

MARTIAL ARTS INSTRUCTOR

Krawz Almarip, you have done quite a bit in a short period of time. Your body has been severely strained in performing at the level you are doing. I want you to drink another energy drink before you start form-number seventeen.

Evo Kaplan was more than happy to comply because the drink did taste good, and it really seemed to help. The instructor handed Krawz Almarip (a.k.a. Evo Kaplan) another energy drink.

MARTIAL ARTS INSTRUCTOR
Please sit down on the bench. I want you to rest your legs a bit
while you consume that energy drink.

It seemed like a reasonable guidance to Evo Kaplan. The instructor obviously
knew what he was doing. The instructor kept Krawz Almarip (a.k.a. Evo Kaplan)
at the table for ten minutes.

MARTIAL ARTS INSTRUCTOR
Okay, we better start again, your muscles are building up lactic
acid.

It was pay me now or pay me later and Evo Kaplan knew it. Evo Kaplan continued
with the rest of his forms, feeling the best he ever had while doing number twenty,
the last one. The crescendo occurred in the last moves. He was finally done and
was probably going back to the classroom soon.

On cue walked two men wearing martial arts workout clothes that looked very
similar to a Japanese Karate Gi.

MARTIAL ARTS INSTRUCTOR
Okay, now that you have practiced your forms, you will fight
these two men.

KRAWZ ALMARIP (a.k.a. EVO KAPLAN)
Okay.

MARTIAL ARTS INSTRUCTOR
They are professional fighters and are trained in how to protect
themselves. Your job is to defend yourself against them.

KRAWZ ALMARIP (a.k.a. EVO KAPLAN)
Certainly.

MARTIAL ARTS INSTRUCTOR
We are going to simulate an attack by one where the other joins
in. You must be on the alert for another enemy showing up and
figure out how to deal with the two of them at once.

KRAWZ ALMARIP (a.k.a. EVO KAPLAN)
What if I accidently kill them?

MARTIAL ARTS INSTRUCTOR
They will know your moves and anticipate them. You will not
kill them, but when you hear me blow the whistle that means
stop immediately.

MONTAGE. MARTIAL ARTS FIGHT.

Note to the cinematographer:

During the next voice over sequence, three stunt men do the fighting Evo Kaplan is in workout clothes the other two men are wearing clothing that resembles a Karate Gi. There should be shots from various angles including possibly using a drone at about 10 feet in the air circling the fight scene.

The following voice over should take approximately one minute and fortyfive seconds.

<u>MUSIC.</u> Background music during the fighting: Johann Strauss Sr. - Radetzky March

VOICE OVER (MALE)

One of the two men walked over to the side seemingly out of position to offer any threat. The other fighter stepped forward and gave Evo a wakeup-call to his face. Evo did his ninjalike escape, just like he had practiced in form number fifteen to come back for an attack. The smack he received on his face still hurt and it gave him a dose of reality as the two men went at each other.

Evo Kaplan had the added complexity of checking his opponent's moves at blinding speed, as well as keeping an eye on the other person for when he would enter the fray. After five minutes fighting just one person, the instructor gave the nod to the second fighter, who then charged Evo rather quickly.

Evo had to avoid this man because if he had succeeded in tackling him and throwing him to the ground, in real life the two of them would kill him very abruptly.

In martial arts the axiom of staying alive is staying off the ground where you will be choked out or kicked by several people with lethal blows.

The jump almost seven feet in the air while maintaining situational awareness of the opponent's location at all times was an extraordinary achievement. The attack was unsuccessful, though the second person proceeded into a profile to assist in coordinated attacks.

So now it was four arms and four legs Evo Kaplan had to block or be worried about. It was now more defense than offense. But he also knew he had to take one of them out to even the odds.

It was time to *Kill Like an Eagle*. Evo quickly worked out the strategy in his head. He faked toward one fighter and landed on the other a devastating blow. Evo Kaplan knocked the guy out, and now it was down to just Evo and the original fighter.

Evo let his mind scan through the advocacy of the various forms he had practiced with a high level of precision and quickly decided a strategy and executed it.

The instructor could not ever be so proud as his student showed great finesse in the successful attack and the second fighter was on the ground. Just before Evo would have killed him out of natural response to the series of moves, the instructor blew the whistle a couple times to stop Evo just in time. Otherwise, Krawz Almarip (a.k.a. Evo Kaplan) might have killed they guy.

The two men were immediately attended to by the medical personnel, and the unconscious man was brought back to consciousness. The two men were then carted off to get X-rays and treatment. They knew from past experiences these doctors were extremely good at reducing pain and enhancing the healing. They would be ready for the next guy tomorrow.

MARTIAL ARTS INSTRUCTOR
You did well today. It's time you go back to your quarters and take a shower and change for more classroom training.

KRAWZ ALMARIP (a.k.a. EVO KAPLAN)
All right. On my way.

NOTE TO THE CINEMATOGRAPHER.

The next voice over lasts about two minutes and 30 seconds. Sometimes sound has proven by *psychoacoustics* has more advantages than visual effects. This Voice over glues the story together.

In the background, with the voice over showing the video depicted in the scene a specific music played would add greatly to the psychoacoustics impact on the audience. [ Richard Wagner - Ride of The Valkyries Bing Videos ]

Evo Kaplan went to his living quarters, took a shower, changed into street clothes, and prepared to receive the trainers. Doctors showed up with the trainers and wanted to check Krawz Almarip (a.k.a. Evo Kaplan) for any injuries sustained in the fighting. The guys Krawz Almarip (a.k.a. Evo Kaplan) beat up were in bad shape.

Looks like he nailed you one good one to your face. Good bruise. We'll put some medication on that now, should be okay by morning. Here's a pain killer so that you don't feel any of it." The doctor handed Evo Kaplan a pill, which he swallowed, and took a drink offered. Soon he felt no pain, but the medication seemed to not blur his thinking ability.

The training consisted of more information on the planet, the operation, and now they were getting down to the nitty gritty: exactly what he needed to look into and precisely how he was going to transmit that information off the planet without being caught. This was all about military intelligence. Evo Kaplan now knew for a fact he was in over his head. He was indeed a major spy involved in espionage. If caught he would be executed after they tortured any useful information out of him.

Krawz Almarip (a.k.a. Evo Kaplan) would be very far off where he could expect no help. He was on his own. He had to be careful and patient. Hustling to get a trip home wasn't going to work. He had to be subtle and resounding. Two hours were jammed full of an incredible amount of data and areas to focus on. The guess work was laid out for him. His job was to confirm what the speculators feared was occurring.

For future planning, they didn't want to step into a trap and lose half the fleet just because they underestimated this outpost that had to be taken down as it was essentially the modern-day pathway to the *silk road.*

What laid on the other side of the nebula and beyond was distant solar systems that contained valuable planets like Earth.

Evo Kaplan was wondering when the ship was going to leave. He'd like to get at least one more day of workouts before he was stuck on the inter-planetary transport where such physical activity wasn't really feasible.

Suddenly it was time to eat again, and to make use of his valuable time since he could be deploying immediately, the trainers had his dinner brought to his quarters where he dined while receiving more training, more videos, more *expose's* including information on various types of space craft and what differences there were. Essentially in a few hours Evo Kaplan was shown the video equivalent of the Dranzonian Empire Janes Spaceships.

A half hour after dinner it was decided Evo could go and do some more physical training. This would be limited to running and calisthenics. Interestingly the two women were there again working out. As Evo Kaplan worked on his calisthenics for thirty minutes, a martial arts instructor arrived and had the women both doing martial arts forms.

*Better them than me now*, Evo thought as he felt for them as they went slowly through all twenty of the forms he had done. They were mostly done when he left the area and went back to his quarters, where he once again showered and felt good.

A doctor came by and looked over his bruised face, put some more ointment on it, then gave him a pill and told him to drink the drink he provided with the pill.

DOCTOR
The pill will make you sleepy. We want you to rest now. We'll wake you up in the morning at the appropriate time.

VOICE OVER
Shortly after the doctor left, Evo Kaplan (a.k.a. Krawz Almarip) felt sleepy and crawled between the sheets. He was soon out like a lamp. He had another one of those strange dreams. But he felt delightful, then he was abruptly awakened to discover several people around his bed.

FIRM STAFF MEMBER
Krawz Almarip, we have some good news for you. Your flight is in a few hours. All your preparations are complete. We have a change of clothes for you to put on now after you use the bathroom. You will then be driven to the space port.

NOTE TO THE CINEMATOGRAPHER.

The next voice over lasts about two minutes and 30 seconds. Sometimes sound has proven by psychoacoustics has more advantages than visual effects. This Voice over glues the story together.

In the background, with the voice over showing the video depicted in the scene a specific music played would add greatly to the psychoacoustics impact on the audience.

[ Richard Wagner - Ride of The Valkyries <u>Bing Videos</u> ]

VOICE OVER MALE

The moment of reality had finally struck. Evo Kaplan soon to play the role of Krawz Almarip was on his way. Never in the five hundred missions Evo Kaplan performed for the Dranzonian Empire Secret Service did he feel quite as uneasy as this.

DELAY IN VOICE OVER 5 SECONDS FOR EFFECT WHILE THE WAGNER MUSIC CONTINUES PLAYING .

When Evo Kaplan was a patriot spying on the Revolution, being killed in the line of duty didn't bother him. But now possibly dying for the enemy did!

Evo Kaplan playing the role of Krawz Almarip knew this mission was highly scripted and he had to perform the next steps; otherwise, the message that Conrad Fanzui gave him would come to pass: he would wish he were dead.

The staff awakened Krawz Almarip (a.k.a. Evo Kaplan) in plenty of time so as not to rush him.

The doctors wanted Evo Kaplan to have good bowel movement, shower, shave, brush his teeth, and feel clean and ready.

Evo Kaplan came out of the bathroom with a towel on and in front of him was a clothing rack with his outfit he would wear to the spaceship. The clothes made him look downright sleazy. He had to look and play the role of the black marketer Krawz Almarip.

As such, the wardrobe they packed for him looked almost identical to what he saw in many of the videos they secretly made of Krawz Almarip so they would have a photographic survey of his natural tendencies and dress. Evo Kaplan said to himself, *they did a great job making me appear as Krawz Almarip and not look out of place in the role I will now play.*

FIRM STAFFER<br>Are you ready?

KRAWZ ALMARIP(a.k.a. Evo Kaplan)
I guess I'm as ready as I will ever be.


FIRM STAFFER
We have a cart outside to take you and your luggage to the front
entrance.


KRAWZ ALMARIP
Alright.


Krawz Almarip (a.k.a. Evo Kaplan went outside his quarters with the several
staff personnel who carried his luggage for him. He got in the passenger side of
the electric-powered cart and soon it was underway driving a short distance and
around the mansion to the front entrance where a vehicle was waiting for him. The
driver opened the door for him and the staff put his luggage into the rear of the
van-like vehicle. They were soon on their way to the space port.


ZANZILTAR TO PRAXISVLASIA, CLAUDETTE RAMSEY


The driver pulled up to the Zanziltar Space Port, got out and opened the door for
Evo Caplan, and handed him his luggage. A porter immediately descended upon
Evo, asking him if he could carry his luggage for him.


KRAWZ ALMARIP
Sure.


PORTER
I'm cleared to carry on board with you.


KRAWZ ALMARIP
That's great.


Krawz Almarip walked beside the porter who had his luggage on a small carrying
cart. They walked through Customs. The porter was cleared he could walk through
with the passengers just for this purpose. They were soon up on the spaceship with
the porter helping Krawz Almarip place his luggage in the four-square feet storage
he was allowed and cleared to board and assist paying customers on Intergalactic
Transport.


PORTER
That will be five credits.


KRAWZ ALMARIP
Charge ten.

Krawz Almarip handed the porter his credit token, which the porter scanned and showed Krawz Almarip the transaction amount. Krawz Almarip approved the transaction with a thumb print on the device.

PORTER
Thank you, sir.

The porter then turned away and walked off the ship and out to the entrance with a big smile from the gracious tip to help the next customer.

INT. INTERGALACTIC PASSENGER TRANSPORT ZANZILTAR (a.k.a. SANCTUARY CITY) – NIGHT

THE SONG A SPY IS GONE PLAYS IN THE BACKGROUND.

Note to the director:

A Spy Is Gone is one of Paul D. Escudero's songs that was composed for a future James Bond Song. Since Welcome to Sanctuary City is a Spy Novel, this is the perfect place to debut it, The song requires a concert pianist like Yuja Wang and an orchestra backup and a singer, preferably Jennie Kim.

VOICE OVER
(During takeoff and flying out into space)

Krawz Almarip sat down at his assigned seat and strapped in his safety harness, as he knew the ship would be leaving soon. There were not a lot of people. It was clear the *FIRM* had purchased all the unsold seats to get the ship underway. Since only half the ship was full, completing preparations were greatly simplified.

EXT. CGI. INTERGALACTIC PASSENGER TRANSPORT LEAVING ZANZILTAR (a.k.a. SANCTUARY CITY) – NIGHT

This transport rolls down the runway and flies out into space like an aircraft. It has huge rocket engines in the back using special fuels for range and velocity.

In no time at all they departed Zanziltar and were soon out in space, heading for Praxisvlasia.

Nobody out of the ordinary was around Krawz Almarip; he got no stares. In the cargo hold were his black-market items, which would provide a lot of credits including some of that energy drink he enjoyed recently during his work outs and Martial Arts Forms.

Krawz Almarip also had a dozen cans of energy drinks packed in his carry-on luggage that would help him improve his alertness, and if he felt he had a reason why he needed to stay awake for long periods of time in route, they would help greatly.

If Krawz Almarip detected surveillance, that would be the case: lack of sleep. He also had a few energy drinks for crewmembers, which Krawz Almarip gave them, according to his interviews. The trip from Zanziltar to Praxisvlasia would not be as boring as it was relatively short.

Expected arrival time at Praxisvlasia Space Port was within seventy-two hours. Since only half of the ship was full of people and cargo (commonly referred to as the Pigs and People run), they had extra fuel to accelerate quicker off the planet and more fuel available to slow down at the other end, which allowed them to travel at a much higher than normal velocity for this leg of the trip.

Most likely they could shave off several hours and arrive as early as just two and a half days. Since a lot of extra seats were purchased to allow an earlier flight, they would not be stuck on the planet waiting for more passengers.

The Intergalactic Passenger Transport would leave Praxisvlasia on its way to Arzon with the posted schedule already advertised.

Being on the planet a few hours would allow a more casual loading, topping off their fuel tanks and those passengers who wanted to get off could stretch their legs in the space port.

Even though this was a blockade runner and a ship that violated a lot of intergalactic laws and regulations, the fact remained it was registered as a Zanziltar Intergalactic Passenger Transport.

Because of intergalactic treaty, the Dranzonian Empire Secret Service would not be allowed to board the ship and detain any passenger. The only way that passengers could fall into their hands would be if they left the ship.

The minute they left the ship to cruise through the terminal, they were fair game. That is one of the reasons why during the FIRM training Krawz Almarip was directed not to leave the ship while it was in Praxisvlasia.

The fact Evo Kaplan  was portraying an infamous black marketer Krawz Almarip easily played into the con he had to stay on the ship.

Crew members who had seen Krawz Almarip on trips in the past knew he would not be getting off the ship because they also knew the Dranzonian Empire Secret Service held him as a person of interest. Krawz Almarip had ostensibly engaged in gun running to the Revolutionaries in their formative years.

There was one occasion before when the Dranzonian Empire Secret Service illegally boarded a Zanziltar Intergalactic Passenger Transport and detained a passenger of reported affiliation with the Revolutionaries.

The Dranzonian Empire Secret Service could not stop the captain of the ship immediately sending off a distress signal. Zanziltar banking officials who then threatened to reveal the bank account information of several Dranzonian Empire officials, including secret rendezvous with organized crime figures and gun runners if the person was not immediately put back on the Zanziltar Intergalactic Passenger Transport.

One of the chief parties involved in the assault on the ship was none other than Reginald Heiqishi and his field operative that had warned him not to do it was none other than Evo Kaplan.

This was one of the events in Reginald Heiqishi's past that grew the animosity toward Evo Kaplan because it almost got Reginald Heiqishi fired. Instead of destroying Evo Kaplan, including a second attempt during Evo's vacation to *Shen de Huayuan*, the opposite happened when Egor Pataslia's secret police informed the Zanziltar banker how Reginald Heiqishi's flagrant affair with his wife Glacy Spencer manifested a contract that allowed Evo Kaplan to end Reginald Heiqishi's life.

Evo Kaplan wasn't joyous that he took Reginald Heiqishi's life. In fact, Evo Kaplan had periods of remorse.

However, the scenario played out was necessary for Evo Kaplan to save his own life. Had Evo Kaplan refused to shoot Reginald Heiqishi, it was most likely Conrad Fanzui's men would simply had shot them both and they would have ended up in the same location: the hog farm.

Krawz Almarip (a.k.a. Evo Kaplan knew it wasn't safe for him to get off the ship. If someone had leaked his new identity to the Dranzonian Empire Secret Service, the facial recognition technology would immediately identify him. Within an hour after DNA confirmation Evo Kaplan would be hauled off to a Dranzonian prison that was no more humane than the Revolutionaries were with their swimming pool and crematorium.

So, what did the real Krawz Almarip do during the delay at space ports en route? It took a while for the FIRM to identify all the flight attendants who flew on this blockade runner, but with insiders working with port authority giving them access to security recordings, and with the use of facial recognition technology, they were all identified. None of them were threatened but they were certainly bribed.

When you live in a den of thieves, being another form of thief was not unexpected. Hence, they were willing participants in discovering everything Krawz Almarip did on those flights so that Evo Kaplan could be trained to copy him to reinforce his cosmetic surgery that took his identity thanks to biological 3D-printing techniques.

Just like the real Krawz Almarip would do, during the flight Krawz Almarip (a.k.a. Evo Kaplan) approached one of the flight attendants Krawz Almarip trusted, Ruth Marradi, and asked her for a favor.

KRAWZ ALMARIP

Ruth, when we land in Praxisvlasia, I want to go to my bunk and sleep while we are on the planet. I sleep much better with real gravity.

RUTH MARRADI

Okay Krawz, understand. Same deal as before?

KRAWZ ALMARIP

Ruth, I'm not sure about the deal. Perhaps I might have something better this flight.

RUTH MARRADI

Those Zanziltar health enhancers are good enough. I can sell them and make get a lot of credits.

Evo Kaplan, during his training, had been informed Krawz Almarip had been giving flight attendant Ruth Marradi a half dozen of these Zanziltar health inducers, which allegedly greatly improved the health of cancer and cardiac patients. Some takers of them claimed they appeared five years younger in a short period of time. Whether true or not, the fact they were willing to pay astonishing amounts for them made it hugely profitable.

KRAWZ ALMARIP

I no longer have those items, but I do have something better. When is your first shift after we leave Praxisvlasia?

RUTH MARRADI

I'll be on duty during Praxisvlasia and twelve hours into the flight.

KRAWZ ALMARIP

So, toward the end of the flight you will be dog-ass tired?

RUTH MARRADI
Probably.


KRAWZ ALMARIP
I'll give you a sample when you wake me up after takeoff. You will not feel tired at all even twelve hours later.


RUTH MARRADI
Okay, I'll give it a try.


KRAWZ ALMARIP
One other thing, make sure nobody snoops around my bunk while I'm sleeping.


RUTH MARRADI
I never have. You can be assured of that. One of my jobs is to always watch the entrance to the ship and I have a direct view of your bunk from there.


KRAWZ ALMARIP
Excellent.


VOICE OVER
Evo Kaplan stayed awake for over a day. He used the time to reconnoiter the passengers and clear his surroundings for potential Dranzonian Empire Secret Service agents or verify that Conrad Fanzui's men were aboard as watchers.

Just like Brenda during the Coy's Ridge operation, a watcher was probably in the cabin with him to report back any issues that should come to the attention of Conrad Fanzui. Evo Kaplan assumed there was a watcher aboard the ship and might even get off at Praxisvlasia and possibly another watcher come aboard to relieve that person, just to keep him and any possible Dranzonian Empire Secret Service agent from detecting the surveillance.

Krawz Almarip (a.k.a. Evo Kaplan) would probably never know for sure, but he was a good judge of body language and if a watcher was aboard, he would catch that person doing observations. He would then know. However, there was a distinct possibility a Dranzonian Empire Secret Service agent unrelated to Krawz Almarip's (a.k.a. Evo Kaplan) mission could be put aboard for other reasons, and thus he would be a target of opportunity if Evo could confirm his suspicions in time. The target of opportunity could work both ways. It would be who discovered who first.

After a full twenty-four hours of vigilance, Evo Kaplan went to his bunk, which was in an arrangement with others. To some it might appear as a bunk bed; to others it might seem like stacked coffins. To the pilot and the crew, they preferred people in the bunks as much as possible because they consumed less oxygen, and the environmental controls were easier to maintain if over half of the passengers were sleeping.

For this flight they had the bonus: half the seats were empty, so atmosphere controls operated significantly easier. Evo Kaplan had identified several black marketers who he recognized from his training videos. As expected, they kept to themselves and most likely viewed the other black marketers as a potential threat or even a snitch.

Just like the French officer in the Casa Blanca movie, the crew of the blockade runner saw no contraband, ever!

Krawz Almarip slid his security privacy slide into position and locked it. It had interlocking metal panels that when locked in place formed what appeared to be a solid wall. A blaster could shoot through it and kill someone, but knives and other weapons would not be strong enough to penetrate.

Inside the bunk with the security privacy slide locked, a person had adequate ventilation with air pumped in and lights they could turn on to read if required. Depending on where the ship was, some communicators worked if a planet was nearby. However, in the open stretch of space they traveled, there would be no planets or any such communications.

People like Krawz Almarip and the other black marketers slept in their clothes just in case they had to get out in a hurry. Other travelers would go to the restroom and change into sleeping clothes and be more comfortable. Evo at least took off his shoes but had them at the foot of his comfortable bed. The mattress sat on a metal tray and was six inches thick and designed for comfort and long hours of sleeping, as some passengers took sleeping pills to pass out for a day or longer to make the trip feel shorter.

Krawz Almarip (a.k.a. Evo Kaplan) was no different and soon saw that white spot at the end of the tunnel getting smaller until he was unconscious. He would wake in about twenty-four hours due to hunger and the need to urinate. His rest period was what the doctor ordered. His dreams were full of color and full of Brenda Broyals, whom he now missed. *I must be falling in love with Brenda Broyals.*

Just like he expected, twenty-four hours later he awoke due to hunger pains and the incredible need to urinate. As he climbed out of his bunk, he noticed Ruth Marradi who was being bribed to look out for him, seeming somewhat focused on him and the surroundings. She gave him a smile and moved her head up and down once, which apparently was her secret signal, everything was all right. After taking care of his business in the bathroom, Krawz Almarip made his way to the lounge where they served space food.

Due to cramped conditions, atmosphere controls, and other reasons, all food was prepared and in tubes or special containers the flight attendants could roll up into a ball like aluminum foil and place into the recycler press that flattened it, then they slid it through a slit to the recycler storage that would be off-loaded at their destination and traded for credits used to purchase return trip-prepared foods.

The meals and everything aboard Intergalactic Passenger Transports was provided for free, no cash or credits necessary. Krawz Almarip selected the food items he had been schooled to do. Even though he might not like these food items, since the real Krawz Almarip always ate them, Evo Kaplan had to play along consuming those items as to not draw any undue scrutiny by potential passengers who had traveled with him time before, including all the black marketers, who were usually very keen on detecting inconsistencies.

The food items were not bad, just not Evo Kaplan's preference; nevertheless, he consumed them out of sheer hunger and out of professionalism of paying attention to detail like a good spy with an ID transplant would emulate. A female entered the lounge and made her way to the food selectors and grabbed several items and an eight-ounce drink.

The crew did not encourage water consumption because in a full ship, they had to conserve waste storage until they traveled somewhere that wastewater could be dumped, like on the edge of an asteroid field where they would maneuver and then out-chop allowing the debris to hit the asteroids where it would not become a menace to intergalactic travel.

It was also against intergalactic rules and regulations to dump trash and wastewater in shipping lanes because those materials could pose a threat to future transport traveling in the area. On the main asteroid fields found between Zanziltar and Praxisvlasia, there were debris fields of trash, waste, and wrecked space craft. One day as materials prices soared due to scarcity and the profitability of recycling, there would be robotic ships harvesting these rich debris fields as the early years in space travel used much thicker and richer composites.

The scrap value of a first-generation intergalactic transport was worth about five times as much as newer models that used thinner materials with more ingenious engineering. They also had more metal and less carbon nanotubes and graphene content.

The woman sat down with her back to the wall behind her at the next table facing Krawz Almarip and smiled. He returned a smile. Krawz Almarip had a reputation of latching onto women on his way to far off planets and used them while he was there making his profits. As soon as he had completed all his transactions and collected his credits, he usually hopped on the next space craft leaving and abandoning the woman who thought there was more to the relationship than what existed.

A couple of women out on planets he never intended to visit again would no doubt attempt killing him if he was ever spotted on their planet. To really play the role of Krawz Almarip, Evo Kaplan had to be flamboyant at times and what would be considered a womanizer.

KRAWZ ALMARIP
Hello. Are you on your way to Praxisvlasia?

FEMALE PASSENGER
No. I'm going to Arzon.

KRAWZ ALMARIP
No kidding! So am I.

FEMALE PASSENGER
What will you be doing on Arzon?

KRAWZ ALMARIP
I have some items I plan on selling.

FEMALE PASSENGER
Seems like a long way to go to sell something.

KRAWZ ALMARIP
Arzon, being a provincial capital and cut off from the Empire,
has a lot of need for special equipment and materials. I provide
what they need and want and make good money at it.

FEMALE PASSENGER
Have you traveled there often?

KRAWZ ALMARIP
Oh yes, several times. How about yourself?

FEMALE PASSENGER
I grew up in Arzon and was sent to Zanziltar for higher education
and ended up getting hired there for a good job. The money was
right so I stayed.


KRAWZ ALMARIP
Going home to Arzon to visit your family?


FEMALE PASSENGER
Yes, my mother is ill and I want to see her before it's too late.


KRAWZ ALMARIP
I'm sorry to hear that.


FEMALE PASSENGER
I should arrive in plenty of time to spend some quality time
with her.


KRAWZ ALMARIP
What if the Revolutionaries capture this ship?


FEMALE PASSENGER
I'll plead my case with them and beg them to let me get to my
mother before it's too late.


KRAWZ ALMARIP
There's no transportation between Revolutionary Planets and
Arzon. All that gets to Arzon are these blockade runners.


FEMALE PASSENGER
I'll stay optimistic and we'll make it.


KRAWZ ALMARIP
What's your name?


FEMALE PASSENGER (a.k.a. Claudette Ramsey)
Claudette Ramsey. How about yourself, sir?


KRAWZ ALMARIP
I'm Krawz Almarip.


CLAUDETTE RAMSEY
Pleased to meet you Krawz Almarip.

KRAWZ ALMARIP
Claudette, same to you. What kind of work do you do on Zanziltar?

CLAUDETTE RAMSEY
I work as an analyst for one of the large Zanziltar banks.

KRAWZ ALMARIP
Which one is that?

CLAUDETTE RAMSEY
It's the Zanziltar Central Bank. I work directly for Randolph Spencer.

KRAWZ ALMARIP
That name sounds vaguely familiar.

CLAUDETTE RAMSEY
Well, since we are alone and I don't have to worry about the news media recording our conversation, I can probably tell you why you have heard his name.

KRAWZ ALMARIP
Okay.

CLAUDETTE RAMSEY
There has been a lot of leaks concerning his friend, a major politician, and him going down to Orgy Island quite often. And there is rumors now swirling around his wife was involved in a scandal at a provincial planet named *Shen de Huayuan*. He's been acting strange ever since there were leaks about all this to some yellow journalist media sources.

KRAWZ ALMARIP
Sounds kind of shocking.

CLAUDETTE RAMSEY
It was to me when I first heard about it.

Krawz Almarip spent a couple hours chatting with Claudette Ramsey and it was soon apparent to both there was some mutual attraction. Claudette Ramsey was the type of woman who would like Krawz Almarip even more after she discovered he ran a sordid operation. The psychology of some people created an attraction to negative individuals whether it be pirates, killers, embezzlers, crooked politicians, and lawyers. *Perhaps that's what drove her to work for Randolph Spencer?*

If it wasn't for the fact, he had Ruth Marradi looking out for him and he missed Brenda, he would have offered Claudette Ramsey to sneak in his bunk with him. It would not be the first nor the last woman to join the twenty-million-mile club with the real Krawz Almarip.

However, part of the caricature he was to develop to emulate Krawz Almarip demanded he follow such a course. Evo Kaplan was briefed and indoctrinated by the FIRM, but also by the Dranzonian Empire Secret Service where he worked as an agent before his purge and eventual defection: all spies use all their weapons as necessary and if a woman had to sleep with a man to fulfill her espionage, she was not sinning, she was merely using some of the tools of her spy craft as the ends justified the means.

That message rings true for all politicians and quite a few lawyers. No doubt there are good people in all professions, but experience shows power corrupts. After a few hours as the testosterone was wearing off and Claudette Ramsey was showing signs of space lag fatigue setting in, she said.

CLAUDETTE RAMSEY

Will you please excuse me, Krawz Almarip. I'm feeling like I
want to take a nap. I was awake many hours and couldn't sleep.
I think now I'll be able to.

KRAWZ ALMARIP

Not a problem. I'll be seeing you around.

Claudette Ramsey stood up and walked out of the lounge back toward her seat and bunk. Krawz Almarip went back to his own seat, which reclined forty-five degrees where he could either listen to music or watch entertainment. He saw Claudette Ramsey get into her bunk, which it turns out was the one just forward of his. This might get interesting later.

On the viewer that came down from directly above his seat and provided surround sound and incredible 3D video capability, he selected some entertainment that would prescribe him a journey to a temporal escape. One thing was certain, the blockade runner didn't fly a piece of crap space craft. This was indeed luxury. But he also knew this one cost quite a phenomenal amount. Claudette Ramsey is spending a fortune to get home to see her mother. She might be as corrupt as the banker she works for.

Evo Kaplan started to think about the name Randolph Spencer. He then unexpectedly made the connection. At the captain's dining table on the cruise liner, there was Lady Spencer. That was his wife. And the guy she was flagrantly having a soiree with a Mr. Blane Jiandie, a.k.a. Reginald Heiqishi! It all made perfect sense now. Randolph Spencer is the person who gave the FIRM the contract to kill Reginald Heiqishi.

There are strange twists in life. It was Lady Spencer who delivered Reginald Heiqishi to him so he could exact his sweet revenge. The ironic part of the story it now seems is that Reginald Heiqishi would be alive today had he not purged Evo Kaplan in revenge.

Traveling to Arzon with Claudette Ramsey just spiced up the trip a few notches. He would get closer to her because INTEL on Randolph Spencer just might be of some value in the future. Evo Kaplan started to think he might even find a way to blackmail Randolph Spencer and retire lavishly. Maybe he could use Claudette to help set up Randolph Spencer for blackmail?

Out traveling in space between two worlds is a lonely period. At least they were at the halfway point now. In thirty-six hours, he would be on Praxisvlasia. How would he feel? After watching some parabolic hypnotic series on the view scanner, which is used along with psychoacoustics in synchronization to trigger endorphin releases, Evo Kaplan thought for a few minutes about Brenda and the special time he had with her. Would he ever see her again?

Krawz Almarip was a flamboyant bachelor and fun-seeking guy. Evo Kaplan could not portray him in a melancholy mood so he decided it would be best if he took another one of those special pills and go lay down for another twelve hours. Then when he came about, he would only have twenty-four hours to be highly observant of his surroundings. Maybe another meeting in the lounge with Claudette Ramsey?

Evo Kaplan pushed the view scanner up and then stood up to walk around a bit, which is what the real Krawz Almarip would do on these long trips according to the reports. It was also not out of the ordinary for him to go up to the cockpit and talk to the duty pilot and co-pilot. Even though modern-day intergalactic transport ships were fully automated and did not require pilots, the public was never able to accept pilotless Intergalactic Passenger Transports.

There was also union pressure from the pilot's union to not do away with their jobs. It got really dicey during the outbreak of the Revolution. The pilot's unions then cemented their positions for good. They had a really simple solution: Either agree to the permanent presence of pilots in the cockpit or we'll simply fly all the transports to the enemy! That carried over to even specialized transport such as the blockade runners.

Evo Kaplan had been warned that some of the pilots knew Krawz Almarip, as he had bribed them in the past with women, credits, energy drinks, et cetera. If one of them called him by his name, that was one of them he needed to be very like-minded to and play along as if they were old pals.

Krawz Almarip (a.k.a. Evo Caplan) decided he would now go test the waters of this multi-crew cockpit. These guys ran in twelve-hour shifts and switched out. However, during planet re-entry, they were all in the cockpit sharing the load in communications, navigation, and control. The computer handled the transport space craft, but the pilot had to oversee and apply common sense and judgement in the event some computer glitch occurred, mainly to retain proficiency.

Some transports were all automated; the pilots were too scared to ever control the craft because even the slightest screw-up resulted in termination of their employment. The unions didn't fight it because the junior officers loved the quick promotions when an old geezer was sent packing. The old geezers figured it out: Never come out of autopilot and you have no worries. It took a short period of time to walk past the lounge and up into the forward area. The crew lived up here and they didn't like passengers walking up there, but they knew who Krawz Almarip was.

Krawz Almarip got lucky: it was shift-change, and the outgoing pilots opened the door just as soon as he arrived.

COPILOT

Hello, Krawz Almarip. I heard you were on the flight.

KRAWZ ALMARIP<br>Yep

COPILOT

Say, come back in about twelve hours with one of your energy drinks and I'll let you sit in my seat for a while.

KRAWZ ALMARIP

That's great, but when will I get to sit in the left seat?

Evo knew their rankings and that he was talking to the junior right seater.

COPILOT

Well, you know there are two things you never do on a space transport: Sit at the captain's chair in the wardroom or in his seat in the cockpit.

KRAWZ ALMARIP

But when you make captain, I'm sure we can work out a deal where I get to just sit there for a moment so I can see how it feels.

I can't promise you anything I might get in trouble for, but when I get promoted to captain and you are on my flight, if you don't tell neither will I.


All right, I'll make that flight just for you.


Good. Your buddy captain Buck is at the controls now. He probably wants to talk to you about some of the schemes you came up with, or at least one of those fancy energy drinks that will keep him vigilant for the next twelve hours.

The pilot standing ahead of them at the door held it open knowing Krawz Almarip had no way to open it, and once it shut those two would be locked in until the next watch relief. Despite what the public thought, they each did have a piss bottle, but if they had to poop, they asked a flight attendant to wake up the other captain for a bathroom relief. And yes, that happened occasionally if the crew got some food-born illness.

In a way it felt kind of spooky. All these guys knew Krawz Almarip well and he had only limited knowledge of what they had done together, including smuggling and black marketing. Captain Buck was apparently the worst offender; close to forced retirement, he wanted that big score so he could stretch his retirement a lot further.

KRAWZ ALMARIP
*What the phuc, Buck,* Krawz Almarip stated as he had been briefed that was one of the banters they did and easy to remember.

PILOT
Well, what do you know, here's the Zanziltar Gypsy.

KRAWZ ALMARIP
Are we safe or should I get on my parachute?

VOICE OVER (MALE)
That apparently was another line Krawz Almarip had used and only became one of the many golden nuggets he confessed to Conrad Fanzui only after advanced interrogation techniques that compelled him to spill a lot of information. It took him about five tries to realize he couldn't beat their lie detectors.

A couple trips to the swimming pool, feet first in the crematorium where he got some nice burns, then being thrown out of a VTOL at ten thousand feet and held by a small cable got him to be very careful of every word he chose going forward.

Krawz Almarip knew he was dealing with some very sick bastards who gave him the choice of luxury living or a god-awful ending. Based on how well their lie detecting equipment worked, Krawz Almarip had no choice but to cooperate fully.

CAPTAIN BUCK<br>
Did you bring me one of those energy drinks?

KRAWZ ALMARIP<br>
I just now figured out it was shift-change.

CAPTAIN BUCK<br>
You can't look at a chronometer?

KRAWZ ALMARIP<br>
I'll tell you what, if you can have your COPILOT Fursungtarwum hold the door open for me, I'll go back to my bunk and bring us some energy drinks.

CAPTAIN BUCK<br>
Hurry it up, we are behind schedule.

KRAWZ ALMARIP<br>
I'll be right back.

Krawz Almarip walked back to his bunk, opened the four-square footlocker, and pulled out one of the bags he had full of energy drinks he was told would come into great use. This was just one of the uses. He had a small carrying bag he could fold up and put in his rear pocket after delivery. He promptly went forward and almost pissed off a flight attendant who would have stopped him had Fursungtarwum not been standing there holding the cockpit door open.

FURSUNGTARWUM<br>
It's okay, Sammyret, he's bringing us some things up to the cockpit.

Moments later Krawz Almarip was sitting in the fourth seat of the six-seat cockpit so he could look and talk to Captain Buck in seat number one. Seat number two was the copilot just ahead of him, seat three was behind the captain. Five and six were behind him and were not occupied unless they were entering the atmosphere in preparation for landing. Having six men in the cockpit helped split up the tasking so the pilot could concentrate on flying, with the copilot assisting. Seats three, four, five, and six maintained situational awareness, weather observation, and affirmative back up to air traffic control and collision avoidance.

All six pilot workstations had similar glass display panels. Complex instrumentation gave these well-trained men extraordinary ability to travel great distance at super high speeds. The rear seaters paid close attention to the *cosmic spatial normalizer data*, especially nearing a planet where air traffic could expand exponentially. Praxisvlasia, being the seat of the Dranzonian Empire, had to make extra effort to prevent a sucker punch and therefore had to maintain a credible space force.

Praxisvlasia's enhanced security posture alone created collision hazards. Due to high speeds and Doppler radar, contact correlation was almost impossible without instruments such as the *cosmic spatial normalizer*, and pilots would not be able to cope.

On board computational equipment processing hundreds of billions of *cosmic spatial normalizer coefficients* every second was really doing all the collision avoidance.

The rear seaters were just monitoring the automated process and talking the pilot down to the planet, who sometimes needed adjustments along the way unless he was like one of the old geezers and said the heck with it and allowed the computers to do all the work.

There were actual reported cases of flight crews playing cards during a landing because they had that much faith in the computer, which always gave them a softer landing. With the boys in the cockpit drinking those special energy drinks, a whole new dynamic began.

INT. INTERGALACTIC PASSENGER SPACESHIP COCKPIT.

C.U. DISPLAYS SHOWING *COSMIC SPATIAL NORMALIZER DATA*

C.U. CAPTAIN BUCK

C.U. KRAWZ ALMARIP

MONTAGE OF C.U. OF *COSMIC SPATIAL NORMALIZER DATA,* CAPTAIN BUCK, AND KRAWZ ALMARIP DURING FOLLOWOING VOICE OVER AND SUBSEQUENT DISCUSSION.

VOICE OVER

The Zanziltar flagged Intergalactic Passenger Transport was in autopilot and, the *cosmic spatial normalizer data* showed no spacecraft ahead at their velocity of 200 million meters per second, which is two-thirds light speed. They couldn't go faster because of the fuel financial constraints to slow down.

A military ship, on the other hand, didn't have to worry about fuel costs and exceeded 300 million meters per second often. It took them several days to make the journey, while a top line military craft would make it in a day.

CAPTAIN BUCK
Are you getting off at Praxisvlasia?

KRAWZ ALMARIP
No, I'm going all the way to Arzon.

CAPTAIN BUCK
Selling some of your wares there?

KRAWZ ALMARIP
If we make it and do not get stopped by the Revolutionaries.

CAPTAIN BUCK
I would think by now that you made enough money to retire.

KRAWZ ALMARIP
Well, yes and no.

CAPTAIN BUCK
Let's start with the no.

KRAWZ ALMARIP
Remember when I told you I was going to take a big load from *Shen de Huayuan* to Zanziltar?

CAPTAIN BUCK
Yeah, you were going to get filthy rich.

KRAWZ ALMARIP
I almost made it, but the Revolution caught our ship and confiscated all the shipment. I could have retired had I sold the material to my customer on Zanziltar.

MONTAGE OF C.U. OF *COSMIC SPATIAL NORMALIZER DATA,* CAPTAIN BUCK, AND KRAWZ ALMARIP DURING FOLLOWOING VOICE OVER AND SUBSEQUENT DISCUSSION.

VOICE OVER

Krawz Almarip knew he would not be caught in a lie because the Revolution did, in fact, confiscate the real Shen de Huayuan goods off one shipment recently when he was abducted by Conrad Fanzui's people.

Pilot Buck and his copilot Fursungtarwum were now starting to feel the effects of this super enhanced energy drink.

Aside from giving a person a lot of energy, it also gave them ultra-sensitivity, which further enhanced their vigilance and bravery. The energy drink also opened old memories that were forgotten long ago, that gave a splendid happiness as they recalled special events in their lives.

Old jokes were suddenly recalled and soon jocularity and banter flourished. The pilot Buck and his copilot Fursungtarwum traded old stale jokes for a while at the same time the memories flourished, including the desires to do things they always planned on doing but never got around to do.

Sadly, as the drugs wore off that were contained in the energy drink, so would they lose those desires to do things they always planned on doing. But for now, and the remainder of their twelve-hour shift, these pilots were super animated, and happiness prevailed.

Krawz Almarip was the purveyor of these marvelous moments and memories. Evo Kaplan' portrayal of Krawz Almarip was convincing and Buck and Fursungtarwum were totally consumed and convinced their friend Krawz Almarip was sitting there in seat number three, loosely participating in what was going on.

KRAWZ ALMARIP
I see on the scanners nothing out in front of us.

CAPTAIN BUCK
Towards the end of our shift, we expect to start picking up some Praxisvlasia traffic and so we should start to see some cargo or transport ships.

KRAWZ ALMARIP
Will it be boring until then?


CAPTAIN BUCK
Not really, I got a few more jokes up my sleeve.


CO-PILOT FURSUNGTARWUM
Just what we need, jokes you told already fifty times


Captain Buck turned to Krawz Almarip.


CAPTAIN BUCK
Krawz, did you meet any pretty ladies on the flight yet?


KRAWZ ALMARIP
I certainly did, and I hope to bag her before we land in Arzon.


CAPTAIN BUCK
You're a slick dog. I wonder how you manage to get all those
women?


KRAWZ ALMARIP
Well Captain Buck, it's like this. I studied statistics and
probabilities. One way you can control the degrees of freedom
is to change the sample rate. I believe increasing sample rate
offers you more opportunity.


Buck and Fursungtarwum laughed momentarily, then Fursungtarwum got serious
for a minute and asked a great question.


FURSUNGTARWUM
Seriously, Krawz did you ever find a woman you really adored
and loved?


This was an easy answer for Krawz Almarip as he allowed himself to think of
Brenda Broyals for a moment and knew he didn't have to give any names but
would leave no doubt in their minds.


KRAWZ ALMARIP
I think I fell hopelessly in love with a woman. Unfortunately,
she and I are heading in opposite directions, and we may never
meet again.


CAPTAIN BUCK
That's how we pilots feel.

KRAWZ ALMARIP
Yes, it's a sad life for a traveling guy. We meet suitable partners
one week and they are out of our lives forever in just a week.

CAPTAIN BUCK
I always wondered if you purposely meet gals, you know you
will not be able to see again?

KRAWZ ALMARIP
Not really, it just ends up that way. I wish a few of them I met
were still with me.

CAPTAIN BUCK
But would you give up your traveling gig to be domesticated
by a woman?

KRAWZ ALMARIP
For my most recent friend, yes. If she and I could go off
somewhere together and live the rest of our lives together, I
would be happy to sell my holdings for a reasonable amount
and leave all this behind me.

CAPTAIN BUCK
But since that's not possible, do you have designs on one of the
passengers?

KRAWZ ALMARIP
Definitely. She lives in Zanziltar, and if we both make it back
there alive, I will pursue her with all vigor.

CAPTAIN BUCK
What about the gal you are in love with? What if she comes
back suddenly?

KRAWZ ALMARIP
She's rapidly changing. She will not be the same woman when
she gets back and may or may not wish to have anything to do
with me.

CAPTAIN BUCK
So, you are going to play the odds in your favor and get hooked
up with the female passenger?

KRAWZ ALMARIP
At least for a temporary gratification.

                            CAPTAIN BUCK
              Good luck with that one. Let us know how it works out.


                            KRAWZ ALMARIP
           It's already worked out well. We talked for several hours. I like
           her and she likes me. I think we are meant for each other.


                            CAPTAIN BUCK
             A shifty character like you would settle down with her?


                            KRAWZ ALMARIP
           Yes, after I make a big score and move to some tropical planet
           like *Shen de Huayuan*.


                            CAPTAIN BUCK
                       Have you ever been there?


                            KRAWZ ALMARIP
                         Yes, it was nice.


                            CAPTAIN BUCK
           I've never been there but I hear all kinds of good things. What
           do you recommend to a person going there for the first time?


                            KRAWZ ALMARIP
           If you stay at the Lantiane Resort, you will have the best quality
           on the planet.


Krawz Almarip then discussed some of the other points of interest such as the
Hupu Waterfalls, club Banma Julebu, the ocean liner tours, Quanqiu Museum,
and the beaches and Barracuda and Cougars that hang out at the swimming pools.


                            CAPTAIN BUCK
               I wouldn't mind a Cougar, but at my age she would have to be
               around eighty.


The only interesting aspect of flying out in space between planets going at high
speed was observing the stars and other planets move along the horizon; even
though they were only going two-thirds light speed. It was just enough velocity to
see the whole complexity of the galaxy unfold before their eyes.


                            KRAWZ ALMARIP
              Do you guys ever get tired of being up here in the cockpit?


                            CAPTAIN BUCK
               Almost every flight we have some excitement.

Captain Buck didn't admit  terror as they barely missed several meteorites and space debris at least once or twice per flight.

VOICE OVER (FEMALE)

The conversations with Captain Buck and the three other pilots lasted without a break until the next watch relief. As soon as the oncoming pilot unlocked the door from outside, Krawz Almarip was able to leave the cockpit.

Krawz Almarip was a little hungry and decided to get a snack before he crawled into his bunk for a rest period, then he would get up and stay up until they landed. After all the departing passengers were off the ship, he would crawl into his bunk and rest until takeoff time, thanks to his prearranged help from flight attendant Ruth Marradi.

As Krawz Almarip walked away from the cockpit control room, he made his way into the lounge and unexpectedly ran into Claudette Ramsey.

Claudette wasn't looking quite as cute as when he first met her. She had evidently cleaned up, washed off all her makeup, and now he got to see the natural woman as she really was. Claudette Ramsey new appearance seemed more like a big girl than the woman she appeared as earlier.

<u>INT. INTERGALACTIC PASSENGER SPACECRAFT CAFETERIA</u>

<u>SPLIT SCREEN SIDE BY SIDE</u>

C.U CLAUDETTE RAMSEY AND KRAWZ ALMARIP REPEATEDLY DURING CONVERSATION

CLAUDETTE RAMSEY

Hello again.

KRAWZ ALMARIP

Enjoy your sleep?

CLAUDETTE RAMSEY

Yes, I think I got a total equalizer. I hope I don't suffer much space lag. How about yourself?

KRAWZ ALMARIP

I was busy visiting my pilot friends in the cockpit.

                         CLAUDETTE RAMSEY
                            You know them?


                         KRAWZ ALMARIP
            Yes, I've taken some long flights with them before.


                         CLAUDETTE RAMSEY
                             To Arzon?


                         KRAWZ ALMARIP
                  No, but to many other locations.


                         CLAUDETTE RAMSEY
                           From Zanziltar?


                         KRAWZ ALMARIP
                   Yes, also from Praxisvlasia.


                         CLAUDETTE RAMSEY
          What were some of your most interesting locations to visit?


                         KRAWZ ALMARIP
         I'd say the Lantiane Resort on the planet *Shen de Huayuan*.


Krawz Almarip noticed the distinct body shift in Claudette Ramsey. He knew he
touched a hot button somehow.


                         CLAUDETTE RAMSEY
                            What's it like?


                         KRAWZ ALMARIP
     The Lantiane Resort there is the best I've ever stayed at, and
     there are a lot of fun things to do.


                         CLAUDETTE RAMSEY
        If I went there, what kinds of things would you recommend?


                         KRAWZ ALMARIP
     They have good ocean cruise liners worth taking. There are a lot
     of good restaurants, one of the Empire's best museums and the
     Dewaltracen Art Gallery, exciting night clubs for dancing, and
     interesting things to visit like the Hupu Waterfalls and Guilong
     Aquarium at Pangu Bay.


                         CLAUDETTE RAMSEY
                           Sounds lovely.

KRAWZ ALMARIP

*Shen de Huayuan* planet is mildly primitive, but out-world travelers nicknamed *Shen de Huayuan* it the GARDEN OF THE GODS. Are you interested in Shen de Huayuan?

CLAUDETTE RAMSEY

I wasn't until my boss's wife went there with a couple of her girlfriends. He got really upset as rumors of a scandal were circulating.

KRAWZ ALMARIP
How did that turn out?

CLAUDETTE RAMSEY

When his wife first came home from Shen de Huayuan, he appeared really upset, then a short time ago he suddenly acted happy again as if nothing happened.

KRAWZ ALMARIP
How about the wife?

CLAUDETTE RAMSEY
She's been acting kind of strange apparently.

VOICE OVER

Krawz Almarip knew exactly why Randolph Spencer appeared happy since he fulfilled the contract to kill Glacy Spencer's lover and his former despicable boss Reginald Heiqishi.

Perhaps that might be a way to blackmail Randolph Spencer? Threaten to tell his wife her husband arranged to have her lover murdered? The conversation continued and Claudette Ramsey seemed to get friendlier.

Claudette Ramsey's smile was genuine, her intelligence was obvious; otherwise, she wouldn't be an analyst working for Randolph Spencer. Claudette Ramsey was wholesome and not ugly with her makeup removed. She almost looked like a teenager, which meant she had many good years ahead of her before she would morph into an old hag.

Krawz Almarip knew he would not be around to watch Claudette Ramsey grow old. The sense of affection and attraction intersected Evo Kaplan's (a.k.a. Krawz Almarip) thoughts, which gave him the ammunition and resolve to lubricate the relationship a bit and conceivably invite Claudette Ramsey to the twenty-million-mile club in his bunk.

Evo also started thinking that since Arzon was Claudette Ramsey's home planet, she could be someone he could exploit and use for his purposes in espionage. Claudette Ramsey might know people who could further his ability to move around and acquire information.

In a brief amount of time, Captain Buck and his Co-Pilot Fursungtarwum arrived in the lounge still wearing their uniforms, seeking something to eat before they turned in or did whatever they planned on.

Captain Buck and his Co-Pilot Fursungtarwum gave Krawz Almarip space and realized this woman was his next conquest, another notch in his belt. Observing Krawz Almarip in action with the ladies did more than enough to give Captain Buck and Co-Pilot Fursungtarwum a false sense of reality, as they had no idea they were observing an imposter, a top-level spy from the FIRM.

Captain Buck and his Co-Pilot Fursungtarwum kept their distance and allowed the black marketer to continue his conquest. In private later they would make bets on when or if he managed to get this attractive woman into the twenty-million-mile club.

For the time being, Captain Buck and Co-Pilot Fursungtarwum, now more interested in getting some restful sleep knowing collision avoidance work in the next watch would be a pain in the ass. The two pilots left the entertaining exhibit where Krawz Almarip would achieve his conquest as easily as the lions got to the sheep in Roman coliseums.

They two pilots left the passenger lounge to turn in and knew by the time they came back on watch in twelve hours, the sheep would be eaten alive.

Suddenly Krawz Almarip and Claudette Ramsey were alone.

CLAUDETTE RAMSEY
What are you going to be doing next?

KRAWZ ALMARIP

I'm going to my bunk and rest for a few hours. Want to come along?

CLAUDETTE RAMSEY
What are you talking about?

KRAWZ ALMARIP
Twenty-Million-Mile Club.

CLAUDETTE RAMSEY
What's that?

KRAWZ ALMARIP
Knock on my security privacy slide three times and I'll unlock
it and you can hop in so I can teach you all about the twenty-
million-mile club.


CLAUDETTE RAMSEY
Wouldn't you be ashamed if someone saw me climbing in your
bunk with you?


KRAWZ ALMARIP
Odds are you will never see any of these people again for the
rest of your life.


CLAUDETTE RAMSEY
I would be too nervous to try something like that.


KRAWZ ALMARIP
If you want, I'll have a flight attendant come get you and escort
you to my bunk to make it look all proper.


CLAUDETTE RAMSEY
You have got to be kidding.


KRAWZ ALMARIP
I bribe them well.


CLAUDETTE RAMSEY
Well, first of all I would never consider.


In a short while Krawz Almarip and Claudette Ramsey went their separate ways.
Krawz Almarip never assumed that Claudette Ramsey would ever get the wild
notion to join the Twenty-Million-Mile Club; he was merely having fun with her.


Krawz Almarip was soon laying in his spacious and comfortable bunk that could
easily hold two people, which sometimes was necessary on the "pigs and people"
runs long distance where there were not enough room for all their luggage so the
families gave up a bunk to store all their personal affects and shared a bunk, which
had plenty of room as long as one of them didn't hog all the space.


VOICE OVER (FEMALE)
Thanks to the sleeping pill, Krawz Almarip (a.k.a. Evo Kaplan)
was soon sound asleep. Evo Kaplan had a restful period and
was in a deep dream when suddenly there were three knocks on
his security privacy slide. Even though he was well under with

the help of the narcotics in the pill he took to enhance sleep, he was also a trained spy, and the three knocks immediately alerted his brain, which swung into action.

Semi groggy, he unlocked the security privacy slide and opened it a few inches. The cabin area was somewhat dark, as the flight attendants made artificial nights for the passengers to help them keep a mental semblance of night and day.

INT. INTERGALACTIC PASSENGER TRANSPORT BUNK ROOM.

Claudette Ramsey had approached Ruth, the right flight attendant, one who had many dealings with Krawz Almarip on past flights and was looking forward to making a lot of money on this flight thanks to his presence and the quid pro quo he was going to provide.

Well, I'll be damned, Krawz Almarip thought for a moment as he saw Claudette Ramsey. Closely behind her was the flight attendant Ruth Marradi blocking the passageway, but also keeping prying eyes away. He then slid the security privacy slide back further, allowing Claudette Ramsey in his bunk, then slid it shut again and locked it. He knew this was going to cost him a little more, but it was worth it as he now would exploit Claudette Ramsey to get a back door to get access to Randolph Spencer.

It was slightly crowded but manageable. The security privacy slide had acoustic baffling as part of its construction. The noise that happened inside the bunk stayed inside the bunk, originally designed so that people could listen to music or play videos without bothering other passengers.

INT INSIDE KRAWZ ALMARIP'S (a.k.a. EVO KAPLAN) PRIVATE BUNK

ANGLE SHOT FROM THE CORNER OF BUNK LOOKING DOWN AT EVO KAPLAN AND CLAUDETTE RAMSEY.

C.U. DURING KISS

AFTER THE KISSING SCENE THEY GET INTO THE SPOON POSITION WHILE LOVE MAKING WITH EVO KAPLAN'S ARMS ACROUND CLAUDETTE CUPPING HER BREASTS WITH HIS HANDS.

Claudette Ramsey had on a very evocative perfume. Krawz Almarip was big about scents. In the Dranzonian Empire Secret Service he was trained to recognize scents because in some cases it might come in handy. Just like teaching a sonar technician how to distinguish sound, teaching a spy to recognize scents was just as important, as a spy had to use everything available to them in many instances.

CLAUDETTE RAMSEY
Tell me about this Twenty-Million-Mile Club.

Claudette Ramsey statement affected Evo Kaplan in the most provocative manner.

KRAWZ ALMARIP (A.K.A. EVO KAPLAN)
Let me demonstrate it first. We can talk about the club's goals later.

VOICE OVER (FEMALE)
About then Claudette Ramsey embraced Krawz Almarip and did one thing that was considered offensive to a lot of people: she began kissing him on his lips in the hungriest fashion. Coming from a provincial world like Arzon, this form of behavior was considered normal.

Vergentia, a Dranzonian Empire World where Evo Kaplan grew up, had similar customs so he wasn't offended. Men on Praxisvlasia would have kicked Claudette Ramsey out of the bunk. It didn't take the two long to figure out the best way to proceed and soon the twenty-million-mile tango was being performed.

Claudette Ramsey was long overdue for a physical embrace with a man. As an analyst working for someone like Randolph Spencer, holding other people's-money image was very important. Claudette Ramsey could not afford any scandals or involvement with an immoral and unethical character. She had a high visibility job, therefore had an existence as modest and as a celibate as a Knights Templar.

Krawz Almarip had a scandalous reputation confirmed by Ruth Marradi, which made the lust and desire more intensive and led Claudette Ramsey to act in quite an illogical manner. But Claudette Ramsey realized what Krawz Almarip said as she threw caution to the wind.

KRAWZ ALMARIP

You will never see any of these people again for the rest of your life.

VOICE OVER (FEMALE)

A brief period of ecstasy then transcendence into an ulterior lifestyle before Claudette Ramsey had to confront her mother's illness on Arzon made the decision to do this despicable and illogical act even more appealing.

As the splendid euphoria set in from the psychophysical responses manifested by the twenty-million-mile stimulus, Claudette Ramsey's gratification achieved a level that made her feel it was all worthwhile. To her delight she discovered how unusually strong Krawz Almarip was. His muscles were out of this world. He never touched such a strong man in her life before.

Claudette Ramsey had no idea she experienced coitus with one of the most dangerous spies in the galaxy and now near the top of the Dranzonian Empire Secret Service top ten list which equated to *kill on sight any way possible and collateral damage should not be taken into consideration in carrying out the execution.*

Krawz Almarip sucked all the energy out of Claudette Ramsey before they both collapsed into a euphoric state and drifted into an almost coma-like deep sleep. It was several hours before Claudette Ramsey came to, feeling extremely satisfied and somewhat emotionally attracted to Krawz Almarip. She couldn't believe what she had just done, but she was happy she did.

Claudette Ramsey realized Krawz Almarip was probably a heartbreaker and here today and gone tomorrow. But she felt invigorated having the courage to try this illogical and, in many ways, considered denigrating toward women, except for those who wanted to live on the wild side and taste the dangerous fruits of a sleazy man such as Krawz Almarip.

Claudette Ramsey would never be able to see anyone like Krawz Almarip on Zanziltar. If Randolph Spencer discovered such a liaison, she feared what that powerful man could do to her. She also knew there was a distinct possibility of strange behavior on the part of Glacy Spencer, his wife, who probably thought Randolph Spencer had her lover murdered and disposed. She too could experience similar treatment if investors pulled out over a scandal, he attributed to herself.

Claudette Ramsey and Krawz Almarip slowly recovered their consciousness and awareness.

CLAUDETTE RAMSEY
I think I should go now. The cabin will be rigged for nighttime
for a while, and I would feel better if people didn't see me
leaving your bunk.


KRAWZ ALMARIP
No problem, I'll let you get out first and maybe in a while we
can meet up in the lounge.


CLAUDETTE RAMSEY
Sounds good.


The security privacy slide was then unlocked and slid open, and Claudette Ramsey
slid out. She then went and took care of female matters and took a quick shower
and changed. Claudette Ramsey decided that since she was happy to become a
member of Krawz Almarip's Twenty-Million-Mile Club, she would put on some
makeup for him and be pretty.

Claudette Ramsey morphed into a glamorous banking official and no longer
looked like a kid when they met soon afterward in the lounge. The lounge allowed
passengers to get away from other passengers who preferred quiet and meet family
members or friends or new acquaintances to have discussions and avoid upsetting
those who didn't want to have to hear noise from others. Krawz Almarip was in
the lounge well before Claudette Ramsey, who took her sweet time putting the
exclamation point on the inductee to the Twenty-Million-Mile Club.

Captain Buck, had a few hours' sleep, had to get up and use the restroom. He
felt thirsty and went to the lounge to get a drink. He found Krawz Almarip there,
sitting by himself.


CAPTAIN BUCK
Hello Krawz, how goes it?


KRAWZ ALMARIP
Really good so far. Enjoying the trip, met such a nice lady.


CAPTAIN BUCK
I saw her with you earlier. She seemed young.


Captain Buck sat down at the table with Krawz Almarip and was enjoying his
drink, just taking it easy and getting ready to go back to his own bunk and attempt
getting a few more hours of sleep in before he had to go back to the cockpit.

Moments later, while Buck and Krawz Almarip were deep into a discussion
about Arzon, Claudette Ramsey appeared, and she was dressed to kill. Claudette

Ramsey felt she had to leave a lasting impression on Krawz Almarip to remind him of her stature during the induction into his twenty-million-mile club. She arrived with a *flaming* smile.

CLAUDETTE RAMSEY
Hello Krawz.

VOICE OVER (FEMALE)
Claudette Ramsey surprised Evo Kaplan (a.k.a. Krawz Almarip) with her fantastically upgraded elegance. Claudette Ramsey realized Krawz Almarip was giving her a huge reassessment.

Claudette Ramsey studied body language, her employer felt necessary in the banking industry as an analyst and had to confront corporate execs and quiz them about their earnings statements, she had to know how sincere they were or if they were just blowing hot air up her skirt.

Krawz Almarip did seem to appear thunder struck and striking body reaction to Claudette Ramsey's stunning metamorphism that immediately altered his demeanor and tempered with his ego.

Krawz Almarip had no idea he was dealing with a highly educated female analyst working for Randolph Spencer, where her findings could impact trillions of credits in a single day.

Some of Claudette Ramsey's decisions had a net value that exceeded the entire wealth of some planets. She was the cat playing with her mouse Krawz Almarip, just before the kill and the digestion.

One of the galaxy's premier spies just met one of the premier banking analysts for the Switzerland of the galaxy. Claudette Ramsey's clothes were not formal—they were casual— but they were very expensive and exotic and several steps above couture.

The exquisite perfume, attire, makeup, pretty hair, and a beautiful face struck Krawz Almarip so much that he felt weak and wondered if exploiting Claudette Ramsey to get a back door to Randolph Spencer might, in fact, turn out to be a bigger chore than he imagined.

Claudette Ramsey just made her fashion statement.

If Krawz Almarip wanted to swim with the sharks and not be eaten alive, he better be very careful with this woman, who now exposed a side of her that was diabolically quite a departure from his earlier estimate.

KRAWZ ALMARIP
Claudette, this is Captain Buck. He'll be flying us all the way to Arzon.

CLAUDETTE RAMSEY
Why are you here and not in the cockpit, Captain Buck?

CAPTAIN BUCK
Claudette, we have three flight crews. We rotate watches. Normally we only use one pilot and copilot at a time for a twelve-hour shift, then the second shift comes in to relieve.

CLAUDETTE RAMSEY
Why so many pilots?

The third set of pilot and copilots is for emergencies, and they do other functions on the ship in transit and only work the cockpit with all the other pilots and copilots when we descend to a planet's surface.

CLAUDETTE RAMSEY
I see. So, you are off watch now?

CAPTAIN BUCK
Yes, I'm off watch and got thirsty so I came to the lounge to get a drink and I noticed Krawz Almarip here. We have been on numerous flights together, so I sat down to talk with him for a few minutes about some of our trips in the past.

CLAUDETTE RAMSEY
I bet those trips were interesting.

Claudette Ramsey then winked at Krawz Almarip in a way that gave Captain Buck a notion something had happened between the two.

CAPTAIN BUCK
Nice meeting you Claudette, but I'm about ready to go back to bed to get a few more hours sleep before I must go back into the cockpit as the pilot.

Captain Buck looked Claudette over good and instantly knew this was a quality woman of high taste and stature, and incredibly beautiful. He was even more surprised when she sat down next to Krawz Almarip and gave him a little hug and a smile.

VOICE OVER

*I'll be damned*, Captain Buck thought. I bet Krawz has already worked his magic.

Krawz Almarip (a.k.a. Evo Kaplan) understood instinctively; he only did the *Twenty Million Mile Club* action to emulate the real Krawz Almarip, to give with a high degree of certainty, everyone would be convinced he was the man he portrayed in stealing his identity.

Evo Kaplan also knew he had to draw the line. As a good spy he would not allow this woman to entangle him into an emotional bond. But sitting here looking at her, it would be very difficult not to grow some tendrils into her in ways he couldn't avoid.

Suddenly becoming the mouse, Evo Kaplan suddenly had less power than he realized controlling his emotions.

Claudette Ramsey wasn't a spy; she was just a banking analyst, but she indeed was a better chess player than Krawz Almarip, and it would come down to spying verses analyzing to see who wins the war of the sexes and love.

Conrad Fanzui would certainly be happy if Claudette Ramsey could break the spell Brenda Broyals had on Evo Kaplan. He wanted to break up the two lovers, as such behavior generally created many problems, which led to avoiding sending them on the same mission together and logistics nightmares.

However, the reality was that after this mission, it was an extremely rare possibility that Evo Kaplan would ever swim with the great white shark like Claudette Ramsey again.

Claudette Ramsey's demeanor was deceptive yet genuine at the same time. Her focus was her mother who was ill, but she also had a life of her own, and living like a modest Knights Templar, like in the past, no longer appealed to her. She wanted to live now. Her bank accounts in Zanziltar were growing exponentially since she was the analyst with insider information, she always knew where to place her bets for sure wins.

VOICE OVER (FEMALE)
As a hobby Claudette Ramsey traded securities at lunchtime and made more income doing so than her seven-digit credit income as a banking analyst. Simply put, she was set for life now, with more wealth than she could possibly ever spend. But the downside was she had no mate, and she was lonely. And here Claudette Ramsey was fooling around with such a despicable example of human flesh, a black marketer, a seedy individual who probably had a girl in every port.

But there was something about Krawz Almarip that didn't add up. Claudette Ramsey was a good investigator and would in due time discover who he was and what he really was. They talked for quite a while. It felt so comfortable and refreshing in many ways. Krawz Almarip was a good listener and at times Claudette Ramsey exposed her soul and her life.

Evo Kaplan, on the other hand, could not describe anything about his life. He was in a precarious situation, soon landing on an Empire space port.

Evo Kaplan had to be careful to only reflect upon Krawz Almarip's life, much of it hidden from society as Krawz Almarip himself had changed his own identity several times. The information on Krawz Almarip's life was a hybrid composition. It had so many holes in it that it simply was like Swiss cheese.

CLAUDETTE RAMSEY
Are you going to get off the ship during our stop over at Praxisvlasia?

KRAWZ ALMARIP
I can't leave the ship because the Dranzonian Empire Secret Service has accused me of gun running to the Revolutionaries.

CLAUDETTE RAMSEY
Did you really do that?

KRAWZ ALMARIP
I purposely can't remember anything beyond a week ago. I don't want to remember the past as I strive forward.

After two hours of chatting, Krawz Almarip wanted to go back to his bunk and sleep.

KRAWZ ALMARIP
I'm getting sleepy. I'm going to go lay down for a bit. You can
join me if you want, but I'll just be sleeping.


CLAUDETTE RAMSEY
They will be turning the lights on in the main cabin. I think I'll
pass. I'm going to go watch some videos. I'll see you when you
wake up later.


Krawz Almarip got his rest period and when he woke up he figured it was time to
S/S/S and put on a change of clothes, which would be his clothes for the stopover
to Praxisvlasia.


Krawz Almarip took his change of clothes and all the other items he needed and
proceeded to one of the empty bathrooms with a shower. After taking care of
his business, he stepped into the shower that had three buttons on the wall of
the shower labeled wash, rinse, and dry. They couldn't have towels on board for
a variety of reasons, so after showering a body blow dryer blowing air down
from the ceiling dried a person, including their hair. A person could do multiple
wash and rinse cycles, but artificial intelligence cut the time down in half on each
subsequent activation to help conserve water.


Eventually when the time got down to a minimum there was a thirty-minute
delay so people would be forced to exit the shower. There were no Hollywood
showers on this spaceship. The shower left Krawz Almarip feeling good, and he
quickly dressed. One of the items he had was a sleazy male cologne, which was
emblematic of what Krawz Almarip usually wore.


Evo Kaplan  played the role of Krawz Almarip one hundred percent, including
simple items such as a cologne that the flight attendants detested and were getting
tired of smelling because it overwhelmed a person if he was near them long,
including himself! Evo Kaplan  could not stand the smell and cringed every time
he put it on, but he knew damn well that spies including himself went through
major scent training and this part of his disguise was essential. If he didn't wear
the cologne, some people might question his identity.


Evo Kaplan also didn't like the flamboyant hair style that the real Krawz Almarip
wore that he now had to wear as part of the disguise.


The hair style included applying a gel-like substance to glue the hair in place.
Back on Earth, men of a bygone era would be called "greasers" wearing similar
hair enhancers. And finally, the clothing was another item.


In real life most people would not be caught dead wearing Krawz Almarip's types of clothing apparel. On Earth Krawz Almarip would be considered someone who looked like a pimp in the inner cities. One item he did not wear was Krawz Almarip's hat, as he said he normally didn't wear it on the ship, but when he got off the ship, he always wore it to give him those *Panama Paul* looks.

After Evo Kaplan (a.k.a. Krawz Almarip) completed all his activities in the restroom, he went back to his bunk and restored all his items, then walked forward to the lounge. Not unexpectedly, Krawz Almarip found Claudette Ramsey there reading.

KRAWZ ALMARIP<br>Hello.

CLAUDETTE RAMSEY<br>Sleep well?

KRAWZ ALMARIP<br>Yes, excellent.

Claudette Ramsey sat there looking at her new conquest and immediately knew what she had to do.

As soon as they got to Arzon—and hopefully Krawz Almarip wasn't doing a "hit and run"—she would purchase him some new cologne so he could stop wearing that atrocious smelling stuff he was now wearing.

Other than that, he would be perfect for a female banker's husband. Krawz Almarip (a.k.a. Evo Kaplan) was an intelligent person.

CLAUDETTE RAMSEY<br>Krawz, are you hungry?

KRAWZ ALMARIP<br>Maybe a little.

CLAUDETTE RAMSEY
I was waiting for you to eat my meal because I wanted your company.

KRAWZ ALMARIP
It's not much of a meal, but I guess it will have to do.

CLAUDETTE RAMSEY
If you want, when we land on Praxisvlasia, I can get some carry-out meals and bring them on the ship, since you don't intend on getting off.

KRAWZ ALMARIP
That would be marvelous.

The two got their food items and drink and set back down and proceeded to have their picnic in space. Conversation flowed and Krawz Almarip enjoyed looking at Claudette Ramsey. She was a beautiful woman and while he was sleeping, she redid her makeup and looked and smelled very fresh. If there ever was a time, he enjoyed being trapped on a ship with a woman like this, including his travels with Brenda Broyals, this was perhaps the most satisfying.

Evo Kaplan (a.k.a. Krawz Almarip) had to keep reminding himself he was a spy and would fail as a spy if he allowed himself to get emotionally intertwined with a person of interest and a future pawn in a blackmail scheme.

Conceivably Evo Kaplan could get enough money out of Randolph Spencer where he could pay for his own cosmetic surgery and live on another sanctuary planet, and if he could find Brenda Broyals and bring her along, that would be just fine too.

But would Brenda Broyals be willing to go? Could she? After several hours the next set of pilots were up and about, eating and preparing to go into the cockpit. All three sets of pilots and copilots would be manning all six seats in their preparation to land on Praxisvlasia.

Captain Buck got his food items and drink and walked over to the table where Krawz Almarip and Claudette Ramsey were sitting. Observing they had their food trays that had been sitting there for a while, he asked,

CAPTAIN BUCK
May I join you?

CLAUDETTE RAMSEY
Sure, Captain Buck, please have a seat.

Captain Buck enjoyed looking at the pretty woman. He could only imagine the intense satisfaction and gratification must have if Krawz Almarip managed to coax her into joining him on the twenty-millionmile club. He would talk to the flight attendant Ruth Marradi later, whom he knew was taking bribes from Krawz Almarip, and confirm his suspicions.

Claudette Ramsey's disposition clearly articulated a well-satisfied lady. One day he would have to query how Krawz Almarip managed to seduce such intelligent beautiful women. The guy must be a silver-tongue devil!

The meal was considerably more enjoyable while looking, talking, and smelling such a delightful woman. Unfortunately, Krawz Almarip's cologne was a little annoying, but heck, maybe that was the secret!

In all his travels, Captain Buck had met a lot of men talking at bars who bragged about conquest. Krawz Almarip didn't brag, he just did it. The fact these two were heading to the same ultimate destination meant their short tryst could extend into a longer event because it normally took Krawz Almarip a month to dispose of all his black-market items and return on another transport back to Zanziltar.

Captain Buck had the pleasure of transporting Krawz Almarip to planets and back. They had numerous interesting discussions in the past. This trip would obviously be another, and the woman Krawz Almarip had seduced was as glamorous and beautiful as any other he had ever seen him with. She clearly exposed her essence of an *Eager Beaver*.

Captain Buck hated to leave the couple he was having such a delightful experience talking to. The exceptionally intelligent woman and his old friend Krawz Almarip, but duty called.

CAPTAIN BUCK

I'm sorry to leave you two, but I need to get up into the cockpit
now.

KRAWZ ALMARIP

Maybe I can join you guys up there for a brief period.

CAPTAIN BUCK

Go see the chief purser. He can let you in and out later.

KRAWZ ALMARIP<br>Will do.

Captain Buck stood up and disposed of his meal wrappers and put the tray on a stack that would be later washed by a flight attendant and put back on a dispenser for other passengers.

Claudette Ramsey and Krawz Almarip were alone again in the passenger lounge.

CLAUDETTE RAMSEY

I hope that when you go to visit the cockpit you do not mention
you invited me to the twenty-million-mile club.

KRAWZ ALMARIP
No, I would never mention something like that.

Somehow Claudette Ramsey thought that would be the very first thing the pilots, who were called Hoggers for multiple reasons, would ask.

They continued. small talk for another thirty minutes.

CLAUDETTE RAMSEY
Why don't you go visit your pilot buddies? I want to do some more reading.

KRAWZ ALMARIP
Sure.

Krawz Almarip stood up and walked aft, hoping to find the chief purser without a lot of effort. He could be anywhere. Luck was on his side. Not far from his bunk was the Chief Purser conversing with his flight attendant friend Ruth Marradi, discussing items they had to accomplish prior to landing on Praxisvlasia.

While the Chief Purser and Ruth Marradi were talking Krawz Almarip pulled out some energy drinks from his locker and put them in the carrying bag he could later fold up. He then approached the flight attendant and purser.

KRAWZ ALMARIP
Hello Chief Purser. I would like to go up to the cockpit to visit the pilots for a few minutes. Captain Buck said you could let me in.

CHIEF PURSER
Perhaps for about ten minutes because they are going to be getting busy soon tracking inbound and outbound traffic in the space lanes we are approaching.

KRAWZ ALMARIP
All right, that works. I probably only need ten minutes anyway.

CHIEF PURSER
Follow me, Mr. Almarip.

The chief purser knew Krawz Almarip quite well since he had met him on quite a few flights. At one point he was going to tell him he would have to refrain from any more twenty-million-mile club activity since he had received complaints from families whose kids asked their parents, "Why is the man and woman going into the bunk together?" That put the parents on the spot to come up with some lie they felt they shouldn't have to tell their children.

Krawz Almarip got away with it on this trip since the craft was only half full and there were no children onboard. The two walked forward through the lounge and crews breathing area and the chief purser put his hand on the palm reader, which scanned it and activated the solenoid activated door lock. He opened the door for Krawz Almarip and admonished him,

                        CHIEF PURSER
        I'll be back in ten minutes. You'll have to leave the cockpit, as
        they probably shouldn't have any distractions as we arrive in
        the transport lanes.

                        KRAWZ ALMARIP
                        No problem.

As soon as Krawz Almarip was in the cockpit standing behind seat number six and almost against the rear wall, predictably Captain Buck, now sitting in Seat Number One, turned around to ask a question.

                        CAPTAIN BUCK
        Say, Krawz, did you get that woman up to the Twenty-Million-
        Mile Club?

                        KRAWZ ALMARIP
        Well, Captain Buck, you know that gentlemen never tell.

Krawz Almarip then balled up his fist and stuck his thumb through his index finger and the next finger, which was a secret symbol between men.

                        CAPTAIN BUCK
        Krawz Almarip, you're a lucky dog.

                        KRAWZ ALMARIP
        Listen, I didn't do anything, I swear, but show her my stamp
        collection.

                        CO-PILOT FURSUNGTARWUM
        Krawz Almarip The last time you ever saw a stamp collection
        was in grammar school.

                        KRAWZ ALMARIP
        I can't confirm nor deny that!

Krawz Almarip then passed out energy drinks to all six pilots and copilots, who were eager recipients as the enhanced awareness it created would indeed make the planetary re-entry far more pleasant.

Krawz Almarip could see over their shoulders and onto the *Cosmic Spatial Normalizer Display DATA* showing distant contacts they would need to avoid. It was kind of interesting. The computer display said, "CPA for CTA number 2387 is ten minutes on a course of 155.663.989 and a speed of 0.75 LS." The Closest Point of Approach would be as close as the transport would pass the other ship.

The Contact Target Analysis (CTA) performed on data received via radio beacon information such as its intergalactic hull number 2387 all non-combat ships were required to transmit or they would lose their immunity from immediate attack. Transmitting the CTA information also put them in peril in that an enemy ship that wanted to destroy a precious cargo bound to their enemy could be located and destroyed by such exposure.

The CTA derived target course was normalized three vector coefficients that provided a three-dimensional spatialized relative motion, hence three numbers and multiple decimal points. The CTA information traveled the speed of light plus the relative motion combined. Hence the CTA broadcast to hull number 2387 arrived at 1.75 LS.

Like Einstein said, it's all relative, but Einstein didn't appreciate how much it could add above light speed.

The pilot's display provided a popup of imagery of hull number 2387 to get an official observation of the structure and hull dimensions of the spaceship. This cargo spaceship designated CTA 2387 was a 150,000-ton transport that did not do atmosphere penetrations. Its cargo was transshipped via shuttles. Shuttles and space tugs made a lot of money servicing such ships. Captain Buck looked only briefly at the CTA data then closed the window. The pilot on 2387 was no doubt looking at their own transport hull number 6809. Five minutes later the first glob of CTA data labels on the *Cosmic Spatial Normalizer Display* (CSND) data started separating and relative motion almost appeared like snow coming toward the windshield on a car traveling in a storm. Just about the time the contact density reached a level the pilots should not be distracted, the chief purser unlocked the cockpit door.

CHIEF PURSER
Krawz, would you please leave the cockpit now?

KRAWZ ALMARIP
Sure, not a problem. See all of you later.

CAPTAIN BUCK
See you, Krawz.

Krawz Almarip walked aft through crews berthing and into the lounge area where Claudette Ramsey was still reading. *I wonder if she's reading some sort of romance novel.* Krawz Almarip thought.

He was closer to the truth than he realized and Krawz Almarip's actions on board this space transport was in line with what she was reading! A provocative parallel indeed.

CLAUDETTE RAMSEY
Did you enjoy talking with your pilot buddies?

KRAWZ ALMARIP

Yes. I took them some energy drinks. Helps make the trip shorter.

CLAUDETTE RAMSEY
You were not with the pilots very long.

KRAWZ ALMARIP

They are now entering the space lanes to Praxisvlasia. The congestion is beginning, and the pilots must concentrate and can't be distracted. The chief purser chased me out of there, but I realized it was time for me to leave since they were getting busy.

CLAUDETTE RAMSEY
Did they spot any other spacecraft?

KRAWZ ALMARIP

Oh yes, in the space lanes there is a blizzard of ships they must avoid collision with.

CLAUDETTE RAMSEY

I would think with all the computerization that should no longer be a problem.

KRAWZ ALMARIP

I'm sure the pilots like to keep up their proficiency just in case they need to do contact management when the computer systems suddenly have a snag.

CLAUDETTE RAMSEY
That seems like a rather remote possibility.

KRAWZ ALMARIP
I don't know what the pilots experience. They obviously want
to keep up their proficiency for some reason or another.

CLAUDETTE RAMSEY
Probably.

KRAWZ ALMARIP
How's the book coming?

CLAUDETTE RAMSEY
I'm about halfway done. I want to finish it before we land. I
have a few more books to read on the trip from Praxisvlasia to
Arzon. Plus, I can get more at the space port terminal.

KRAWZ ALMARIP
I'd get some books too, but something tells me I'm going to
have my hands full taking you on additional rides up to the
twenty-million-mile club.

CLAUDETTE RAMSEY
You never know, I might just have to take you up to the forty-
million-mile club.

Claudette winked at Krawz Almarip as she was relieved his cologne was wearing
off a bit and not quite as offensive as he first showed up in. She knew what she had
to do. When she was in the tax-free section of the space port shopping, she was
going to buy him a cologne she really loved. If she could have sex with that man
wearing Chunlang, her utmost favorite, it would all be worthwhile.

They talked for about an hour then Krawz Almarip excused himself to go use
the restroom, then came back and wondered if he should invite her to his club or
wait for her to invite him to her forty-million-mile club. It didn't take long before
Claudette Ramsey put down the book.

CLAUDETTE RAMSEY
You probably didn't take me seriously when I suggested I could
take you to the forty-million-mile club?

KRAWZ ALMARIP
I would never assume or disbelieve anything about you.

CLAUDETTE RAMSEY
Okay, come with me. You have your work cut out for you.

Krawz Almarip followed Claudette Ramsey to her berth, which smelled a lot better than his, and a flight attendant had just rigged the cabin for nighttime operations, which was always done for planetary re-entry so that passengers could enjoy the view of the approaching planet, the moons, and any solar view if they were on that side of the transport.

Evo's favorite flight attendant Ruth Marradi, whom Claudette Ramsey got to know while Krawz Almarip had joked with her and informed her she had every intention of taking Krawz Almarip up to the forty-million-mile club and teach him a lesson about women. As she watched the two walking to Claudette's bunk, she assumed the event was just about to occur, so she positioned herself to block off foot traffic in that direction long enough for the couple to assume their launch position to the forty-million-mile destination.

CLAUDETTE RAMSEY
Would you mind taking off your shoes first? Give them to me
and I'll put them in my locker.

KRAWZ ALMARIP
Sure, no problem.

Krawz Almarip shortly handed his pair of shoes to Claudette, who stowed them for him.

CLAUDETTE RAMSEY
You get in first.

The following voice over happens during the love making scene:

VOICE OVER

Krawz Almarip hopped into Claudette's bunk, and she followed immediately afterward and closed and locked the security privacy slide. Claudette placed her back to Krawz Almarip and initiated immediate spooning.

Between the heavy-laden pheromones in her perfume and a special cream she had just in case she got lucky, Krawz Almarip was soon transfixed into an explosion of gratification unlike he ever recalled.

At first, Evo Kaplan (a.k.a. Krawz Almarip) felt guilty he had expired before she could get her gratification, but he was in for a big surprise. There was plenty of room for her to turn and reposition herself on the "Pigs and People" mattress.

Claudette climbed up on top of Krawz Almarip and soon demonstrated what lonely women who had to live a private life developed with robotic help: surreal vaginal muscles. Claudette then proceeded to perform unlike anything Krawz Almarip had ever experienced, nor the duration.

Due to the special cream Claudette put on her vulva area, Krawz Almarip was essentially drugged as if he had taken a dozen doses of Viagra. He was not able to stop, and Claudette had the stamina of a Chita that could run seventy miles an hour for prolonged periods.

Chita woman Claudette kept on pounding Krawz into submission. Krawz Almarip just was "trumped" by a woman and was now a member of her forty-million-mile club.

Moving forward, Evo Kaplan would have a different attitude toward women. After Claudette Ramsey finally ended her Chita burst, the two slowly eased into a post orgasmic evolution of feelings that broke the inner fabric of their emotions.

Krawz Almarip (a.k.a. Evo Kaplan) was in deep trouble now, far more so than he could ever imagine. The thought of him breaking a woman's heart was a huge downer on him. It was as if he could mentally think of Brenda Broyals flying off into space, lifeless, as if she was expelled from a crippled ship floating aimlessly to her demise. It was a feeling he never wanted to have again in his life.

Breaking the heart of a woman he adored and truly loved.

VOICE OVER (FEMALE)

Claudette Ramsey, the master chess player, was now three moves ahead of Krawz Almarip, playfully having fun with her mouse before she swallowed him whole.

Krawz Almarip was desperately trying to throw himself a life preserver with his vast indoctrination of a spy.

Now Evo Kaplan was failing as Brenda Broyals herself had. The two were slowly becoming failures as spies because they allowed their emotions to deviate outside the sphere of a spy whose success relied upon compartmentalizing every aspect of their missions and their private lives.

Never shall the two meets, was Axiom number one of the spy businesses. Evo Kaplan's failed to compartmentalize early enough now dangerously slipped over the line. One image he indelibly had printed in his mind now was the girlish look that Claudette Ramsey had when she had her makeup off.

The tender, sweet, and delightful woman had purposely exposed the fabric of Claudette Ramsey's youthful essence unintentionally and just like Brenda Broyals he could not bear to bring himself to break her heart as well.

Caught up in this war of love where there would end up being serious casualties, there was no safe way out.

Evo Kaplan had built his home, and now he had to live in it, for the rest of his life.

It was heartbreaking business, and Evo Kaplan's own heart would also feel the tremors as one or both were stripped away from him forever for reasons out of his control or simply due to failure of the mission he was now just about to execute.

Perhaps there was some satisfaction knowing he would be close to a woman he fell for when he met his demise?

As Claudette Ramsey and Krawz Almarip crossed over that boundary of celestial delights into a realm of unequivocal post-orgasmic paralysis, they jointly succumbed to the psychophysical reaction that induced sleep and were subsequently transcending into another universe or domain that neural processes that were mankind's biggest mystery took them.

The paralysis lasted several hours until they slowly experienced rational and coherent thoughts beyond the dream world.

One stirring aroused the other, which further elevated their awareness of their surroundings. The sleep period had deflated the emotional explosion that a combination of guilt and disturbing consequences flooded Krawz Almarip (aka Evo Kaplan), who had built up remorse from the choking nostalgia that his experiences with Brenda Broyals had created.

After two hours of sleep and a break from all those thoughts, Evo Kaplan was less incapacitated from the emotions and allowed his training and indoctrination take over his mental processes that fulfilled the need to compartmentalize those emotions as to not interfere with his life-or-death venture that was now unfolding.

Even now though as Evo Kaplan compartmentalized his feelings, he could not help but feel slight sorrow for Claudette Ramsey, who was a special woman and deserved a partner worthy of her.

As soon as Claudette Ramsey was fully alert, she threw Evo Kaplan a lifeline he needed for psychological transcendence to escape the moral dilemma he found himself in.

CLAUDETTE RAMSEY
Now that I have got my spurs into you, why don't we go back to the lounge where I can do some reading and we can hang out?

KRAWZ ALMARIP
Sounds good to me.

The two slithered out of her bunk and got themselves ostensibly together and made their way to the lounge. In passing, Claudette Ramsey smiled at Ruth Marradi, who had raised eyebrows as she Claudette gave the thumbs-up signal while Krawz Almarip was walking forward and out of position to catch the secret semaphore. They arrived to an empty lounge, which had been somewhat the case until now.

However, shortly after a couple arrived and obtained their food and drink and sat down at another table. There wasn't much being discussed between Krawz Almarip and Claudette Ramsey, as she was once again reading, and he was simply hanging out thinking about what he could or should be doing. Claudette Ramsey was facing the couple and due to the confined space of the lounge, it was impossible to not overhear the other conversation.

They were clearly lovers and full of passion and happy they were almost home from their vacation to Zanziltar. Their exposure and carrying on as two younger lovers were expected to exhibit had an appeal to Claudette Ramsey, which made her thoughts of her just completed forty-million-mile trip feel even more pleasant.

Exposure to love has a strong influence to others. It psychologically creates thoughts and passions that would ordinarily lay dormant and unrecognized. These influences encapsulated the moment which would be endearing and indelibly etched in Claudette Ramsey's mind. And here her mouse was in front of her as she playfully entertained him, just like a real cat would its prey.

The couple stayed until they were all admonished to take their seats for planetary landing. Krawz Almarip and Claudette Ramsey followed the couple aft to the passenger cabin seating area and took their assigned seats to get strapped in. Krawz Almarip reassessed his plan. He would wait until all the other passengers got off the ship. He assumed he would be the only one waiting onboard.

KRAWZ ALMARIP

When you finish and come back aboard, I'll be in my bunk sleeping. If you want to wake me up, knock three times on my security privacy slide.

CLAUDETTE RAMSEY
Sure thing, sweetie.

Evo Kaplan noticed the tone in Claudette Ramsey's voice. He was now trapped in a whirlpool of love or something else, and he didn't know this woman too well, other than she was a target he planned to exploit to get to Randolph Spencer.

Krawz Almarip (a.k.a. Evo Kaplan) was closest to the window and could raise the window shade and look out. It was certainly dark, but he also observed more and more ships pass by as they approached the planet and the space lanes merged into major space transport paths required for security observations to prevent the Revolution from doing a surprise attack.

All ships went down in single file passing space buoys who identified them and verified they matched their CTA data. Otherwise, the Dranzonian Space Force would have an interceptor right on it ready to blast it out of the sky if necessary.

Up in the cockpit Captain Buck and the five other pilots and copilots now witnessed an extraordinary sight they would never have seen five years ago: on the *Cosmic Spatial Normalizer Display Data*, appearing as a solid stream as the outbound ships were in a perfect line accelerating to precise speeds required until they fanned out a good distance away from the planet and began independent courses to multitudes of different worlds within the Empire and some outside the Empire.

Directly in front of the ship in direct alignment with the planet was a blob that overlaid on top of each other as the arrivals were in perfect alignment as they passed several space buoy identification devices checking registration and originations. This transport would be automatically a ship of interest since it originated in Zanziltar, the *Sanctuary Planet*, which meant the possibility of money launderers and Revolution spies aboard.

Everyone leaving the ship would be far more scrutinized than arrivals from Empire planets where they were already pre-screened. Captain Buck, up in the cockpit, was merely watching the display graphics as the ship was in full autopilot. Each one of the six pilots would love to grab the controls and fly the ship manually.

Automation was called for because the air controllers in Praxisvlasia demanded absolute abeyance of instructions and any deviation could result in them being shot down over fear of a Revolution ship sneaking in and laying waste to a city or an industrial complex. Because they were now in direct sunlight, the outbound ships could be observed and earlier as they were fanning out on new courses pointing their destination planets, the plumes from their rocket exhausts were very bright as the also no longer had speed restrictions.

The ships now passing in single file still under speed restrictions only had small rocket exhausts and plumes were very short and diffused right away. All the CTA information slid by on the departing ships on icons they could expand to read if they wanted. But in reality, it would waste time especially after they passed their CPA and were opening. CTAs would become more important in space traveling through the Revolutionary Empire zone.

The blockade runner would be running dark during the next leg of it's travel. They would not be transmitting any CTA information and under intergalactic convention rules could be considered a warship and attacked without any repercussions. Their only hope was the Revolutionary Guards, or the Dranzonian Empire Space Force would first inquire who they were and where they came from and just detain the ship and the crew for possible criminal prosecution.

In the case of the Dranzonian Empire Space Force detaining the ship, it would be a horror story for Evo Kaplan, so he might as well commit suicide and avoid the torture should that occur. He was prepared to do so. A smart spy always carries a way out with him. Sometimes death is preferred over the treatment a spy receives. He would speculate that since the FIRM was probably Revolutionaries, he would not be subjected to such harsh treatment. At least not until they no longer had any use for him.

Dead ahead was the planet the cockpit crew observed. It was also now being shown on video displays in the cabin, which was done to give the public something to look at and help comfort them at the end of a long multi-day journey.

Part of the departure space lane was in view as well so the passengers could see many ships passing them in the opposite direction. Several miles ahead they were simply growing dots out of the stream of transports departing, but as they got within a couple miles, they buzzed past at very high velocities and only could be observed for a little more than a second before they passed and were no longer in view.

Praxisvlasia slowly grew in size. Meanwhile, Praxisvlasia's moon *Yaoyuan de Zhenzhu* was then observed off the port side of the transport. Unlike Earth's moon, Yaoyuan de Zhenzhu had many lights on the dark side that were easily observed, showing it was occupied. A large portion of the fleet was on Yaoyuan de Zhenzhu so they would not be all wiped out in a sucker punch and could be quickly launched so that an enemy had to fear being attacked from two simultaneous directions, which complicated any strategy of attacking Praxisvlasia.

*Yaoyuan de Zhenzhu* also had ample gravity, water, and vast green areas. It could and did sustain life. No people lived on that moon until well over five hundred years ago. The ship slowly closed in on the space port that had a seven-mile-long runway, which allowed large transports to land. It took them some time to slow down, using ground effect on the high-speed wing and forward thrusters.

The transport would arrive into the atmosphere around seventeen thousand miles per hour and continue down at approximately a 45-degree angle, bleeding off speed through dynamic breaking of the auxiliary turbines powering forward facing thrusters. The amount of dynamic breaking was proportional to speed, so the faster they were going, the more breaking action. When they slowed down below Mach 4.0 the amount of dynamic breaking available was less than 25 percent of initial re-entry speed and had less effect.

The method to bleed off the rest of the speed was simply to fly horizontal for a while; hence the landing patterns were a lot longer than for commercial airliners. Touchdown speed was nearly 300 miles per hour, hence the need for a seven-mile-long runway. Flying four feet above the ground using the ground effect on the wing provided enough friction to effectively slow the transport, usually within three and a half to four miles.

The additional length of the runway was to accommodate ships that had pilots who overshot the runway and had to get down be enough fuel to do a circle and come back and try it again. This only occurred in a manual landing instead of a computer landing, which always touched down exactly on an imaginary point of the runway within a few feet of where any other automated landing occurred.

The transport filled with more light as they were in the atmosphere and slowing down. Soon Evo Kaplan was looking out at the planet and observed sights they passed over. Oddly enough, Evo Kaplan spotted Coy's Ridge and the mansion where the ultra-rich industrialist Abniler Manther lived.

That sight brought back a lot of memories of Brenda, which hit him in the gut like a ton of bricks. But instead of suffering more remorse, he used his spy techniques and compartmentalized it all and then focused on the mission and a future endeavor with Randolph Spencer.

*Will I become a "runner" and escape the FIRM?* Who would they send to sanction him if they discovered him hiding out in an off-world paradise?

*Brenda perhaps?*

As they got closer to the space port, all the landmarks he could see were just like he last remembered them. Too bad corruption landed him in the hands of the FIRM. With the satisfaction of finally dealing with Reginald Heiqishi, he no longer exhibited the bitterness he once had toward the Dranzonian Empire Secret Service.

But Evo Kaplan was a realist; in due time they would attempt to nab him. He wondered why suddenly; he was on the top ten list of Kill on Sight orders? Did the Revolutionaries betray him to coerce him into remaining in their service?

He was having many thoughts and mixed emotions as the transport came down on the runway. It flew just a few feet off the runway without touching down to bleed off the speed using the ground effect, which could either slow you down or allow you to float along forever, depending on the aperture of the wing structure.

Three hundred miles per hour a few feet off the ground is somewhat scary for someone who has never experienced it before. But for a race car driver or a transport pilot, it was a joyous occasion—part of the perks of being in the business. The transport bled off speed pretty quick and at the prescribed speed, the computer automatically deployed the landing gear. Using precise computer control and aerodynamically stabilized landing gear with wings, the contact to the runway was so smooth that even the most sensitive accelerometer could barely pick up the force of the contact.

However, tires on the runway started to slow the Intergalactic Passenger Transport through more dynamic breaking as the electric motors mounted individually on the multiple wheels provided constant reverse pressures. The wheel electric motor generators had more slowing effect than the ground effect earlier, especially when the full weight of the transport was sitting on them.

Just as Pilot Buck hoped, they were down to maneuver speed at the three and a half-mile marker with a perfect landing, allowing them to turn off the main runway onto the service ramp and over to the Intergalactic Customs Terminal.

Looking around, Evo Kaplan could see the passengers were extremely pleased to be getting off the transport and to their ultimate destinations. Claudette Ramsey sat in her seat until all the other passengers had stood up and marched to their bunks to retrieve their personal items out of their lockers. Almost all of them would be leaving and not returning. Only a few would remain for the continuation flight. She didn't need to get into her locker; she was prepared to exit the transport spaceship but wanted a moment of privacy with Krawz Almarip.

Since passengers sitting near Krawz were now gone, Claudette Ramsey sat in one of the seats right next to him.

CLAUDETTE RAMSEY
While I'm off the ship, is there any specific food items you would like me to get you?

KRAWZ ALMARIP
Surprise me. Pick something you like.

CLAUDETTE RAMSEY
Okay.

KRAWZ ALMARIP
Do you need any credits?

Claudette Ramsey smiled.

CLAUDETTE RAMSEY
Listen, darling, I have all the credits I will ever need. You are lucky you met me.

Claudette Ramsey then stood up and walked off the intergalactic passenger transport and out into the duty-free zone, looking for souvenirs to give to her mother and friends. The transport being half empty so many of the passenger lockers would be empty, so there be plenty of room to store her purchases. Claudette Ramsey realized a little bribe might also help her get one of the flight attendants to help her carry it off the ship since she assumed Krawz Almarip, being a black marketer, would have a lot of his own articles to carry.

The ship was empty except for Krawz Almarip's favorite flight attendant Ruth Marradi that always took bribes from him. Krawz Almarip walked to the bunk area and took his shoes off, and hopped in and immediately shut and locked the security privacy slide. He would pop a pill and take advantage of all the down time to sleep so he could do a lot of surveillance on the new passengers and look for potential spies. Especially any that might be sent to find him.

Claudette Ramsey walked through the delightful terminal, enjoying having her feet planted back on terra-firma. There were multitudes of shops hawking their junk to gullible passengers. People just passing through always wanted to pick up souvenirs from the Empire's Capital Praxisvlasia to take home.

Everything imaginable was there to purchase. And if you didn't have room on the ship, for a price they would ship it to you on a regular serviced planet carrier. A lot of people traveling to Zanziltar made such purchases. People traveling to Arzon could not take advantage of this service since there no longer was regular service, nor could it be guaranteed since the Intergalactic Passenger Transport to Arzon had to travel through Revolution Empire areas.

It took several hours for Claudette Ramsey to find enough articles. She decided she would re-board, stow her articles in her bunk, then go back out and find some delicacies she could share with Krawz Almarip, her perfect mouse she loved toying with.

Claudette Ramsey bumped into Krawz Almarip's favorite flight attendant Ruth Marradi when boarding the Zanziltar Intergalactic Passenger Transport

CLAUDETTE RAMSEY
Hey, I purchased some souvenirs and need some extra space for the flight. If you could help me store some of this in an unused bunk for this flight, I'll make it worth your while.

The flight attendant, who knew damn well who Claudette Ramsey was and what she was doing with her mouse, smiled.

RUTH MARRADI
The bunk directly above your bunk does not have any reservations for this flight. Go ahead and store it all in there.

CLAUDETTE RAMSEY
Wonderful. Say, I'm going back off the ship to get some food in the courtyard. Is there anything you would like me to get you?

RUTH MARRADI
If you are going to pick up some items, I'm kind of looking forward to Styrolian Sponges served on a bed of Zanziltar Shuidao.

CLAUDETTE RAMSEY
All right I'll get that for you. Say, I have one other question.

RUTH MARRADI Yes?

CLAUDETTE RAMSEY
Do you know what Krawz Almarip's favorite food is?

RUTH MARRADI
I've stayed at the same hotel with Krawz Almarip a few times
and he always seem to order Kao Zhurou.


CLAUDETTE RAMSEY
Okay thanks!


Claudette Ramsey was off the ship and out food shopping. She was lucky she found a restaurant that did takeout that had everything she needed on the menu and didn't have to go to multiple locations. As soon as she was loaded up, she went back to the Zanziltar Intergalactic Passenger Transport, where she quickly noticed a sign that said to passengers, "If you are bringing food items onto the ship, please eat them before we depart the space port so that we can remove all waste products prior to take off."

She hoped Krawz Almarip would not be upset if she woke him before takeoff so they could comply with the sign. She went up to Krawz's bunk and knocked three times. She waited about a minute and the security privacy slide slid open and Krawz Almarip appeared to adjust his eyes, focusing in on Claudette Ramsey.


CLAUDETTE RAMSEY
I got your meal, but we must eat it before the ship takes off so
they can dispose of the trash.


KRAWZ ALMARIP
All right.


Krawz Almarip  opened up the security privacy slide and hopped out and put on his shoes. Krawz Almarip and Claudette Ramsey headed toward the passenger lounge, and ran into the flight attendant Ruth Marradi.


CLAUDETTE RAMSEY
I brought you what you requested. Would you like to join us in
the lounge?


RUTH MARRADI
Thanks. I have about an hour before we start pre-boarding new
passengers.


The three went to the lounge where they all sat down, and then Claudette Ramsey dished out the contents to everyone.

CLAUDETTE RAMSEY
Good thing I ran into Ruth. She said you like Kao Zhurou.

Evo Kaplan, mindful this flight attendant knew more about the real Krawz Almarip than he did, simply went along, even though it really wasn't one of his personal favorites, and responded like someone would who liked the selection.

KRAWZ ALMARIP (a.k.a. Evo Kaplan)
Thanks.

Soon they were all eating and Evo Kaplan, eyeballing the flight attendant's meal, sure wished he had the Styrolian Sponges instead. They had only been eating for a few minutes when another flight attendant took Ruth Marradi away for an issue.

RUTH MARRADI
I'm finished. If you guys want to try the Styrolian Sponges, help yourselves.

Krawz Almarip finished half of the serving of Kao Zhurou.

KRAWZ ALMARIP
I kind of like those Styrolian Sponges. I'm going to have some of them.

After Krawz Almarip finished the sponges, he felt full.

KRAWZ ALMARIP
I think I'm done.

CLAUDETTE RAMSEY
Me too. Let me take care of all the trash, dear.

Claudette Ramsey stood up and systematically cleaned off the table, placing each item in the trash bin that no doubt would get emptied in a short while.

KRAWZ ALMARIP
Thank you for bringing me the meal. It was very pleasant.

Krawz Almarip gave Claudette Ramsey's a lovely smile.

CLAUDETTE RAMSEY
My pleasure, dear.

In many ways, Claudette Ramsey's personalization of the statements was endearing, but in another way was also troubling since it spelled out the remarkable speed to which they had evolved into a relationship of some sort, whether Krawz Almarip was ready for it or not. He crossed over the line when he ate the forbidden fruit, and now he would have to integrate all those circumstances into his strategic plan, conducting his mission on Arzon.

Krawz Almarip (a.k.a Evo Kaplan) also looked at the time, which was shown on digital displays on the walls in the lounge. He had about thirty minutes before he had to crawl back in his bunk before customers from Praxisvlasia boarded the transport so they would not see him until they were underway and out into deep space accelerating to Arzon. By then it would be extremely difficult for the Dranzonian Empire to stop and search the craft unless they had a military vessel out in front of them in the path to Arzon. The two chatted for about thirty minutes, enjoying each other's company, which included some veiled flirting and cat-and-mouse play time.

KRAWZ ALMARIP

I'm going to my bunk for takeoff. If something goes wrong, I prefer to die in my sleep.

CLAUDETTE RAMSEY

Don't be silly, dear. Nothing is going to happen.

KRAWZ ALMARIP

What are you going to do?

CLAUDETTE RAMSEY

I'm going to stay here and do some more reading until they direct me back to my seat.

KRAWZ ALMARIP

All right, I'll see you in a few hours.

CLAUDETTE RAMSEY

Sleep well, honey.

<u>*WELCOME TO SANCTUARY CITY* THEM SONG STARTS PLAYING LOW VOLUME UNTIL THE VOICE OVER COMPLETES, THEN IS SLOWLY RAISES IN VOLUME FOR EFFECT DURING THE CREDITS.</u>

VOICE OVER

Krawz Almarip stood up and went to his bunk. He looked around. Nobody was within his eyesight. Krawz Almarip took off his shoes and climbed into the bunk, which had been remade while he was eating. Probably his favorite flight attendant

Ruth Marradi, who was not allowed to give her real name to passengers for security reasons. Her name tag only said, "flight attendant."

Krawz Almarip knew the truth: her real name was Ruth Marradi, whom the real Krawz Almarip privately called Ruthless. And in his interviews, describing all the possible flight crew on CTA number 6809, Evo Kaplan had been advised this was probably the only flight attendant he could trust, though she expected a big payoff.

Krawz Almarip also conveyed Ruthless expected one day to receive sexual favors as well as substantial credits. Sexual favors would become nearly impossible from now on while Claudette Ramsey was aboard the transport.

Perhaps on the return leg if he was able to get back to Zanziltar? Pills for this, pills for that. Perhaps the reason why they wanted a six-year contract is they figured that's the duration it would take to burn me out on all these pills? Evo Kaplan wondered. He then took another pill that would put him under for a while. Perhaps Brenda Broyals would come to him in his dreams. Will he ever see her again?

Paul D. Escudero

December 2023